Consequences

Consequences

Skyy

www.urbanbooks.net

Urban Books, LLC
78 East Industry Court
Deer Park, NY 11729

ISBN 13: 978-1-60162-316-4
ISBN 10: 1-60162-316-X

First Trade Paperback Printing October 2011
Printed in the United States of America

10 9 8 7 6 5 4 3 2 1

This is a work of fiction. Any references or similarities to actual events, real people, living, or dead, or to real locales are intended to give the novel a sense of reality. Any similarity in other names, characters, places, and incidents is entirely coincidental.

Distributed by Kensington Publishing Corp.
Submit Wholesale Orders to:
Kensington Publishing Corp.
C/O Penguin Group (USA) Inc.
Attention: Order Processing
405 Murray Hill Parkway
East Rutherford, NJ 07073-2316
Phone: 1-800-526-0275
Fax: 1-800-227-9604

Dedication

This book is dedicated to my precious niece Karai, and nephew London, my superstars.

Dedication

Acknowledgments

I want to first say thank you for purchasing or borrowing this book, lol. I hope you enjoy the read. These characters are a part of me, and I hope they become a part of you.

Now I'm singing "No Day But Today" from *Rent*. Live every day as if it was your last.

I really love my fans. Keep sending those emails and responding to my crazy posts on Facebook. You all keep me smiling.

Meshanna "Shunta" Jones, I remember when you were just a straight girl working at Storage USA. Now you have blossomed into a beautiful gay, lol. I can honestly say you are one of my besties, even though you aren't into my weirdness.

Tiffany "Tip-Tip" Graham. I don't really know how you managed to stay around so long, but I'm glad you did. You are a super dork, but I love you anyway.

Catherine "Rosario" Evans, my favorite Happy Mexican, ha ha ha. Thanks for all the support and by support, I mean financially, lol. Without you I would probably have starved a long time ago.

Redd Redd Redd . . . There are no words. Actually there are. You are a great friend, awesome writer and super awesome P.R. guru. You make me sound so good on paper.

Super Fun Friends: Cat, Tiffany, Bimbim, Chereny, Cassie, my tarot reader Byrd, Shanna, Cache, Kira, Angel,

Acknowledgments

Precious, Skylar, you are the crazy bunch that keeps me laughing on a daily basis. I can pretty much depend on one of you doing something crazy every day. Love you lots.

My family, both real and extended, thanks for putting up with me.

Thank you, Kelly Frey, for taking the time to assist me with the legal side of this business. I wouldn't be writing this without you. Robin White, I really wouldn't be writing this without you. I can't even explain how much I appreciate everything you did for me. Farrel McClure, thank you for all of your assistance as well. I can't wait to pay you all back for all of the support.

Chapter 1

"Showtime," Lena said to herself as she looked at her image in the mirror. The Manolo Blahnik stilettos lengthened her five foot three inch frame to nearly five-and-a-half feet. Her long hair flowed perfectly under the veil, and her Vera Wang wedding dress fit perfectly around her curvaceous body. She looked down at the five-karat, princess-cut ring on her finger that was about to have a beautiful platinum band to go along with it, and smiled. She had made the right decision.

"Lena, it's time," Carmen said when she walked into the room. She helped Lena place the Swarovski crystal-studded veil over her face. "Next time I talk to you, your name will be Lena Redding." She hugged Lena, and they headed out of the room.

The New York Philharmonic began playing the traditional Mendelssohn March as the guests turned to watch the procession enter the orchid-filled chapel. The bridesmaids glided one by one down the aisle in their creamy white dresses accented with Tiffany-blue sashes. A groomsman dressed in a white tuxedo with a matching Tiffany-blue cummerbund received each. Brandon stood at the altar in the middle wearing an enormous smile on his face.

Lena walked down the aisle as David Hollister's "Forever" began to play. The guests stood as Lena slowly made her way down the aisle. Lena glanced at her soon-to-be husband. Brandon's tall, athletic frame looked amazing in his white tuxedo. She was about to marry "one of the sexiest men alive," according to *Essence* magazine. She looked to the right and noticed many of her friends from St. Benedict High School and some of her new sorority sisters of Chi Theta. She looked to her left and saw mostly Brandon's teammates and their wives.

Finally she made it to the altar, and her father proudly gave her hand to Brandon. The ceremony began.

"Is there anyone who objects to these two joining hands in holy matrimony?" the preacher asked.

Lena smiled as she looked at Brandon and resisted the urge to wipe the tear sliding down his left cheek.

"Yeah, I do!"

Commotion ensued as someone burst into the church.

Lena's body started to tremble at the sound of the voice. She turned around to see Denise headed toward her in jeans and a black wife-beater.

"Lena, you don't love him! You love me!" Denise yelled as every bit of her toned body fought to break through the bodyguards holding her back.

"Denise, what are you doing?" Carmen yelled at her friend.

"Bitch, have you lost your mind?" Brandon yelled as his groomsmen held him back.

"I am sorry, Brandon, but Lena loves me, and she knows it!" Denise exclaimed.

Lena turned to Brandon. "I'm sorry, Brandon, but it's true. I do love Denise." She turned around and ran toward Denise.

Instantly they embraced each other, sharing a passionate kiss. The church was in hysterics.

"Well, if you want her, y'all can have each other," Brandon said, walking up to the both of them. "In hell!"

Two shots rang out, and everything suddenly went black.

Lena abruptly woke up in a sweat. Her heart was pounding as she turned to see Brandon in his usual deep sleep. "It was only a dream," she thought to herself. She eased out of her bed and quietly went into the bathroom and splashed cold water on her face.

"Lena, what is wrong with you?" she questioned herself. The dreams were becoming more frequent as the wedding date drew closer. She was losing more and more sleep.

She headed back into her bedroom in the new loft that Brandon had purchased for her. He had signed a 9.5 million-dollar contract with the Memphis Grizzlies basketball team. Even though he was a rookie, it was well known that he was going to be one of the star players.

Lena grabbed a bottled water out of her brand-new Sub Zero Refrigerator at the morning bar and sat on an oversized leather couch. She looked out of the large double-hung windows at the beautiful view of the Mississippi River and Memphis Bridge.

Lena looked down at the massive rock on her hand. Brandon had upgraded her original ring as soon as he signed his contract. Lately she felt the weight of the ring not on her finger, but in her heart. She couldn't stop thinking about Denise. She took a deep breath, knowing she had to suppress her feelings.

Lena crept back into bed and stared up into the pitch-black space. Denise came into her mind again. She couldn't stop herself from thinking of her. The school year was approaching, and she was going to be faced with her skeleton again. Lena said a silent prayer for strength to overcome her impure desires for Denise. She looked at Brandon again and felt she was where she was meant to be. She only hoped that she remembered that the entire school year.

"Get a grip, Dee." Denise stared into her bathroom mirror. This was becoming a nightly routine. She splashed cold water on her face and looked at herself in the mirror. Droplets rolled down her brown cheeks. She could see the stress in her dark brown eyes; small red lines filled them from lack of sleep.

"Baby, you OK?" a voice called from the other room.

Denise didn't want to answer. She pulled her ponytail holder off of her head and ran her hand through her thick, long hair.

"Yeah, I'm good," she replied through the door. Denise sighed and brushed her hair back before placing the ponytail holder back on it. She wiped her face and walked back into the other room.

Rhonda stared at Denise as she illuminated the bedroom with the light from the bathroom. She smiled. She loved everything about Denise, especially her frame. She watched Denise's toned arms sway. She noticed from day one how great Denise's body looked in clothes, and she couldn't wait to see how it looked naked.

"Baby, I know you're stressing about school, but I know something that can relieve that stress," Rhonda hinted, caressing Denise's arm. She quickly began to massage Denise's broad shoulders.

Although it felt great to Denise, she knew it would lead to something she didn't want.

"Rhonda, we already had this conversation." Denise sighed.

"I know, but it's been three months. School is about to start. I just want to show you how much I care about you."

"And I told you I don't get down like that." Denise turned away from Rhonda.

Rhonda looked down at Denise. "Fine, baby, I am willing to wait," she said, turning her body toward Denise so she could put her arm around her.

That's what I'm afraid of, Denise thought to herself as she closed her eyes, hoping to quickly fall back to sleep. Before she knew it, she was.

Denise turned over and wrapped her arms around Rhonda. She loved holding Rhonda in her arms. "This is how things are supposed to be," Denise whispered in Rhonda's ear as she kissed her on the cheek. She felt Rhonda caressing her hand. Things were perfect, just how they were supposed to be.

Chapter 2

The smell of bacon and eggs aroused Denise's senses long before her body woke up. Rhonda was cooking breakfast, something Denise had become used to every morning. She got up and headed into the kitchen. The table was filled with all of her favorites.

"Damn, did you cook everything in the fridge? It's only two of us," Denise said. She didn't know why she was annoyed with Rhonda.

Rhonda placed a heaping plate of food at Denise's seat at the table. "I'm sorry, Denise. I'll buy some more food to cover what I used. I know it's a lot. I just wanted to do something special for you since you made me feel so special last night."

Denise gave Rhonda a curious look. "I did?"

"Yes, woman, remember what you told me?" Rhonda kissed Denise on her forehead. "That laying next to me was the way things are supposed to be."

Denise immediately felt guilty. She knew she was not thinking about Rhonda last night. She yawned. "Yeah, uh, I was real tired. I'm not even sure what I said last night. This looks good." She quickly began to eat to avoid any more questions.

Rhonda's heart stopped. It wasn't the answer she expected. "Well, you know I gotta feed my girl." She sighed as she sat down with her plate.

They heard the door open.

"Bruhhhhh!" Cooley yelled as she burst into the room.

"Oh, snap. I thought I was picking you up tonight," Denise said as she hugged her best friend.

"Well, maybe if you would check your voice and text messages, you would know I caught an earlier flight. What the fuck did I get you a Sidekick for anyway?"

"I've been checking my messages whenever I get them. I haven't had any," Denise said, looking down at her phone.

A loud noise erupted.

"Oh, sorry," Rhonda said, picking up the pieces of a plate that she threw into the sink. She wasn't expecting Cooley to show up till later. Erasing Denise's messages hadn't worked after all.

Cooley's expression changed. She threw Denise an evil stare. "Oh. Hey," she said to Rhonda with as much attitude as possible.

"Hi," Rhonda said, returning the same amount of attitude. "Well, I need to get home, so Denise I will see you later, OK," Rhonda said as she headed to Denise's room to put her clothes on.

Cooley looked over at Denise. She frowned. "Why is she still here?" She did not like Rhonda at all.

"Shhhh. She might hear you," Denise answered.

"Whatever, man, I'm definitely going to have to hook you up with someone else. I preferred that ho-ass Crystal over that bitch," Cooley responded.

"Man, come on, I know you don't like her, but . . ." Denise stopped talking when Rhonda walked back into the room.

"Do you need me to bring anything to your practice?" Rhonda leaned down and placed a long, sensual kiss on Denise's lips.

Cooley made a gagging expression.

"Nah, I'm good. I'll just see you later. There is actually no need to come to my practice."

Rhonda looked confused. She loved watching Denise play during practice. "But—"

"After practice, OK! Bye, Rhonda." Denise knew she had to cut her off.

"All right, if that's what you want." Rhonda tried to kiss Denise, but she moved her face. Rhonda looked up at Cooley ,who was trying to hold in her laughter, and stomped out the door.

"Man, come on, she is so damn phony! You can do so much better," Cooley remarked as she headed to her room.

Denise followed.

Cooley sighed when she walked into her room. She didn't realize how much she had missed home. Her room was decked out better than most bachelor pads. A large black and white abstract painting of a woman's body hung on her wall. Her colognes and shades were lined up perfectly along her dresser. The collection of fitted baseball caps decorated another side of the wall, each in its own spot. A king-sized bed sat in the middle of the room against the back wall. The black and white Ralph Lauren bed set accented with red throw pillows was one of her favorite things in the room. Cooley had an unmistakable sense of style.

"Cooley, she isn't that bad." Denise remembered that when Rhonda met Cooley, she immediately had an attitude with her. Rhonda always questioned why Denise was friends with Cooley and Carmen, as she didn't like either one of them.

"Man, that girl is bad news, but the pussy must be nice 'cause you're still with her stank ass."

"She isn't that bad, and I wouldn't know about the pussy thing," Denise said as she leaned against the wall in Cooley's room.

Cooley stopped unpacking. "You been shackin' up with the bitch all these months and you haven't fucked? Bro, what the hell is going on with you?"

Before Denise could answer, Cooley responded, "I know you are not still stuck up on Lena."

Denise remained quiet.

"Damn bro, you either need to go fuck her or let her go, but all this pining over her isn't going to get you anywhere."

"Who you tellin'? I'm trying to get over her. Shit, I can't get that kiss out of my head."

The image of Lena kissing Denise immediately entered her mind. She couldn't forget the kiss they'd shared on the last day of school last year. She couldn't forget the intensity and passion that was filled in the minute-long kiss.

"We haven't spoken all summer. I haven't seen her. She's gonna be married at the end of the semester." Denise sighed. "I know she's made her choice, but I don't know what to do to get over her."

"Well, maybe if you find a girl to take your mind off of her." Cooley threw a bag to Denise.

"That's what I got with Rhonda for," Denise said. "What's all this?" Denise asked and started pulling things out of the bag. It was filled with CDs and a bottle of cologne.

"Oh, some things I got for you this summer. Check that scent out. It's Unforgivable by Sean Jean. Hot shit."

Denise nodded in approval of her gifts.

"And I meant a real woman." Cooley laughed. "Seriously, man, if you aren't gonna get wit' Lena, then you need to let it go. Hey, since we have this phat-ass crib now, how about we throw a back-to-school party? I got some great mixes from Jam Zone. What do you think?"

Cooley had spent the summer interning at Jam Zone Record Label. She got the connection when she met Sonic, one of the label's artists, last year in Atlanta.

"If that's what you want to do, then fine. I'm down for it," Denise said over her shoulder as she walked out the room.

Denise lay down on her bed and looked around the room. She didn't decorate her room like her lavish best friend. The only thing they had in common was how neat they kept their wardrobes. Her fitted hats lined the side of her wall, hanging on individual nails. Her shoe collection was lined up perfectly in her closet, complete with almost every color of Air Force Ones. She looked out of the window and wondered what Lena was up to.

"I have died and gone to heaven," Carmen said as she looked at the long table filled with miniature cakes.

"Lena, you are going to have to take my dress out 'cause I plan on tasting every last one of these bad boys," Misha added as she looked at the table.

The baker came out of the back room. "Well, Ms. Jamerson, these are the crème de la crème. Please take your time tasting all of them. You may mix and match whatever you would like for your wedding. After all we are here to please you."

Lena smiled. "Thank you. Please leave me and my friends, and we will ring when we are finished." She walked up to the table as the woman politely left the room. "Let's get started."

Carmen and Misha looked at Lena as they grabbed forks and began to sample each small cake.

"Damn, the perks of marrying someone rich. Damn, I am mad as hell about it," Carmen joked as she sampled a piece of a cake that tasted like coffee.

"Yeah, well," Lena said as she sampled something with a strawberry on top. "Who better to share this with than my girls?"

"I still can't believe it's only a few months until you're a married woman," Misha squealed in delight. "Oh my God, this vanilla cream is unbelievable."

Carmen ran over to try a piece of Misha's discovery. They looked up at Lena, realizing she was standing still, a concerned look on her face.

"Lena, are you OK?" she asked.

Lena turned around when she heard the question. "Yeah, I'm just a little light-headed. I haven't been getting much sleep lately."

"Girl, you better slow down before you wear yourself out. You don't have to do everything. You should hire that Mr. Fabulous guy to do your wedding. His shit is off the chain," Misha added.

"No, I wanted to do my own wedding. I do have a wonderful wedding planner, but certain things I want to do myself. I just need a good night's sleep." Lena smiled. She knew that was not her only problem. "So are you all ready for your senior year?" she asked Carmen and Misha, both seniors.

"I am so ready to be done with school. When I finish, me and Nic are moving to L.A.," Carmen said. She was still with her girlfriend Nicole. Carmen had never been so happy before.

"I'm not too excited. Once I graduate I still have law school," Misha said as she headed into the dressing room to change.

"At least you're done with most of it. I'm just a junior, and I am only a junior because of the summer school classes and overload from last year," Lena said.

"Yes, but you are finishing in three years instead of four," Carmen yelled from her dressing room. "Hell, at least you're smart enough to finish. Most girls about to marry a millionaire would be barefoot and pregnant by now."

Lena knew that Brandon wanted her to quit school and start working on the home, but she was determined to finish, in case she and Brandon didn't make it.

Carmen's phone rang 50 Cent's "P.I.M.P."

Misha and Lena both stopped what they were doing. They knew Cooley's ring tone.

"Hey, bro, you're back!" Carmen squealed. "How was Atlanta?"

Lena continued to sample cake as Misha tried to pay attention to Carmen's conversation.

"Misha, are you all right?" Lena asked when she noticed the expression on her face.

"I'm fine. I just, well, I guess I forgot that I was going to be around Cooley again," Misha said, putting her head down.

"You don't have to be around her too much. I'm sure Carmen will understand if you pass on a few events. I have to as well." Lena almost caught herself mentioning Denise, but it was too late.

"Why, Lena, because of Denise?" Misha looked Lena straight in her face.

Lena had to tell the truth. "Yes, OK, it's 'cause of Denise. So what?" Lena said, walking out of the dressing room. Misha followed her.

"Girl, did something go on between you and Dee last year?" Misha questioned.

Lena had never told Misha about the incident last year. She had planned on sleeping with Denise the night of the athletic banquet, but things were changed when Brandon asked her to marry him. When she got to her dorm, Denise had changed her mind, knowing that having sex with her would complicate her life.

"Nothing happened. We kissed, but that's it." Lena thought about the kiss; it was the most intense and passionate kiss she had experienced. The only problem now was, kissing Brandon was not enough for her. She always desired more.

"Misha, can we drop this please?" Lena said, noticing Carmen walking out of the dressing room.

"Hey, guys, we've been invited to a welcome back to school party at Cooley and Denise's new apartment."

"We? Does Cooley know I would be coming?" Misha questioned.

"Yes. She asked me to tell you. Oh, and you too, Lena." Carmen looked at Lena, who was grabbing the name cards off their favorite cakes.

The wedding cake maker walked back into the room.

"I can't make it. I have to go to a dinner with Brandon, but I'll send them a housewarming gift." Lena looked at the baker. "I need to have samples of all of these sent to my house for Brandon to try." Lena handed the woman the cards. "I gotta finish up here. I will talk to you women later, OK? Take whatever cakes you want with you."

The baker grabbed some boxes and bags and gave them to Carmen and Misha. Lena quickly followed the woman into the office, leaving Carmen and Misha surrounded by the leftover cakes.

"I wonder what that was all about," Carmen said as she packed up her favorite samples.

"Oh, come on, girl, you already know, don't you?" Misha replied, sneaking another piece of the strawberry cake.

Carmen looked confused.

"Did you know they kissed last year?"

The comment caused Carmen to stop dead in her tracks "What? Misha, are you serious?" she asked Misha, who kept walking. She ran to catch up. "Bitch, you better answer me."

Misha smiled. "Yes, OK. Lena just told me they kissed last year. From the look on her face it was a pretty damn good kiss."

"Oh, hell no. I am going to kick Denise's ass," Carmen replied. "Damn, maybe that's why she has been shacking up with that bitch-ass Rhonda."

Carmen hated Rhonda more than Cooley did. Rhonda had asked Denise to stop hanging with Carmen because she didn't think a femme and a stud could be real friends. Denise didn't do it, however, and from then on Rhonda always had an attitude with Carmen, and Carmen had one with her as well.

"I know, right. That girl is so not Denise's type," Misha added as they got into Carmen's car. "Seriously, I wondered why Denise was messing with her."

"Well, now I know, and now I can squash that shit. So, are you coming to the party?" Carmen asked Misha.

"I don't think so, girl. I don't think Tay would like me going to a party at my ex-girlfriend's house." Misha had started dating Tay, a very popular stud on campus. Cooley and Tay both could pass as men. They were studs personified.

"Speaking of why people date who they date, you need to dump that loser and give my buddy another chance. You know Cooley isn't over you." Carmen didn't approve of Misha being with Tay either, who was known for hitting her girlfriends. She also knew if Tay ever laid a hand on Misha that Cooley would go to jail for attempted murder.

"Really? Is that why she slept with two girls the last day of school? Carmen, we hadn't been broken up twenty-four hours yet."

"Misha, Cooley was hurting very bad. That's the way she dealt with the pain. She couldn't let you or anyone see how hurt she was. Why do you think she actually took that internship? To get away from Memphis and away from you. Hell, every time she called, she wanted to know stuff about you."

"Well, a little too late to tell me that now," Misha said. "If Cooley wanted me, she knew my number, so let's drop this convo now please."

"All right, it's dropped." Carmen pulled up in front of the dorm. "Well, see you later girl. I gotta go meet Nic." Misha got out of the car and headed into her dorm as Carmen drove off.

Chapter 3

Misha sat on the bed while Tay primped herself in the mirror. She laughed to herself, remembering how long it used to take Cooley to get ready. Misha knew that Tay was cute but didn't have anything on Cooley. She looked Tay up and down. Misha had never realized just how short Tay was. Tay didn't have the captivating effect on her that Cooley did.

"Misha!" Tay yelled.

"Yeah." Misha jumped, realizing she had been daydreaming.

"How this look?" Tay said as her mouth shined with a gold grill.

Misha watched Tay turn around, showing off her Sean Jean outfit.

"It looks fine. But I wish you would take that damn grill out." Misha rolled her eyes. She would never understand the fascination with wearing grills. She liked to see white, healthy teeth, not a metallic grin.

"Whatever, girl. I'm keeping my grill in." Tay folded her arms and flashed her teeth in the mirror. She popped her collar. "I need to be better than fine. I gotta be the flyest stud tonight," she said, brushing her waves down.

"Why you wanna be so fly to go to a movie?" Misha asked as she stood up.

"Oh, shit, we're going to a welcome back party." Tay placed her fitted blue cap on. She gave herself another complete look over in the mirror.

Misha looked at Tay. "What if I don't feel like going to a party?" Misha paused. "Wait, the only party I know of tonight is at Cooley's place."

"Yeah, that's it. I can't wait to see the look on that nigga's face when I walk in lookin' like this." Tay smiled at the thought of out-dressing Cooley at her own house. She knew Cooley was the only person standing in the way of her being the hottest stud in Memphis.

She looked at Misha, her most recent victory. She got the girl Cooley actually settled down with the year before. Tay knew Misha still cared about Cooley, but wasn't afraid. Misha had left Cooley because of all the drama that followed her. By the end of last year all the stares, gossip, prank phone calls and psycho chicks had gotten to Misha. Tay knew she would never put herself back in that situation, and being with Cooley was always going to bring drama.

"Wait, you want me to go to Cooley's party?" Misha snapped.

Tay looked at her with a confused expression.

"Did it ever occur to you that I might not be comfortable going to a party at my ex-girlfriend's place?"

"What? Misha, the only reason that shit should matter is if you still want to be with her. But we know that's not the case. Cooley ain't got shit on me."

If only you knew. Misha thought to herself. "You still should have asked me."

"My bad. So you wanna go or what? We need to be showing off how fly we look together. Shit, I know my outfit is going to be the hottest. I paid a grip for this. Cooley gone be hatin'. I know it."

"Why the fuck do you always gotta bring her up? Damn, you act like you in some kind of competition or something," Misha said, while rummaging through her closet. She had to find an outfit to show Cooley exactly what she was missing.

Over the summer Misha had made some changes. She took out her frustration in the gym, causing her body to tone up. She cut her hair to her shoulders and began wearing her natural curls. She also changed her style a little. She always knew she was sexy, but with her new tone body, she began to show off her sex appeal even more.

"No, I don't. Man, she be the one thinking she the best thing going and shit. She always think she so fly. She think she the hottest, but she's not. I am. Shit, wait till the stud competition this year. I am going to win." Tay held her head up high, imagining the look on Cooley's face when she won.

"Tay, it is not that serious." Deep down Misha knew that for Tay and many other studs it was.

"Man, OK, so you ready to go?"

"Let me change real quick, and we can roll out," Misha said.

Tay sat on the bed, constantly looking in the mirror until Misha was ready to go. Tay smiled when she saw Misha's new look.

"Damn, baby, you went and got Rihanna fine." Tay wrapped her arms around Misha while Misha put her finishing touches on her lip-gloss. She knew Cooley was going to be pissed when she saw her arm wrapped around Misha, and made a mental note to rub on Misha's ass in front of Cooley. She might even kiss her.

Valentino looked great on Lena, but she wanted to have on jeans. She had quickly grown tired of the dinner parties and special engagements she had to attend on Brandon's arm. She secretly wished she was at the party Denise was throwing.

"Baby, you are wearing that dress." Brandon kissed Lena on her cheek. He looked at himself in the mirror.

His black suit was tailor-made for his tall physique. "We are one attractive couple." He smiled.

Lena smiled. She had to admit, they looked great together. They were quickly becoming local celebrities. Lena didn't want all of the attention on her, but Brandon loved it. She knew she had to play the part.

"Sweetie, do we have to be out all night? I have school starting and all."

"Lena, you know I have to be at this event."

"I know. I just hoped we could leave a little early."

Brandon sighed. "If that is what you want, then fine. I don't know why you insist on going back to school anyway."

Lena rolled her eyes. Brandon had expressed his opinion of her schooling numerous times. He preferred his woman to be at home. "Please not tonight."

"I'm not saying anything else. Let's go." Brandon walked out of the room, leaving Lena standing there.

She looked at herself one more time. "OK, Lena, it's show time."

Cooley and Denise's apartment was packed with all of the who's who of the black gay community. The music had everyone rocking. There were new tracks that Memphis had not been privileged to hear yet. The living room floor was packed with women shaking their butts, trying to see who could shake it the best. Cooley's internship over the summer ensured that her popularity with the women increased, and she had excess attention to show for it.

More women than usual were also checking out Denise because she was now the super star senior basketball player. Rhonda refused to leave Denise's side, thinking she had to defend her territory.

"Bro!" Carmen yelled as she and Nic walked into the party. She ran up to Cooley and gave her a big hug. "I have missed you so much."

"I missed you too, baby girl. Nic, are you treating my girl right?" Cooley asked.

"Hell, the question is, how is she treating me?" Nic joked. She and Carmen, hooked up again at the end of the school year after the big falling out with Carmen's ex, Tameka. They had been happily in love ever since.

Nic had her own little fan club as well, being that she was one of the most attractive studs in Memphis. And the fact that she was still considered new to Memphis made all the girls want to be the first to get her. Carmen worried sometimes, but her self-esteem was rising so much that it was starting to not bother her anymore.

"Hey, C, is Misha coming?" Cooley asked Carmen as they walked to get something to drink.

"Um, Cool, there's something that I have to tell you. You see—"

Cooley interrupted Carmen before she could finish. "What the . . ." Cooley's facial expression changed quickly. Her heart began to beat rapidly when she noticed Misha. She could feel her nature rising just looking at how sexy Misha looked. Misha had never looked this way before.

Cooley remembered telling Misha she should dress a little sexier, but she never wanted to. Now Misha looked like she had stepped out of a Jam Zone music video.

Cooley smiled, rubbing her hands together, ready to get her girl. Her smile quickly changed when Tay walked in and placed her arm around Misha. "What the fuck!" Cooley said as her blood began to boil. "I know that is not Tay with Misha!" Cooley exclaimed while staring Misha down.

Tay looked in Cooley's direction and smirked. She pulled Misha closer to her side.

Cooley wanted to go beat her down, but held her composure. She never let a woman see her sweat.

"See. That's what I needed to tell you . . ."

Cooley headed in Misha's direction before Carmen could finish her sentence. She approached Misha and touched her on her neck, one of Misha's hot spots.

"Hey, Misha," Cooley said in her seductive voice.

Misha quickly turned around. She knew if Cooley stayed too close to her she wouldn't be able to control herself. "Nothing much, Carla. How are you doing?" Misha said, returning the comment in her seductive voice as well.

"It's all good on this end. Damn, bae, I almost didn't recognize you. You looking hella—"

"Tay, this is Cooley," Misha said, cutting off Cooley.

"Yeah, we know each other," Cooley casually replied. "Whut up, Tay?"

Cooley and Tay stared at each other. Tay's face dropped when she saw Cooley's shirt. She knew her Sean Jean out-fit didn't compare to having a shirt worth over a hundred dollars, even if it was just a T-shirt.

"Not shit. Can't complain," Tay said, putting her arm around Misha. She knew she might not be the flyest, but she still had Misha.

Cooley could feel the anger starting to rise.

Misha sensed the tension in the air. "Well, I guess I will see you around, Cooley," Misha said as Tay guided her into the house.

Cooley stood at the door as Carmen walked up to her.

"Why didn't you tell me, Carmen?" Cooley said.

Carmen could tell she was hurt, but trying to hide it. "Cooley, I didn't think it was going to be serious. You know I don't like Tay. I just thought it was a fling."

"Does she know about Tay's rep? Man, I have seen her hit girls before."

"She knows, but she told me Tay has been nothing but nice to her," Carmen said, putting her arm around Cooley.

"Yeah, well, I ain't going out like that. Especially not over that fake-ass nigga," Cooley said in her regular cool voice.

"Don't do nothing stupid, Cooley," Carmen warned and followed Cooley into the living room.

"Oh, I won't do anything crazy, unless I see Tay lay a hand on her. Then you better call the cops." Cooley walked off to greet more guests.

Denise looked over at Carmen. She hadn't spoken to her yet. She wondered how she was going to get away from Rhonda to go talk to her friend. Rhonda was involved in a conversation with a few members of the gay family she wanted to join. Rhonda wanted to be a member of the Premiere Family, but they never showed interest in her.

Gay families were big in Memphis, and the Premiere Family was the largest in the city. Families consisted of an older lesbian couple that invited younger lesbians from the community into their homes as a safe haven. Older lesbians would be considered mothers, fathers, uncles, and aunts, depending on whether they were more masculine or feminine. The family members were also called son or daughters, depending on their gender classification as well.

The Premieres always wanted Denise and Cooley to join. Cooley was always asked to perform at the shows at the club. She was a favorite of the women, always making large amounts of tips whenever she preformed.

"I'll be back," Denise whispered to Rhonda.

"No. Where are you going?" Rhonda questioned.

"Just to get something to drink. Stay here. I'll be back." Denise walked off before giving Rhonda a chance to respond. She made her way to her room.

Cooley noticed Misha standing alone by the window. Cooley walked up and caressed the back of Misha's neck, causing her to shiver. She turned around, and Cooley smiled. "Guess I still have that magic touch. Where is your li'l date?"

Misha took a step back, knowing if she stood too close she would not be able to control herself. "My girlfriend went to the car to get her phone." She looked Cooley up and down. Cooley lined her hair, and her curls were sitting perfectly. Misha also noticed that Cooley's arms looked a little more cut through her shirt. "Have you been working out?" Misha inquired, trying not to lust over Cooley's sexy body.

Cooley smiled. "That's not your girlfriend. You can't have a girl 'til I give you up completely." She stared at Misha, "I've been doing a little something. Atlanta treated me right this summer, but I was ready to come home."

Misha wanted to smile, but held it in. "Why? Ran out of ass in Atlanta?" She rolled her eyes.

"Yeah, OK, I guess I deserved that. But to answer your question, Atlanta is cool, but it was missing what I truly wanted." Cooley walked toward Misha until she was against the wall. They were now standing face to face, the sexual energy rising every second.

Misha tried to contain herself. "And what . . . did you want?"

Cooley gazed into Misha's eyes. "You of all people should know that." She leaned in, ready to kiss the lips of the only woman she ever loved.

Misha quickly moved away. "Cooley, don't go there. You know we can't do this. I won't do this with you again. I'm with Tay."

"Well, since you brought the fake-ass nigga up, let's talk about that. What's the deal, Misha? You go get wit' the bitch that wants to be me more than anyone else."

"She doesn't want to be you. Tay is a cool person." Misha knew she was lying.

"Whatever, Misha, that girl is—"

"That girl is walking in the house. Bye, Carla." Misha walked off just as Tay was coming back into the house.

Cooley watched her whisper into Tay's ear. They walked back out of the apartment.

Cooley shook her head. She wasn't giving up that easily. She headed over and joined the spades game that was about to start.

"This is pathetic. You have to hide in your room just to get away from that ho," Carmen said as she walked into Denise's room. She looked at Denise, disgusted with the relationship she had with Rhonda.

"Give me a break tonight, OK. Hey, why didn't Lena come? Did you tell her about it?"

"Yeah, I told her. She had some fancy dinner to go to with Brandon." Carmen could see the disappointment in Denise's face. "Dee, why didn't you tell me about you and Lena?"

"I don't know. I guess I wanted to forget it."

"Forget it? Girl, you can't get it off your brain, can you? Why would you do that, Dee? You knew—"

Denise interrupted. "I know, OK, I know. But you know it was supposed to be more. She wanted me to have sex with her. I almost did it, but I couldn't."

"And you should be happy you didn't. The girl is going to be married in two months. You both need to get over your feelings for each other real damn quick," Carmen said.

"Both? Carmen, what do you know?" Denise's eyes brightened.

Carmen knew she had put her foot in her mouth.

"Denise, I know that Lena cares about you, but you know it can't happen. Let it go, boo. And while you're at it, let Rhonda go too."

"Well, isn't this a sight?" Rhonda said as she pushed the door open. "Guess you just had to get my woman away from me long enough to try to break us up!" she exclaimed.

"Girl, you better get up out my face—That's all I know," Carmen countered, holding her ground.

Denise knew she had to intervene before something went down. She went to get in between Rhonda and Carmen, but it was too late.

"I'll be in your face all I want to," Rhonda challenged and walked toward Carmen.

Denise grabbed her hand. "Rhonda, come on."

"Yeah, Rhonda, you best listen to Denise on this one," Carmen responded, adding fuel to the fire.

"The only thing I better do is whip your ass."

Rhonda charged at Carmen, but was met by Carmen's fist. Instantly Carmen was on top of Rhonda, pounding her in the face.

"Cooley, Nic, come help me. These girls are fighting!" Denise yelled, running into the kitchen where the poker game was in progress.

Nic jumped up, but Cooley remained seated.

"Who is winning?" Cooley casually asked while looking at her cards.

"What?" Denise yelled. "Carmen is on top of Rhonda. I can't break it up alone. Get up, bruh!"

Cooley remained seated and started to laugh. "Fuck that. I hope Carmen kicks the dog shit out of that bitch." She laughed as she placed more chips in the middle of the table. "I just know y'all bet not break shit!"

Denise ran back into the room, where Nic had finally pulled Carmen off of Rhonda. She helped Rhonda get off the ground. Carmen was still fuming, but Nic had begun to calm her down.

"I think we need to go," Nic told Denise. "All right, Ali, let's go."

Nic grabbed Carmen's hand. Everyone else in the party began to disperse as well.

Denise looked at Rhonda. "What the fuck is wrong with you?"

"What? I told you how I feel about her," Rhonda said, sitting on the bed.

"Rhonda, Carmen and Cooley have been my family for years, and no woman is about to make me stop kicking it with them!" Denise was fuming.

Rhonda looked at Denise. "Oh, so it's like that? OK, then, I'll roll. I don't want to be anywhere that I am not respected." Rhonda grabbed her bag and walked toward the door, passing Cooley, who was sitting on the couch with three girls.

"You leaving, Rhonda?" Cooley asked in her sarcastic voice.

"Fuck you, Cooley. Go to hell!" Rhonda said, causing Cooley to laugh even harder. She slammed the door.

"I'm going to make it an early night," Lena said as she pulled her shoes off and walked into her house. "That is, unless you want to come and join me." Lena looked at Brandon. His manhood was already beginning to rise.

"As much as I want to take you up on that," Brandon said as he hugged Lena, allowing her to feel the stiffness in his pants, "I have got to do a little work. But, trust, I will be waking your ass up soon." He smacked Lena on her butt as she headed to her room.

Brandon headed into his study. He opened his desk drawer and a picture fell out. He looked at the small photo. He then glanced at the picture of Lena sitting on his desk. She was the most wonderful thing in his life. He picked up the phone and made a call.

"We need to talk. I will be over there in three hours." Brandon hung the phone up and headed into his bedroom.

He crawled into bed next to Lena. She was wearing one of his oversized Grizzlies T-shirts. He slowly rubbed his hand up her leg till he made it to her butt. No panties. She was ready for him.

Lena turned over and looked at Brandon. "I guess you didn't have to wake me up after all."

He leaned down and kissed her. He could feel her becoming wet as he caressed her clit.

"You ready for Papi?" Brandon said as he made his way face down in between her legs.

He reached up and stroked the soft mound of curly hair before parting her wet lips and slipping his thumb in and out. He eased his mouth around the hard knot of her clit and licked it, flicking it softly at first before slowly stroking it with the broad length of his tongue.

Lena moaned and stroked her fingers over his hair. He could feel her pussy pulsating as he thrust his tongue into her narrow opening and felt the salty juices flowing out of the corners of his mouth. Then he devoured her, sucking her clit harder and pushing his tongue farther in as he took all of that sweet nectar into his mouth.

"Brandon," Lena moaned in ecstasy as she felt the weight of his body press against her. Slowly, he entered her, pushing her open with his large manhood. Her fingers tightened and curled around fistfuls of his hair as she gasped open-mouthed and her body arched up to meet him.

He watched her face contort as he easily overpowered her, while he pressed himself farther inside. Her walls closed around his thickness and pulled on his sheath as he rode her while pushing his rock hardness deeper inside each time.

She gave herself to him, letting him have her body, feeling his hands roam her terrain, smacking her ass as he rode.

Pressing her thighs wider and higher with each stroke, he grasped her breasts in his wet, cum-soaked mouth and pinched her hard nipples with his teeth. Lena groaned and grabbed at his shoulders. He pulled her hands away and held them by her wrists above her head with one hand as he grabbed the firm flesh of her ass with the other.

"This is mine," he softly hissed under his breath.

Those words sent chills throughout her body as she neared her climax. She watched Brandon's eyes widen as he neared his and wrapped her legs around his waist as he rode faster and harder, his balls slamming against the tiny opening in the crack of her ass. She loved every moment of his claiming her as they exploded together.

"God, I love you, woman," Brandon panted as he got out of the bed and got into the shower.

Lena looked at the bathroom door. It was the first time he had ever gotten up after laying a sexing on her like that. She decided to let it go until he walked out fully dressed.

"Where the hell are you going at three in the morning?" she snapped.

Brandon jumped on Lena and kissed her. "Calm your ass down. I am going to the store. I like going to Wal-mart in the wee hours. You know that."

"What do you need from Wal-Mart that much?"

Brandon gave Lena a funny face. "Lena, stop tripping. Damn, I don't get to just enjoy my life anymore. I'm always getting stopped and shit. I just want to go to Wal-Mart, browse the DVDs, and buy some unnecessary shit. Can't a man do that, please?"

Lena looked at him suspiciously. "I guess. But since you're going, buy me some tampons . . ."

"Hell naw, Lena, I ain't buying that shit!" Brandon yelled, disgusted by the idea of even going on the aisle.

Lena laughed. "I'm just playing with you. But do get any Disney DVDs that I don't have, OK?"

Brandon kissed Lena again and left the room.

Lena turned over on her back and stared into the darkness. She wondered how the party was, secretly wishing she was there.

Denise walked into the room. Cooley could tell Denise was pissed. Cooley asked the remaining girls to leave.

"Cooley, that was fucked up," Denise said as she grabbed a garbage bag to clean up some of the mess from the party.

"Man, please . . . you did the right thing. That girl wasn't for you, and you knew it."

"That's not the point. She was serving her purpose."

"Oh, really? She had a purpose? Oh, I get it; she was supposed to take your mind off of Lena," Cooley said. "Well, the problem is that it didn't work, so why the fuck was you still with her?"

Denise sat down in the chair. "I don't know."

The room became silent.

"Look, bruh, I hate to see you fucked up like this. I say if you want her, go to her."

"You know I can't do that," Denise responded.

"Whatever. The only one stopping you is you. So tell me, Carmen was kicking her ass, huh?" Cooley smiled.

Denise smirked. "She did whip her ass."

They both started laughing as they continued to clean the apartment.

Chapter 4

The first day of school was more like a fashion show than an academic day. Women and men wore their best outfits as if they were headed to the club instead of campus, especially freshmen. Older students laughed as new students wore their stilettos on campus, not realizing just how much walking they would be doing. The smart ones knew how to look fly and to be comfortable at the same time.

Music blared from the speakers set up in the university center for the first step show of the year. Sorority girls strutted while fraternity men yelled their various calls. It was a freshman's paradise, the one place they could see everyone, Greeks, jocks, artists, and more.

Cooley looked herself over one time, making sure her pink and white striped polo shirt hung just right. She brushed the back of her neck while she patted down one side of her curly, mini Afro.

Nic shook her head; she wasn't as big on fashion as Cooley. She was comfortable in her jeans and T-shirt.

They could hardly tell it was nearly autumn. The sun was beaming down, causing most to pull out their shades and short-sleeved gear. Frat brothers walked around with their towels to match their Greek colors. Women still sported their skimpy summer clothes and flip-flops.

Denise patted the top of her head. "These braids are about to kill me." A brief autumn breeze rushed through the quad, giving Denise's scalp temporary relief.

"Stop patting them, bruh. They're hot," Cooley said. "I told you she was gon' make you look like you are headed to the pros."

"Well, if I have to endure that type of pain to look like a ball player, I'll keep my ponytail," Denise said, hoping for another breeze.

"How I end up hanging with y'all two non-dressing fools?" Cooley teased. She pulled out a mirror to check her short curly Afro. She had let her hair grow out from the short boy cut. Even though her hair was naturally curly, she placed a mild texturizer in it to give it just the right amount of curl.

"Whateva. I don't know about you, but I'm going to class and practice. I'm not getting fly for that. I am happy sitting here in my shorts," Denise said.

"I feel you, Dee. This is supposed to be school, not a runway. Besides, my girl likes the way I dress." Nic smiled.

"Y'all crazy. You are your appearance. Nic, you need to let that hair down and put on something fly. And, Dee—Fuck it! You're just hopeless."

"Fuck you!" Denise laughed.

"Like I said, my girl likes it," Nic boasted, holding her head high.

"Aww, there you go with that sappy shit," Cooley said. "Damn, this is the last year. I'm so ready to be up out this bitch," Cooley said, placing her shades on her face. That was one thing they all agreed on.

"What's up, Cooley?" A petite girl walked up. You could tell she cut her shorts herself by how uneven they were. They showed the majority of her butt cheeks.

"Ahh, shit, Bree, what's up? What the deal, mami?" Cooley stood up and gave the girl a hug. She had messed around with Bree, but never went the entire way.

"You got it. Word on the streets is that you doing it big boy-style, working at Jam Zone," the girl said, batting her long, fake eyelashes.

"I was doing it big before Jam Zone, and you know it."

"You right, you right. So what's up wit' cha? Heard you not wit' ole gal anymore."

"Damn, you sho do hear a lot about me," Cooley said.

Nic and Denise attempted to hold back laughter.

"You know I like to make sure I keep up with what I want." The girl leaned her body up against Cooley. "So what's up? You wit' her or not?"

"That's a negative, but I'm in chill mode right now, shorty. But I'll get at cha when I'm able again," Cooley said.

Denise and Nic were amazed.

The girl looked over at Nic. "Your name is Nic, right?" She smiled.

"Um." Nic looked confused. She had never seen the girl a day in her life. "Yeah."

The girl smiled. "Yeah, I saw your show last year. That was hot. My friend Peaches is crazy about you. She thought you were just so fine. I can give you her number if you like."

"Um, thanks, but no thanks. I got a girl." Nic timidly looked down at her book.

Denise couldn't help but laugh.

"Well, looks like all the sexy studs are off the market. Dee, you just don't give no girl a chance. My girl Tee been trying to get at you since freshman year."

"You already know the deal, Bree," Denise said.

"Well, I will see you all lata. Let me go break the news to my girls. Holla." Bree walked off.

"You in chill mode?" Denise questioned Cooley. "What's up with you?"

"Nothing. I'm just not looking to mess around right now," Cooley said.

"I never thought I would see the day." Denise laughed.

"Damn! Y'all act like a nigga just can't get right." She smiled, pointing at Nic. "Look at this mutha over here.

Girl's finna start throwing the panties at you. They would throw them at Dee, but she already turned them all down." Cooley laughed.

Denise threw up her middle finger.

"Well, they can just throw them at someone else 'cause not a girl on this campus or in this city interests me more than what I already have," Nic said.

"I know I said chill with that sappy shit. Aww, damn!" Cooley slumped down in her chair a little as Carmen and Misha approached. She watched Misha glance at her through her shades.

"You all are never going to believe this," Carmen said as she and Misha walked up to them.

"Believe what?" Denise questioned.

"Lo is back to dick now," Carmen said as she sat on Nic's lap.

"Whuuut?" Denise and Cooley said at the same time. Lo was a hard stud. There was nothing feminine about her.

"Yeah, she goes by Loretta now. She married some club owner or DJ something," Carmen added.

"Get the fuck out of here!" Cooley was shocked, "She was a bigger ho than—"

"You?" Misha interjected.

Cooley threw her a smirk.

"Yeah, and Tisha is pregnant, but I always knew her ass was going," Carmen said.

"Oh, not miss 'I can't stand dick' Tish. That bitch claimed she was so gay. Fucking sike-a-dyke." Misha rolled her eyes.

"Hey, if the girl wants to be back with men, then y'all gon' let her go back to men. It's not like y'all fuckin' any of them," Nic said, noticing how upset Misha seemed.

"Nic, you don't understand. Women like that make it hard for women like me. They are the reasons that men feel like they can talk to me any kind of way. 'Cause these bitches will yell they are gay but in the same breath will drop the panties. So, men think all of us are the same way."

"Not to mention, that's the reason that all these STDs are starting to hit the lesbian community more. 'Cause these bisexual women are sleeping with men and then having unprotected sex with women. And it's usually the ones that aren't up front about who they are."

Cooley and Denise listened as Carmen, Misha, and Nic talked. Denise thought about her experience with her ex, Crystal. She'd caught her in bed with a man. Her mind then went to Lena. She was crazy about her, and she was sleeping with a man every night.

"And look who's headed our way," Cooley said as two women walked toward them. Both were passing out flyers to everyone who passed their way. "These bitches get on my la—What's up, Nyla?" Cooley said to the petite feminine woman.

"Man, so much. How are all of you black people doing today?" Nyla responded.

"Yeah, how is everyone?" the other girl said. She was much taller than Nyla and wore long locks. "How are you, Carmen?"

"I'm good, Neo. How are you? Loving the locks," Carmen said to the stud.

"Things could be better." Neo handed Carmen a flyer. "You know the majorette choreographer, Devin, was bashed a couple of days ago."

"Get the fuck out of here!" Misha said. "Was it on campus?"

"Yeah, it was. You know, over by the drama department. We're having a planning meeting to figure out how to deal with the way things are getting on campus." Neo handed Misha and Carmen flyers. "You two should come. Carmen, we missed you in the Gay Student Alliance last year."

Cooley cleared her throat. "Um, what about us?"

"What about you?" Neo said with a slight attitude.

"Why you gon' single out C and Misha but not us? Maybe I'm wrong, but I think it's three gay-ass studs sitting at this table too."

"Cooley, come on, like you're really interested. You haven't been in the Alliance any year you've been here," Neo responded.

"Just 'cause I'm not joining the Alliance doesn't mean I wouldn't participate in anything with an issue like this. I was cool with Devin. Not to mention, if someone was to get bashed again it would probably be one of us before Carmen or Misha. After all they can pass, we can't. You of all people should understand that."

Neo sighed. "Fine, Cooley, if you want to come, then come." She handed Cooley a flyer. "I will see you all later."

"Fake-ass nigga," Cooley said when Neo and Nyla walked away.

"Cooley, why you have to act like that?" Carmen asked.

"I want to know why she had to flirt with you like that," Nic said to Carmen.

"She was not flirting." Carmen smiled.

"How was I acting?" Cooley interrupted. "The girl is fake. Just a few years ago she was just like Misha's little girl Tay, trying to jock my style. Hating on me and shit."

"Whatever," Misha said.

"But you don't have to act like that. People change," Carmen added.

Nic ignored her. "She was completely flirting with you."

"How was I actin'?" Cooley said again.

"Oh, Nic, I love it when you're jealous." Carmen kissed Nic.

"Dammit, how the fuck was I actin'?'" Cooley yelled.

"Like you really give a fuck about coming to the meeting or the alliance," Misha said.

"Wait, how do you know I wasn't? Damn, that's fucked up that you all don't think I care about gay rights and shit."

"Cooley, so you would join the Gay Student Alliance?" Nic asked.

"Hell naw. Man, the only people who join that are newly out and proud lesbians, curious women who want to act like they really give a damn about bridging the gay and straight gap, when they just trying to find a date, and ugly chicks, 'cause that's the only way they can meet people."

"That's fucked up, Cooley. I was in the G.S.A. my freshman and sophomore year," Carmen said.

"My point exactly. I didn't see you joining last year when you went off and thought you were sexy all of a sudden and when you got with Pretty Tony over here," Cooley said.

Nic threw up her middle finger at Cooley.

"Whatever. I was just busy," Carmen said.

"Exactly. We aren't nerds without lives like the people who join the G.S.A." Cooley put her shades on and smiled.

Misha shook her head.

"And what's that all about, Misha?" Cooley asked.

"You are pitiful," Misha said.

"Anyway, new subject." Cooley looked over at Misha. "Mish where yo' little gal at?"

Misha rolled her eyes. "She is in class. Where is your groupie of the week?"

"Ahh, you got jokes. No groupies, shawty. I'm gon' wait for you to get ya shit together and come back where you know you supposed to be." Cooley smiled.

"Changing the subject again," Misha said. She knew she had to get off the subject before she got any weaker in the knees. "So are y'all going to see Oohzee perform at Escapade this weekend?"

"Hell, yeah, you already know! Me and my bruh here are on the show," Cooley said, giving daps to Nic. Oohzee was the most popular exotic entertainer in the lesbian nation. She was notorious for pulling studs up on stage with her and flipping them over onto their backs with her acrobatic moves. Many up-and-coming entertainers had tried to copy her style, but few of them had the pull that Oohzee had. After pulling Cooley on stage the last time she was here and having her way with her. Cooley had been in love.

"Who is Oohzee?"

Everyone turned to see Lena walk up. Denise's heart began to beat rapidly.

Lena looked at Denise and could feel the butterflies fluttering around in her stomach.

"Oohzee is my future baby mama." Cooley looked at Misha. "Well, that is, since Misha won't act right." She grinned.

Misha rolled her eyes at Cooley. "Whatever, fool. Well, I guess I will see you there," Misha said. "I gotta get to class. See y'all later." She started to walk off.

Cooley jumped up and followed. "Misha, hold up," Cooley yelled after her. She felt as though history was repeating itself. She had run after Misha the first time they met.

"What, Carla?" Misha responded with a hint of attitude.

"Damn, Misha, why you gotta act like that with me? I thought we are better than that."

"Sorry, Cooley, I just can't be all around you like that. Tay doesn't like—"

"Misha, why are you dating that clown anyway? You know about her rep—"

"Oh, no, you didn't say anything about reps. After all, I did date you, and your rep is ten times worse than hers." Cooley knew she was right. She was still known as "Killa Cap Cooley."

"Man, Misha, that's not fair. You know how much I care about you. I changed all that for you."

"Yeah, and you reverted back to your old ways the next damn day! Yeah, Carla, I know about your little fuck fest the last day of school," Misha snapped.

Cooley knew then that Misha still cared about her.

Cooley lowered her head in defeat. "Misha, look me in my eyes and tell me that you don't still care about me."

"Cooley . . ."

"You can't do it, can you?" Cooley walked closer to Misha. Her eyes were piercing Misha like a knife. The heat began to rise between them. They were electric.

Misha cut Cooley off and backed up. "Cooley, we can't do this. I can't go there with you. I am with Tay now. I am happy. Let's just agree to work on our friendship. That's all we can have."

Cooley took a step back. She refused to show just how hurt she really was. "A'ight, dig that then. See you around, shorty." Cooley turned around and headed back to the courtyard. She refused to give up that easily.

"Hey, Dee." Lena finally mustered up the nerve to speak.

"How are you, Lena?" Denise asked. She had almost forgotten just how beautiful Lena was. Denise tried not to stare at Lena's frame. She noticed how Lena's short Baby Phat shorts were hugging her thighs and butt perfectly. She wondered if it was the breeze that was giving her chills.

"I am good," Lena said. She tried not to pay attention to Denise's brown skin. She wanted to feel up and down her muscular arms. She loved seeing Denise in wife-beaters; they hugged her body, showing off just how toned she was. "Hey, want to walk and talk?"

Carmen and Nic watched as Denise and Lena walked off.

"Soooo, are you thinking what I am thinking?" Nic said.

"Yup, that's disaster waiting to happen."

Denise and Lena walked in silence for a while. They made small talk about each other's summers. Lena could feel herself being drawn toward Denise and tried to fight it. They sat down on a bench in front of the library.

"I have, um, really missed you this summer," Lena admitted.

Denise's heart skipped a beat. "Really? I have missed you too. I didn't want to bother you. I know you've been real busy."

"Yeah, wedding planning and—"

"Yeah, wedding planning and Brandon." Denise could feel her stomach sinking.

They both became silent.

"Dee," Lena whispered.

Denise looked at her. Their eyes met.

"Do you think about, you know, what happened last semester?"

All the damn time. Denise thought to herself. "Well, yeah, sometimes I do. But I know it was just a kiss."

"Do you really think it was just a kiss?"

"What do you think it was, Lena?" Denise looked at Lena.

"I was just wondering. That's all."

"Lena, like I told you last year, you were just a little curious. It's no big deal. We made the right decision not to act on that. Hell, you are about to be married after all."

"Yeah, I guess you are right. So, are we still friends?" Denise asked.

"Yeah, of course, you are one of my best friends."
Denise hugged Lena. Neither one of them wanted to
let go.

They parted ways, both trying to shake the feelings
before they got around anyone who would notice.

Cooley stood in front of the bookstore bulletin board
hoping to find a band or two to check out. She wanted
to have something interesting to take to Atlanta during
Christmas break. She knew she'd made a great impression over the summer at Jam Zone and hoped to secure
a job over Christmas break.

"You don't see any ads for a freshman English book,
do you?"

Cooley turned to see an attractive girl staring at the
bulletin board.

"Naw, I don't. You know what, I think I have a freshman English book in my dorm. You're a freshman?"
Cooley sized the woman up. She was definitely great potential, but she hadn't gotten the gay vibe from her yet.

"No. I'm a senior, but I am trying to help a girl from
my church out. She was a Katrina victim. Lost most of
her family."

"Well, in that case, follow me."

Cooley and the girl headed into the bookstore. Cooley picked up a new freshman English book and bought
it. She could tell the girl was impressed. They headed
out of the bookstore.

"Wow, that was really nice of you." The girl smiled,
exposing two rows of perfect, white teeth.

Cooley smiled back. "My pleasure. I am always about
helping people."

"And who should I say helped her get this book?"

Cooley figured the girl couldn't be gay. All the gay
girls on campus knew who she was. "My name is Carla,
but most people call me Cooley. And your name is?"

"I'm Lynn." Lynn shook Cooley's hand. "I thank you again, Carla."

Cooley watched as Lynn walked away.

Damn shame, Cooley thought to herself. She hated to see straight women pass her up.

Before Denise could make it into her room, there was a knock on the door. She opened it to find Rhonda standing there in a long black coat.

"Can we talk?" Rhonda asked her as she walked into the apartment before Denise could answer. She headed back to Denise's room.

Denise closed the door and slowly followed Rhonda back to her room. "What's going on, Rhonda?"

"I fucked up, Denise. I am sorry about that. Let's not throw away what we have over a small argument," Rhonda said, turning her back to Denise.

"Man, I can't deal with you getting all pissed over my friends. They have been there for me for years, and your feud with them is bringing me stress." Denise sat on the bed. "I'm too damn blessed to be stressed."

Rhonda was still turned away from Denise. "I agree. It will never happen again." She turned around slowly. The jacket was now unzipped and exposed her nude body.

Denise was in shock.

Rhonda walked up to her and began to sensually kiss her neck. She pushed Denise back onto the bed and straddled her.

Denise felt funny. She put her arms between Rhonda and herself.

"Rhonda, I am not ready to be doing this," she said as she sat up, causing Rhonda to get off of her.

"Denise, we have been dating for almost five months and you have never put a hand on me. What's up with you?" Rhonda was quickly becoming upset. She jumped up and put her jacket back on.

"Man, I told you from jump that I am not looking for anything serious, and now you wanna act all brand-new."

"Denise, I have been waiting on you for five damn months. I figured maybe you were fucking another girl, but we spend all our time together. So what's the deal? It must be that bitch you were all hugged up with by the library today!"

Denise's eyes widened. "Oh, so now you spying on me?"

Rhonda knew she was caught. "No, it's not like that. I saw you walk away with the girl and my friend saw you at the library with some girl—"

Denise cut her off. "You know what, Rhonda, save it. This isn't going to work."

"Denise, I'm sorry," Rhonda said.

"Rhonda, come on now. I can't do this. Let's just be friends."

Rhonda looked at Denise and sighed. "You know what, fuck you, Denise!" She stormed out the room.

Denise heard her slam the front door. Denise sat back down on her bed. *Drama*, she thought to herself. She decided to make the vow she made to herself again. *No more women until I graduate.*

Lena heard her phone ring. It was Brandon. She pressed ignore. She wasn't in the mood to talk to him. She picked up the phone and called Carmen instead.

"What's going on, girl?" Carmen said when she answered the phone.

"Nothing much. Hey, what are you and Nic doing this weekend? I was thinking you all could come over this Friday and have dinner with Brandon and me."

"Oh, Friday won't work. Remember we're going to the club to see Oohzee perform?"

"Oh, yeah. I still don't know who Oohzee is," Lena said.

"Girl, she's the baddest damn dancer in the land. You want to venture out to the gay club with us again?" Carmen laughed.

"No, I don't think that would be a good idea. I saw Denise today." Lena expected a response, but didn't get one. "Carmen, did you hear me?"

"Yeah, I heard you. What did you want me to say?" Carmen responded. She knew that Lena was still feeling Denise.

"I don't know. I told her that I still think about her," Lena confessed.

Carmen's mouth dropped. "Really now. What did she say?"

"She turned me down. Told me to go home to Brandon." Lena felt her eyes starting to water.

"Oh, I'm sorry, Lena. You may not like what I am about to say, but she's right. That is something you need to let go of. You know curiosity kills many cats."

"Carmen, it's not that easy. I have been trying to all summer."

"Well, I suggest you try harder. Maybe you should talk about this to someone who is impartial. After all we're talking about my best friends here. I love you, girl, and I want the best for you. And the best is your fiancé."

Lena knew Carmen was right. "You're right, C. I just need to try harder."

Chapter 5

The club was packed, just like it always is when Oohzee comes to town. Denise walked into the club with Cooley. Cooley immediately saw Misha hanging on Tay's arm.

"Are you OK, bruh? Don't pay her any attention," Denise said to Cooley.

"Dude, I'm not trippin' on that girl. I got somethin' fo' her ass tonight. Now, let me go see my wife." Cooley walked off to go to the dressing room.

Denise found Carmen and Nic sitting down near the stage.

"Hey, people," Denise greeted Carmen and Nic, grabbing a seat next to them.

"Hey, baby, where is your little girlfriend?" Carmen asked, rolling her eyes.

"I wouldn't know. I broke it off with her." Denise saw the smile form on Carmen's face. "Damn, C, you could ask me if I am OK."

"Oh, fuck that. I am going to find you a real girlfriend. That's one down. I got one more to go," Carmen said as she saw Misha and Tay walking to the bar.

"Baby, behave tonight," Nic said to Carmen.

They heard the announcement for the show entertainers to come to the dressing room.

"Well, I guess I gotta bounce." Nic kissed Carmen on her cheek and headed to the back.

"Hey, Denise."

Denise turned around and was speechless as her teammate Stephanie walked up. She had never seen

Stephanie dressed like a woman before. She usually wore sweats.

"Stephanie, damn, is that you? Why aren't you in Spain?" Denise asked.

"Spain wasn't working out for me, so before I signed I decided to come back to school to finish off the year with you all."

"Dig that." Denise felt an instantaneous attraction for the first time, but she shook it off. That was team drama in the making.

"Well, I will see you at the meeting next week." Stephanie smiled and walked away.

Carmen noticed Denise watching her walk away.

"Now, that is the teammate you should have hooked up with in the first place," Carmen said to Denise.

"Whatever, man. I never noticed her before. Damn, what a difference a skirt makes."

They laughed as the show music began to start.

Instantly people stopped dancing and turned toward the stage. Lip synching shows were huge in Memphis. The Premiere family ran the Friday night shows at Escapade. Studs always performed male songs, and feminine women performed songs by women. The first number on the show was a group number featuring the mother of the Premiere family. She and a few of her gay daughters pranced around to Destiny's Child's "Bootylicious."

A few more numbers passed. Two studs performed a Jagged Edge song together, and a femme performed Heather Headley's "In My Mind."

Denise tipped her five dollars because she was feeling the song's lyrics. She lowered her head and closed her eyes, taking in the words of the song.

The announcer walked out on stage. "That bitch did that song, didn't she? Well, now I want to bring to the stage one of my new baby daddies." The male MC snapped his fingers. "This muthafucka here gon' make me go straight for her. I will be her bitch, you feel me? Give it up for Cali Nic!"

J. Holliday's "Bed" began to play.

Carmen smiled, as Nic's tall, slender body appeared on stage in a pair of black silk pajamas. The women in the crowd began to flock to the stage as Nic began to lip synch the words. Women held up their dollars, hoping that Nic would sing to them personally. Carmen watched as the girls screamed and smiled.

Nic pulled off her ponytail holder and let her long, wavy hair fall down her shoulders.

"You all right, C?" Misha asked and placed her arm around Carmen.

"My baby is fine as hell. Ain't . . ." Carmen paused when she saw a girl named Jamela walk on the stage. "What the fuck?" She watched as Jamela began to throw dollars on Nic one by one.

Jamela was one of the hottest women in the community, and she knew it. She wore her weave long and wavy to make it look like she was mixed with something. She showed her body as much as she could without being naked, but she could pull it off. Her pink dress was short, hugging her butt just right with a slit right down the middle for easy access to her breast.

Nic turned to Jamela and began to dance with her.

"Oh, hell no." Carmen walked up on the stage and began to throw dollars on Nic. She gave Jamela a look that let her know to get back. Nic then turned around and began to grind on Carmen. Carmen dropped the rest of her dollars on Nic and left the stage.

Misha laughed. "Girl, you was claiming your shit, huh?"

"You know it." Carmen looked out at the crowd. She no longer felt proud. All the girls were now looking like competition. She wondered which ones would actually try to get with her woman.

Nic's show ended, and she began to pick up her dollars as the MC walked back on the stage. "Damn, I will pick your dollars up for you. I will cook, clean. What you want me to do?"

Everyone including Nic laughed as she gave the MC a hug. He kicked his foot back while receiving the embrace.

Nic swaggered off the stage.

"How many of y'all liked that?"

The girls screamed.

Carmen watched Jamela smile and shake her head in approval. Jamela looked over at Carmen and rolled her eyes.

Misha grabbed Carmen's hand. "Girl, don't trip. Fuck that bitch."

"I'm just gon' move on with the show so I can go change my panties after that last one," the MC joked. "I'm wet. Now it's time to get you bitches wet. Y'all know what time it is. Coming to us straight from D.C., the bad girl herself. Y'all give it up for OOOHHHZEEEE!"

People crowded around the stage as the music began to play. A petite dancer came out in an all-white jacket. She lip synched to the beginning of her music. Suddenly she ran, flipped, and landed in a split. The crowd went wild.

Nic walked from backstage still in her show outfit. "That's my dog. I'm gonna tip her on stage, OK, baby?" She said to Carmen.

"Oh, go right ahead." Carmen smiled. She hoped that her wish would come true.

As soon as Nic walked on stage, Oohzee approached her. She laid flat on the stage and placed her foot between Nic's legs. She raised her leg up, pushing Nic into the air with her foot. Oohzee then flexed her powerful leg, causing Nic to fly into the air and land on top of her. As soon as she landed, Oohzee rolled her around the entire stage.

Carmen loved every minute of it.

Oohzee then put a dollar on Nic's face. She jumped down and back up again, pressing the dollar into her G-string.

The crowd was on its feet, screaming at the top of their lungs and chanting, "Oohzee, Oohzee."

Carmen was laughing in hysterics as Nic walked off the stage blushing. Other studs nodded approvingly as Nic walked through the crowd toward her.

Carmen could feel herself getting moist at the thought of what was in store for her later with Nic. She would have to thank Oohzee later.

It took the crowd a minute to get come down off of their frenzy. Nic and the MC helped to clear the money and clothes left from the performance off of the stage.

"Now, baby daddy, I don't know how I feel about you letting these other women feel on you and shit," the announcer joked with Nic as she left the stage. "I'ma have to get these bitches right. Y'all can't have my man," he said, looking at his show list. "And y'all can't have my other baby daddy either. I'ma have to get you bitches right when it comes to my men. Please welcome to the stage my original baby daddy, Cool!"

The women in the club went crazy when they heard J. Holliday's "Pimp in Me" start to play.

Cooley walked out in an all-black suit. The girls in the crowd went crazy running to the stage and pulling out their money to throw at Cooley. Cooley lip-synched the words to the song. Her eyes flashed and burned with focused intensity.

Carmen walked onto the stage and started tipping her, throwing dollar after dollar into the air.

Cooley got into the song. Misha watched with her arms folded as the song talked about not being a pimp anymore. She knew the song was directed at her. She could feel the steam rising from Tay, who was not happy about the song.

Suddenly the music faded out, as Avant's "Don't Say No" began to play.

Cooley walked to the back of the stage, took her jacket off, and unbuttoned her shirt. The girls screamed when she took her shirt off, leaving her wife-beater on.

Cooley turned her head in Misha's direction. Misha was standing up with her arms crossed in front of her chest. Cooley knew the song was getting to her. That was one of the songs they had sex to the first time.

Misha left Tay and walked to the stage. Tay reached for her hand but missed. Misha stood at the front of the stage with a dollar in her hand.

Cooley got on her knees and took the dollar, holding Misha's hand as she sang a piece of the song to her. They were in their own world.

Suddenly, Tay stormed up to Misha and grabbed her arm. She jerked Misha away from the stage so hard that she almost fell.

Cooley continued to perform the rest of the song, but she was also watching Misha and Tay walk off.

Denise and Carmen looked over at Tay and Misha, who were now involved in a heated argument.

The crowd near them stopped watching the show and started to focus on them, wondering if a fight was going to break out. The crowd soon got their wish. Misha tried to walk away from Tay but was met with a hard smack to her face.

Cooley instantly jumped off the stage, stormed up to Tay, and punched her in the face. Nic and Denise ran over to the scene, trying to break up the fight between Tay and Cooley. Misha was also trying to charge Tay, but Carmen held her firmly in place.

Three security guards eventually broke up the fight, and Tay was escorted out of the club.

Cooley turned around to see Misha standing with Carmen. "Misha," Cooley said as she grabbed Misha's arm, "baby, are you OK?"

"Yeah, Cooley, I am fine. It really wasn't that serious, you know."

Cooley was shocked. "What do you mean, not that serious? Misha, she put her hands on you!"

"Yeah, and, Cooley, I am a grown-ass woman. I don't need you rushing to help me. I was about to get in her ass all by myself," Misha said, looking down.

"Misha, I was just trying to protect you," Cooley said as she put her hand on Misha's face.

"Well, that's not your job anymore!" Misha snapped back. She looked at Cooley. "Look, I am sorry, all right. I didn't mean that. Thank you for coming to my rescue, but this doesn't change anything."

Cooley felt strange. She was looking at Misha completely differently. "Yeah, whatever." Cooley walked off, trying not to show any emotion.

Misha turned around and walked toward the dance floor, immediately regretting what she said.

Cooley walked into the game room of the club. She noticed a few faces that were new, but all looked too young for her to get involved with. She turned around when she thought she felt someone looking at her. She noticed a familiar face and smiled.

"Well, well, well, Miss Lynn, didn't expect to see you here," Cooley said as she approached Lynn. Lynn had a natural beauty just like Misha. Cooley could tell there was a lot of potential there.

"I didn't expect to see you on stage or fighting. Guess we both got a surprise tonight, huh?" Lynn smiled.

"Why didn't you tell me you were family?" Cooley stared into Lynn's eyes. One thing that always worked for Cooley was her natural grey eyes.

"Because I don't walk up to people and say, 'Hi, I'm Lynn. I'm gay.' And besides, I don't know you like that."

Cooley looked at Lynn in disbelief. "So, you really didn't know who I am?"

"No, I really didn't know. This is actually my first time coming to the club, and it's my first semester at Freedom. I transferred from Christian Brothers." Lynn smiled at Cooley, who tried to keep her cool face on. "I didn't know you were the head stud around here." Lynn laughed.

"Ha, ha, ha, very funny. I'm not the head of anything, I'm just Cool. So what are you getting into after the club?" Cooley looked Lynn in her eyes again. It made them weak. She could see it was working on Lynn.

"Nothing. Just going back to my room, unless I find something else to get into." Lynn gave Cooley a seductive grin.

Cooley licked her lips. "I think I have something we can do. Watch a movie or something. Let me grab my things, and we can head out." Cooley headed to the dressing room. Suddenly her night was taking a turn for the better.

Carmen scanned the crowd, looking for Nic. She noticed her standing at the bar. Carmen's heart dropped when she saw Nic talking to Jamela. She quickly began to make her way to the bar.

"So, your show was off the chain," Jamela said to Nic.

"Thank you. Thanks for the tips," Nic said. She hoped the bartender would quickly give her the drinks she ordered.

"So, what's up with you anyway, Nic?" Jamela batted her fake eyelashes. "What's a girl got to do to get to know you a little better?"

"Now you know I got a woman," Nic said, handing the bartender the money.

"So, you can't have friends?" Jamela batted her fake eyelashes.

"I already got those too. But thanks."

"Jamela, what the fuck do you think you doin'?" Carmen said as she jumped in front of Nic.

"Carmen, chill." Nic attempted to grab Carmen's arm, but she jerked away.

"What you mean? I think I'm talking."

"Bitch, don't make me hurt you. You know Nic is mine and if you come by her again, I'm gon' beat you worse than Teka did," Carmen threatened.

Last year a girl named Teka had attacked Jamela for sleeping with her girlfriend. Teka beat her and pulled all her clothes off of her in the middle of the parking lot. Jamela had to run to her car naked.

"Whatever, bitch," Jamela retorted.

Carmen began to swing, but Nic grabbed her hand.

"Come on, let's go!" Nic said in a stern voice as she pulled Carmen away.

"Carmen, what the fuck is wrong with you?" Nic asked as they drove home.

"What you mean, what's wrong with me? What the fuck is wrong with you, all up in her grill and shit!"

"Carmen, I can handle my own shit. You don't even know what I was saying. Why you trying to go off? Before you tried to jump bad, I had just told her that I had a girl."

"She don't care. She was gon' try you anyway."

"She can try all she want to. That don't mean I am going to let her. Shit, Carmen, you ain't got to worry about these scandalous bitches out here. I'm with who I want to be with."

"But—"

"There isn't any buts to it. Carmen, you can't try to fight every girl that tries to talk to me, just like I can't try to fight every girl that tries to get with you. I know you aren't going anywhere."

"And you know girls not gon' try to talk to me like they try to get with you." Carmen fought to hold back her tears.

"Carmen, please, that isn't the point. The point is that I don't want any of them. I got who I want. You gon' have to get up off that jealousy shit."

Carmen fell silent. She knew Nic was right. She didn't know how to react to those situations. "I just don't want to loose you."

"You aren't going to." Nic kissed her hand. "Wit' yo' crazy ass."

They both laughed.

"I love you, shorty."

"Love you too." Carmen smiled, but deep in her mind she couldn't get the sight of Jamela and Nic talking out of her head.

Cooley made it back to her room, intending to rock Lynn's mind.

Lynn walked in and began to look at their DVD collection. "You have some great movies." She pulled out *Finding Nemo* and looked at Cooley.

"That's my roommate's," Cooley lied. She loved *Finding Nemo*.

Lynn squealed, "I love *Harlem Nights*! I haven't seen it in forever. Can we watch this?" Lynn smiled like a kid in a candy store.

"Yeah, that's cool. Let's take it back to my room," Cooley said. She didn't plan on making it past the infamous "pinky toe" scene.

Cooley gave Lynn one of her large shirts to get comfortable in and looked at her. She could tell the girl was really innocent.

She decided not to give her the full "Killa" experience. She didn't want another crazy chick like Cynthia on her like last year. Cynthia had gotten a job in the housing center to ensure she was roommates with Cooley. When she fucked her within the first thirty minutes of meeting her, it ended up being the worst mistake of her life. Cynthia had caused the most of the drama in her life last year, including making the whole campus believe Cooley had herpes.

Lynn lay in the bed next to Cooley. Cooley began to rub on her leg. Lynn took notice. "Um, I hope you don't think it's going to be that easy. I don't give it up on the first night."

Cooley looked at Lynn with amazement. She wanted to tell her to leave if she wasn't giving it up, but she knew many girls who said the same thing. "Girl, it's not that type of party. You gotta earn this."

Lynn appeared surprised by Cooley's response. "Is that right? You make a girl wonder if it is really worth trying to earn."

Cooley gave Lynn a "girl, please" look. "Girl, you better ask someone."

"I prefer to find out for myself one day, just not tonight." She smiled.

Cooley actually found that cute. She decided not to try her that night after all. They watched the movie and fell asleep.

The next morning Cooley woke to a mouth-watering smell coming from the kitchen. She walked into the kitchen and found Denise eating a full breakfast. Lynn was standing in front of the stove, frying bacon.

Denise looked up from her plate. "Damn, bruh, your girl is cooking her ass off in here."

"I see that. I smelled that all the way in the room." Cooley looked down at the table. There were pancakes, eggs, and bacon on the table. "Girl, what are you trying to do to us?"

Lynn smiled. "Nothing. I just like to cook. I hope you don't mind that I did it."

Denise took a sip of her freshly squeezed orange juice. "Mind? Hell, you can move in if you gon' cook like this." Denise got up from the table. "I gotta get to practice. I hope I can move after this." She walked out the room.

Lynn served Cooley. "So, Cooley, can I ask you a question?" Lynn said as she put the fresh bacon on the table. "What are you actually looking for in a woman?"

Cooley paused. She wasn't ready to answer that question. "Actually, Lynn, I am not in the market for a girlfriend or anything. I am just kicking it right now. I just got out of a relationship, and I am not looking to commit again anytime soon."

Lynn didn't want to hear that answer, but she accepted it. "Oh, that's cool. I totally understand," she lied. "I was just making sure that we were on the same page."

Cooley gave a sigh of relief. "I am glad you understand. I mean, I am feeling you and would like to get to know you better, but I am dating around and just like to keep it real, you know."

"Yeah, I know." Lynn smiled.

Cooley smiled back. "Now sit down and enjoy this breakfast." Cooley was glad Lynn understood. She planned on keeping her around, even if it was only for the food.

Chapter 6

"*Hola*, Rico Suave."

Nic turned around when she heard a familiar voice giggling behind her. "What's up, crazy-ass girl?" Nic gave a big bear hug to the tall and slender girl named Larissa. "How are you? I love the new haircut," Nic said, noticing Larissa's new do. It was cut in the inverted bob Victoria Beckham made famous.

"I'm good." Larissa smiled. "This is my friend Sophie."

Nic shook hands with the short, round girl. She laughed to herself. Carmen and she had previously made fun of the plump friend for wearing a dress that was two sizes too small at a Chi Theta party.

"I've seen you around before. You date Carmen Taylor. She is Vice-President for Chi Theta, right?" Sophie's eyes were bright.

"Yeah, she is," Nic responded. She could tell that the girl was one of the eager girls wanting to pledge. She was the kind that got taken advantage of by sorority members. They loved meeting girls who were too eager simply so they could use the membership as leverage to get whatever they wanted from the naive women. "So how did your class come out, LaLa?"

"Great!" Larissa smiled. "Thanks to you. Nic helped me pass that damn math class. I swear she could do the problems in her head."

"Smart, huh?" Sophie added.

"Not with everything. I'm about to not graduate over this literature class I'm taking. I ended with this professor who is focusing on Shakespeare. I don't know shit about Shakespeare."

"Professor Drumm," Larissa said.

"Yeah. You had him?"

"Yeah, because I love Shakespeare. I'll look through my things to see if I still have my notes."

Nic grabbed Larissa's arm. "Girl, don't play with me. Are you serious? Please do. I will be forever in your debt."

"I got you. I love Shakespeare, so I can help you with whatever you need. After all, you helped me last year."

Nic threw her arms around Larissa and scooped her up in a tight embrace that left her feet dangling above the ground.

"Thanks so much. Now Carmen won't kill me for not graduating. Oh, shit, how is your dude doing?" Nic asked as they walked out of the campus café. She opened the door and held it for both ladies.

"Oh, we're, um, good. It's a couple of things I have to work on him with, but we're good.

"Wow, that's wonderful, girl. I hope everything works out for you two. Wait, let me get that for you," Nic said as Larissa went to open the door to leave the University Center. Nic again held the door for both girls.

Larissa looked at Sophie. They both smiled.

"Well, Nic, I will call you if I find the notes, or probably text you."

"Thanks, La. See you two later. Nice meeting you, Sophie." Nic turned around and headed back into the café.

"Girl, you weren't lying. She is fine as hell. I thought she was a boy at first," Sophie remarked.

"I told you. When I saw her in my math class I was so attracted. Then I found out her name was Nicole. That fucked me up, girl. Especially when I started to get to know her. I swear she is a better man than damn near every man I know, including my own."

"I see. Shit, I haven't had a guy open a damn door for me since my father."

They laughed.

"Tell me about it. Man, if Nic was a fucking guy, I would so have to take her from Carmen. I am not gay, but hell, I see why so many women like to try the shit."

"I wouldn't say that much. I don't care how fine a bitch is, it ain't gon' make me want to stop getting dicked down," Sophie said as they gave each other a high-five.

"I swear, if I ever meet a man anywhere near as good as Nic, I am going to hold on and never let go," Larissa said.

"Dig that," Sophie added as they headed to the library.

Denise sat next to Stephanie and Michelle listening to their coach's spill about bringing another championship home. Denise snuck a glance at Stephanie. She still couldn't believe her changed appearance. The new players and scrubs headed to the floor, hoping to land one of the open starting positions.

"Man, doesn't it feel good to be seniors now?" Michelle said. "Look at them. Remember when we were like them, trying to make starter?"

"Hell, yeah. I was so damn nervous," Stephanie added. "Well, you know Denise here didn't have any problems. She was golden from jump."

Denise smiled. "Whatever. I had to try just like everyone else."

"Whatever, nigga. Coach had your ass ready to start from jump." Michelle looked over at Stephanie. "Steph,

I wouldn't be the person I was if I didn't ask what the fuck is up with your new look?"

"What do you mean?" Stephanie said smiling.

"Girl, please. You was harder than Dee here last year. Now you come back all fish and shit."

"Man, I just wanted to try something new."

"New, my ass," Michelle said.

"OK, check this out. I need to dress for success now, and y'all should think about it too."

"What you mean?" Denise asked.

"OK, so I was talking to some people when I was in Spain. It seems that showing I was gay as hell wasn't a good image. Dee, when you go pro, it's gonna happen to you too. Don't nobody want a dyke as a role model for their little girls."

"That's bullshit," Michelle spat. "The majority of the WNBA is gay, and you know it."

"Yeah, but they don't say they're gay, now do they? They walk around with their little boy toys to make the public think they're straight."

"What about Sheryl?" Denise said. "She is my idol, and she is out."

"Yeah, but it took her years to come out. And it's not like her coming out has caused a chain reaction. Then think about those reports of gay players coming on and messing with other players. From what I'm understanding, people just don't want those type of issues." Stephanie stood up. "So, I am going to play my role and try to get my ass on a WNBA team."

"Fuck that. If I can't be myself, I don't want to do it. What's the fun of being pro and not being able to be myself? I'm not hiding anything." Michelle walked down the bleachers and headed to the locker room.

"Don't you agree with me, Dee?" Stephanie asked.

"Sorry, I can't say that I do. I mean, don't get me wrong, I don't advertise who I sleep with to the world.

But if I was to have a girl, I'm not going to hide her away. I came out a long time ago, and I'm not going back in the closet."

They both headed to the locker room.

Denise froze when she walked into the locker room. There was a large exotic bouquet of flowers filled with pink orchids and purple callalilies, and a large teddy bear with a small jersey on it. "Who did that?" she asked, pulling the card out from under the bear.

> *Dee,*
> *Please forgive me. Let me show you how much*
> *I care about you. Talk to you later.*
> *Rhonda*

"Damn, Dee, what you put on that girl?" Michelle asked as she read the card over Denise's shoulder.

Denise folded the card and put it in her bag. "Not shit."

"I can't tell," Stephanie teased.

"You know, I don't know . . . it's something about that girl that just doesn't sit right with me," Michelle cautioned.

"Cooley and Carmen don't like her either." Denise tried to push the flowers into her locker, but they wouldn't fit.

"I feel them on that. She is too jealous or something. Look at how she acted at your party. I hope you don't get back with her."

"The only thing I am trying to think about is how to get rid of these flowers."

They all laughed.

Lena opened the door to her apartment and was taken over by a wonderful smell coming from the kitchen. She smiled and ran into the house, hoping to catch Brandon cooking.

"Brandon, what are you cooking?" she yelled out. She rushed into the kitchen, only to find an older black man cooking. Before she could question him, she felt arms reach around her waist.

"Surprise, baby," Brandon said as he put his arms completely around her. "This is our new chef, Max. And Junaita is our new housekeeper, but she is out at the store right now."

Lena turned around to Brandon. "Baby, if they cook and clean, what exactly am I supposed to do now?"

"You are supposed to go to school, shop, and do volunteer work to make me look good." Brandon smiled.

Lena didn't like the sound of her new schedule.

"But, baby—"

Brandon interrupted before she could finish. "Now, Beyonce has asked me to star in her new video, so I am going to L.A. for the weekend. Go pack your bags. We leave first thing tomorrow."

"Baby, I can't go to L.A. I have class."Lena was growing tired of Brandon's lack of interest in her schoolwork. He always wanted her to attend late-night functions and go out of town, which would cause her to miss school. He made the comment more than once about her quitting school. She refused. Just in case she ever had to leave him, she wanted something to fall back on.

"Damn, can't you miss a few classes?"

"No, boy, I can't. But have fun with Beyoncé and don't let Jay-Z kick your ass, OK?"

"Well, how about you invite your crew over for the weekend? You know, Misha and Carmen. Order like one of those come-to-the-house spas or something."

Lena squealed with happiness. "Baby, that's a great idea. I know they will love it." She hugged him and gave him an intimate kiss. "Why don't you come back here and let me give you a little something to remember me by?" She pulled his hand toward the bedroom.

Brandon hesitated. "As tempting as that is, I have to go meet with my agent before heading to the airport, so I will have to just make sure to get doubles when I get back, OK."

He kissed her again and headed out the door, leaving Lena wondering what just happened. Brandon never turned down the chance for a quickie.

"How are you, girl?" Carmen asked as she sat next to Misha.

"I'm fine. Girl, the bitch had the nerve to come to my room last night and apologize." Misha laughed. "I must have slapped the shit out of her before closing the door. I am so glad I didn't make her my roommate like she wanted me to."

"I am glad too 'cause I don't need you or Cooley going to jail," Carmen said.

Misha looked at Carmen. "I think I need to apologize to her."

"You need to do more than that. I wasn't going to say anything, but that was real fucked up, Mish."

"I know. I just was pissed off. But I think I finally pushed her to the limit," Misha said.

"Yeah, she was pretty upset. And you know how she reacts to rejection."

"She hooked up with someone?" Misha asked.

Carmen shook her head.

"Well, typical Carla. Can't wait one day before fucking someone."

"They didn't fuck, Misha. Just watched a movie or something. Misha, I know you don't want to hear this, but Cooley really does love you. She doesn't want anyone but you."

"She had her chance. She didn't even try to fight for me."

"She fought for you last night."

Carmen and Misha looked at each other.

"I'll talk to you later. I got some business to handle." Misha gave Carmen a hug and headed out.

"What do you want?" Cooley opened the door, letting Misha into her house.

Misha had waited a few weeks before coming to Cooley. She knew she was wrong for reacting the way she did at the club. Misha could tell that Cooley was still upset. "Carla, I just wanted to apologize for what happened. It was real wrong of me to act like that. I know you were just trying to help."

Cooley looked at Misha. She noticed how her jeans were fitting perfectly around her petite body. "Oh, so really, you noticed that, huh?"

"Carla, I am sorry things are sticky right now, but I do want us to be friends."

Cooley stared at Misha. "Mee, I don't know if I want to be your friend." She stood up and walked toward Misha.

The body heat was rising between both of them.

"How can I be friends with you when I want to be the one holding you and caressing you?" Cooley caressed Misha's arms. She could sense that Misha wanted her just as badly as she wanted her.

Misha could hardly contain herself. Her panties were soaking wet from the sight of Cooley. She moved back before she lost control. "Cooley, we don't need to do this. We weren't good together."

Cooley grabbed Misha's arm and pulled her close to her. "I think we were dynamite together." She pulled Misha to her and kissed her. She let all of her passion rush into the kiss, hoping that the transfer of emotions would help Misha remember where she belonged.

Misha couldn't resist. She wrapped her arms around Cooley, letting Cooley take complete control of her body and soul.

Cooley picked her up and carried her into her bedroom. Slowly she removed every piece of Misha's clothes, determined to lick every inch of Misha's sexy body. Misha moaned as Cooley lifted her leg up and devoured her toes. Cooley kissed her way up Misha's leg to her thigh. She sucked on the inside of her thigh and branded her with a Cooley love mark.

Misha's pussy was throbbing, completely wet and hot, ready for Cooley to take it, and she quickly obliged.

Cooley entered Misha's pussy and stroked her with sensual familiarity. Slowly she started turning her fingers as Misha's walls expanded and closed around them, pulling them farther inside of her. Cooley pushed another finger and then another, until Misha felt like she couldn't bear any more. She sucked on Misha's clit, reclaiming it as her own, while her hand slowly disappeared inside. She licked her around the lips of her pussy stretched taut from the force of Cooley's hand inside her and slowly then more quicly sucked back and forth, extending the length of Misha's hardened little clit.

"Oh shit!" Misha yelled, unable to control her moans. It had been so long since she had it done right. Tay couldn't' hold a candle to Cooley. Misha knew that no one would ever sex her like Cooley could. She fit Cooley like a fine leather glove.

Cooley continued stroking her and sucking on the hard, little knot, occasionally flicking it with her tongue and nibbling gently, pulling on it as she sucked.

Misha moaned louder and arched her back, lifting her ass into the air.

Cooley slipped her free hand around Misha's ass and cupped her cheeks together. She rubbed, smacked, and stroked them. She teased the small entry in between with the tip of her thumb.

It sent shivers through Misha's pussy and made her groan uncontrollably. "Oh, fuck, oh fuck, I'm gonna, gonna . . ." Her moans became inaudible as she started to tremble.

Cooley's body responded to Misha's moans and quaking body. Her clit throbbed and grew. It pulsated and pushed between her own lips. As Misha yelled and her body began to shake, Cooley began to ejaculate. She withdrew her fingers and wrapped her arms around Misha's ass, making sure that she didn't miss a single drop of the sweet cum pouring down Misha's thighs as she exploded with an intense orgasm.

Cooley licked one last droplet and kissed the inside of her thigh as she stood up. Misha was still panting heavily from the orgasm. Cooley reached down and petted Misha's soaking wet pussy.

Misha twitched and laughed as she pushed Cooley's hand away. "Don't you dare, Killa." She laughed while still trying to catch her breath. "You ain't gon' have me out there looking for no damn inhaler," she said, referring to the night Cooley got her nickname, Killa Cap, when she made a girl have an asthma attack.

They both laughed.

"Damn, Misha, when was the last time you had it done right?" Cooley smirked, knowing she just gave Misha some super head.

Misha smiled.

"When was the last time you had it?"

Misha looked around and grabbed various pieces of her clothes.

Cooley smacked Misha on her butt as she headed to the bathroom.

Misha looked at herself in the mirror. She knew that she still loved Cooley, but she wasn't convinced that was where she needed to be. She walked out of the bathroom and looked at Cooley lying on her bed. "Cooley, this does not mean that we are back together."

Cooley looked at Misha. She was still not used to having the shoe on the other foot. Cooley was used to those words coming out her mouth. "Damn, Misha, did you hear me say anything about that?"

"No, but I wanted to ."

"You wanted to fuck up the mood, and you did a good job of it." Cooley stood up and put a T-shirt on.

Misha watched Cooley give her the cold shoulder. "Come on, Carla, you know what I mean. After all, the sex was always great. It was the relationship we had a problem with."

"Last time I checked, you had the problem with the relationship." Cooley could feel herself getting angry. "I gave up a lot for you, and I am still willing to do so again. You couldn't handle it."

Misha looked at Cooley. "And I don't think I can handle it now. I don't want us to fight. I want us to come to a conclusion."

Cooley sighed and sat down in her chair. Deep down she knew Misha was right. "Look, shorty, you know I got feelings for you. I am not willing to give you up completely."

"And I am not willing to give you up either," Misha said as she stood in front of Cooley. "So what do we do?"

Cooley wrapped her arms around Misha's waist. "Look, I say that we do our own thing, but when we get together, it's all about us. I mean, honestly, I did meet this girl that seems pretty cool."

"That's good, but, Cooley, you can't be fucking every bitch on campus and thinking that you gon' come back to me," Misha responded.

"I know. It's not even like that anymore. So, we agree to see other people, but still get down like we used to on occasion?"

"Yeah, that's good." Misha smiled. She leaned down and kissed Cooley. "So how about another round?"

"As much as I want to say yes, the girl is going to be over here soon." Cooley hated telling Misha no.

"Dig that. I'll see you later, Carla." Misha turned around and walked out of Cooley's room.

Cooley smiled. Things couldn't get much better than that.

Chapter 7

Denise woke up to the sound of her phone ringing. She listened to the answering machine pick up.

"Denise, this is Ms. Wallace from across from your grand's house. I think something may be wrong here—"

Denise jumped to pick up the phone.

"Hey, Ms. Wallace, what's going on?" She said, clearing her throat.

"Now, baby, I don't know for sure, but there has been a lot of people in and out of there. I know you busy with school and your mother is living there and all, but I wanted to let you know 'cause I figured you didn't know. It's not the right kind of people either," Ms. Wallace said with concern in her voice.

Denise immediately felt herself getting angry. She always questioned why her grandmother would leave the house to her mother. Denise's mother had been a junkie her entire life, but after the death of Mema, she thought that Tammy was finally getting her life right. She attended rehab just like Mema said she would have to do to live in the house. Denise hoped that she didn't go back to drugs, but she knew that was probably the case.

"Thank you, Ms. Wallace. I will be over there soon." Denise jumped up and put her clothes on. She walked into Cooley's room to find her in the bed with Lynn.

"Cooley, something's up at Mema's house," Denise said as Cooley woke up.

"Dude, give me ten minutes." Cooley jumped up out of the bed and started to get dressed.

Denise called Carmen and told her to meet her at Mema's house.

"Do you need me to leave?" Lynn asked as she watched Cooley hurrying to get dressed.

Cooley looked up, forgetting that Lynn was at the house. "Yeah, I'll call you later, all right?"

Lynn took the cue and immediately got dressed to leave.

As they arrived at the house, they noticed the grass obviously had not been cut in months. There were beer bottles and litter all over the yard. Denise's blood was boiling. Cooley and Carmen noticed her intensity growing.

"Denise, please calm . . ."

Before Carmen could finish, Denise charged into the house. Cooley ran in after her while Carmen called the police.

"Tammy!" Denise yelled out. "Tammy, where the fuck are you?" Denise looked around the house; it was filthy. There was trash all over the ground. She noticed most of Mema's furniture was missing, including her trophy case and all of her trophies earned over the years.

Carmen walked in the house and gasped. She looked around the destroyed place as tears began to form in her eyes.

Suddenly they heard a noise from the back. Denise looked at Cooley. They both ran to the back of the house. They noticed the door to Mema's room was cracked. Denise opened the door to see Tammy having sex with a man. There was another man on the floor shooting smack into his arm.

"Who is that?" the man said as Tammy rode on top of him, obviously so high she didn't hear anyone come into the room. Tammy turned around to see Denise standing there. Her eyes widened.

"Denise!"

Before she could finish, Denise lunged at her. She started to tighten her arm around her mother's throat. "How could you! How could you!" she repeated as she watched the life start to drain from Tammy's sunken face.

Cooley ran to grab Denise and struggled to get her friend's arm loose from her mother's neck.

"No, Denise, this isn't the way!" Cooley yelled as she pulled Denise off of Tammy, who was trying to catch her breath.

Denise was breathing hard. She looked at Tammy crying on the floor.

Denise stood up and walked toward Tammy, who began to plead with Denise.

"Denise, please, baby, I am sorry," she cried.

Denise continued to stare at her mother.

Carmen walked in to see the display. "Denise, the police are here," she said. She had never seen Denise so angry.

"Don't ever come around this house or come around me again. You're dead to me." Denise left the room to the sound of Tammy's cries.

Carmen and Cooley watched as the police put Tammy and the other men in the squad car. Carmen heard her phone ring. She realized the ring was Lena.

"Um, Lena, can I call you back?" Carmen said, keeping a close eye on Denise.

"Sure. Well, I have this whole little spa thing set up over here, so when you get free come get you a massage, OK?" Lena replied.

"Yeah, OK." Carmen hung the phone up. She looked down at her phone and smiled.

Carmen walked over to Denise and put her hand on her shoulder. "Sweetie, you need to relax, Lena has something for you at her house. Go over there and relax OK? Me and Cooley will take care of everything here."

Denise looked at Carmen. She knew something was up, but she didn't question her. She just wanted to get away from the scene. Denise hugged Carmen and headed to her car.

Cooley walked up to Carmen. "What are you up to?" she questioned as she looked at Carmen. She also knew she was up to something.

"I am just giving Denise what she needs right now." She picked up her phone and called Lena back. "Lena, I can't make it, but Denise is headed over there. She has had a very rough day. Please let her have my massage, OK?" She hung up the phone before Lena could respond.

"What was that all about?" Cooley asked Carmen, who was smiling.

"Nothing, Cooley," she said as she headed back into the house.

Cooley grabbed her arm. "Carmen, you got one second to tell me."

"I just wanted Denise to relax. And there is only one person who can help her with that." Carmen looked at Cooley. Cooley smiled, realizing what Carmen did.

They both laughed as they headed in the house to clean it up.

Lena looked at herself one last time in the mirror when she heard the doorbell. She knew that her new staff would open the door. She walked into the front room and found Denise looking around.

"Damn, girl, I thought our dorm room last year was tight," Denise said as she gave Lena a hug. She smelled the Creed on her body, the same perfume that used to arouse all of her senses.

A small dog ran up to Denise and started jumping in the air. "What the hell is that?" Denise wasn't a fan of small dogs.

Lena picked up the little dog. "This is Kovu. He's a Pomeranian."

"What the fuck kind of name is Kovu?"

"I got it from the *Lion King II*. You know, the lion that married Simba's daughter." Lena smiled.

"Whatever. I guess, you really are living that glamorous life. Got the little mutt and everything."

"Yeah, a thousand-dollar mutt." Lena laughed.

"You paid a *G* for a dog that's gonna put hair everywhere? Hell, naw, Lena." Denise laughed.

"Whatever. Come. Let's eat before I put you out."

They headed into the dining room. They sat down as the cook brought out their T-bone steaks with sides of garlic, mashed potatoes, and mixed vegetables.

Lena looked up at Denise, who was barely eating her steak. She had sadness in her eyes.

"Denise, is everything all right? You look like something is troubling you."

"My mom ruined Mema's house. She's back on that shit and she ruined Mema's house." Denise forcefully poked at her steak. "The fucked up thing is that I can't blame anyone but myself. I knew better. I knew she wasn't going to get her life together. I knew she was going to still be a fuckin' junkie!" Denise stabbed the steak so hard, it bent the fork. "Shit. I'm sorry, Lena."

"It's fine, just a fork." Lena handed Denise another one. "Denise, you just did what your grandmother wanted you to do. Don't blame yourself," Lena said. Her heart dropped when she noticed a tear fall from Denise's face. "You can't blame yourself, Dee. Don't do that to yourself."

"I just feel like I'm letting my grandmother down."

"Dee, your grandmother is looking down on you and smiling. She knows you are doing all that you can. Dee, you're so driven. You are the most driven person I know."

"I miss her so much." Tears rolled from Denise's face.

Lena wrapped her arms around Denise.

"I can't believe my mother did that shit. I don't know what I'm going to do about the house. It's ruined."

"Hey, hey, let's not think about that right now. I want you to relax. Come watch a movie with me in our theatre. I got *Love Jones*." She reached her hand out to Denise.

Denise smiled and took her hand. Lena's hand was soft and warm. She felt butterflies. Denise swallowed hard, hoping to make them go away.

Denise laughed. "You would have a theatre!"

"Shut up." Lena laughed.

Denise hugged Lena.

Lena laid her head on Denise's chest. She loved to hug Denise. She felt so safe in her arms.

Lena dismissed all of the staff and locked up behind them. They headed into the theatre.

"Now don't say shit when you go in here."

"OK."

Denise couldn't believe her eyes. The large screen took up most of the wall space. The white carpet was so plush, it left the imprint of footprints when you walked. There were two oversized micro-suede, brown couches along with a working replica of an old-fashioned pop-corn popper on wheels.

"Man, Lena, you are really doing it big. I hope I get to this level one day," Denise said with approval as she sank into the couch.

"You will. You are going to be famous like Sheryl Hoops."

"*Swoopes*, Lena. Sheryl *Swoopes*." Denise shook her head and laughed.

"Whatever. You know what I meant." Lena laid down and placed her head in Denise's lap.

Denise took a drink of her beer. She looked down at Lena, who was deep into the movie. She smiled and noticed all the curves in Lena's face. Denise felt a warm sense of comfort that she hadn't felt since the end of last semester.

Denise and Lena watched as Darius and Nina had their first date. They stood in the doorway, right before the infamous sex scene. The smooth sound of Maxwell played as the movie got to the sexual part. They watched as Darius and Nina got it on for the first time.

Lena sighed. "Now that's how lovemaking is supposed to happen." She looked up at Denise. "Don't you agree?"

Denise looked down at Lena. Their eyes met. They began to kiss.

Denise wrapped her arms around Lena, slowly caressing her back. Lena could feel her panties becoming soaked from Denise's soft stroke.

Denise pushed Lena on her back, causing the couch to shift. Suddenly there was a loud crash as one of the vases on the end table shattered on the floor. They both jumped up. The dog began barking loudly at the broken vase.

Lena looked around the room and remembered where she was.

Denise could see the fear in Lena's eyes. "Lena—"

"Oh, no!" she said as she leapt off the couch. "Oh, no! What have I done? What the fuck is wrong with me?" She began to cry as she ran to her bathroom.

Denise heard the door slam. She put her head down. She realized she had made a terrible mistake.

"I'm going to leave, Lee," Denise said as she headed toward the front door. Denise felt a strange feeling in her stomach. She knew she couldn't leave.

She walked back to the bathroom door and heard Lena's sobs on the other side. She opened the door to find Lena staring in her mirror. Tears had streaked her makeup.

"Lena, baby, it's going to be OK," she reassured as she put her arms around her.

"Denise, I'm sorry. I don't know what I have done. I shouldn't have done it. I don't know what do to. Brandon . . . Damn, I just kissed you in our house. What have I done?" Lena began to cry harder.

Denise put her arms around Lena and picked her up. She carried her into the master suite and put the sobbing Lena in her bed.

She took her shoes off and climbed into the bed next to her. "You didn't do anything, Lena. I am your friend and I am here for you."

Denise held Lena until she fell asleep. Denise got out the bed, headed toward the door. She noticed a pad on the table. She jotted down a quick note and laid it on the table next to Lena's bed before heading out the door.

I am always here for you as your friend. —Dee

***

It was almost midnight when Denise made it back to her apartment. As soon as she made it inside, she heard a knock at the door.

"What do you want?" she said to Rhonda, who was standing at her door.

"Can we talk?" Rhonda asked.

Denise reluctantly let her into the house.

"I have been waiting on you for about an hour. I was just about to leave when I saw you pull up. Denise, I don't want us to be over. I will work on my attitude, if you give me another chance."

"Rhonda, I don't know. You be trippin' too much for me. I told you before, I don't do the drama," Denise said, walking into the kitchen.

"I know, Denise, and I promise to be better. We have a lot in common. We are good for each other, and you know it."

"Rhonda, we really don't. Yeah, you like some of the same music as I and shit, but that isn't enough to make a relationship off of. You don't like any of my friends, and they are a major part of my life."

"I am willing to put all that in the past. I didn't really give them a fair chance, and I was wrong for that. Come on, Denise, don't leave me. Don't do that to me," Rhonda cried out.

"Rhonda, I just don't . . ."

Before Denise could finish, Rhonda began to unbutton her shirt.

"Denise, I belong to you. This will always belong to you. You can have it whenever you want it." Rhonda dropped her blouse.

It was the first time Denise actually looked at her breasts.

Rhonda walked up to Denise and began to kiss her on the mouth. Denise wrapped her arms around her, and they headed to her room.

Denise finally gave up. If she couldn't be with the right girl for her, she would be with the girl that was there right now. She took Rhonda into her room and began to fuck her. There was no love involved, no passion in it for Denise. It was the first time she had used the strap that Rhonda had bought for her a few months back. She pounded against Rhonda, taking all her stress out on Rhonda's vagina.

Rhonda moaned, yelling Denise's name. She loved every minute of it.

Denise closed her eyes, and Lena popped into her head. She started to grind on Rhonda, who was on her second orgasm. Denise kept her eyes closed, imagining Lena's body. She licked her lips, savoring the taste of Lena.

Denise began to quiver as she climaxed. She lay down on the side of the bed and felt arms wrap around her.

"Baby, that was amazing. I knew it would be worth the wait," Rhonda purred as she got up and headed to the bathroom.

Denise opened her eyes, realizing what she'd done. She felt a twinge of guilt. She closed her eyes. She wanted to make sure Rhonda thought she was asleep when she got back, in case she was expecting some oral sex from her.

Denise took a deep breath. Her mind drifted back to Lena. She wondered if she was all right. She wanted to go back to the loft, but knew it would be a bad mistake. She closed her eyes, hoping to drift off into her dreams. Dreams always filled with Lena.

Cooley closed the door to her bedroom. She had been kicking it with Lynn for a while, and it was finally time to take it to the sexual level. Cooley looked at Lynn's body. She couldn't wait to see her naked.

"So, Cooley, what happens after this?" Lynn said as she slowly unbuttoned her shirt.

"We could get something to eat if you like." Cooley walked toward Lynn and began to nibble on her neck.

"No, crazy. I mean, what does this make us? I mean, we have been kicking it every day, and I was just wondering, where do we go from here?"

Cooley pulled back. "Baby girl, I am digging you, but like I said when we met, I am not looking for a relationship."

"I'm not asking you to marry me. I'm just trying to see what happens from here." Lynn put her shirt on the bed.

Cooley noticed her big breasts, but tried to resist the temptation to take her right then.

Cooley stood up. "I hear you, and, Lynn, I love kicking it with you. But if a relationship is something that you want, then we need to cut this out now 'cause I don't want a girlfriend anytime soon."

Lynn walked back up and put her arms around Cooley. "Let's just talk about this another time. Why don't we focus on today?" Lynn raised her head and began kissing Cooley.

Cooley placed her arms around Lynn, gently rubbing up and down her back. She made it to her bra and quickly unbuttoned it. She felt Lynn jump.

Cooley stopped and looked at Lynn. "Are you OK?" She noticed apprehension in Lynn's face. "Lynn, you have been with women before, right?"

Lynn looked at Cooley, realizing that Cooley sensed her nervousness. "Yeah, I have." She smiled. "I just have heard that you are something to experience, and I just wanted to brace myself.

Cooley grinned. Her reputation preceded her. "Just relax, boo." Cooley unbuttoned the last clasp, and Lynn's bra fell to the floor. She picked her up and laid her on the bed. She began to nibble all over Lynn's body, giving the right combination of tongue and lip action.

Cooley grazed her hand up Lynn's thigh, until she made it to her pussy. Lynn's entire body was trembling. "Lynn, baby, you have to relax."

"I'm trying to. What do you need me to do?" Lynn questioned.

The comment threw Cooley off. The only time women asked questions like that was when they were inexperienced.

Cooley sat up. "Lynn, you have to be real with me. How much experience do you have?"

Lynn looked at Cooley. "OK, the truth is, I have only been with three women, and they all did things the same. You are something new. But don't let that stop you. Take me, Cooley."

Lynn sighed in ecstasy as Cooley decided to go for it. Her tongue began to devour Lynn's clit. Lynn had never felt anything so orgasmic in her life. Her body began to tremble all over. She felt an intense sensation taking over her entire body.

She scooted her butt back, but was quickly grabbed by Cooley. "Don't run. Take it," Cooley said as she came up for breath. She grabbed Lynn and pulled her even closer.

"Shit!" Lynn screamed as her body began to shiver. She couldn't hold back anymore. She let go, letting Cooley take in all her nectar.

Cooley sat up and looked at the exhausted Lynn. "Don't give out on me yet. I'm not through with you yet." She began to strap her harness on.

"No, Carla, I can't take that right now. Let me have some time to breathe." Lynn turned over in the bed.

Cooley looked back at her back in disbelief.

Hell no, this is not going to work, she thought to herself as she realized Lynn had fallen asleep. Cooley was used to going for hours, and this girl couldn't hang for forty-five minutes.

Cooley poked Lynn, but she didn't budge. Realizing it was a lost cause, Cooley headed into the bathroom. Guess she wouldn't be getting her nut that night. She made a mental note to start looking for a replacement quickly.

Cooley headed to the kitchen to get something to drink.

"Hello, Cooley."

Cooley stopped in her tracks. She knew the voice. Cooley didn't want to turn around. She hoped she was dreaming. She turned around to see Rhonda standing in her kitchen completely naked.

"What the fuck are you doing back here?" Cooley exclaimed, disgusted by Rhonda's appearance.

"Well, I was just taking Denise some water." Rhonda took a sip out of one of the glasses. "Boy, she just wore me out. I would have tried to get it a long time ago if I knew it was going to be that good." She smirked as she walked up on Cooley. She got so close, her breasts rubbed against Cooley's chest.

"I'm about to go back in here and see if the nickname Killa Cap should belong to you or her." Rhonda smiled as she switched back toward Denise's room.

Cooley felt sick to her stomach. She picked up her cell phone and called Carmen. "Your damn plan backfired," Cooley complained as she fell down on her bed.

"What are you talking about?" Carmen said as she turned over in her bed.

"The wicked witch is back," Cooley said.

Carmen began to shout obscenities.

Cooley hung the phone up. She knew then that the worst was yet to come.

Lena woke up and turned to see Denise was gone. She noticed a small note on her dresser. She smiled when she realized how much Denise cared about her. Lena knew that Denise would always be there for her.

Lena jumped when she heard her doorknob turning. She quickly tore the note up and threw the paper on the ground. "Brandon!" She yelled as Brandon walked in and put his bags on the ground.

"Yeah, it's me. Damn, you act like you've seen a ghost," Brandon teased as he plopped down on the side of the bed next to her. "Baby, how are wedding plans going?"

Lena yawned. She noticed a piece of paper laying on her nightstand. "Oh, um, they're done. Just sit back and relax now."

"Well, what do you think about moving the date up some?" Brandon asked.

Lena turned and looked at him. "Why? I didn't think you wanted it any sooner."

"Baby, if it was up to me, I would fly us to Vegas right now and elope. I'm just ready to call you Lena Redding." Brandon kissed Lena.

She felt a twinge of guilt enter her soul. "Baby, you know what . . . I think that is a great idea. Fuck the wedding. Let's elope." Lena smiled.

Brandon couldn't believe what he was hearing.

"Are you serious? Lena, you have never done a spontaneous thing in your life."

Lena got out of the bed. "I am dead serious. We can elope and come back and have a big reception." She looked at herself in the mirror.

Then she glanced down at the picture of her parents and suddenly changed her mind. "No, we can't. My mother and father are looking forward to this wedding. I can't rob my father of the chance to walk me down the aisle." She turned around and crawled back into bed with Brandon.

"You're right. It was just a dream. But I know one thing I can start on."

"Really, Papi, and what is that?" Lena smiled at Brandon. She knew what that look in his eye meant.

"I can start putting my seeds in your belly. Come here, girl."

Brandon grabbed Lena and kissed her. They began to make love. It was the first time in a while they had done it without a condom.

Cooley woke up and headed into the kitchen.

"Damn, it wasn't a nightmare," she said when she saw Rhonda fixing Denise a plate of food. Denise looked at her friend to let her know not to start any mess early in the morning.

"Well, hello, Cooley. Would you like something to eat?" Rhonda smiled at Cooley.

"Nah, that's OK. My girl will fix me a real breakfast when she gets up." Cooley made sure to add as much attitude as possible.

"Since when do you have a girl? What girl in her right mind would want anything more from you than a quick nut?" Rhonda smirked.

"Whatever. I'm going to shower. Bruh, you need to come talk to me soon." Cooley headed back to her room.

Denise quickly entered and closed the door.

Cooley looked at Lynn, who was now awake. "Can you fix me something to eat?"

Lynn quickly nodded her head and hurried out the room.

Denise sighed. "Look, man, I know you don't like Rhonda. But she is good to me, and I am going to keep her around."

"Bruh, have you lost your damn mind? Man, if that girl is good, then I am a damn saint," Cooley responded. She snatched her outfit for the day out of the closet. "I know you wanna get over Lena and all, but, shit, you can do better than her!" Cooley realized how upset she was. She knew her friend was headed for trouble.

"Look, I don't bother you about the bitches you have in and out of here, so please do not get on my one girl that I have over," Denise replied, feeling herself getting angry. "And I would appreciate it if the Lena shit could be dropped, OK!" She sat down on Cooley's bed and put her head down.

Cooley turned around and looked at Denise. She began to smile.

"You fucked Lena!" Cooley yelled.

Denise jumped up and put her hand over Cooley's mouth. "Hey, quiet. Rhonda may hear you," Denise whispered while she checked to see if Rhonda was standing near the door. "No, I didn't fuck Lena. We just kissed . . . a lot."

Cooley fell on her bed laughing. "Damn, man. When, where, and how the fuck was it?"

Denise pulled up Cooley's chair. "I told you we didn't fuck. We just made out a lot. Man, last night, when I went over there. She had this great meal cooked and a masseuse. We were watching *Love Jones,* and next thing I know, I was on top of her, kissing her." Denise smiled when the thought of Lena's legs trembling while she was kissing her entered her head.

"For real? Gotdamn, *Love Jones*, I swear it works everytime." Cooley's eyes lit up. "Man, I am so damn proud of you, dog. It's only a matter of time before you get the pussy." Cooley gave Denise daps. "I bet she's saying 'Brandon who?' right about now." Cooley laughed.

Denise sat back in her chair. "I doubt it. She may be crying again. After the vase broke, she got a quick reality check and realized that she fucked up. She ran into the bathroom crying. I had to put her in the bed. I hope she is OK. I gotta have Carmen call and check on her."

"Oh, damn. So, where does that leave you all now?" Cooley asked Denise.

"Friends. I thought something was going to happen, but it's just over. It was over before we had a chance to begin. Now, I have Rhonda, and I gotta move on."

Cooley sighed when Denise said Rhonda's name.

"Move on, yes. With that bitch? Hell no! Man, you can do so much better. I swear I get bad-ass vibes from her. I think she's up to something. You need to watch her sneaky ass."

"Man, she's harmless. You and Carmen are just going to have to get over this feud y'all have with her. I'm comfortable with her, so I'm going to keep her around." Denise got up and headed to the door.

"I hear you, dude, but I am telling you, sleep with one eye open." Cooley stood up as Denise walked out the door. She knew Denise wasn't going to listen, so she was going to have to look out for her friend.

Chapter 8

Carmen stared at Nic as she brushed her hair. Nic turned around and looked at her. "Why the hell are you staring at me?"

"'Cause you are too gotdamn fine." Carmen laughed.

"Whatever, girl. Every day I realize more and more it's something seriously wrong with you." Nic smiled.

"Whatever, you like it."

"Love it." Nic smiled as she walked to the door. "Let me go get one of those newspapers before they run out." She walked out and gently shut the door behind her.

Carmen sat on her bed. She smiled to herself thinking about how lucky she was. Nic was one of the most desired women in the Memphis life and she was with her.

Nic's cell phone began to go off. Carmen pushed a button to try to stop the ringing, but ended up opening the text message. It was from Larissa.

I got what you want. See you lata.

Carmen felt her heart breaking. Her hands began to tremble.

"I got one of the last ones. I hope the coupon is still in here," Nic said while flipping through the pages.

"Who the fuck is Larissa, and what the fuck does she have for you?" Carmen yelled.

Nic looked confused. "What?"

Carmen threw the phone on the bed. "Larissa has what you want. Who the hell is she?"

Nic picked up her cell phone. "Carmen, are you fuckin' serious?"

"Answer my question!" Carmen snapped.

"You know wha . . . I'm not. I'm gon' let you answer your own damn question. Read the other texts. Read the messages I sent." Nic threw the phone back on the bed.

Carmen grabbed the phone and began going through the messages that Nic sent to Larissa.

Please tell me you have notes on Othello. This Shakespeare class is going to kill me.

Carmen read the next text from Larissa.

Lol how bad do you want it? Bad enough to take my online math quiz?

Nic responded.

Hell yeah I got you on that. Just tell me you got the notes and it's on.

The last text was the original one that Carmen read. She looked up at Nic.

"Yeah, pick ya face up off the ground," Nic said.

"I'm sorry."

"Whatever, Carmen." Nic sat on the bed.

"Nic, I'm sorry. I don't know what is wrong with me."

"You keep trying to put me like that muthafucka you were with before. I am not going to cheat on you. How many times do I have to say that?"

"That's the same thing Tameka said." Carmen instantly wished she didn't say Tameka's name.

Nic's face began to turn red. "You know what, Carmen, I am not going to spend the rest of our relationship trying to prove to you I'm not like that bitch. If you don't learn how to trust me some more, we are headed for the end."

"Don't say that, Nic," Carmen cried.

"No, Carmen, it's the truth. I am not that bitch, and I'm not gon' let you take out the shit that she did to you on me. You don't see me going through your phone questioning you and shit about muthafuckas. And you did cheat on me. Remember that shit, Carmen?" Nic yelled.

Carmen couldn't say anything. She cheated on Nic with her ex, Tameka, the year before, and Nic took her back.

Carmen tried to wrap her arms around Nic, but Nic pulled her off. Carmen's face broke. "Nic, I'm sorry. It's hard for me, but I'm trying," she sobbed.

"Well, try harder. Take some time to think about what I said. I gotta go get the notes from Larissa." Nic walked out the door, leaving Carmen standing alone.

Lena couldn't concentrate on the wedding business in front of her. Her mind drifted off as her wedding planners went over the details of her grand affair. She no longer cared about how many thousands of orchids were being flown in. She could care less about the Tiffany china being ordered, or mood lighting being designed for her special day. All she could concentrate on was Denise.

"Miss Lena." Drako, flamboyant wedding coordinator extraordinaire, snapped his fingers, hoping to bring Lena back to reality.

"Oh, yes, that's fine," Lena mumbled, unaware of anything that was going on.

"Miss Lena, I know you have a lot on your mind, but I really need you to work with me a little bit here. We want everything to be fabulous, darling," he said.

"I'm sorry, Drako. I'm just very tired. Now, what were we going over?"

Lena left the office exhausted from all of the wedding details. She couldn't wait to get the day over and done with. Her phone rang; it was her mother. She didn't answer.

A few moments later the phone rang again. She knew her mother wouldn't stop calling until she answered.

"Yes, mother."

Karen sat back in the spa chair while a woman attended to her feet. "Darling, I have been calling you like crazy. Why didn't you speaker phone me on the meeting?"

"Because you weren't needed for it. I think I can plan my own wedding."

"Lena, what is with that tone? Are you on your period?"

"Mother!" Lena exclaimed as she got in her car.

"Well, what is going on? Do you need me to come down there early?" Karen she took a bite of a small cucumber sandwich.

"No! I mean, no, Mom, everything is going just fine. I have my final fitting in a few days, and Drako has everything else ready."

"What about PR, sweetie? I got *InStyle* to cover the wedding."

"What about TV One?" Lena said.

"What about them? Fine, Lena, I will get them as well if it makes you happy." Karen sighed. She didn't understand her daughter's fascination with the black television station. "But *InStyle* should have the exclusive."

"Whatever, Mom, I just really don't feel like talking about this right now. I have a lot to do, so we will finish this later."

"OK—"

Before Karen could finish, Lena hung up the phone.

Lena made an illegal turn and headed to the campus.

"Lena, what are you doing here?" Carmen questioned as she held the door open for Lena to walk in. Carmen lay back on her bed.

"Carmen, I really need to talk to you about something. Carmen, are you OK?" Lena said, noticing Carmen's blood-shot eyes.

"I'm going to lose Nicole," she explained.

After psychology, Carmen had headed to University Café to get a coffee and relax before her next class. She noticed three girls sitting at a table near her looking in her direction. She soon realized they were girls from the gay club, but she didn't know their names. She pulled out a book to read while drinking her coffee. The girls began to talk loudly enough for her to hear.

"So that girl is fine as hell. I am going to try my hardest to get her before the end of the year," one of the girls said. She fingered the long, wavy extensions in her hair.

Carmen had to admit, she was pretty.

"What makes you think she would ever leave her girl for you?" another one said. She wasn't nearly as attractive as the first girl. Her hair was short with blonde streaks and looked like it hadn't been styled in weeks.

"'Cause her girl don't have shit on me. Besides, you should see how we flirt with each other in class. She is goin'."

"Do ya thing, Sheka," the shortest of the three added. "She is fine."

"Shit fine," Sheka said. "I haven't seen anyone nearly that fine. And for her to be with her girl, that girl don't have shit on any of us. Hell, she don't have shit on anyone I have seen. She used to be fat as hell. You can tell."

Carmen felt her body become tense. She had a feeling they were talking about her. She continued to listen as the girls stood up.

"All I'm saying is that it wouldn't take much for another girl to get her, especially not me. She need to be on the arm of someone as fine as her," Sheka said as they gathered their things.

"Well, I guess we will see," the short-haired girl said.

"We will. Trust, by the end of this semester, that fine-ass Cali Nic will be mine." Sheka looked at Carmen.

Carmen's body began to tremble.

The three girls laughed as they walked away.

Lena put her arm around Carmen. "Girl, why didn't you say something to her?"

Carmen wiped the falling tears from her eyes. "What could I say? Honestly she is right. Nic is too fine. I am nowhere near as fine as her."

"Shit, Carmen!" Lena stood up. "Why do you do this to yourself? Girl, look at Brandon. He's fine and a fuckin' athlete, but I don't let what bitches say bother me."

"Lena, 'cause look at you. I have yet to see a girl on this campus, hell, or around Memphis, that looks as good as you."

"Damn! Have you been to Miami? How about New York or L.A.? Carmen, even Atlanta. There are women ten times better looking than me, and they try to get him just like everyone else. But I am not going to let any of them make me think bad about myself or question what I have with my man. Brandon is mine. He loves me, and Nic loves you."

"That's easy for you to say. You're pretty."

"Carmen, you are too! Shit, I wouldn't hang with you if you were busted. Trust."

"I don't know what I would do if Nic left me." Carmen sat up in her bed. "I don't know what is wrong with me. What if she does me like Tameka?"

"See. That's your problem right there. You hold the shit that Tameka did against Nic. That's not fair, Carmen. That's not fair to Nic. You need to let all that shit go, sweetie."

"It's easier said than done."

"No, Carmen, it isn't. Let it go. You have a woman who loves you, and you are going to fuck it up if you don't let it go," Lena said sternly.

Carmen knew Lena was right. She knew how frustrated Nic got when she accused her of doing things. "I am going to work on it."

"You do that," Lena said. "And I came over here to talk to you about something."

"Girl, I'm sorry. What was wrong?"

Lena looked at herself in the mirror. She saw Carmen's maid of honor dress hanging in a bag on the door. "Um, girl, just wedding shit is bothering me. I just wanted to know if you all were still going with me to the final tasting for the food and the dress fitting."

"Of course, we are." Carmen looked at Lena. "Lena, are you sure that's the only reason you came here?"

"Girl, yeah, I'm sure. Just wanted to vent about the wedding planning, that's all. Do you want to go see a movie or something?"

"Actually, I was going to go to a poetry reading. Go with me?"

Lena consented as Carmen grabbed her bag, and they headed out the door.

Lena looked around the unfamiliar area. She parked in a small lot next to a little building. "Where the hell are we?"

"It's called Rhyme and Reason. It's a little artist spot. Come on, you'll like it."

They walked in the small building. It reminded Lena of the poetry spot in *Love Jones*. There were pictures of various revolutionaries and artists on the walls. A large red, black, and green mural of Africa with a black fist in front of it was painted on one wall. The other wall had the Jamaican colors with pictures of Bob Marley. The smell of incense filled the air.

A tall guy with long locks and a picture of Africa on his shirt was on stage doing a revolutionary piece.

Carmen tapped a girl with long locks on the shoulder.

She turned around and smiled. "You came," Neo said as she hugged Carmen.

"Yeah, I told you I would. This is my friend Lena."

Lena and Neo shook hands. Lena noticed the expression in Neo's eyes as she looked at Carmen.

"Great. Let me get you all to a table and get you something to drink."

They listened to various poets doing pieces on everything from politics to love. Three poets did a piece about Hurricane Katrina that almost made Lena cry. They finished by talking about the experience of going to New Orleans to help the rebuilding effort.

Suddenly, it turned into a small testimonial session. The room was silent as a girl stood up and talked about her experience of being a Katrina refugee. Tears filled her eyes as she recounted waiting days for aid. She watched an older woman die because she couldn't get her medicine.

Tears rolled down Lena, and Carmen's faces. Lena made a mental note to have Brandon donate to Katrina victims.

Others discussed the poverty in Memphis.

They took up a collection to raise money to feed the homeless. Lena pulled out two hundred-dollar bills and handed them to the gentleman in the front.

"Thank you, my sister. She has just donated two hundred to our fund. You are a blessing, Nubian queen."

Lena smiled as the crowd clapped.

The guy turned the show back over to the MC.

A tall, slender, dark-skinned guy with long locks walked to the stage. "We want to thank everyone again for coming out to Rhyme and Reason. We took a pause for the cause, but now we are going to get back into the rotation. Let's bring up my nigga—I mean, sista."

Everyone laughed. "Y'all, I can play with her like that. She's like a little sister to me.

Y'all give it up for Neo."

Carmen and Lena clapped as Neo walked to the stage.

"I was going to do a different piece, but since there is someone special in the crowd, I'm going to read something else I have been working on. It's a work in progress, but y'all know how it is."

I wonder if she knows
How intense my
Infatuation with her is
I wonder if she knows

I'm watching her every move
I wonder if she knows
The slightest touch sends
Chills up my spine
And that infectious laugh
I hear in my sleep
I wonder if she knows
The curves of her smile
Like I do
I wonder if she knows
I like a woman with a little
Meat on her bones
I wonder if she knows
Her scent gets me
A little wet
I wonder if she knows
When she looks at me
That my
Whole body starts to shake
And I can't shake this
Feeling
The feeling of being on cloud nine
Every time she passes by
I wonder if she knows
I could be the one
I can be the one who
Sends her to her highest level
Climax
Without sex
I wonder if she knows
I adjust my day for her
Just so I can get a fix
Cuz I feel like an addict
Addicted to her touch,

Her smile, her laugh, her style
She's the one for me
I wonder if she knows . . .

Carmen couldn't believe what she was hearing. Neo
had stared at her almost exclusively while reading the
poem. Lena was in shock. She didn't know if she was
supposed to be happy or concerned.

The crowd snapped and clapped as Neo left the
stage. She looked at Carmen and walked off to the bar.

"Um, if that wasn't a *Love Jones* moment right
there," Lena said. "And you thought no one wanted
you."

"You really think that was for me?" Carmen said.

Lena gave her a sarcastic look. "Girl, if that poem
wasn't about you, my name isn't Lena."

The crowd began to disperse after the last poet. Soft
Neo Soul music played as people chatted with each
other. Lena and Carmen stood up to leave.

"So, you leaving?" The sound of Neo's voice gave
Carmen goose bumps.

"Yeah, we have to get back to campus," Carmen said.
"Um, that was a very, um, interesting poem."

Neo smiled. "It was interesting? That wasn't the response I was hoping for. I was hoping to get a date out
of it."

"Um, Carmen, I'll meet you at the car." Lena quickly
walked out the door.

"Neo, I like you as a friend, but I have a woman, and
you know that."

Neo lowered her head. "Yeah, I know, but things like
that could change, right?"

Carmen shook her head. "Not things like this. We are
very happy and moving to California after graduation.
I'm sorry."

"I am the one that's sorry. I guess I'm a little too late. Well, I will see you around, Carmen. Hope you liked the poem."

"I loved the poem. See you around, Neo." Carmen turned around and walked out the coffee shop.

"Well, look at you, wit' your bad ass," Lena teased.

"Whatever, girl."

"Whatever, my ass. How does that make you feel? That girl was a cutie."

Carmen smiled. "I feel pretty damn good. Now, get me home to my woman."

They laughed and headed back to campus.

Chapter 9

Cooley knocked on the thick dorm room door. She had been messing with Lynn for weeks and still was sexually frustrated. Misha opened the door. Cooley felt her pressure rising at the sight of Misha in her boy shorts.

"Cooley, what is—"

Before she could finish responding, Cooley began to kiss her. She slammed the door with her foot as she held onto Misha and made her way to the bed. Cooley fumbled with Misha's boy shorts, until she decided to just rip them off, out of sexual frustration.

Misha didn't know what was up with Cooley, but she didn't care. She let Cooley take full control of her body. It was some of the most intense sex they had ever had.

Cooley fucked Misha until she got all of her tension out. She sighed afterward. That was how sex was supposed to be.

Afterward Cooley lay in Misha's bed as Misha got up to get a new pair of underwear.

"You know you are buying me another pair of those, right?" Misha said as she threw away the torn panties.

"I got you," Cooley responded. She laughed when she thought about ripping the boy shorts.

"Good. So now you want to tell me what that was all about?" Misha looked at Cooley.

"Sorry, baby, I just had to have you."

"What about Lynn? Isn't she giving you enough?" Misha asked. She knew that Cooley had been seeing Lynn pretty much exclusively, except when she was with her.

Cooley sighed. "The sex with that girl is horrible, Misha. She doesn't know what to do at all."

"Damn! Are you her first or something?" Misha said, trying to hold back the laughter.

"You know I thought I was, but I asked her, and she said she has been with, like, three girls before me. But I swear that girl fucks worse than any straight bitch I have turned out."

"Well, Carla, you should talk to her about it. Maybe she doesn't know she isn't doing a good job. Put your shirt on," Misha said as she threw Cooley's shirt at her.

"Whatever, man."Cooley looked at Misha. "Hold up. Are you kicking me out?"

"Pretty much. I have somewhere to go," Misha said as she grabbed her robe and towel.

"Where you got to go?" Cooley felt herself getting heated.

"Why?"

"'Cause I asked, that's why. You sitting up here trying to treat me like a booty call and shit. Where you have to go that's soooo important that you kicking *me* out?"

Misha sighed. "If you must know, I have a date."

"You got a what?" Cooley felt jealous. "Wit' who?"

"I'm sorry. When did you become my mother?" Misha said sarcastically. "Damn, with this chick I met. You don't know her. Why you trippin'?"

Cooley stood up. "I'm not trippin'." She looked at the wall. "Who is the girl?"

"I said you don't know her, and you are trippin'. So what's the deal?"

"You a trip, Misha. I thought we were being honest with each other. I just get finished fuckin' you and you 'bout to go be wit' some random bitch and shit."

"I have been honest with you. Hell, I just met her. I don't even know if I like her yet. Damn, chill out." Misha looked at Cooley, who was fuming.

Cooley tried not to look at Misha. She didn't like how vulnerable she felt. Her feelings for Misha were making her weak. Cooley began to pick her hair. She always picked her hair to relax. "You know what? Dig that. Do you then, Misha," Cooley said as she headed to the door.

"Cooley, what is up with you?" Misha said as she grabbed Cooley's arm. "Aren't you seeing Lynn? Why are you tripping over this, girl?"

"I'm not. Just let me go." Cooley tried to open the door, but Misha stood in front of it.

"No, Carla, talk to me. What is really wrong?"

"You really want to know. Well, I don't want no one touching you!" Cooley felt herself losing control. "Damn, Misha, this shit is not working out. I can't just fuck with you like this."

"Carla—"

"Fuck! You got me buggin' for real."

"But we had an agreement," Misha said.

"That's not working."

"Why?"

"'Cause I am still in love with you!" Cooley paused. She finally said the words she had been tryng to hold back.

Misha's eyes brightened. She couldn't believe what she heard. "Carla, talk to me." She wrapped her arms around Cooley's neck.

Cooley knew she couldn't fight it anymore. She took a deep breath. "Misha, I love you. I have always loved you. I don't just want to be your friend. I don't just want to fuck on occasion."

Misha looked down at the ground. She looked back up into Cooley's grey eyes. "Cooley, I hear you, but I am not ready to commit back to you. Maybe we need to take a little more time apart. Make sure this is what we both truly want." Misha looked Cooley in her eyes. She had never seen Cooley so vulnerable.

Cooley tried to maintain her composure and not show her face breaking. She sighed. She never had to try so hard to be with a girl in her life. "Fine, Misha, whatever."

"Carla, don't act like that. I'm not saying never. I'm just saying I'm not ready yet."

Cooley knew this was a battle she wasn't going to win by pressure. She pulled Misha close to her. She could feel Misha's heart beating. Cooley looked into Misha's eyes and planted a sensual kiss on her.

"Misha, you know where to find me when you want to."

She opened the door and walked out. Cooley hated what she was becoming; she knew she had to do something about her feelings.

"Great job, ladies. See you all later," Carmen said to two of her sorority sisters. They had put the finishing touches on their informational display in the University Center. "I will see you all later, OK."

They walked off as Carmen looked over the display one more time.

Carmen felt a strange feeling come over her body. She knew something was not right. She turned and looked around the U.C. but didn't see anything out of the ordinary. However, something was telling her she needed to leave.

Carmen grabbed her bags quickly and headed toward the door. "Shit," she said as she realized she left a bag. She walked back into the center and felt her heart drop. She saw her ex, Tameka, standing in front of the Chi Theta board with a girl. Carmen soon realized it was the same girl that she'd caught Tameka with last year during the sports ball. She decided to leave the bag, but it was too late. Tameka spotted her.

"What's up, shorty?" Tameka said as she flashed a devilish grin. "Hey, my girl is thinking about Chi Theta. What does she need to join?"

Carmen grabbed the bag from off the floor. "She needs class," Carmen said as she turned to walk away.

"They didn't require that when they let your stupid ass in!" the girl snapped back.

Carmen tried to ignore the comment, knowing she couldn't throw down in her letters. She continued to walk off, until she heard Tameka respond.

"Yeah, fuck her, baby. She just mad 'cause I don't want her dumb ass anymore."

Carmen turned around just in time to see Tameka lay a deep kiss on the girl. Carmen's body began to shake. She dropped all her bags and began to walk toward them, until someone grabbed her shirt.

"Hey, baby?" Carmen turned around to see Nic looking at her. Nic leaned down and planted a deep kiss on Carmen. "Is everything cool?"

"Yeah, everything is fine," Carmen responded. She turned to see Tameka looking surprised.

Tameka grabbed the girl's arm and headed in to the cafeteria.

Carmen began to pick her bags up. Her body was still trembling.

Nic grabbed her arm. "What was that all about?"

"Nothing, baby," Carmen said, fidgeting around. "They were trying to start some shit."

"And it looks like you were going to walk right into it," Nic said sternly.

Carmen noticed Nic's expression. She could tell she was not happy.

"Nic, it's not what you think."

"Carmen, save it, OK? Look, baby, I know you are still going to care for that girl, but I am telling you now, if you even think about going back, hell, if you even think about letting her affect us in any way, you can kiss me good-bye for good this time." Nic picked up the rest of Carmen's bags.

Carmen realized that Nic had a reason to feel that way. She had left Nic alone the year before to deal with Tameka again, but Nic forgave her when things with Tameka predictably went sour.

"Nic, you are right. Even though she treated me like shit, I am always going to care for her. But I love you, and now I know what real love truly is." She wrapped her arms around Nic's tall torso. "I am not going anywhere."

Nic kissed Carmen on her forehead. "I hope not."

They walked out of the U.C. Carmen knew she had a prize that she wasn't going to mess up again.

Denise landed another three-pointer. Nic and Cooley were both out of breath. Denise hadn't even broken a sweat.

"You know. Fuck this. I'm done," Cooley said, dropping the ball in the dimly lit gym. They would come to the gym late at night to play ball and talk. "It's not fair, playing with your ass."

"Aww, bruh, don't be mad 'cause I got skills." Denise laughed.

"Fuck that. I'm a lover, not a jock," Cooley said, sitting on the bleachers. Cooley noticed the look on Nic's face as she practiced her jump shot. "What tha deal, Nic?"

Nic turned around. "Man, you won't believe who we ran into today. Tameka."

"Oh, really now? How was Carmen?" Denise asked.

"How was Tameka's face? I was hoping I left a mark last year," Cooley said.

"I don't know, but I wanted to leave a few this year," Nic said as she sat down. "I walked up on her starting static with Carmen."

"Don't tell me no shit like that," Cooley said. "I already had to do enough community service."

"You didn't do no damn community service. You had that girl—you know that own the daycare say—you worked there," Denise said.

"It's the principle of the thing. They said if I get into it with her again I'm out of school."

"The messed up part was Carmen. It's like she is still affected by the girl. I don't know what to do to stop that shit," Nic said.

"Carmen loves you, Nic. She isn't going anywhere again."

"I hope not, but to make matters worse, the girl does not trust me at all. Man, she was ready to jump that girl who tipped me on the show when Oohzee was there."

"Well, you know Carmen has been hurt real bad," Denise said. "And she has always had low self-esteem."

"Yeah, but I haven't done anything to make her treat me like that. I haven't as much as yelled at her." Nic angrily bounced the basketball.

"Look, man, you just gotta realize something. Carmen is damaged. She is trying to guard herself from getting hurt again."

"Well, talk to her for me, 'cause I love that girl. I'm not going to cheat on her. Hell, my biggest fear is that she is going to let Tameka back in again. I don't even want her to consider it."

"Fuck that. Tameka bet not think about it. She knows I will kill her ass if she comes near C again," Cooley said as Denise's phone began to rang.

She quickly pressed ignore.

"Now look at this nigga here. One guess who that is. You need to get rid of that bitch."

"Cooley, don't start," Denise said.

"I have to agree with Cool on this one. Denise, something's not right with that girl. Have you paid attention to the look she gets sometimes?"

"That's 'cause y'all just can't stand her."

"Now, Dee, that may be Cool and Carmen, but not me. The girl is a little strange. Have you seen the little spacey way she looks sometimes?"

"She is a lot strange. I think the ho is psycho, personally. Dee gon' wake up and be tied to the bed like in *Misery*."

"No, I'm not." Denise stood up. "But don't worry. I'm not really feeling it anymore anyway."

"You weren't feeling it from day one," Cooley said. "You need to drop her for good and let it go. Stop this back-and-forth shit."

"I agree, Dee. If you leave her alone again, let it stay. A girl ain't gon' take too many times of you leaving her and coming back."

"I hear y'all."

"No, you really need to hear us," Cooley said. "Handle your shit, Dee. With Rhonda and Lena."

"Oh, snap," Nic laughed.

"What's that supposed to mean?" Denise said.

"You know what it means," Cooley countered.

"Whatever. There isn't anything between Lena and I. I've told you that."

"Except you kissed her last year, " Nic said.

"She almost fucked her this year," Cooley said. "Personally I say fuck her and get it over with. Y'all are worse than a fuckin' movie."

"Waiittt a minute! You almost fucked Lena? Damn, Carmen didn't tell me that," Nic said.

"Carmen doesn't know 'cause it's not like that," Denise said. "Look, we had a moment, but that's all it was. I have let go of Lena. She is about to be married. She loves him, so I've moved on. We are just friends."

"That's bullshit, and you know it. Dee, that girl is as much in love with you as you are with her. Y'all are going to fuck. It's going to happen, and I know it. It will happen when you stop acting like a pussy and give Lena what she has wanted since day one." Cooley shot the ball toward the goal but missed. Denise grabbed the ball.

"True, true," Nic co-signed. "But, honestly, Cool, you ain't no better. Misha and Lynn."

"Thank you!" Denise said. "How you gon' give advice when you fuckin' Misha and Lynn?"

"Look, I am single. I can fuck who I want to fuck, and they both know it."

"Well, when are you going to get out of denial about how you really feel about Misha? Every time the girl comes around, you light up like a kid in a candy store," Denise said.

"Whatever. Y'all don't know shit." Cooley shot the ball again and missed.

"You know you love Misha," Denise continued. "You need to tell her, and y'all need to get back together. Maybe you need to get rid of that 'cool nigga' act and let her truly know how you feel. I bet once you actually tell her how you feel, she is going to run back to you with open arms."

"Trust me, I got this with Misha. I'll admit I care about her a lot. I'm not giving up. By the end of this semester I am going to have her back. Trust that," Cooley said.

"And you need to let Lynn go. As much as I would hate to let that cooking go, you need to handle her. That girl is falling hard for your ass."

"You notice that too?" Cooley said. "I got it."

"Well, let me get my ass home before Carmen gets back. She's at some poetry reading."

"Oh, not with that nigga Neo. Fake-ass nigga right there. I knew Neo back in the day when she was just Nedra, trying to fuck around like I was. These bitches kill me, trying to be in competition with me, like Pooh weak ass." Cooley sneered.

"She don't seem to be like that no more," Denise said.

"Please, she is still the same Nedra. She just is taking a more realistic approach. She still wish she could pull half the amount of hoes I could pull. She just like to use her poetry to pull them. I'm not buying this whole act she got going right now. All of a sudden she's all about gay pride and revolution and shit. Whatever."

"Cool, you think everyone is the same," Nic said.

"Not everyone. Just most of the weak-ass Memphis studs. I can't wait till I get the fuck up out of here," Cooley said.

"Dig that," Denise said. "I've had too much shit happen recently. I can't wait to move on to something new."

"We gon' be doing big thangs in other cities, just like we do them here," Cooley added.

"And good riddance." Denise shot the ball and made a clean basket. She looked at Cooley and smiled. Nic began to laugh.

"Man, fuck you, wit' yo' hoopin' ass." Cooley hit Denise.

They headed out the gym.

Chapter 10

Nic sipped on a coke as she attempted to understand her Shakespeare assignment. She wiped the sweat off of her head.

"You look stressed." Larissa laughed. "It's not that serious."

"That's easy for you to say. I can't get through this shit," Nic said.

"OK, I'm going to let you in on a little secret. There are movies of *Othello, Romeo and Juliet,* and *Midsummer's Night Dream.* Rent them and watch them. Maybe then you can make it through the book better."

"You think he will know if I only watch the movie?" Nic said.

"Hell, yeah, he will." Larissa laughed. "He asks questions that they don't discuss in the movie. Shit. Where the hell is my man?"

"Oh, Thomas is on his way?" Nic said. "How are y'all doing?"

"It's all good. Let me go wait for him outside."

"I'll walk with you." Nic stood and packed her books.

Larissa looked at Nic as she opened the cafeteria door for her.

"Nic, you know you are a true gentleman. You act more like a man than half of the men I know."

"Umm, OK. Is that a good thing?" Nic laughed.

"Yeah, it is. You do the little things. You open doors, pull out chairs. I can't get Thomas to open a door for me. Hell, I bet if there was a puddle you would put your jacket over it."

"Naaa, I'm not fuckin' up my clothes. If it's that serious, I'd just pick you up." Nic smiled.

"See, that's what I'm talking about. If you were a man, you would be fucking perfect."

"Aww, thanks, but seriously I'm not. I just believe in letting women be women. I guess a lot of men forget that women are supposed to be treated with pure respect."

Larissa smiled. "I know Carmen isn't going anywhere. She is a lucky girl. Well, let me go. See you later, Nicole."

Nic waved good-bye. She sighed. She only wished Carmen could see her the way other women did.

"OK, are you all ready?" Lena yelled from out of the dressing room.

Carmen and Misha let her know to come out.

Lena stepped out the dressing room. It was her final fitting and she was now completely flawless.

Carmen and Misha were speechless. Tears began to form in Carmen's eyes.

"Carmen, don't start," Lena said.

"What, girl? You look so beautiful. I am going to be no good at your wedding. I already know it," Carmen said, wiping the tears from her face.

Lena turned around and looked at herself in the mirror. "One month. One month till my wedding." Lena took a deep breath and looked at herself in the mirror again. She felt butterflies starting to form in her stomach.

"Actually, it's only twenty-four days," Misha corrected as she smiled at Lena. "And I have planned the best bachelorette party. Exams will be over on that Thursday, and we are going to party all night long!"

They all laughed.

"Oh, my goodness, look at my baby."

The girls turned around to see Lena's mother, Karen, standing in the door. She walked up and hugged Lena.

"Mom, I didn't think you were supposed to be here for another two weeks," Lena said, still in shock at seeing her mother.

"Oh, I decided I needed to be here with my baby. Oh, you look so beautiful, but—" Karen looked at the dress on Lena. She snapped for an attendant. "Look right here, it is missing a bead."

Carmen, Lena and Misha looked down at the dress.

"Mrs. Jamerson, how did you spot that?" Misha said, surprised at the small defect Karen noticed.

"Oh, sweetie, it's called a trained eye. Everything needs to be completely perfect for my baby's wedding, so I am going to go over everything with a fine-tooth comb."

Lena headed back into the dressing room to change. "Mother, it's not that serious. That's why I hired wedding planners."

"Wedding planners are there to assist. You are to make sure that everything is perfect. It's your day, after all," Karen corrected, grabbing Lena's wedding dress out of the dressing room. She handed it to the attendant. "I expect you all to go back over this dress thoroughly. If I see any mistakes, there will be hell to pay."

Karen walked back over to Misha and Carmen. "So, ladies, how are your dresses?"

"Absolutely beautiful. We already had our final alterations," Carmen replied.

"Great. Well, if you don't mind, can I have a few minutes alone with my daughter?"

"Sure. We will head over to the restaurant and get a table. See you soon, Lena."

The two headed out of the dress shop.

Lena came out of the dressing room. "Mother, what's going on? Why are you really here?" Lena enquired. She noticed a worried expression on her mother's face.

"Well, after that last disturbing call that we had, I realized something was not right with you. So I decided to check on the wedding details myself."

"Mom, I told you I was just stressed. Is everything all right with you?"

"I was going to ask you the same thing. What is Denise's name doing on the guest list?"

It was no secret that Karen was no longer fond of Denise. Once she found out she was gay, she was always suspicious of Lena's and Denise's dealings together.

"Mother, that is my friend. I am not going to not invite her to my wedding." Lena was irritated by her mother's constant bashing on Denise. "You know, before you found out she was gay, you thought she was pretty nice."

"Yes, before I knew she was gay, and trying to ruin my baby's future."

"Mother, she has not tried to ruin anything! Denise and I are friends. What part of that don't you understand?"

"The part where you sent her a love letter this summer when you were at my house." Karen caught herself too late.

Lena remembered sending Denise a letter but never receiving a response.

"Mother, what are you talking about? What did you do?" Lena demanded. She could feel herself starting to tremble.

"I saved your relationship. I got the letter before you sent it, and I must say, how could you even think about doing something so . . . so . . . Well, it doesn't matter now that you are about to be married."

"So, you mean to tell me you not only got my letter, but you opened it as well? Mother, how could you do this?" Lena stormed out of the store.

"I did it to protect you!" Karen said, grabbing Lena's arm. "I knew when I walked in that dorm room that there was something between the two of you. Lena, you are not some damn dyke!"

"I know I am not, but—"

"But nothing. If you would have sent that letter, that girl would have been coming to try to break you and Brandon up in a heartbeat!"

"Denise is not like that." Lena felt her eyes watering. "She is a wonderful friend, and I am so privileged to have her in my life. This conversation is over, mother."

Lena got in her car, but her mother grabbed the door before she could close it.

"Baby, I am sorry. I just wanted to look out for you. It is perfectly normal to be curious about the other sex, but it's not acting on it that is important. In a few days you will be a married woman."

"I know that. But if the only reason you came here was to pry into my personal life, then you might as well go home. I will see you in a few weeks. Good-bye, Mother." Lena closed the door and sped off, leaving her mother standing on the sidewalk.

"Damn, I can't believe I actually have to study for this test. I've barely had time to kick it at all!" Cooley said to Nic as they looked over their notes.

"Yeah, I feel ya, and on top of that, I barely see my baby. She is so busy with Lena's wedding, that sorority, and work. I don't see how she does it."

"Yeah, Carmen is the super worker. So how are you all doing?" Cooley asked as a group of girls walked by the table.

Cooley caught the eye of one of them. She was thick in all the places Cooley liked. The girl smiled at Cooley, instantly giving Cooley the go-ahead to approach her.

"We are doing fine. I want her to quit her job and let me support her, but you know Carmen is not going for that," Nic said. She noticed Cooley's attention was gone. "Go catch the girl before you fall out your seat looking." Nic laughed.

"Yeah, I'll be right back."

Cooley walked briskly to catch up with the girl, who was looking at the Chi Theta information board. Her friends had headed into the food den.

"You know my best friend is president. If you give me your name and number, I can give a good word for you."

The girl looked at Cooley and smiled. "Is that right? What if I don't need your help?"

"In that case I should give you my number, in case you need my help with anything else." Cooley gazed into the girl's eyes. She knew that she had her just where she wanted her.

"I honestly don't think I will need your help with anything."

"Well, just in case, call 569-COOL. Dig that?" Cooley said, making sure to keep her eyes on the girl's face. She knew that women hated it when people were checking them out. She always focused right on their faces, so that they would think she was interested in them and not just their bodies.

The girl laughed. "Are you serious? That's your number?"

"I am dead serious. I like to keep it simple. If it's one thing I know you will never forget my name, and I made it so you could never forget my number either. Oh, and your name would be?"

"Tara!" a deep voice yelled from behind them.

Cooley turned around to see a large guy headed toward them. She could tell he was not happy with what he was seeing.

"Hey, baby," Tara responded as the man stared Cooley down. "This is Cooley. Her best friend is the president of Chi Theta. She is going to arrange for me to meet her."

Cooley smiled at the guy. Something told her that he didn't believe her.

"Look, no offense, but if I want my girl to meet the president, I will take care of it. She don't need any help from you," the guy responded.

Cooley knew that he was feeling threatened by her. She smirked.

"Yeah, OK. Well, anyway, it was nice to meet you, Tara, and, um, I didn't catch your name."

"Don't worry about my name. You just keep your ass away from my woman!" The man grabbed Tara's hand and stormed off.

Cooley could tell they were arguing once they got outside. She shook her head and headed back to the table.

Nic was standing up watching the whole thing. "Is everything cool? I was right here waiting on him to try some shit," Nic said as they both sat down.

"Yeah, everything is good. Looks like she has a jealous boyfriend," Cooley said casually as she looked down at her notes.

Nic could tell that Cooley was hiding something. "Dude, I would advise that you not fuck with that girl. Unnecessary drama."

"Yeah, I hear you," Cooley said, excusing Nic's warning. Something told her that it wasn't going to be the last time she heard from little Tara.

"Well, I will admit one thing. It's actually good to see you back to your old flirtatious self."

Cooley smiled. "What's that supposed to mean?"

"It means that you have been walking around looking a little off lately. I never see you looking at other women. I was starting to worry about you." Nic looked at Cooley, who appeared shocked.

"I can't believe you noticed that."

"I notice everything," Nic said. "Like your girl walking her way toward us."

"Fuck," Cooley said when she saw Lynn out of the corner of her eye.

"Hey, baby!" Lynn said, putting her arm around Cooley from behind.

"Hey, Lynn, what's going on?" Cooley hugged Lynn. She was going to let her go, but after they'd had sex, she woke up to a great meal that Lynn fixed. She had to keep her after that.

"Nothing much. Just got out of class. What time are you coming home?"

Cooley and Nic looked at each other, both catching what Lynn said.

"Home?" Cooley responded.

"Yeah, to your home. I was going to go to the grocery store and make steaks tonight." Lynn realized Cooley wasn't happy with her previous response.

"Actually, I am kicking it with Nic and Carmen tonight. But maybe tomorrow, OK?" Cooley realized that the girl was getting too comfortable. She usually never let a girl stay over so much, but she couldn't help it. Cooley was digging the big breakfasts and dinners Lynn was making every day.

Lynn's face became sad. "Oh, OK. Well, I guess I will see you tomorrow. I need to go to my dorm anyway. I've been at your place so much, I think I forgot what room I stay in," Lynn said, trying not to seem to hurt.

"Yeah, OK. Well, I'll talk to you later." Cooley didn't care about Lynn's feelings at that moment. She still couldn't believe the girl called her apartment *home*.

Lynn walked off, and Cooley dropped her head. Nic started to laugh.

"That shit isn't funny, Nic."

"Like hell, it isn't. You better take care of that," Nic responded. "You been making that girl wifey for the whole semester. She ain't gon' put up with that shit for too much longer."

"Yeah, I know, but the girl can cook her ass off. She got a nigga sprung on that damn cooking."

"You're a mess." Nic laughed.

"Yeah, well, I just gotta put her ass on a schedule, 'cause a nigga gotta eat that good-ass food at least once a week."

Cooley and Nic laughed as they continued to study.

"She did what!" Misha exclaimed as Lena relived the incident with her mother earlier.

"Wait. What I want to know is, what the hell was in the letter?" Carmen said and Misha quickly co-signed.

Lena sighed. "You guys, I thought about Denise all summer. Kissing Brandon hasn't been the same since we kissed. I didn't know what to do, so I wrote her a letter. I told her that I thought I was in love with her. But I realize now that it was just a curiosity. I have gotten it out of my system now. Shit!" Lena said as she realized that she slipped up.

Misha and Carmen quickly caught what she said.

"Oh, hell no, Lena. What does that mean?" Misha exclaimed.

"Nothing."

"You are so fuckin' lying. You better spill it, girl," Carmen added. "Have you and Denise done something?"

Lena lowered her head.

Both girls began to scream. All the people in the restaurant looked at them, some frowning at their display. They quickly quieted down when they realized they were in an upscale restaurant.

"OK, OK. Yes, a few months ago when Denise came over after the incident with her mother. One thing led to another, and we ended up getting a little hot and heavy. She did a few things," Lena said, quickly taking a sip of her martini.

"Some things like what?" Misha and Carmen said in unison.

"Well, we were kissing. It was a real, real passionate moment. But then the couch moved and made a vase fall and break. We stopped then." Lena started to blush.

"Denise kissed you? Y'all was making out?" Carmen exclaimed. "I am going to kick that bitch's ass for not telling me this."

"So, how did you feel? Did you want to do more?" Misha said, smiling from ear to ear.

"It was great. The best kiss I have ever had. For a moment I wanted to do more, but when the vase broke, I knew that was a sign. Me and Denise are not supposed to go that far." Lena gulped her martini, finishing it in one swallow.

"Damn, girl, you are turned out," Carmen teased. "*Dos* strikes again."

They all laughed. Denise had the nickname *Dos* from giving her ex multiple orgasms in two minutes.

Their food arrived, and the conversation was put on hold.

Within minutes, Misha broke the silence after the server left.

"So, Lena, if you have messed around with Denise and you liked it, are you sure that is going to be it? Or do you think that you all are going to end up doing it?"

Lena swallowed her food. "Look, I admit the kiss was amazing, so passionate. But afterward I realized just how much I love that man. I love Denise, but as a friend. She was there for me, and we shared something special. But she will only be a friend to me. I don't regret what happened. I think it needed to happen for me to know that I truly love Brandon and want to spend the rest of my life with him."

The table became silent as they contemplated what Lena said.

Lena looked over at Carmen. "So, I guess the next wedding will be Carmen and Nic." Lena smiled.

"Girl, I don't know about all that. I do know I love that woman, but sometimes I get the feeling that she is holding back on me." Carmen looked at the both of them. "It's like there's something in her past that she hasn't told me about, but I think it bothers her."

"Have you asked her about it?" Misha said to Carmen.

"I am just going to let her tell me when she wants to. I am not forcing anything on her."

"Good deal. Now all we have to do is get Misha back with Cooley, and things will be all good." Lena smirked.

Misha shook her head. "Oh no, that ship has sailed. Did I tell you all that Cooley told me that she loves me?

"What!" Lena and Carmen said in unison.

Misha smiled. "Yeah, you know we have been getting down most of the year. But when I was getting ready for a date, she tripped out and told me that she didn't want another girl touching me and that she loves me."

"Damn, Misha, so why are you trying to fake like you don't want to be with my brother? She told you something that she has never told another person." Carmen looked at Misha. She knew Misha was the one for Cooley.

"Because things were too complicated with Cooley. I love her, but I can't deal with the drama."

"Misha, she hasn't had any drama all year. The girl has changed. She is all calm now. The only person she is messing with is that Lynn chick."

Misha finished her daiquiri. "Carmen, I hear you, but I can't. I do plan on giving her another chance, just not right now. I don't think it is the right time."

"Well, you better think fast, 'cause that Lynn chick is ready and willing. She cooks like a professional chef and is not planning on leaving Cooley anytime soon."

Misha smiled. "Girl, please, she may can cook, but she can't fuck for shit. Trust me, when I finally get my shit together and feel like Carla is ready, then we will do our thang." Misha turned to Lena. "And, Lena, I think that you need to fuck Denise."

Lena almost choked on her bread. "What!"

Carmen looked at Misha, wondering as well what made her say that.

"Carmen, before you say anything, hear me out. Right now you and Denise are both holding back emotions and shit. Y'all have unfinished business. You need to fuck her one good time and get it out before you get married."

"Hell, no, she doesn't. What happens when she likes the shit?"

"Then she stops herself from making a bigger mistake in marrying Brandon. But I personally think that it's something she will do and get over."

"Why are you all talking about me like I am not sitting here?"

Misha grabbed Lena's arm. "Just think about it, OK? Until you finally let that girl do something, you are always going to be wondering what if."

Lena wondered if that was true.

They dropped the Denise talk and focused on the wedding for the rest of the meal. The three left the restaurant full and tired and headed toward Lena's car.

A light-skinned woman with reddish-brown hair walked up to them. She was attractive, but looked very stressed. Her eyes had bags under them like she had been crying for months.

"Aren't you the woman marrying Brandon Redding?" she asked Lena.

Lena was shocked to have someone recognize her. "Um, yes, I am. Do we know each other?" Lena asked her.

Misha and Carmen remained in their spots, in case something was about to go down.

"No, I don't know you personally." The woman looked at Misha and Carmen. She backed down when she realized she was outnumbered. "Congratulations on the wedding. I am just a big fan of his." The girl quickly walked away.

Misha and Carmen looked at Lena. All of them had a very funny feeling about the woman. Something was telling Lena that she was going to see her again.

Chapter 11

"Damn, I'm coming!" Denise yelled at whomever was beating at her door.

"How you gon' sell Mema's house?" Denise's cousin Shemeka said as she invited herself into Denise's apartment.

"What you mean? I am not going to live there, so why keep it?" Denise asked and sat down on the couch.

"Denise, that house has been in our family since it was built. Our granddaddy built that house!" Shemeka yelled as she paced the floor.

"I know the history of the house. I don't need you to tell me. I can't afford to keep it, Shemeka."

"It's paid off, Denise."

"I know, but my mom fucked up a lot of stuff in there. And there are taxes to pay on it every year. There is no other alternative."

Shemeka sat down in the chair in front of Denise. "Look, I know that we have not been too close, and I have done some pretty fucked up things to you."

Denise looked at Shemeka.

"OK, yes, I have done some real fucked up things. But, Denise, I am trying to live right with the Lord and by my kids. And having seven kids in a three-bedroom apartment isn't working."

"Meka, what are you trying to get at?" Denise said, already knowing where the conversation was heading.

"Let me get the house. It's four bedrooms and perfect for me and my kids."

"You must be out of your mind. Hell, no, Meka. You don't keep a job, and the second you don't pay right that shit is coming back on me."

Shemeka looked at Denise. "Dee, I know you don't want to believe me, but that shit Mema said in her will really messed with me. After I got over being mad, I realized that she was right. I haven't done shit, and my kids are suffering because of me. I went and got a job and have been working at FedEx for almost a year. And, with the money I get from child support, I have more than enough to pay the taxes. If you will just sign the house over to me, you don't have to worry about it at all."

Denise regarded the serious look on Shemeka's face. She knew that she was being genuine. "It's funny that you treat me and my friends like shit, and now you come over here all humble 'cause you want something." Denise remembered all of the nasty comments Shemeka made about her lifestyle.

"Dee, I was jealous," Shemeka said dejectedly. "I was envious as hell of you."

"What the hell for?" Denise said, shocked by the revelation.

"Look at you, Dee. Mema treated you like you were gold. She never treated me like that. You was living with Mema, getting true love, and I was stuck with my ho of a mother and my dad, who only came around when he wanted to sweet-talk my mother into not making him pay his child support. There is so much you just don't know, Dee."

"Why don't you fill me in?"

"Dee, you know who the father of my first child is?" Shemeka asked.

Denise shook her head.

"My mother's ex-boyfriend, Dante. I guess he wasn't satisfied with just screwing my mother."

"Meka, why you didn't tell us?" Denise asked. "Why didn't you say anything?"

"'Cause there wasn't any way to prove it. Plus, I had already been labeled to be just like my mother."

"Damn, Meka, but you were sixteen."

"I know, but that's old water under the bridge. I just was envious of you. I wanted to be the good student, the basketball player and all, the apple of Mema's eye. But now I have gotten my life right with the Lord, and I am trying to get right in every aspect. I want to do right by my kids. That's why I want to have the house."

Denise stared at Shemeka. "All right, I will sign it over to you 'cause I know that is what Mema would want me to do. But you better keep shit right. I'll call the lawyer in the morning. I got two weeks of away games coming up, so I won't be able to do too much until afterward. But you can go ahead and move in."

Shemeka stood up, hugged Denise and headed to the door. She turned around and looked at Denise. "Um, Dee, I heard about what Tammy did. But, um, I think you should know that I saw her recently, and she is looking real bad, thinner than ever."

"Man, whatever. If she stay up off that shit, she wouldn't look like shit," Denise said as she walked to close the door behind Shemeka.

Shemeka grabbed Denise's hand. "Denise, something I learned is that you gotta forgive. It's a book called *In the Meantime* by this lady name Iylana or something. It's powerful, and you really should pick it up. You gotta forgive her 'cause in the end she's still your mother. And, Denise, I really think you need to contact her. I think it's more than just the drugs."

"I hear you. I'll think about it," Denise said as she closed the door behind her. She thought about what Shemeka said. *Naw, fuck that, she made her bed, now she gotta lie in it*, Denise thought to herself as she headed to her room. She had to get some sleep.

Carmen could feel, the tension when she walked into the room.

"You got a message," Nic said, never looking up from her book.

Carmen looked at Nic and pushed the play button.

What's going on, shorty? I just wanted to apologize for that whole ordeal in the U.C. You know a nigga still find it a little hard seeing you with old gal. Anyway you know who this is. Get at me.

"Nic, I didn't—" Carmen said to Nic in her sweetest voice.

Nic pulled her head out of the book. "I don't even want to hear it, OK?"

"Nic, I have been in the same room for two years. It's not like she doesn't know the—"

"How can I get her out of your life?"

Carmen walked over to Nic and put her hands on her neck. She began to massage Nic's broad shoulders. "Baby, there is nothing Tameka can say or do to get me to go back to her. It is all about you and not about her. I am yours."

Nic stood up. "I hear what you're saying, but it wasn't—"

Carmen smiled. "Nic, I am yours. What can I do to make you feel better?"

Nic wrapped her arms around Carmen and smiled. "I know something that will make me feel better."

Carmen knew what that smile meant. Her panties began to get wet. "Well, I am willing to do whatever it takes to make you happy." She pulled her shirt off, exposing her breasts.

Nic picked Carmen up and placed her on the bed. She began to kiss her sensually. They could kiss for hours before making love. Their Cancer-Scorpio love connection included some very passionate sex.

Nic devoured Carmen's breasts. She licked just the way Carmen liked it. Carmen squirmed as her pussy got hotter and hotter. Nic unbuttoned Carmen's jeans while they kissed. With Carmen's constant moving, the pants fell to her ankles. Nic yanked the pants off and pushed Carmen's legs up in the air, almost making her feet reach her face.

Nic stuck her tongue deep into Carmen's walls. She sucked on Carmen's clit, causing Carmen's whole body to tremble.

"Shit, shit!" Carmen yelled as Nic's tongue danced all around her walls, hitting every one of her hot spots. Carmen took her hands and grabbed her legs, pulling them out so that Nic could use her hands to rub on her nipples. She raised her butt. The yoga class she was taking gave them even more positions to try.

Nic looked at Carmen. "Damn, baby, I am glad you took yoga." She took her tongue and continued to lick Carmen's rim up and down before settling in.

Nic was the first to toss Carmen's salad, and Carmen loved it ever since. Carmen let Nic's finger enter her asshole and pushed her booty back as she begged Nic for more.

Nic edged another finger into the tight hole as she continued to lick around the rim. The pressure of Nic's fingers inside and the softness of the feel of Nic's tongue stroking around her anus was almost too much for Carmen to bear.

Carmen reached across her belly and began to stroke the protruding button between her wet lips. She moaned softly and trembled as Nic went at it, stroking, licking and teasing her, then sucking the juices pouring from her pussy as well.

Nic reached up, pushed Carmen's hand away and began to stroke the hard little clit herself. At this point Carmen could no longer rein in the convulsions that erupted from her body. Her face contorted as orgasmic spasms took control of her body.

Nic looked at Carmen and laughed at her facial expression. Nic loved the looks that Carmen made after she had a hard orgasm. She climbed up on the bed and kissed Carmen.

"I love you, shorty," Nic said as she held Carmen in her arms.

Carmen closed her eyes. "I love you too."

Chapter 12

"Lynn, what are you trying to do to me? I am supposed to be in training," Denise said as she devoured another piece of Lynn's fried chicken.

Cooley looked at Denise and smiled. "Bruh, can't she cook her ass off?" Cooley said as she took a gulp of the red Kool-Aid. "Bae, this is off the chain."

Lynn smiled. "Anything for my *papi*." Lynn continued to fry chicken.

"Coach is going to bench my fat ass if I keep on doing this." Denise got up from the table and hugged Lynn. "Thanks again, boo."

Lynn turned and looked at Cooley, who was only paying attention to her plate. She sat down at the table and watched Cooley eat.

Cooley looked up when she felt Lynn's eyes on her. "What? I got something in my teeth?"

Lynn smiled with a dreamy-eyed look. "No, I just was thinking of how great this semester has been going. Don't you think so?"

"Yeah, it's cool."

"We have been having a real good time, right?" Lynn asked Cooley.

Cooley nodded her head. "Fa sho, you know how to treat a nigga right." Cooley took a bite of her mashed potatoes.

"Cooley, I was wondering if you wanted to come home with me for Christmas?" Lynn asked, still looking at Cooley with her dreamy eyes.

Cooley almost choked on her Kool-Aid. "Um, I hate to say no 'cause I'm sure ya mama taught you how to cook like this. But I will be in Atlanta during break." Cooley looked at Lynn, "Plus, you don't take niggas like me home. You take your girlfriend home"

Lynn's face dropped. "Well, I mean as much time and all that we spend together, I figured we were getting to that—"

Cooley quickly cut her off. "Shorty, I told you in the beginning that I am not looking for a relationship. It's not something that I am going to do."

Lynn got up from the table. "I know that's what you said, but it's like I'm over here like almost every day and all. We're practically in a relationship now."

"Well, do we need to stop kicking it so much? Because if you want time to see other people, I understand." Cooley got up from the table and put her dishes in the sink. She could see the hurt in Lynn's face.

"No, everything is fine," Lynn said, trying to hide her disappointment. "But you're right, my girls have been complaining about me being with your ass all the time." Lynn smiled.

Cooley wasn't buying her excuse. "If you say so, shorty. I like spending time with you, but you just caught me at the wrong point in my life. I swear last year I actually tried the relationship thing, but it's not what I want now." Cooley kissed Lynn on her forehead and walked back into her room.

Lynn finished cleaning up the kitchen. She wasn't giving up that easily.

"Is coach trying to kill us?" Stephanie said.

"I don't know, but I know my body is killing me right now," Denise said as they walked out of the dressing room. "Hey, are you all right to make it back to your room this late?"

"Yeah, I am fine. Michelle is going to wait on me," Stephanie replied. "Dee, can I tell you something?"

"Yeah, what's up?"

"I wasn't completely honest with why I dress more feminine now." Stepanie looked down at the ground as they walked. "There was more."

"Spit it out then," Denise said, noticing how nervous Stephanie looked.

"Well, to be honest, I have always been a tomboy, but not a stud."

"What do you mean? You always date femmes."

"That's because if I went up to a stud they would be ready to slap the shit out of me," Stephanie said.

Denise knew she was right. Studs just didn't date other studs in Memphis.

"When I was in Spain, I realized something was really missing. Then I realized I could never have it, dressing the way I dressed."

"So you are saying that you're crushing on someone?" Denise said as she tossed her bag in her car. "Do I know the person?"

Stephanie smiled. "Oh yeah, you know them very well."

"Don't tell me it's Cool."

They laughed.

"No, it's not Cooley."

"Well, who?"

Stephanie looked into Denise's eyes. "I thought it should be obvious." Stephanie grabbed Denise's hand.

Denise felt a warm sensation flow through her body. "Steph—"

"Denise!" Rhonda yelled, storming up toward them.

"What's up, Rhonda?" Denise said, slightly irritated that she interrupted her conversation.

"That's what I want to know," she retorted, looking Stephanie up and down.

"Look, I'm 'bout to roll out. I'll see you tomorrow at practice, Dee," Stephanie said and walked off.

Rhonda immediately started in on Denise. "What the fuck was that, Dee? Why was she holding your hand and shit?"

"Rhonda, you need to calm down." Denise sighed. She noticed a few people beginning to watch.

"No, I don't need to calm down! Stop telling me to calm down when you are doing shit like this! You need to tell me what the fuck is going on! So you fuckin' your teammates now?"

Denise took a deep breath to try to keep her cool. "Rhonda, this is not the time."

"Yes, the fuck, it is." Rhonda pushed Denise.

Denise grabbed her arms. "You know what? Fuck this shit!" Denise let go of Rhonda. "Number one, I don't have to explain shit to you. Two, you know I don't do this drama bullshit, so you need to calm the fuck down," Denise said in a very stern voice.

Rhonda could tell Denise wasn't playing, but she continued to try her anyway.

"Fuck that, Denise! You not finna play me for a fuckin' fool. I bet not catch you up on her again or it's gon' be both of yo' asses!" Rhonda said as she rolled her neck and threw her hand around in Denise's face.

"You know what, fuck this shit. You are fuckin' crazy!"

Rhonda's face turned quickly. "What did you call me? Take it back. I'm not crazy. Take it back!"

"Whatever, Rhonda, I'm done. Do not call me anymore. Do not show up at my practice. Leave me the fuck alone!" Denise got into her car.

Rhonda hit the window as Denise drove off. "It's not over 'til *I* say it's over!"

Nic was amazed by how quickly Larissa could type. She watched as Larissa never looked down at the keys. She was glad she had come into her life.

"So, did you need me to type anything else?" Larissa asked Nic, still amazed by how quickly she typed the paper.

"Um, no, speed racer. Girl, I would have been here all night typing those pages." Nic smiled.

"It's all good. I'm good at typing."

"You're excellent at typing. Damn, it's late. We need to get going," Nic said.

They headed out of the computer lab.

"Where are you parked?"

"Over the tracks. Goodness, I didn't know it was ten."

"Yeah, I didn't know it was so late either. I'm not getting you in trouble, am I?" Nic smiled.

Larissa blushed. "Um, no. Hell, I had my own work to do. Your paper took like five minutes."

"Great. Make me feel real shitty, why don't you? Come on, let me walk you over these tracks."

"You don't—"

"La-La, you already know I am walking you."

Nic and Larissa headed out of the building.

"Larissa, how are things at home?"

"Um, they are OK. How are things with you?"

"Can I confide in you?" Nic asked.

"Of course."

"Man, I love Carmen to death. You know that, right?" Nic said.

Larissa nodded her head. "It's Carmen's ex.

It's like I can't shake the feeling that Carmen still has feelings for her."

"Damn. Have you talked to Carmen about it?"

"Hell, yeah. She knows how I feel about the situation. The other day the girl left a message on our dorm phone. I swear I wanted to go kill her. But at the same time I couldn't shake the feeling that Carmen liked hearing from her."

"Nic, I don't know. I personally don't know why any woman would want anyone over you. I mean, any straight woman would kill for a man that acted like you. Lord knows I would." Larissa looked at Nic. "Have you ever been completely cool with something, until someone shows you the better side?"

"What do you mean?" Nic asked.

"You know, like you are used to drinking the cheap vodka. Then one day you have Grey Goose. It's like you don't want to go back to drinking the cheap shit. It just doesn't compare anymore."

"I feel you on that."

"Well, it's like lately my eyes have been opened up to more. And I don't know if what I have is worth keeping anymore." Larissa looked at Nic. Their eyes met. "You understand what I am saying?"

"Yeah, I do. Um, is that your car?"

Larissa jumped back into reality. "Yeah, it is. Well, I'll see you later, Nic."

Nic closed the door for Larissa and began to walk off. She heard Larissa call her name.

"Nic, remember that you deserve someone who loves you just as much or more than you love them." Larissa smiled and drove off.

Chapter 13

"I officially wish I hadn't waited till this year to take my last math," Carmen said to her friend Brian, who also went by Brandi.

"It's all good. You help me get through keyboarding, and I got you in math," Brian said as they sat typing away in the computer lab.

Brian was the star of the majorette squad. He could twirl a baton better than all the women on the team.

"Look at Derek over there, with his gay ass."

Carmen looked over at the large football player. "Since when is Derek Smith gay?"

"Since he started fuckin' me at least twice a week." Brian snapped his neck. "Girl, he can't get enough."

"Brian, you better stop, and if I was you, I wouldn't tell anyone else. I am sure he don't want the world knowing he's gay."

"I know, right. Girl, his dumb-ass girlfriend is so fuckin' clueless. I tell you about these dumb broads around here. She think she got something special. She just don't know I'm getting it too."

Carmen shook her head. She hated the idea of down-low brothers. "I really hope you're using protection with these scandalous men."

"Umm-hmm, girl, you know it. 'Cause I know they will pick up trade as easily as they pick up me," Brian said.

"How is Devin?" Carmen asked.

"She is OK, you know, a little fucked up over the whole thing, but you know you can't keep that diva down."

"Why weren't you at the protest?"

"Girl, please, these muthafuckas around here don't give a damn about us. Hell, you can't even get the gays to come out. We handle our shit our own way, by coming back to school and being as grand as eva. These homophobic niggas up here don't stop no show."

"So she's coming back to school?"

"Yep, next semester, talking about she gon' wear full drag in one of the dance team outfits. She planning on out-dancing all those bitches. You know it was trade that did that to her."

"You think so?" Carmen asked. "A student?"

"Hell, yeah. You can't tell me no different. Probably someone who was mad she wasn't fucking him no more. But that's OK. They will get theirs in the end."

"What's up, Carmen?"

The familiar voice caused Carmen's flesh to crawl.

"You fuckin' with he-shes now?"

"What the fuck you call me, tramp?" Brian stood up.

The computer lab attendant quickly walked over.

"Take this outside, people."

"No, there's nothing to take outside. So what is this, Tameka? Now, you want to jump new after the little message you left on my phone. Tameka, do you have, a life or are you just content with trying to fuck with me?" Carmen said, refusing to back down.

Tameka's grin turned to a frown. "Well, look who finally got some backbone. You maybe got a little spine now, but you still ain't nothing but a fat-ass girl."

The comment hit Carmen like a blow to the chest. She continued to hold her composure 'till Tameka left the room.

"Cece, are you all right, girl," Brian said. "That bitch better be glad we on this damn campus. I bet not see her at the club."

"I'm fine, fuck it. I need to roll." Carmen grabbed her bag and headed out the lab. She needed to get back to her room, back into the arms of someone who cared.

Denise looked down at her phone. Five missed calls, all from Rhonda. She shook her head as she cleared her call log.

"I told you that bitch was crazy," Michelle said, grabbing her gym bag.

"Man, tell me about it. I don't even do this kind of drama." Denise picked up her gym bag. "Yo', where is Steph?"

"I'm right here," Stephanie said, stepping out of a bathroom stall.

Denise couldn't help but stare at her thick legs in the shorts she had on.

"Damn, is there something on me?"

Denise looked up. "Damn, naw, I just—"

"She was looking at your thick-ass legs." Michelle laughed as Denise hit her on her arm.

"Well, Dee, you're welcome to look." Stephanie smiled as she walked out the locker room.

Michelle looked at Denise. "You know she wants you, right?"

"You think so?"

"Dee, she's my roommate. She wants you, dog. Too bad y'all can't get down."

"Yeah, coach would kill us both."

"Exact—Oh, shit. Homey, you being stalked," Michelle said as they noticed Rhonda sitting up against Denise's car.

"Rhonda, don't start this shit today," Denise said, trying to get past her without using force.

"Denise, please just talk to me." Rhonda grabbed Denise's arm, but she quickly jerked away.

"Man, look I told you—" Denise turned her head when she heard a horn beep. She smiled at the sight of Lena. Denise walked away, leaving Rhonda in a huff.

"What's going on, Lena?"

Lena pulled her shades off. "Hey, I was, um, in the area and just wanted to come by and see if you were still in practice."

"Dee," Rhonda called out, but Denise ignored her.

"Did I interrupt something?" Lena asked, looking at the anger on Rhonda's face.

"Hell naw. So, what's up?"

"I wanted to see if you would take a drive with me."

Denise couldn't resist. She heard Rhonda call her name again. "Give me one second." She walked over to Rhonda. "Look, I have told you more than once to leave me the fuck alone. All this blowing my phone up and shit is doing nothing, but making me really not want to talk to you. I will call you when I want to talk to you."

Rhonda's face dropped. Tears began to roll down her face. "Fine, Denise." She threw her hands up in defeat and stormed off.

Denise got in the car with Lena.

"So, this is your city. Where is somewhere we can go to talk?" Lena asked.

Denise knew the perfect place.

They drove over a small bridge to Harbor Town, the exclusive Mud Island neighborhood, where many of Memphis' wealthiest citizens lived. The area had numerous places along the river for people to park for some alone time; it was the perfect place to creep for many.

Lena guided the car through perfectly planned neighborhoods filled with homes in stately Victorian, Craftsman and Federal architecture styles. She drove through the town square, slowing for the many pedestrians strolling along the brick-lined crosswalks. Lena smiled at the quiet, nostalgic feeling the town square had. It was almost as though they had driven into another century when they crossed the bridge.

Lena drove down to the last parking lot for the park on the river. They parked all the way down at the end. "This is a peaceful place," Lena commented while staring at the muddy water of the Mississippi River. Her iPod was playing random songs by her favorite artist.

Denise sighed. Their taste in music was just another reminder of how much they had in common.

"Look, Lena, I really wanted to—"

"Denise, don't apologize. That's not what I want to hear right now."

Denise looked out at the water. "Lena, I don't know what to say."

"Dee, that kiss, our kisses. They are unlike any kiss I have ever had. So much passion. I have feelings that I, I just don't understand them, or how to deal with them. I just don't know anything anymore."

A single tear fell from Lena's eye, causing Denise's heart to break. She hated seeing women cry especially about something she did.

"Lena, please, I don't want to see you cry," Denise said as she wiped the tears that were now flowing heavily from Lena's face. "This is why I didn't want to go there with you. I don't want you hurting because of me. Let's try to just move on from it."

"Denise, you don't undersand. I had to do it. I have had these feelings since last year. I just didn't know what it was. You and those damn wife-beaters. God, I used to love to watch you work out. I love watching you play basketball."

"Lena, please don't do this," Denise said, trying to hold back her feelings.

"Dee . . ."

"Lena, no, you can't do this. Shit, I shouldn't have come with you. You are with Brandon. You finna marry that nigga in two weeks. I can't do this. It, it . . . I just can't do it." Denise turned her head from Lena. She couldn't bear to look at her. She wanted to tell her everything, but she had to hold back.

Lena could tell Denise was just as affected as she was. She knew deep down she was right. She sighed. "When did things become so complicated?"

"They aren't. We are cool, you are my friend, and that's how things have to be." Denise felt her heart breaking inside, but she held her composure. "Look, I hate to cut this short, but I really need to get back to campus."

Lena cranked her engine as Jazmine Sullivan's "Lions, Tigers and Bears" began to play. Denise and Lena sat in silence as they listened to Jazmine's smooth voice. They held back emotions as the words got to them.

Chapter 14

"Do you see the shit on this list? We can't afford this shit," Cooley remarked, looking down Lena and Brandon's registry list, as they walked around Bloomingdale's, looking at the expensive china.

Denise was in her own world. She couldn't get Lena off of her mind.

Cooley snapped her fingers in front of Denise when she realized Denise wasn't listening to her. "Bruh, are you OK?"

"She is getting married in two days." Denise sighed.

"Man, damn, I was hoping you were getting better. Are you OK to go to the party?"

Denise sighed. "Yeah, man, I'm good. I have to let go, right?"

"You know I wouldn't be myself if I didn't say this. You do realize she isn't married yet. You still have time to get her if you want her."

"I can't do that to her."

"But what if she's making a mistake? What if she is the one for you, and you are supposed to be together?"

"Man, no. Brandon can offer her so much more than I can—"

Cooley cut Denise off. "You know what? I love you, dog, but you have become such a pussy."

"What you call me?"

"A pussy. Dee, you act like you don't have anything to offer her. Shit. So what, that nigga got money? That ain't shit in the end. He may have money, but you have heart."

They stood in silence for a moment. Denise's mind went back to Lena. "Man, I love that girl."

"I know."

"Cool, I love her so much, I am willing to let her go. If it's meant to be, she will come back."

"Dig that," Cooley said. "So, um, considering that everything on this list will cause us to become homeless, how about we buy a bottle of Grey Goose and Patron and call it a day?" Cooley smiled, causing Denise to smile as well.

"So, are we going to have male and female strippers?" Carmen said.

"Hell, I think she would be cool with just female." Misha laughed.

"I heard that, bitch." Lena giggled as she joined them at the table. "So, is tonight planned?"

Carmen rolled her eyes. "Yup, we have the two-bedroom suite at the hotel so that Nic and I can get one room, you get the other, and Misha can sleep on the couch."

"Yeah, just put me on the couch." Misha rolled her eyes.

"You think Denise is going to come?" Lena asked.

"Carla told me she was coming for sure," Misha reassured her.

"Don't look now, but there is the infamous Lynn," Carmen said as she motioned for Lynn to join them.

Misha cut her eyes at Carmen then looked at her competition.

"Hi, Carmen, how are you." Lynn smiled. "Hello, I'm Lynn, Cooley's girl."

"Girl?" Misha said.

Carmen hit her under the table. "So, how are things with you and my bro?" Carmen said.

Lynn pulled up a seat. "Oh, it's good. Hey, aren't you Misha? It's nice to finally meet you."

"Likewise." Misha pretended she was reading a magazine.

"Well, it's nice to meet you, Lynn. I'm Lena."

"Oh yes, the one getting married to Brandon Redding. One of my friends is so in love with him."

"I will tell him he has a fan."

"Awesome!" Lynn smiled.

"So, Lynn, how did you manage to bag Cooley?" Misha asked.

"I am not sure, actually. I guess she saw something in me. It was real interesting 'cause I never thought we would make it this long. She is so experienced, and being that she was my first I know that—"

"What?" Carmen cut Lynn off. "You have never been with a girl before?"

Lynn realized she stuck her foot in her mouth. "Well, actually I had never been with anyone before."

"Does Carla know that?"

"Um, well, not necessarily. I didn't want to scare her off."

Carmen was pissed. "Lynn, that was something you really should have shared. Cooley would have been gentler with you."

"No, I was fine. I didn't want her to treat me like some inexperienced girl. That's why I didn't tell her."

Misha wanted to laugh but held it in. She buried her head in her book. She knew it was the end for Lynn.

"Well, um, I have class. Can we finish this later?" Lynn asked.

"Cool. Hey, come to my wedding if you want. I'll give Cooley an extra invitation for you," Lena said, hoping to clear some of the tension in the air.

"OK." Lynn hurried off.

Carmen looked at Misha, who started to laugh. Lena couldn't do anything but shake her head.

Carmen picked up her phone and called Cooley.

"Hey, you," Larissa said.

"What's up, girl? I haven't seen you around that much." Nic said, giving Larissa a hug.

"Yeah, I know. I had to get a job. My so-called man wants me to start helping pay some of the household bills."

"Damn."

"Tell me about it," Larissa said as she sat at Nic's table. "I really hate that I'm taking eighteen hours next semester."

"Damn, girl, are you going to be able to make it?" Nic asked. She was concerned about Larissa.

"I have to. I want to graduate on time. I had a class I forgot about taking. I don't know if I will be able to pledge now. I don't know when I would have the time." Larissa tried to hide her disappointment. "How does Carmen do it all? You know, being in school, working and the sorority? She's so active in it."

"Oh, C doesn't work. I won't let her," Nic said.

Larissa was shocked. "You won't let her? Why?"

"'Cause I take care of mines," Nic said, packing up her bag.

Larissa smiled. "Nic, you never cease to amaze me. You are truly one of a kind."

Nic smiled. "Oh, don't go there. I just don't like my woman to work unless she absolutely has to or just wants to. Lots of men are like me."

"No, they aren't." Larissa stood up. "Well, it's pretty late. I need to get going."

"Let me walk you to your car." Nic stood up, but Larissa stopped her.

"No, I'm right outside. Got a good spot. I guess I will see you next semester, Nicole."

"Bye, La." Nic gave Larissa a hug.

Larissa looked Nic in her eyes but quickly turned around and walked off.

Larissa's phone began to ring as she left the library. It was her man. She pressed ignore, suddenly annoyed by the thought of talking to or seeing him.

Chapter 15

Denise stared at the bathroom wall in the hotel. She did not want to leave it.

Cooley looked at herself in the mirror once more. She was going to get Misha if it was the last thing she did. She bought a baby blue and white button down shirt and a new pair of dark blue jeans. Baby blue was Misha's favorite color.

Cooley cocked the collar of the shirt up and placed her baby blue sweatband around her curly Afro. She placed her shades back on her eyes. Her look was complete.

"Dee, how do I look?" Cooley asked as they stood in the bathroom.

"Fine," Denise mumbled without looking at Cooley.

Cooley grabbed Denise's arm. She began to pull on Denise's clothes.

"What the fuck are you doing?"

"I'm making you look presentable. Shit, you need to walk in there and make Lena's panties wet. Take that white tee off. I'll be right back."

Denise watched Cooley walk out the bathroom. She wondered what she was up to.

Cooley walked back into the bathroom holding a bag. "Put this on."

Denise pulled the muscle T-shirt out of the package. "Dude, I don't want to wear this."

"Man, please. If it's one thing I know, Lena loves your arms. This shirt will show 'em off. Put it on. And here." Cooley handed Denise an icy white fitted baseball hat.

While Denise placed the hat on her head, Cooley sprayed her with something.

"Man, that smells good. What is it."

Cooley smiled. "Creed for Men."

Denise instantly placed the familiarity of the scent. She loved Creed on Lena. Denise looked at herself in the mirror. She had to admit, Cooley had an eye for fashion. "Now let's go."

They could hear Beyonce coming from the hallway. Cooley knocked on the door.

Misha opened it, and her mouth dropped. "Carla, you look—"

"I look what?" Cooley said taking her shades off. She stared directly into Misha's eyes.

Misha's knees began to tremble. "Come in," Misha stammered, trying to regroup. "Hey, Dee, you look nice."

"Thanks," Denise said as her eyes quickly caught Lena.

Lena looked at Denise. Her eyes roamed all over Denise's body. She felt herself becoming heated. She'd never seen Denise look so good.

Denise walked over to her. She wrapped her arms around her, and the Creed cologne quickly drifted into Lena's nostrils.

"Is that Creed?"

"Yes."

"Very nice. You look—"

"Thanks."

"Damn, this place is hot," Cooley said, walking around the suite complete with three-bedrooms, a living room, and a dining room. It looked more like an expensive apartment than a hotel suite.

"OK, now we can get the party started," Carmen said, stumbling into the living room. "Dammit, what took you two so long?"

"We had some last-minute preparations," Cooley replied as she stared down Misha's back. Misha could feel Cooley's breath hit the back of her neck. She wanted to take Cooley right then and there.

An hour later everyone in the room was drunk.

Cooley stood up. "All right, all right, since there are no strippers at this shindig, I guess we are going to have to get grimy my way. Truth or dare time."

"Oh, hell no, Carla, I am a married woman now," Carmen protested. She knew Cooley's games of truth or dare were no holds barred.

"Let me explain something to the newcomers. This truth or dare is no holds barred. If you don't do what we say, you have to take three shots in a row," Cooley slurred as she sat back down. "Does everyone agree?"

Carmen looked at Nic.

Nic smiled. "Hell, I'm down. What goes on in this room stays in this room, right?" She kissed Carmen as they all looked at Lena.

Lena looked at the group. "What? I am down for whatever!"

Cooley looked at Carmen. They both smiled devilishly.

Denise looked at Cooley. She knew she was up to something. "OK, let's do this."

Cooley grabbed an empty bottle and spun it on the table. It landed in front of Carmen. "I will start out easy with you. Carmen, if you had to have a threesome with Nic and someone in this room, who would it be?"

Carmen looked at Nic. "That's easy. Misha."

Everyone laughed.

"Why me!" Misha said, shocked by the answer.

"'Cause you were able to keep up with Cooley, so you are the only femme in the room who could probably keep up with me and Nic."

The room roared.

Carmen spun the bottle. It landed on Misha. "Misha, truth or dare?"

"Fuck the bullshit. Dare all the way." Misha took another shot.

"OK. I dare you to let Cooley lick on your titty right now." Carmen smiled.

Misha looked unimpressed. "Is that all?" She pulled her shirt up and exposed her breasts.

Cooley quickly dived toward her, licking all over her nipple.

Lena was intrigued by Cooley's sucking technique. She felt herself getting moist.

Misha pushed Cooley off of her, once her panties were completely soaked. "That's enough."

She spun the bottle. It landed on Lena.

Everyone got quiet as they waited on Lena to decide truth or dare.

Lena decided to go for it. "Dare, please."

Denise couldn't believe Lena asked for a dare. Misha looked over at Cooley. She already knew what to ask for.

"Lena, I dare you to kiss Denise in front of all of us."

Denise began to object when Lena straddled her on the chair. Lena pressed her lips against Denise's. Denise was shocked, but she quickly began to return Lena's kisses. They soon became engaged in a very passionate session of tongue dancing.

Everyone was shocked by the spectacle.

Cooley couldn't stop smiling and nodding her head in approval at the way Denise was handling Lena. "OK,

OK, Denise, it's your turn," Cooley yelled, hoping she could get some more time with Misha.

"Um, I think that it's time for us to call it a night. Someone needs to be rested for her wedding," Carmen suggested. She was unsure of what to think about the kiss, but she could smell trouble.

Lena looked at Denise, who didn't want to let go.

"I guess you're right," Lena reluctantly agreed, while still sitting on Denise's lap.

"Great!" Carmen said. "So, Cool, Dee, are you all staying?"

Lena couldn't stop looking at Denise.

"I don't know. Misha, am I staying?" Cooley stared at Misha. Misha couldn't resist.

"Well, I guess I need to go," Denise said, still looking into Lena's eyes.

Lena finally snapped back to reality. "Oh, yeah, um, I guess so." She climbed off Denise's lap. Lena could feel the wetness in her panties.

"Ooookkkkaaayy. So, Dee, call me when you make it home, all right?" Carmen hugged everyone. "See y'all in the morning."

Nic and Carmen headed to their room.

As soon as she closed the door, Nic looked at Carmen. "Did you see that shit?" Nic said to Carmen.

Carmen shook her head. "You know I did."

Cooley grabbed Misha's arm. "We will see you in the morning, Lena," Cooley said as she pulled Misha toward her room.

Misha and Cooley walked into the dark room. Cooley walked up behind Misha and put her arms around her. She kissed her on the back of her neck.

"Cooley, don't go there. We are just sleeping," Misha said as she slipped a shirt on.

Cooley quickly picked her up and placed her against the wall.

"Cooley!" Misha said as she tried to fight the feelings that were coming over her with each kiss Cooley laid on her neck. She couldn't resist. She wrapped her legs around Cooley as they began to kiss.

Denise opened the door to her empty apartment; it had never seemed so quiet. For the first time in a long time she realized just how lonely she was. Everyone in her life had someone, while she longed for a woman who could never be hers. She fell down on her couch and stared into the darkness. She wondered what Lena was doing at that moment. Was she thinking about her at all? Had Lena felt the same way she felt during the kiss? She laid her head on the back of the couch and stared at the ceiling. Before she knew it, her eyes began to close.

Lena sat on the couch pondering what Denise was doing. Confused thoughts entered her head, what to do or what not to do. Thoughts of Brandon receiving lap dances from random strippers made her wonder; she probably hadn't crossed his mind.

The memories of her and Denise rolled through her mind like a movie. She loved their friendship, but couldn't help but yearn for more.

Misha's phrase repeated itself over and over again, "What if." What if Denise really was the one that she should be with? What if she did what her body wanted her to do? The thoughts consumed her and sounds of Carmen and Misha's moans weren't helping the situation.

Frustrated, she put her jacket on, grabbed her keys, and walked out the door.

It was like she was the only one on the road. She listened to a playlist on her iPod as she drove with no destination in mind. Floetry began to play. She thought about when she and Denise met. Denise caught her from falling off of a chair.

It seemed like Denise caught more than just her body that day. She noticed barricades stacked up on the side of the road. She realized she was in front of the site of her wedding. It was going to be a grand affair, but she could only think about another affair. Lena tried to make sense of it. Brandon, after all, was no saint, and she had been faithful for five long years. Maybe she deserved her chance to fool around before she said I do.

Soon she was sitting in the parking lot, staring at Denise's apartment window. The lights were not on, but she saw Denise's car parked a few spots down. She opened the car door, and the cold, dry Memphis air flew up her little shorts. She closed her coat and ran up the stairs. There she stood staring at the numbers on the door. It was now or never.

Denise woke to the sound of someone beating on her door. She realized that she had fallen asleep on the couch. She attempted to work the kink out of her neck from her awkward sleeping position as she walked to the door. She opened it without looking in the peep hole.

Denise rubbed her eyes, trying to become alert. Her body froze as she saw Lena standing in front of her. Before Denise could say anything, Lena wrapped her arms around her, and they began to kiss.

They walked farther into the house without letting go of each other. Denise closed the door with her foot. She didn't want to let go, but she had to.

"Lena, what is going on?"

"I'm getting married tomorrow." Lena sighed.

"I know that. That's why I'm having a hard time understanding why you are here." Denise rubbed her hands down her braids.

Lena looked at Denise. "I don't know. All I know is . . ." Lena turned around and walked toward Denise's room. "Are you coming?"

Denise stood in the living room dumbfounded. She knew it wasn't right, but she couldn't resist.

Lena dropped her coat on the floor, exposing her little silk sleep set. Lena's body enticed Denise. She followed Lena to her bedroom.

The only sound in the apartment was the ticking of the wall clock. Denise watched as Lena slid her shirt over her head. She wanted to pinch herself to see if she was dreaming. She knew it wasn't a dream; her fantasy was coming true.

As Lena sat her nude body on the edge of the bed, Denise stood in the doorway, almost afraid to enter, but turned on more than ever.

"Lena," Denise said, afraid of what she would do if she was to enter the room.

Lena stood up and walked toward her. She placed her index finger on Denise's lips. "Take me," she whispered.

Denise dropped her head in submission to Lena's request, ready to finally let go and get what she wanted. She picked Lena up and carried her toward the bed, kissing her intensely. Denise placed Lena's body on the bed.

Lena watched as Denise pulled her shirt over her head. Her biceps and ripped stomach aroused Lena like it always did. Lena rose up and began to unbuckle Denise's jeans.

Denise ran her hand through Lena's long hair. Her fingers grazed the nape of Lena's neck causing Lena's whole body to quiver and her nipples to protrude.

Denise gently pulled Lena's hair, causing Lena to let out a moan. Their eyes met. Lena felt as though Denise was looking into her soul.

Denise ran the tip of her tongue from Lena's lips down her neck, kissing her chest, then stopped to indulge on her erect nipples.

Lena's pussy was throbbing harder than ever. She grinded her pelvis against Denise's thigh.

Denise could feel the heat coming from Lena's body. She let her hand walk down Lena's thigh until it made it to her cave. She slowly slid her fingers into Lena's soaking wet walls.

Denise pulled her fingers out and licked them. She knew Lena was going to taste good, but she didn't know it was going to be so sweet. She had to taste more.

She lowered her head and let her tongue explore Lena's walls, stopping to devour her clit like it was her last meal.

"Shit. Oh, shit!" Lena moaned as she began to quiver from Denise's tongue.

Denise was determined to enjoy every moment, knowing it could be the only time. Her tongue worked like a small bullet over Lena's clit.

Lena felt her legs stiffen up, as Denise's tongue fucked her better than Brandon's dick ever did.

Lena needed something to hold on to. She grabbed the bottom sheet, causing it to partially come off the mattress. An intense feeling started to creep from her toes to her legs, which to shake. "Denise!" Lena exclaimed as she tried to squirm away.

Denise locked her arms around Lena's thighs. "Don't run," she whispered as she continued to treat her to the best head she could possibly give.

Lena's whole body shook as she began to climax. "Ahh, Denise!" Lena grabbed on to Denise, digging her nails down into her skin. "Wait . . . wait . . . I . . . can't . . . take . . . it . . ."

Denise wasn't going to let her go until she got every last drop of Lena's sweetness. Lena's body exploded as Denise swallowed her contents as a keepsake of the moment.

Denise rose up and looked at Lena, who was in a state of euphoria.

Lena grabbed Denise and pulled her toward her, placing another intimate kiss on her. She could taste herself on Denise's lips. Brandon never let her kiss him after he gave her head. He would always jump up and go brush his teeth.

Denise wrapped her arms around Lena. She didn't want to let go.

Lena rubbed her hand against Denise's arm. She always had to tell Brandon to hold her; Denise did it naturally.

Lena's mind went to Brandon. She felt a small sense of guilt, but it didn't overtake the feeling that she had for Denise at that very moment.

Lena turned over on her side. Denise wrapped her arm around Lena, cradling her body against hers.

Lena's eyes got heavy as she began slowing falling asleep, exhausted from the workout Denise put on her.

Denise watched as the woman she loved slept, the woman that would never be hers. Looking at Lena's beauty, tears rolled down Denise's face.

***

Misha lay in Cooley's arms after their hours of love-making. She knew she could not hold back anymore. "Cooley, after we all get back from winter break, I want you to leave Lynn alone."

Cooley looked at Misha. "Why is that?"

"Because I want us to concentrate on making us work, if you still want to."

Cooley kissed Misha. "That's all I have wanted to do all year."

They fell asleep in each other's arms.

Chapter 16

The sunlight from Denise's window woke Lena. She looked over, realizing she was still in Denise's arms. She smiled at Denise's sleeping face. Lena slowly got up, trying not to wake Denise. She quietly put on her gown and walked toward the door. She noticed a notepad on the coffee table. She quickly wrote a note and placed it on her pillow. She looked around the apartment one more time and quietly walked out the door.

She walked into the hotel room. Everyone was still asleep. She slowly crawled into bed. Within minutes she was asleep.

Before she knew it, Lena heard the door close. She woke up and saw Misha standing at the door.

"Hey, chick," Misha said, getting into bed with Lena. "How was last night?"

"Wonderful. God, I love that woman." Misha smiled. "I know. I'm glad you were with her last night."

"So, in a few hours you are going to be married. Are you ready?"

Lena thought about the question. She smiled. "Finally, I think I am."

Denise woke up the next day alone. She looked around and noticed that Lena's things were gone. She found a note lying on the pillow where Lena slept.

Denise,

I thank you for last night. I want you to know that you are a very special woman to me. I have never felt for any-one the way I feel for you, but I know now that the feelings I have for you do not surpass the love that I have for Brandon. I hope that you don't hate me after this, because I truly love you. You are my best friend. I hope to see you at my wedding, but if you don't, I understand.

Please remember that I love you.

Denise stared at the letter. She didn't feel upset. She realized Lena was right. She was happy that it happened, but her friendship was the most important thing.

She walked into the living room, a small piece of her hoping to see Lena sitting in there. Denise started to walk back to her room when she heard a knock on the door. She opened it and couldn't believe her eyes. "What do you want?"

Tammy looked at Denise. "I know you don't want to see me, but there is something I need to talk to you about." Tammy had tears in her eyes.

"I have nothing to say to you." Denise noticed a purple blemish on the side of Tammy's forehead. "See you still into your old shit," she scoffed as she headed to close the door.

"Denise, please!" Tammy wedged her foot in the door before Denise could close the door. "I really need to talk to you. Just give me five minutes."

Denise noticed that Tammy had lost a lot of weight. She was looking as frail as she looked a few years ago when she was deep into a crack binge. "You should have thought about talking to me when you fucked Mema's house up. Get the fuck away from my house!" Denise pushed Tammy back and closed the door.

Tammy knocked at the door a few more times before giving up. Denise stood at the door the whole time. A big piece of her wanted to give her a chance, but she couldn't. She couldn't let her back into her life. She turned away from the door and headed to her room.

Cooley opened the door. "I know that wasn't Tammy I just saw. Man, she looks terrible."

"It was nothing," Denise said as she pulled out various pairs of pants, trying to decide what to wear.

Cooley walked into Denise's room. She sniffed the air. "What did *you* do last night?" Cooley said.

Denise laughed. "What?"

"Dude, if it is one thing I know, that's the smell of sex. You was fuckin' last night. Who was it?"

Denise plopped down on her bed. She looked up at Cooley. "Can you really smell sex?"

Cooley laughed. "Oh snap! Who did you hook up with after the party? Wait, it bet not be Rhonda."

"Naw, man, guess again."

Cooley looked puzzled.

Denise smiled.

Cooley's eye's widened. "Lena? Dee, you fucked Lena! How the fuck did you manage that?"

"Man, she showed up over here." Denise smiled at the memory of the previous night.

Cooley could not stop laughing. "Oh my God, I should've come home. Damn, you finally tapped it! Was it good? Give me details."

"Hell no, I am not telling you anymore," Denise declined as she walked to her closet.

"I will kill your ass if you don't tell me what happened," Cooley persisted.

Denise remained silent.

"I bet she sound good as hell moaning. I can hear her ass now, 'Denise, Denise, oh, Denise,'" Cooley teased.

"You are a nut," Denise said as she ironed her shirt.

Cooley realized what Denise was doing. "You mean you're still going to the wedding? You are a bold bitch."

"Man, I will admit fucking Lena was off the chain. But I still feel the same. Our friendship is the most important thing. It happened. Now I can finally move the fuck on."

Cooley patted Denise on her back. "Good for you, dog. I guess I will go too. I thought I was going to have to console your broken-hearted ass. I get to go look at some fine-ass bitches."

"What about Misha?" Denise asked.

"Misha is . . . let's just say I'm only looking at women at the wedding. Don't worry, I'm not about to mess up anything with my boo."

"Oh, your boo, huh?" Denise smiled.

Cooley smirked. "Yeah, whatever. Fuck you," she said, hitting Denise. Inside she was smiling harder than ever.

Carmen and Misha looked around the hotel room, making sure they had everything to head to the church. They buzzed to each other as Lena sat on the couch.

"I had sex with Denise," Lena blurted out.

Carmen and Misha both stopped dead in their tracks, neither believing they heard her correctly.

"Come again?" Carmen said.

"I had sex with Dee," Lena repeated.

Misha and Carmen looked at each other and ran to the couch.

"How the fuck did that happen?" Misha said, still in shock.

"I left last night and went to her house."

"Oh my God," Carmen said, shaking her head.

"How was it?" Misha said, grinning.

Lena smiled.

Misha and Carmen both said, "Oh my God!"

"Damn, give details." Misha hit Lena's arm.

"What's going on?" Nic said, walking from the room.

They all yelled for Nic to go back in the room.

"Damn," Nic said, quickly closing the door.

"Lena, fuck the details right now," Carmen said.

"Fuck that, details now!" Misha cut Carmen off.

"No, Mish, there is something so much more important. Do I need to put this dress on or not?"

They sat in silence waiting on Lena to answer the question.

Lena looked at both of them. "Today I become Mrs. Brandon Redding. I am getting married."

Without saying anything else, they got up and headed out to the church.

Chapter 17

The outside of the church was like a circus. It was the biggest event Memphis had seen in a while. Athletes and celebrities piled into the church. Photographers snapped pictures of all the A-list wedding guests as they walked up the Tiffany Blue carpet rolled out over the steps of the church.

The bride's room was buzzing. Lena stood in one spot as her style team primped her for her special day. Carmen and Misha also enjoyed the special treatment. They were both picked as maids of honor.

There was a knock at the door. Cooley and Denise walked into the room. Cooley was dressed in an all-white suit. Denise wore black.

"Hello, beautiful," Cooley said as she hugged Lena. "You ready to do this?"

"Yes, Cooley, I am ready." Lena turned around and looked at Denise.

Misha, Carmen, and Cooley knew it was time to make an exit. They pulled the style team into the adjoining room.

Denise looked at Lena. It was the first time they had seen or talked to each other since their incident.

"You look beautiful, Lena," Denise said in a sullen voice.

"You look quite dashing as well." Lena smiled. "Look, Denise—"

"Shhhhh." Denise put her finger up to Lena's lips. "There is no need to say anything. I am still your friend, and I love you, Lena." Their eyes locked.

Denise knew it was wrong, but she wanted to kiss her. She leaned in for the kill but heard the sound of someone trying to get into the room.

"Will someone unlock this door!" Karen yelled from the other side.

"Shit!" Lena scuffled to get Misha and Carmen back into the room. "You and Cooley wait in there." She pushed Denise in the small office with Cooley.

Carmen opened the door to find Karen looking upset. "Were sorry, Mrs. Jamerson, we just wanted to have a special best friend moment with her. Forgive us."

"Oh, it's perfectly all right. Now let me look at my baby." She put her hands on Lena's shoulders. "My baby, you are about to become Mrs. Brandon Redding." She hugged Lena.

"Oh, mother, come on." She turned to see Carmen crying. The makeup artist was quickly trying to stop her tears from messing up her makeup.

"Carmen!" Lena exclaimed.

"I'm sorry. This is just so special." Lena walked up to Misha and Carmen to give one last group hug. They heard the sound of the processional music playing. It was showtime.

Cooley and Denise waited till the coast was clear. Cooley looked at Denise.

"Bruh, are you going to be all right?" Cooley asked as she put her hand on Denise's shoulder.

"Yeah, I am going to be fine. But I can't lie. I wish I was Brandon right about now."

They headed out of the room to find their seats.

The sanctuary was draped in the Tiffany colors of white and blue. The white roses were lined with the signature Tiffany Blue ribbon.

Denise smiled at the sight. She remembered Lena saying that she was going to have the Tiffany signature color for her wedding. She remembered them watching a special on celebrity weddings. Lena fell in love with Toni Braxton's wedding cake. It was shaped like little Tiffany and Company jewelry boxes.

The bridesmaids and groomsmen began to come into the church to the sound of Eric Benet singing live at the wedding.

"Damn, I didn't know we were getting a concert too," Cooley whispered and nudged Denise.

Suddenly Brian McKnight approached the front, singing his hit, "Never Felt This Way." It was Brandon and Lena's song. The crowd stood as Brian continued singing. Lena was standing in the entryway.

Denise felt butterflies fill her stomach as Lena began to walk into the church. Denise had never seen a more beautiful sight. Lena made it to the front, and her father placed her hand in Brandon's. Denise took a deep breath. She really had to give her up now.

The wedding ceremony was refined. The preacher talked about love and the union of marriage. Denise tried to concentrate, but was constantly interrupted with Cooley whispering things about the various celebrities in the church. Denise looked at Carmen and Misha. Both of them were crying.

Soon the preacher made it to the famous line. "If anyone objects to the union of these two, speak now or forever hold your peace."

"Bruh, if you speak we will instantly be at the most entertaining wedding ever," Cooley whispered to Denise causing her to snicker. She was glad no one noticed her.

"OK then."

The ceremony went by in a flash. Within minutes it was time to kiss the bride.

"Well, by the power vested in me and the state of Tennessee, I now pronounce you husband and wife. You may kiss your bride."

Brandon leaned in and kissed Lena passionately. Denise felt her heart break. Brandon and Lena turned to the crowd as the preacher introduced them as Mr. and Mrs. Brandon Redding. The crowd went wild with people clapping and yelling. Denise sank down in the pew, trying not to let a tear fall.

There was a loud bang on the right side of the sanctuary. An informally dressed woman rushed into the sanctuary.

"No! I can't be too late. No!" she yelled as she ran toward Brandon and Lena.

Lena took a look at the woman, recognizing her as the same woman who'd approached her in front of the restaurant.

"No! I have something to say."

Brandon looked as though he had seen a ghost.

Suddenly the bodyguards bum-rushed the woman, carrying her out of the church. She yelled the whole way. "No, no, this isn't right, this isn't right!" The woman's cries were finally silenced by the closing door.

Peaches, Brandon's publicist, ran to the front of the church.

"Everyone, let me have your attention. We are so sorry about that spectacle. She was a disgruntled fan who is not too happy about seeing her favorite basketball player marrying someone. But since there are so many of us that are happy about this wonderful union, let's let our happy couple go, and we will see you all at the reception."

Everyone cheered as Brandon and Lena ran down the isle out of the church.

Cooley and Denise sat in their seats for a few minutes. Nic quickly joined them.

"Wow, that was something, wasn't it?" Nic said as she took a seat next to Cooley.

"Hell yeah, but I ain't buying what the lady had to say. I bet that's some bitch that B has been fucking that is pissed that he is married now," Cooley said as she eyeballed a cute girl, who was obviously eyeing her as well. "Well, I am about to head out to this reception so that I can get more acquainted with a few of these high-society bitches up in here. Dee, you coming?"

Denise was in a daze. She looked up at Cooley. "Nah, I think I am going home. I have had enough to last me a while." She got up and headed out the church.

Cooley and Nic headed off to the reception.

"Misha Renee Davis." Misha got goosebumps when she heard a deep voice call her full name. She turned around and smiled.

"Patrick, it really can't be you," Misha said as she looked at the tall, handsome man standing behind her in the cake line.

"In the flesh." Patrick hugged Misha. "I thought that was you in the wedding."

"Oh, my goodness. What are you doing here? Who do you know?"

"The groom. We went to school together. I can't believe I am standing in front of my first love." Patrick smiled.

Misha noticed he still had the most adorable dimples. "I can't believe I am standing in front of my first love as well. This is so surreal."

"Hey, Misha," Carmen said as she walked up to the two. She noticed the large smile on Misha's face. "Wow. Who has you smiling like this?" Carmen looked at Patrick.

"Carmen, this is Patrick Donaldson. Or as I used to call him, Boo Boo." She smiled as she looked at Patrick's eyes. He was blushing.

"Oh my goodness, I can't believe you just did that." Patrick shook Carmen's hand. "Please forgive my beautiful ex. No one called me that but her." Patrick locked eyes with Misha. They couldn't stop staring at each other.

Carmen noticed the connection. "Well, I guess I will leave you all to catch up, OK." Carmen walked off when she realized they did not hear her.

Misha and Patrick quickly made it to an empty table and began to catch up on old times. Patrick was now a sports agent.

"I am so proud of what you have become, Patrick. You know I thought you were destined to be a thug for the rest of your life." Misha laughed.

"No, no. I outgrew that as soon as we got to Atlanta. It was the best decision that my mother ever made."

Patrick and Misha were inseparable for three years. She was the good girl who fell in love with a neighborhood thug. Only Misha was able to see his sensitive side. After his brother was shot and killed, Patrick's mother moved them to Atlanta. He was her first and only male lover, the only man she ever had sex with. "The only regret was that I had to leave you." Patrick looked at Misha with a very serious look.

She felt butterflies in her stomach. She wanted to change the subject. "So where are your wife and children?" Misha said, trying to stop herself from staring into his deep brown eyes.

"No such luck. I have never been married, and I have no children. So where is the man that I am going to have to beat up?"

Misha and Patrick laughed. He always used to beat up any guy who tried to look at her.

"I don't have a man. Actually, um, there is something that I think you should know." Misha knew she had to tell him she was a lesbian. She looked into his eyes. She had forgotten just how beautiful his eyes were.

"Misha?"

Patrick calling her name snapped Misha back to reality.

"What did you want to say?"

"Oh, I think you should know. You should know . . ." Misha looked into his eyes again. "Um, I don't have a man. I am single as can be."

Patrick smiled. "Well, that has got to be the best news I have heard all week."

Misha smiled. She knew she had to tell him, but she didn't want to spoil the reunion.

They spent the rest of the night catching up.

Chapter 18

Denise couldn't sit in her home. The essence of Lena still lingered in the air. She headed to the campus gym. She walked into the gym and heard someone dribbling a ball.

"Stephanie?"

Stephanie dropped the ball. "Dee, what are you doing here?" She wiped the sweat from her forehead.

"I was about to ask you the same question."

Stephanie walked up to Denise. "I come here all the time, you know, just to practice."

"Well, aren't you dedicated."

"Everyone isn't a superstar like you. I have to work hard to even come close to being as good as you." Stephanie smiled.

"Man, you're great. Want a little one-on-one?"

"Only if you give it all you can. I want to go up against the Denise everyone else has to face."

Denise smiled.

They began to play. Denise took it easy on Stephanie, knowing she couldn't handle her to the fullest extent. Stephanie did her best to guard Denise, but she failed on many attempts.

"Dammit, I suck!" Stephanie yelled as Denise got past her to score.

Denise held the ball. "Don't say that. You don't suck."

"Shit. You have scored on me how many times?" Stephanie sat on the bleachers.

"Steph, you are hella good. They wanted you in Spain, remember?"

"I want to be wanted in the States. I want to be in the WNBA. God, why can't I have your talent?"

Denise didn't know what to say. She'd never thought about how good she was. It was mostly natural. She almost took it for granted.

"Stephanie, you have to be the best you can be, not the best that I am. Hell, you think if I played against Sheryl Swoopes I would be good? Hell, no."

"I bet you could give her a run for her money." Stephanie smiled. "It's just that I want this so bad. Don't you want it just as bad?"

"Of course, I would love to play pro ball, but I didn't come to school thinking I was going to go pro. I just wanted to graduate and make my grandma proud." Thinking of her grandmother, Mema, was still very sore for Denise. "I just wanted her to see me graduate. Guess I was a year too late."

Stephanie put her head on Denise's knee. "That's why I like you, Dee. You are so genuine. You don't run across girls like you."

"Well, thank you."

Denise looked at Stephanie. Their eyes locked. Stephanie leaned in to Denise. Denise closed her eyes.

"Wait." Denise put her hands on Stephanie's shoulders. She stood up. "We can't do this, man."

"Why?" Stephanie asked.

"Steph, you are my teammate. We can't cross that line. Also I think that if I was to kiss you, the only reason I would be doing it is to get my mind off someone else."

"Rhonda?" Stephanie couldn't believe it would be her.

"Hell naw, not Rhonda. Someone else, someone I am still in love with."

The words hit Stephanie hard, but she kept her cool. "Well, thank you for stopping. I think I need to get home. You are a special woman, Denise." Stephanie grabbed her things, determined to get out of the gym before Denise could see how she really felt.

"Shit," Denise whispered as the door closed. "Dee, what the fuck is wrong with you?" she said aloud.

"Nothing at all."

Denise looked up when a familiar voice responded in the distance. She stood up when she saw Rhonda walk into the gym.

"Rhonda, don't—"

"Dee, hear me out first, OK?" Rhonda said, walking toward Denise. "I was leaving the computer lab and noticed your car outside. I just wanted to apologize for everything. I don't know what was wrong with me. You are just the most wonderful woman I have ever been with. I let my own insecurities mess it up with you."

"Yeah, you did. Well, I accept your apology."

"Dee." Rhonda grabbed Denise's hand. "Can you find it in your heart to forgive me? We work so well together, don't you think?"

"Rhonda, we really don't. Besides, I should've never gotten with you to begin with. I have a goal, and women aren't a part of it right now."

"Dee, I don't want to mess up your plans. I just want to be a part of your life, enhance your life, help you meet your goals." Rhonda's eyes were filled with tears.

For the first time Denise could see the sincerity in Rhonda's face. *It's better to be with someone than no one*, Denise thought to herself. "Rhonda, if you flip out on me one time, I am through with you for good."

Rhonda wrapped her arms around Denise and planted a sensual kiss on her.

Denise tried to enjoy it, but it didn't compare to the lips of yesterday.

Brandon and Lena settled into their room at the Madison Hotel. Lena changed into an outfit that would definitely send Brandon into a frenzy. She walked out of the bathroom wearing a peach corset with no panties. Her vagina was freshly waxed into a landing strip. She had on peach thigh-highs and high heels.

"Hello, Mr. Redding, are you ready for your wife?" she purred seductively.

"I have been ready for you, Mrs. Redding. Now come over to this bed and let's consummate our marriage."

Lena walked slowly to the bed and crawled over to Brandon.

Soft music filled the beautiful suite. Brandon made a mental note to thank his assistant for making the perfect romantic playlist to play for their special night.

Brandon grabbed Lena and picked her up, placing her on his face.

Lena rode Brandon's face, making sure he got a taste of all her sweetness. She closed her eyes and listened to the music play, trying to completely get into the mood.

Janet Jackson's sensual "Would You Mind" began to play. Lena's mind drifted to the night before. She began to grind her body against Brandon's tongue. She was no longer in her honeymoon suite. Her mind was back in Denise's bed. She really didn't care if Brandon never gave her oral sex ever again. She had better, and now his didn't compare anymore.

She slid down off of his face and placed herself on his rock-hard manhood. Denise was the pro at giving head, but Brandon would always be the best at waxing her with the dick. If only Brandon was blessed with the skills to make her cum just by tasting her like Denise was.

Lena snapped back to reality. She couldn't be thinking about Denise on her wedding night. It was all about her and Brandon. She focused on him for the rest of the evening as they sexed each other in nearly every position all night long.

Lena lay in the bed with her eyes open. She thought about her beautiful wedding. She knew it was going to make it into the *INstyle* weddings issue. She hoped too many people didn't catch wind of what happened with that girl.

"Brandon."

"Yeah?" Brandon responded, obviously groggy from her waking him up.

"What was the deal with that girl? Is there anything that you're hiding from me?" Lena asked. She knew that there was a possibility that Brandon had been messing with groupies. She hoped that he wouldn't, but she knew there was always a big chance that he would.

Brandon sat up and looked at Lena. "Honestly, baby, I don't know who that girl was. Peaches said that the girl had been trying to meet me for a while 'cause she wanted to marry me, but I had never seen her before," Brandon said.

"The funny thing is that the girl came up to me earlier this week."

Brandon's eyes popped. "You mean that she had contact with you? What did she say?" Brandon got up out of the bed.

"Nothing, baby, she was just asking if I was the one marrying you. Carmen and Misha were with me, so I guess she knew that if she tried something that all hell was going to break loose."

"That's not cool. That is not cool at all. I will handle this. From now on I want you to have a bodyguard, and I will get Peaches to get a restraining order against that psycho," Brandon said as he paced back and forth.

"Brandon, I don't want some bodyguard following me around campus."

"Baby, I don't think you should go to campus anymore."

Lena jumped out of the bed. "What do you mean? I told you before that I was not quitting school!"

"Lena, I am not telling you to quit school. I think that you should tele-course and Internet it this semester. We don't know anything about this girl, and I don't want her trying to do anything to you." Lena looked at Brandon. She could tell he was really worried about her.

"All right, I will do Internet classes for the spring semester. But, Brandon, get things together 'cause I want to go to summer school, and I will have to take classes on campus next year." Lena walked up to Brandon and put her arms around him. "I love you, *papi*."

"I love you, Mrs. Redding. Now, let me get my baby back into the bed." Brandon picked up Lena and placed her into the bed.

Chapter 19

"So I guess this is the way things are going to be from now on, huh?" Cooley said as she and Denise sat in their apartment staring at each other.

"I guess so. We're grown-ups now. We are going to be apart more and more."

"I am going to miss you, bruh."

Denise looked at Cooley. "I am going to miss you too."

"Oh, would you two shut the fuck up? It's only a month, for goodness, sakes," Carmen said as she walked into the apartment. "Y'all act as though you are never going to see each other again."

Cooley was heading back to Atlanta to work for the record company, and Denise was going to a basketball camp. Carmen and Nic were going to spend the first half of break in Jackson at Carmen's house and the second half in California with Nic's family.

"Carmen, we're serious here. Next year I will be in Atlanta with the record company. Who knows what team Denise is going to end up on? And you are going to be in California trying to have babies with Nic. Our time is running out." Cooley had a very serious look on her face.

"Just because we will be in different places doesn't mean we don't love—Wait, what the hell am I doing?" Carmen caught herself from falling into Cooley's and Denise's depressed state. "Cooley, you are going to come and visit all the time 'cause you want to get some Cali hoes. And Denise is going to be making mad money in the WNBA, so she can come visit too. This just means we each have somewhere to crash when we want to get away from our regular spots," Carmen reminded them.

Cooley's eyes brightened. "You're right, I can come to Cali and get some Cali pussy. I gotta go pack for my trip." Cooley got up from the table and headed to her room.

Carmen sat down next to Denise. "You know you can be hurt if you want to. I know how much you care about her," Carmen said to Denise, who was staring into space.

"It's written all over my face, huh?"

"With a Sharpie marker." Carmen knew Denise was having trouble dealing with Lena's marriage.

"I'm glad she's happy, you know. Man, I was feeling someone, but I can't do it."

"Yeah, I know, Stephanie." Carmen walked over to the refrigerator and grabbed a soda.

"Damn, C, are you a fuckin' psychic or something?"

"Nope, but I do know you and Carla like the back of my hand." Carmen smiled.

"Yeah, man, we got kinda close last night, but I had to stop it. Oh, and there is something I need to tell you two."

"What's up?" Carmen and Cooley said in unison as Cooley poked her head out of her room.

"I am sorta talking to Rhonda—"

"Don't fucking finish that sentence, Dee!" Carmen yelled.

"Hell no, you aren't dating her again."

"You all don't understand."

"Yes, we do," Cooley said. "The best way to get over one is to get under another. But that ain't the bitch to get wit'."

"Dee, don't do it," Carmen said. "That bitch is twisted, and you know it."

"Well, what else am I supposed to do?"

"Since when do you have a problem being alone?"

Denise knew deep down they were right. Her mind began to race through all the times Rhonda flipped on her. "Shit."

"See, you regretting it already. So call her and tell her you changed your mind," Carmen said.

"I can't just do that. That's mean."

"Give me the phone. I'll tell the bitch," Cooley said grabbing Denise's phone.

Denise quickly grabbed it back. "Fuck, I'll do it. Just not right now."

"Great. Now new subject. C, what was the deal with that girl at the wedding?" Cooley asked about the girl who caused a stir at the ceremony.

"I really don't know," Carmen said, sitting back down at the table. "But check this out. You wanna know something strange? That girl who ran into the wedding, we met her earlier that week."

Denise looked up at Carmen. "Are you serious?"

"Yeah, the girl walked up to us at J. Alexanders. She asked Lena if she was the one marrying Brandon. It looked as though she wanted to say more but backed down when she noticed me and Misha looking at her."

"No shit," Cooley said. "I told you, dog. Brandon was hitting that. Don't no regular fan gon' do no shit like that. That was a booty call gone wrong." Cooley walked into the kitchen with Carmen.

"You know, I didn't want to say anything, but I honestly think Cooley may be right. There is something more to that story," Carmen said.

Denise looked down at the table. "If Brandon ever hurts Lena, I swear I may go to jail that day," she said in a serious tone.

"Please. Brandon is going to cheat. He has too much pussy being thrown at him. But Lena knows the deal. She knew what she was in for when she said 'I do,'" Cooley said, sitting back down at the table.

"That don't make the shit right." Denise looked down at her glass. Vivid images of Lena's naked body entered her head. She heard someone calling her name in the distance. Denise jumped. "Oh shit."

"Damn, bruh, where was your head just then?" Cooley asked, looking at her friend. She smiled. "Oh, I know where your head was—in between Lena's legs."

The comment made Carmen spit out her juice. Cooley began to laugh.

"I can't believe you fucked her," Carmen said, shaking her head.

"Well, shit happens." Denise stood up.

"Good one, Dee." Cooley laughed.

Carmen hit her hand.

"I'm glad you fucked her. Shit, it's about time. I was tired of you being just a bitch about the situation. Get that shit."

"Fuck you, man," Denise said as Carmen and Cooley laughed.

They heard a knock at the door.

"Damn, that's Lynn. Man, I gotta get rid of this girl real quick."

"Cooley, let her down nice, OK?" Carmen said as Cooley answered the door.

Cooley nodded her head as she headed to the door.

Lynn smiled as she walked in. "Hey, baby, I have missed—"

"Lynn, we need to talk." Cooley walked to her bedroom.

Lynn looked confused. She glanced at Carmen and Denise, but they tried to avoid eye contact.

"What's going on?" Lynn asked when she entered Cooley's bedroom.

"Lynn, why didn't you tell me that you hadn't been with anyone before?"

Lynn felt a knot forming in her throat. "Um, I didn't think it was that big of a deal."

"Man, that is a big deal. I flat-out asked you, and you lied. I don't deal with shit like that."

"I am sorry, Cooley. Please don't be mad at me."

"I'm sorry, Lynn, but this isn't going to work. I wasn't looking for nothing serious, and you don't need someone like me."

Tears began to roll down her face. "Cooley . . ."

Cooley tried not to look at her. "I'm sorry, Lynn. I did like you, but this isn't going to work anymore. I hope we can be cool, but that's it."

Lynn's heart was broken. She ran out of the room. Cooley heard the door slam.

Carmen walked in. "Damn."

"*Damn,* is right. Man, fuck it. Besides, Misha and I are going to see what we can do when I get back anyway. I was gonna have to drop Lynn anyway. You know Misha ain't going."

Someone began to knock at the door. Cooley walked over to the door, still trying to shake off making Lynn cry. She opened the door to see Rhonda standing there.

"Damn, what the fuck do you want?" Cooley said as Rhonda rolled her eyes.

"I was invited, thank you very much. So get out my damn face," she said as she pushed by Cooley. "Hey, baby—I mean, Denise. Sorry, I guess it's still a habit," Rhonda said as she took a seat next to Denise.

Carmen looked at Cooley and rolled her eyes.

"So what? You finally begged my bro until she couldn't say no?" Cooley said to Rhonda, causing Carmen to nearly choke on her water.

"Look, I know I have been a bitch in the past, but I love your friend. So hopefully we can get along."

Carmen and Cooley looked at each other and laughed.

"Get the fuck out of here. I don't know what you said to make Dee have a temporary lapse of judgment, but trust, she will wake up soon," Carmen said.

Rhonda was furious but simply smiled."I guess we will just see about that."

"You damn right, we—"

"Carmen!" Denise said, trying to dissolve the conversation before it escalated further.

"Look, I'm gone. I'm going to sign up for Life Support later tonight." Carmen hugged Denise. "I will see you next year, OK." Carmen walked to Cooley's room.

"So are you packed?" Rhonda asked Denise.

"Um, actually, I'm not. Look, Cooley, is going to drop me off on the way to the airport."

"I don't mind waiting. I'll wash up these dishes while you finish," Rhonda offered, picking up a dish.

"No, that's OK. Cooley and I have some things to talk about, so don't worry about it. I'll call you later."

Rhonda looked over at Cooley. She wanted to knock the devilish grin off of Cooley's face. "Fine, call me and let me know you made it, OK." Rhonda tried to kiss Denise on her lips but was met with her cheek." Rhonda walked out of the door.

"That bitch is wacked." Cooley laughed as they both headed to their rooms to continue packing.

"Fucking Cooley and Carmen," Rhonda huffed as she got in her car. "Fuck that. No one is going to stand in the way of me and Denise." Her tires squealed as she sped off.

***

Carmen signed her name on the volunteer list. She planned to get a few hours in before she and Nic left for the holidays.

"Carmen, now you know that we can manage without you. You're about to go out of town, and you should be preparing for that," the attendant at the front desk of the recreational center said.

"Oh, I'm already packed. I'm only signing up for the next Life Support meeting."

Carmen had started volunteering with the Life Support meetings after she watched *Rent*. The meetings were designed as a support group for people living with HIV and AIDS. She started attending the meetings because of the movie, especially the part when they sang "Will I Lose My Dignity." Carmen became attached to the people after the first meeting and began volunteering weekly.

"So how many have signed up for it so far?"

Carmen looked over the list of participants that signed up in advance. She noticed a name that made her heart beat quickly. Tammy Chambers.

Chapter 20

Misha knocked on the door of the hotel room.

Patrick's jaw dropped when he opened the door. "Wow. Damn, girl, are you trying to give me a heart attack?"

Misha smiled. "You don't look bad yourself there." Misha looked Patrick up and down. She was impressed by his black Armani suit. She could tell it was tailored for his slender build.

"Come on in. So where would you like to go tonight, madam?" Patrick asked as he let Misha into the room.

Misha and Patrick had spent the rest of the evening after the wedding catching up on each other's lives. They had also gone out the following days. She felt as though they had never lost touch.

"Oh, I really don't care. It's whatever you want." Misha took a seat on the bed. The smell of Patrick's cologne filled the whole room. She took a deep breath and let the smell fill her nostrils.

"Well, honestly, I'm perfectly fine staying right here. I'm paying for this room. I might as well take advantage of the hotel's services. How about room service and a movie?" Patrick said flirtatiously.

"Um, yeah, we can order room service. I'm sure there is a movie on that we can watch," Misha said as she slipped her shoes off and reclined on the bed.

As Patrick ordered their food, he glanced over the menu at Misha. She was too busy flipping through the channels to notice his gaze. Patrick smiled. "Hey, Misha."

Misha looked up at him.

"Did I tell you how good you look tonight?" Patrick smiled, causing Misha to blush.

"You're silly," Misha said.

Patrick flashed his bright, white smile again.

They began to laugh and joke around. Before they knew it, there was a knock on the door.

"That must be the room service," Patrick said as he headed to the door.

"Good. I'm actually hungry. Oh my God." Misha's mouth dropped when she saw the lavish setup. "When did you do all of that?"

"While you weren't paying attention to me on the phone," Patrick answered as the waiter set up the table. An exotic flower arrangement sat in the middle of the table.

Misha smiled. "Wow, Pat, this is amazing," she said as the waiter lit the two taper candles.

Patrick plugged his MP3 player into the speakers. The mellow sound of Sade began to set a romantic mood.

Misha looked at the table. She didn't know where to begin. Pat had ordered nearly everything on the menu. They sat down and began eating.

"So, Misha, you haven't told me about any of your past relationships. How many hearts have you broken besides mine?"

Misha immediately thought about Cooley. She took a long sip of her champagne. "Not many. I haven't dated much. I wanted to concentrate on school."

"You were always the bookworm. I remember when you would sit out on my stoop and study while I sold weed. Always trying to get me to pay attention to what you were learning."

They both laughed.

"Yeah, and how much you hated me reading my poetry." Misha smiled.

Patrick leaned closer to her. "Your eyes enchant me, making me feel blessed that I can see.'"

Misha's eyes widened. It was a piece of a poem she'd written for him years ago. Her smile was as big as a Cheshire cat's. "I can't believe you still remember that."

The end of the Sade CD came, and the MP3 instantly began to play "Slowly" by Syleena Johnson.

"I remember a lot of things."

Patrick and Misha's eyes met. He stood up and walked over to her. Misha looked up at him. Patrick got down on his knees.

"I remember the main reason I could never let you go was because of those lips. It was the only time I have ever wanted to truly kiss a woman."

Syleena's beat was pounding, the sound her voice echoing in Misha's ears.

Patrick put his hand on Misha's face, pulling her close to him. She closed her eyes as their lips met. Misha stood up along with Patrick, never parting from his lips. Patrick and Misha lay down on the bed. His hands started to explore underneath her dress.

Misha suddenly realized what was going on when his hands rubbed against her breasts. She jumped up.

"No, we don't need to be doing this," Misha weakly protested.

Patrick ignored her and continued to kiss her full lips. She couldn't resist. She let Patrick remove her dress.

Misha slowly closed her eyes and let Patrick take control. Misha let go. She let Patrick take control of her body and her soul.

***

"Maybe it's not her, baby," Nic said as they watched the various people walk into the Life Support meeting.

"I surely hope not," Carmen replied. She had been nervous since she read the name on the paper. That was Denise's mother's name; the thought of telling Denise that her mother was dying made Carmen anxious.

Carmen gasped as the frail woman walked into the room.

Tammy looked around as one of her friends put her arm around her shoulders for moral support. Tammy's eyes widened when her eyes met Carmen's, filled with tears. Tammy quickly ran out of the room.

"Tammy, wait!" Carmen quickly followed, making it just in time to catch her.

"Carmen . . . I . . . you can't. Don't tell Dee." Tammy, filled with fear, looked at Carmen.

Carmen grabbed Tammy's hand. She noticed the large purple lesion on her forehead. "Tammy, how long?"

"A while. About three years." Hot tears streamed down her face.

"Why don't you want to tell Dee? She needs to know—"

"No!" Tammy yelled. "I already tried. I went by there, and she wouldn't even let me in the house. I have hurt her too much. I refuse to hurt her anymore."

Carmen shook her head in disbelief. "How long do you think you have?"

"I'm not sure. Some days I'm OK. Others, I'm not. My B cells have dropped a lot, so they say that's bad."

"B cells?" Carmen said in confusion until she realized the mistake. "You mean your T-cells. Have you been taking care of yourself?"

"I'm a junkie, Carmen. I've messed my body up so bad, there really isn't much to do now but die," Tammy said, sitting down in a folding chair. "Ain't no need of taking pills and shit from people who really need it."

Tears rolled down Carmen's face. She had seen many people with AIDS, but it had never been this close to her. "Tammy, I can't keep this from Denise. I have to tell her, but I really think you should."

"I can't do it. She has her senior year and basketball to worry about. She don't need to be trying to worry about an old, dying junkie. She just dealt with Mama all those years. Please don't tell her."

Carmen thought about all of the work that Denise had to do for Mema. "I'm sorry, but she's my best friend. I can't keep it."

"Well, let me tell her. I'll do it when she gets back from that camp," Tammy pleaded with Carmen.

Carmen hesitated. "Fine, but if you don't tell her, I will." Carmen took Tammy by the hand. "Come on, they're about to start."

The two walked into the room. Carmen realized that there was going to be a long, hard semester to come.

Chapter 21

Cooley sat in the control chair listening to the beat she created. The studio was dark, mainly lit by candles and a few soft lights. Black light posters of Tupac, Bob Marley, and various marijuana leaves covered the walls. The smell of incense and weed filled the air. Cooley finally learned to block the smell out. Sonic was sitting on the couch surrounded by her women as usual. A large tray of cocaine and loose weed sat in front of her.

"Come on, Sonic, I want you to hear something I'm working on for you," Cooley said as she pulled an extra chair up.

Sonic didn't respond.

"Yeah, right," the engineer whispered to Cooley. "I don't know why you even try with her. She's washed up." The man got up and walked out the room, shaking his head when he passed Sonic, who was almost passed out.

Cooley called Sonic's name again, realizing she was not getting up. She started working on the track she was preparing for Sonic.

Cooley zoned out into her own little world. She let the music take her away. She could picture herself making love to Misha to the sound of the track. She could see Misha's naked body moving to the sound as she sat on the bed and watched the private show.

Cooley had zoned out completely. She didn't hear the door open. When she finished the track, she heard someone clapping behind her.

"Wow, Cool Cat, sounds like you just created a hit track." Big Ron, the owner of Jam Zone, stepped closer to Cooley. "I didn't know you were a hit maker."

"Man, I was just playing around, you know, trying to get a feel for every aspect of the business. You really like it?"

"I don't play when it comes to music. Who were you making it for?"

"I was thinking about Sonic, you know, since she's working on her new album," Cooley said as Big Ron took a seat next to her.

"You know something, Cool? You want to know what I told Sonic when she came to me about some lesbo she wanted to work here for the summer? Hell, no! But finally I went ahead and gave you the internship, and I must say I made a damn good decision."

Cooley was surprised. "Well, thank you for taking a chance on me."

"Yeah, and I want to take more. When do you graduate?"

"I have one semester left," Cooley answered. She tried to keep a straight face.

"Well, the day you get your degree, you come back to Atlanta and to Jam Zone. We're opening an office in Miami, and guess who is going to be in the A and R department?"

Cooley's eyes widened. "Are you serious?"

"Dead serious. I ain't about to lose you to another label. You are going to do great things, Cool." Big Ron stood up and headed to the door.

Cooley could hardly contain herself. She attempted to wake Sonic up, so they could celebrate, but it wasn't happening.

Cooley had met Sonic last year when they attended a party hosted by Jam Zone Records, the label Sonic was on. She remembered walking up to Sonic and telling her that she had tight music and fine-ass bitches. Sonic laughed and invited her to join them. Sonic helped Cooley get her internship at Jam Zone during the summer.

Cooley was the first stud that Sonic trusted. They had become good friends over the summer. She even offered Cooley a chance to tour with her, but Cooley decided to come back and finish her last year of school.

Cooley headed out of the studio. She wasn't ready to go back to Sonic's house and fight off the many groupies she let stay around the house. At first Cooley liked the naked women walking around catering to her every need, but it got old quickly. Cooley refused to take any drugs, and so many times she felt a little out of the loop.

Cooley decided to celebrate on her own. She walked down the street and noticed Kittens, a local strip club. She thought she was having déjà vu but quickly realized what she was seeing was real. There was Sahara heading into the club with a duffle bag.

Cooley ran across the street and questioned the bouncer. "Hey, what was that girl's name who just walked in?"

"If you want to know her name, you have to pay twenty dollars like everyone else," the large man grunted.

Cooley pulled out a twenty, paid the cashier, and headed into the club.

Cooley took a seat in a chair near the main stage. She looked around but didn't see Sahara anywhere.

A girl in a black cat outfit finished her routine on the main stage as the announcer began to introduce the next girl. "Now bringing to the main stage, the sexy Siren!"

The light turned red as a girl sauntered onto the stage. Cooley's eyes widened as she looked the familiar body up and down. Sahara had on a red outfit that fit so tight, it looked like it could have been painted on. Cooley noticed that her body was still perfect, just like she remembered.

Sahara worked the pole like a true pro. Men threw bills at the stage as she moved her body to the song.

Cooley walked up to the stage. Sahara was in her own world as she took money out of the miscellaneous horny men's hands. She was zoned out as she turned around toward Cooley.

She froze when she noticed the familiar face standing in front of her. Cooley placed the hundred-dollar bill in her G-string and headed back to her seat.

Sahara couldn't take her eyes off of Cooley for the rest of her number.

"Now this is a pleasant surprise. I never thought I would see you again," Sahara said as she took a seat next to Cooley after her show.

Cooley couldn't help smiling. Sahara was just as beautiful as she remembered. "Tell me about it. I surely never expected to see you in a place like this," Cooley said as she looked at Sahara. She could tell she was tired. "How long you gotta be here?"

"I don't actually. I just came in to make some extra cash. And, thanks to your tip, I'm good for the night." Sahara hit Cooley on her leg playfully.

"Well, in that case, let's get out of here, go get something to eat."

Sahara smiled. " Sounds good. Let me go change, and I'll meet you outside. They can't see me leaving with you, or I'll get fired for prostitution."

Sahara headed to the back, and Cooley walked out the door.

Cooley followed Sahara to the Waffle House. They took a seat in one of the small booths nestled in the back of the restaurant.

"So how long you been dancing?" Cooley took a bite of her waffle.

"Not for long. A few months. Things got tight when me and Michelle broke up," Sahara responded.

"Word? Y'all broke up?" Cooley wanted to smile, but she held it in. "You doing all right?" Cooley noticed that she was eating like it was her last meal.

Sahara looked at Cooley. "I've been better. You know, Michelle didn't want me to have a job while we were together, and my dumb ass did it. So, when she left she, of course, left me with nothing. My home girl got me this job at the strip club. It's cool 'cause it's not grimy like some clubs are. I pretty much been hustling to get by, stripping and shit."

Cooley hated to think what other things she was doing. "Man, that's fucked up."

"Tell me about it. But I'm making it, putting myself through school, studying dance. Trying to break into some of these videos or get on a tour so I won't have to strip anymore." Sahara finished the last bite of her food.

"You really love to dance, huh?"

Sahara's eyes brightened as she smiled. "Man, I love it. Every day I'm either in a studio on campus or at work."

"Maybe I can help you out," Cooley offered. She hated to see Sahara like that. "I'm staying with Super Sonic right now."

"Wow, look at you, doing big things," Sahara said. "Damn, I'm proud of you."

"Thanks. But, seriously, I just got promised a job at Jam Zone when I graduate. Hey, they're having a video shoot this weekend, if you want to come by. I can try to get you in it if you want."

Sahara's eyes widened. "Are you serious, Cooley? I would really appreciate it. I knew you were something special."

"I'm something. Don't know if I would call it special."

They both laughed as they got up to pay and leave.

"Well, thank you again for dinner and everything, Cooley." Sahara gave her a big hug. "So, are you going to call me Friday?"

"Yeah. I'll actually call you tomorrow."

"Great. It was really nice seeing you, Cool." She smiled.

"Likewise, Sahara." Cooley hugged her and watched her walk out. Cooley shook her head and laughed to herself.

Cooley eventually made her way back to Sonic's house.

"Man, Cool, I cannot wait until you are here full time," Sonic said, giving daps to Cooley as she sat down next to her. She had a plate of cocaine in her hand. She offered some to Cooley, but she declined.

The one thing Cooley did not like about Sonic was her drug habit. "Yeah, I know. Just a few more months and I'm done with school," Cooley said, taking the plate from Sonic and placing it on the table. She could tell Sonic had reached her limit.

Three naked women entered the room. They began to make out in front of Cooley and Sonic.

"Now that's what I'm talkin' 'bout," Sonic said approvingly as she watched the women play with each other. "This is the life, ain't it, bruh?"

Cooley barely looked at the girls. She wasn't really interested in them. All summer she played around with groupies that followed Sonic everywhere she went. Cooley quickly became tired of the easy groupies. Ever since Misha, she didn't find a thrill in very many easy women anymore.

"Man, Sonic, don't you ever think about calming down with all of this?" Cooley asked, pointing at the women and the drugs.

"Man, calm down for what? I'm living the life of a superstar."

"All superstars don't get down like this, bruh."

Sonic squinted at Cooley. "What's going on with you? What happened to Cool from this summer?"

"Man, I'm still Cool. I just think you don't need to do so much. I'm not trying to tell you what to do. I just think you need to focus more on getting the album out, instead of on partying and girls."

"You sound like Ron," Sonic said, slumping down on the couch.

"Well, maybe you should listen. Bruh, I love you to death for all that you've done for me. I want to do back for you, show my appreciation. I made a hot-ass track for you, and you couldn't even listen. Shit." Cooley looked down and realized Sonic had fallen asleep. She shook her head and headed toward the stairs.

"Cooley, you want some company tonight?" one of the groupies said as she rubbed on her erect nipples.

"Naw, I'm good," Cooley said.

"Oh, please, baby. I'll let you do whatever you want to me," the girl begged as she walked over to the stairs.

"Hell, naw. Get out of my face." Cooley now realized why some rappers talked so crazy to groupies. They could be a pain.

"Well, if you change your mind, come to my room. We'll be waiting on you."

The three girls headed out the room. One of them grabbed the tray of cocaine before leaving.

Cooley headed to her room. She never thought the day would come that she didn't take easy pussy.

Misha woke up in Patrick's arms. She lay there, wondering what her next move should be. She didn't know what came over her. She hadn't wanted a man since Patrick left her five years ago. Now she was lying next to her first love, who had given her the most intense orgasms she had ever experienced the night before. Misha tried to ease her way out of the bed, but Patrick grabbed her and pulled her close to him.

"Oh, where do you think you're going?" he said, kissing her on the back of her neck.

It sent chills down her spine. "I was going to the bathroom to freshen up." She pulled away and headed into the bathroom. She gently shut the door behind her. "What the fuck are you doing, Misha?" she said to herself as she looked into the mirror.

Misha never had feelings for another man besides Patrick. When he left town she was devastated. She found comfort in a girl named Lauren. Soon the friendship became more, and Lauren became her first female lover. She never looked back, until now.

Misha walked back into the room to see Patrick standing up at the window. She felt her panties getting wet when she noticed his nude body.

"What are you thinking about, man?" she said, walking up to join him.

"You remember when I left? I told you that as soon as I graduated from high school I was coming back for you." Patrick turned around and looked at her. "Well, the week after I graduated, I did. I came back to get you. I saw you leaving the school. You looked so beautiful. Two years had passed and you had turned into a real woman. I knew that someone had to have gotten you, so I lost all my nerve. I left and decided to let you live your life."

Misha put her arm around Patrick. "Are you serious?"

"As a heart attack. It was the biggest mistake I ever made. I never forgot you. Misha, I have never stopped loving you. I will always love you, and I truly want you back. I'll do whatever I need to do to get you back in my life."

Misha's heart began to beat rapidly. Their lips met. Patrick picked her up and carried her to the bed. Misha couldn't resist, all of her old feelings rushing back. She realized she was still in love with Patrick.

Chapter 22

Carmen woke up at three A.M. She felt funny sleeping without Nic holding her. She crept downstairs, hoping her mother didn't hear her. They had been in Jackson for a week, and she was at her wits' end.

It was evident after the first day that they could not be close. Carmen's mother wasn't rude to Nic, but she wasn't nice either. Nic tried on several occasions to strike up a conversation, but it wasn't working.

One day Nic slipped up and called Carmen baby, causing her shocked mother to drop her glass of water. They would be headed to L.A. in two more days. She just hoped she could make it that long.

Carmen walked into the small guest bedroom, where Nic was sleeping. She climbed on top of her, waking Nic up. She started to kiss her, pulling her own shirt off in the process.

Nic protested and pushed her away. "Hell, no, Carmen, we are not about to do this in your mother's house," she whispered, looking around, hoping that no one was going to walk in.

"Baby, it is three o'clock in the morning. She and my sister are asleep. Now, make love to me now." She lifted one of her breasts and rubbed it against Nic's mouth.

Nic couldn't resist. She turned Carmen over and quickly began to pull her clothes off. Grabbing hold of her hips, Nic buried her face between Carmen's thick thighs.

Carmen made her moans as quiet as possible. She put a pillow over her face and tried to drown out the sounds that she was making. She felt an intense orgasm coming on. She wondered if it was the sheer fact that she was in her mother's house that was making the sex so good.

Nic lifted her face. "Did you hear that?"

"Hell, no. Don't stop." Carmen pushed Nic's head back between her legs. She could feel the orgasm coming. She began to shake. She was seeing the light.

Nic instantly stopped.

Carmen turned around to see her mother standing there with her hand on the light switch.

She quickly closed the door, leaving Nic and Carmen frozen in the same spot.

Nic jumped up. "Shit, shit, shit! Carmen, damn I told you. Shit! She is gonna come back and shoot both of us!" Nic fumbled around, trying to find her wife-beater.

Carmen scrambled to get her clothes on. She looked over at the clock, realizing they had been making love for almost two hours. Her mother had gotten up to start her preparations for Christmas dinner that day.

"Baby, calm down. She doesn't even have a gun."

"Then she is going to stab me. Damn, you had to come down here and fuck with me." Nic was freaking out completely.

"Look, I will go talk to her." Carmen left the hysterical Nic and headed to the kitchen. She had no idea what she was going to say. She saw her mother washing greens in the sink.

"Mom."

"Are you coming in here to help me cook?" her mother said, not looking up from the sink.

"Sure, I can help." Carmen grabbed the bag of peas and began to snap them at the kitchen table. "Mother, I am sorry about—"

"Carmen, I do not want to talk about that," her mother said, cutting her off quickly.

"But, Mom, you don't—"

"Carmen, I said I do not want to talk about it. Why would a mother want to talk about walking in on her daughter letting some girl lick on her?" Her mother threw the greens into the sink.

Carmen didn't know how to respond. She was becoming nervous. She decided to drop it and continued to snap peas.

The room was quiet. Carmen knew she had to break the silence. "Mom, can I make the lasagna this year?"

Her mother looked up at her. "When did you learn how to make lasagna?" Her mother knew that she did not know how to cook.

"Well, Denise's grandmother taught me how to cook. I can pretty much cook anything."

Carmen's mother looked at her. Carmen could tell she was surprised.

"You sure learned a lot of things in college," her mother stated.

Carmen knew she was not talking about cooking anymore.

"Actually, I knew a lot before I left for school. Mom, I am about to gradutate with honors. I am the vice president of the most successful year of Chi Theta. I have five job offers, and I have a person in my life that loves me more than I love myself sometimes. Why can't you just give her a chance?"

Her mother looked at Carmen with tears in her eyes. "Yes, Carmen, you have done well. But what about babies? She can never give you those. I will never be a grandmother. You are going to miss out on so much."

"Mom, I can still have children. I still plan on having one. Mom, Nicole loves me so much. She holds me up when I think I am going to fall. Just like Daddy did for you."

Carmen was crying hard. Tears were running down her mother's face as well.

"Carmen, I love you, and I just want what's best for you."

"Nic is what is best for me. Mom, before Nic, I had no selfesteem. I did not love myself. Well, she loves me so much that I couldn't help but start to love myself as well." Carmen put her arms around her mother. "Can't you see that I am happy? Can't you see how in love I am?"

"Baby, I can see that you love her. I didn't realize it was this serious to you." Her mother held her close.

"It is. So please give her a chance."

Carmen's mother wiped her eyes. "Carmen, if you truly love her, I refuse to stand in your way. I will give her a chance."

Carmen looked up at her mother and smiled.

"Now call your little girlfriend in here so she can help us cook."

Carmen called Nic to the room. She peeped her head around the door. Her bright face was red. They could tell how embarrassed she was.

Carmen and her mother began to laugh.

"Girl, come in here and get to helping us cook. But I am telling both of you the only person who can hunch in this house is the one who paid for it."

Nic sighed in relief. Carmen knew that everything was going to be all right. They continued to prepare Christmas dinner.

The meal went surprisingly well for Carmen. Nic couldn't believe how much food Carmen's family made. Carmen and her mother laughed as Nic consumed turkey, dressing, yams and homemade rolls like she had never had food before.

"Nic, are you leaving room for dessert?" Karen said.

"Yes, ma'am, I'm just going to have to run one hundred miles to make up for this."

"Humph." Aunt Sylvia said in her usual bitchy manner. She stared at Nic the entire time.

Her aunt always had an opinion about something. She used to focus on Carmen's weight, but with the new addition of the boyish-looking woman, she had a new thing to question.

Carmen could tell Sylvia wanted to say something but was afraid to bring it up in front of everyone. She was waiting to chime in when someone else did.

Carmen got out of seeing her uncle because he didn't show up before she left to go visit her cousin Marcus. Marcus had stunned Carmen the year before by telling her that he was gay and dating a drag queen named Maylasa. He made up a lie about having to work so that he didn't have to come to the family dinner. Carmen understood. It had to be hard on him trying to find a way to come out, especially with his mother being Sylvia.

Carmen and Nic arrived at the address Marcus gave. It was an old apartment complex notorious for being filled with gay men. There was a group of men and drags sitting out on the stoop in front of the building.

She gasped when one of the men stood up and headed toward her. "I know that can't be my cousin," she whispered to Nic. The man was very thin. Marcus was always a bigger guy.

"Cousin, how are you!" Marcus said as he wrapped his arms around her. "I'm so happy to see you."

Carmen didn't know how to react. She instantly became frightened by his appearance. "Marcus, what the hell has happened to you?" she exclaimed at her younger cousin.

"I know I've lost a lot of weight. It's all the working and going to school. Senior year is hard as hell." Marcus smiled.

Carmen did not buy his alibi. "Are you sure that's all that is going on with you? What are you doing hanging out over here? Are you being safe like I told you?" Carmen was very concerned. She didn't want to see her cousin taken by the plague of AIDS or any other disease.

"Carmen, I'm fine, and these are just my homies." Marcus looked over at Nic. "You must be the famous Nic."

Nic shook Marcus's hand. She also was very surprised by his appearance. "Yeah, man, I am. It's nice to finally meet you." Nic tried to lighten the mood, but she could tell Carmen was not happy.

Carmen and Marcus played catch-up. She made sure that he was still on the right path with school. He told her that he applied to Freedom. She told him to also apply for schools in Los Angeles, since that was where she was moving. She wanted her cousin close, so she could keep an eye on him.

"Well, I really need to pack, so I guess we have to go," she said as she hugged her cousin."

"Yeah, I feel you. Man, Nic, take care of my cousin, OK?" Marcus said as he shook Nic's hand again.

"Oh, most def. It was nice meeting you, Marcus. You should come and visit us real soon," Nic added.

Carmen grabbed her cousin again. "Marcus, please don't ever be afraid to call me if you need anything. I'm always here for you. Please remember to always stay safe. It is too much shit out here taking our young black gay brothers."

Marcus nodded his head and headed back into the apartment.

Carmen sat in the car and looked out the window as Nic drove off.

"Baby, I know what you're thinking, but I'm sure if something was wrong he would tell you," Nic tried to reassure her.

"I hope so. I hope he has been getting tested. He looks terrible. I feel like I should have been around him more or something."

"He's a young man. He's gonna do what he wants. I'm sure he has to be stressed about coming out, in addition to working and going to school. I would probably lose weight too."

Carmen looked at Nic and smiled. "Well, I hope so. Hell, knowing who his mother is, I don't blame him." She decided to let it rest and prayed that God would protect her cousin.

"So did you want to go to your sister's house today?" Patrick asked Misha as they got dressed to find somewhere to eat Christmas dinner.

"Hell no! I don't talk to that bitch anymore," Misha yelled. She hadn't spoken to her sister since last year. She walked in on her sister trying to make a pass at Cooley and hadn't forgiven her since.

"Damn, why is it like that?" Patrick asked.

"'Cause the bitch tried to sleep with my ga—um, man."

Misha caught herself in time. She almost let her secret slip. She had been finding it hard to not let her orientation slip. She almost made a comment about a girl while out with him. When talking about her ex-relationships, she constantly had to make sure not to mention any girl names or use any feminine references to them.

"Damn, sorry to hear that. I guess she never grew out of that. You know she tried to get with me once."

Misha quickly turned her head at the statement he made.

"Yes, it was one day when I was waiting on you at the house and she asked me to fuck her."

"Oh, really? Well, I guess that's an ass kicking that I need to add to my list," Misha said as she combed her hair.

"Oh, it's not like that. I never wanted that girl, and it's always been you, boo." Patrick smacked her on her butt.

Misha hadn't had so much fun with anyone she had dated recently, not even Cooley. She was actually dreading him leaving.

"So, um, Patrick, when do you think you are going to make it back to Memphis?" Misha asked.

"Um, it will probably be a few weeks. I have a lot of work to catch up on," Patrick said as they headed out the door. "I'm going to get back as soon as possible though."

"Oh, OK then." Misha tried to not sound disappointed.

Patrick could sense her feelings. "Baby, I'll be back very soon. I am not going to be away from you for too long. You are my girl again."

Misha's eyes brightened. She realized what he just said. "Are you saying you want me back as your girl?"

"Misha, there is nothing I want more. Will you be my girl again?" Patrick stopped and looked into Misha's eyes.

She forgot about all of her skeletons in her closet. "Yes, I'm yours."

Chapter 23

The director yelled, "That's a wrap!" at the end of a long video shoot.

Cooley looked at Sahara standing on top of a car and couldn't help noticing how sexy she looked in the short, black boy shorts and white halter-top.

Cooley had introduced Sahara to Big Ron and the director on the first video shoot. They asked her to show them what she could do. Sahara blew them away with her moves. They weren't typical stripper motions; she added some serious dance techniques to her movements. Cooley was impressed by her skill. Big Ron and the rest of the men were impressed by her ass and flexibility. She killed them during the first shoot, and was asked to do three more.

Cooley watched as Sahara gave another artist, Killa Krisp, a hug. Cooley could tell by the look in his eyes that he was going to try Sahara. She walked up and put her arm around Sahara's lower back.

"Great video, Krisp," Cooley said.

"Oh, so this is you, Cool?" Krisp asked. "Damn, why y'all get the finest women?"

They all laughed.

"Thanks for rescuing me. You must have known what was on his mind," Sahara said.

"Hell, yeah, the same thing that's on every nigga's mind in here," Cooley said as they walked to the dressing room.

"Well, I only want it to be on one person's mind." Sahara looked into Cooley's eyes. "I'll be right back."

Cooley couldn't help but smile. She had thought about sexing Sahara ever since she saw her on the stage at the strip club.

"Cool!" Big Ron yelled as he walked toward Cooley. His two assistants walked right behind him. "You did it again. That girl was amazing. You should see the tape."

"I told you." Cooley gave Ron daps. "That's my dog."

"Well, ya dog is going to be in the Mike Mike video shooting next weekend in Mexico. You coming?"

"Man, I wish. I gotta get back to school though."

"Oh, that's right. You 'bout to be leaving us. Hey!" Big Ron yelled on the set. "Party at my crib tonight, a farewell for Cool."

Everyone cheered. Cooley couldn't say no now.

Sahara walked out in a tight fitting pair of Baby Phat jeans and a tight-fitting sweater.

"Hey, baby girl, got something to do next weekend?" Ron asked.

"No. Why?"

"We will see you in Mexico."

Sahara looked at Cooley and smiled. "OK," Sahara said as Ron walked out of the door.

"Oh my God, Cooley, thank you so much for everything." Sahara wrapped her arms around Cooley.

Their eyes met, and Sahara planted a sensual kiss on Cooley's lips. Cooley kissed her back, holding Sahara's body close.

"Are you sure you have to leave tomorrow?"

"Yeah," Cooley said. Misha's face entered her mind. She pulled away from Sahara. "Um, so we'll pick you up tonight around eleven to go to Ron's party."

"Um, OK." Sahara looked confused. She had made moves toward Cooley for weeks and gotten no response.

Cooley looked at Sahara. She knew Sahara was wondering what was going on. She gave her another hug and headed out of the building.

Cooley picked up her phone. She had attempted to contact Misha on several occasions but never got an answer. She dialed Misha's number and got her voicemail again. "Misha, you know who this is. Get back at me."

Cooley closed her phone. She wondered what Misha could be doing that kept her from answering her phone calls. Thoughts raced through Cooley's head. She wondered if Misha was seeing someone else during the break. She knew that they were free to do what they wanted until school started back. Maybe Misha was doing just that.

Cooley thought about Sahara. If Misha was free to mess around, she could too.

The tears in Rhonda's eyes blurred her vision. The sound of Me'Shell Ndegeocello's "You Made a Fool of Me" drowned out all noises in the room. She had been playing it for two days straight.

Rhonda picked up her phone. She dialed Denise's number again. The voice mail came on. Rhonda screamed as she flung her phone against the wall. It broke into three pieces as it hit the painted concrete.

Rhonda panicked. She picked up the pieces of her broken phone. Now she wouldn't know if Denise called. She grabbed her purse and flew out of her room, leaving the loud music blaring.

"Rhonda, can you turn that shit down?" one of her neighbors asked.

Rhonda ignored her and continued to rush down the hall.

"Crazy bitch," the girl said under her breath as she slammed her door.

Rhonda picked up the first phone she saw in the store. She urged the agent to hurry with the purchase. She quickly threw her SIM card into the new phone and turned it on. She waited. No text messages, no voice mails. She screamed in frustration.

The mobile phone dealer watched, unaware of what Rhonda might do next. She stormed out of the building in a funk.

Denise will be back tomorrow. Maybe she's really busy in camp, she thought to herself as she pulled up in the apartment complex. She looked up at Denise's window. *I should go in and check on the apartment. Good thing I made myself a key.*

Rhonda quickly let herself into the apartment. She looked around Denise's room and smiled. She ran her hand across the picture collage Denise had. She noticed a picture of Denise, Cooley and Carmen. She frowned. *I gotta get rid of those bitches.*

Rhonda ran into Cooley's room. Everything was completely neat. All of Cooley's hats were lined up on nails around her wall. Her clothes were in her closet by item and color. All shirts were lined up together then separated by colors. Cooley's colognes were aligned perfectly on her dresser. It disgusted Rhonda. Rhonda ran her hand across the dresser, causing all the expensive bottles to crash and break on the ground.

Rhonda felt a great rush. She continued her path of destruction.

"You are what's keeping Denise from me!" she yelled as she threw Cooley's shoes all over her room.

She headed into the kitchen and grabbed the bottle of bleach. She began to sling bleach all over Cooley's wardrobe. She noticed Cooley's Billionaire's Boys Club Shirt. She took a pair of scissors and feverishly sliced it into pieces.

Rhonda looked around at the destruction. She was pleased.

She grabbed a pair of Cooley's shades and put them on. "They look better on me anyway," she said out loud.

She looked back at her destruction one last time before walking out. She locked the door and headed back to her dorm. She felt better already.

Lena was becoming frustrated as she went through her gift list. She realized she should have taken her mother's advice and gotten professional help. Her last pen stopped working. She looked through her bag to find another pen but couldn't.

"Dammit!" she yelled in agony. She got up and headed to Brandon's office. She turned on the light to his little shrine. There were cases of trophies on one wall and framed newspaper articles and plaques taking up the majority of the rest of the walls.

Lena shook her head as she walked to his desk. "Ain't this about a bitch?" she said to herself looking at the drawer full of Grizzly pens. She grabbed a handful.

Something caught her attention. She moved more pens to find a picture of a baby. Clipped to it was a receipt from Babies "R" Us.

"What are you doing?" Lena jumped when Brandon walked in the room.

"Shit, you scared me. I needed some pens, and I see that you have them all in here." Lena held the picture up. "Brandon, whose baby is this?"

Brandon paused. He walked up to Lena and took the picture. "Yeah, I forgot about this. It was a fan from

New Orleans I helped out. I had a bunch of stuff sent to her from Babies "R" Us. When Liz brought the receipt, the girl had also given her this pic. I thought the boy was cute. Hopefully our kids will be as cute." Brandon put the picture back in his drawer and closed it.

"Oh, that was sweet of you. Well, of course our kids will be cute. That's why I married you." Lena kissed Brandon.

Brandon wrapped his arms around Lena. "Why don't you show me why you married me?" He bit his lip.

Lena smiled. Whenever he bit his lip, he wanted to sex her.

She soon felt his manhood rising. Lena pulled her pants down and sat on his desk.

Brandon wasted no time penetrating her walls with his manhood. Lena moaned with pleasure at the roughness of the act. She loved it when they were spontaneous.

Brandon and Lena hit four different positions on the desk before ending back in the position they'd started with. She held on tight as he exploded inside her.

Lena wiped the sweat off the top of his head as she passionately kissed him.

"Oh, I just got you pregnant that time, baby." Brandon laughed as he kissed her on her neck.

"Whatever, fool. Move. I have work to do." Lena pulled her pants back up. She thought about his comment and grabbed her stomach. She realized they had been raw-dogging it for a while. She knew she needed to start taking birth control. A baby was the last thing she wanted in her life then.

Cooley and Sahara were the most attractive couple at the party. Cooley smiled as they soaked up the glamorous life. Cooley loved Ron's house. It was everything she hoped to own one day.

The party was planned in less than six hours, but was fabulous. Beautiful ice sculptures and flowers adorned the long, lavish buffet. The unexpected snowfall created a winter wonderland outside. The biggest names in Atlanta mixed and mingled. People were dressed from casual to semi-formal.

Cooley learned early that the real ballers didn't have to wear huge chains and flashy clothes. Most of the richest men and women didn't dress flashy, but they had a presence about them that screamed "big time." Cooley couldn't believe it was all for her. There was a large cake that said "Farewell Cool Cat" on a table by itself.

"Are you all right?" Sahara asked.

"I just can't believe the life that I have right now. Tomorrow I'm going home to a small two-bedroom apartment that I share with my best friend." They both laughed.

"Well, it won't be for long. You are about to blow up, Cool. This is where you belong." Sahara kissed Cooley.

Cooley felt herself getting heated. "You want to get out of here?" Cooley knew what the answer was going to be.

"Ron, I think I'm going to head back to Sonic's. My flight is early 'cause I wanted to meet my best friend at the airport." Cooley gave Ron daps.

"All right, take care of yourself. See you this summer." Ron gave Cooley a hug. "I'm proud of you, Cool. You're going to do big things."

"Thanks, man." Cooley smiled. She looked up to Ron like she used to look up to her father before he passed away.

***

Sahara and Cooley walked into her large room at Sonic's house.

Cooley walked over to her iPod stereo and programmed it to play her sex folder. "Just get comfortable."

"I already am."

Cooley turned around to find Sahara lying on the bed in a pink lace bra and panty set. Cooley slowly crawled on top of Sahara and began to kiss her. Her hands began to roam all over Sahara's toned body. The smell of Sahara's Victoria's Secret lotion enticed Cooley's senses.

Avant's "Don't Say No" Began to play. Cooley looked down at Sahara. Before her eyes, Sahara's face turned into Misha's face.

"Fuck." Cooley jumped.

"What's wrong?" Sahara looked at Cooley. Cooley's face looked flushed.

Cooley sighed. "Sahara, I can't do this."

Sahara's face dropped. "What's wrong? Is it something I did?"

"Hell, naw, you're great. Sexy as hell. Damn, what the fuck is wrong wit' me?" Cooley stood up.

"There's someone else, isn't it?" Sahara said. Cooley's face said it all. "I knew it." Sahara started to put her pants back on.

"How'd you know?"

"You were always checking your phone and voice mail. The Cooley I met before would have taken me home the first night. It's been weeks and you hadn't laid a hand on me. She must be something special."

Cooley thought about Misha. "Sahara, you have had the craziest effect on me. When we met, I never thought I would want to settle down. You were the first chick who made me even think about it. But Misha is the first to actually make me do it."

"Cooley is in love." Sahara smiled.

"Yeah, I am. I'm so sorry about this."

"It's all good. I am happy for you. Hell, you've helped me realize my dream. How fucked up would it be for me to fuck up yours? I'll call a cab."

"No, you can stay here if you want," Cooley said.

Sahara took her up on the offer.

Cooley put Sahara in a guest room downstairs, instead of near hers, just so she wouldn't get tempted to do something.

It was still dark outside when Cooley checked her bags to make sure she had everything. She walked into Sahara's room. She was sleeping peacefully. Cooley left a good-bye note and then walked down the hall to Sonic's room. She was in the bed sleeping with two other women.

"Sonic." Cooley hit her on her foot.

Sonic turned over and looked at Cooley.

"I'm out of here."

"Oh, shit! What time is it?" Sonic looked down at her cell phone.

"My friend Sahara is sleeping in one of the guest rooms. When she wakes up, please make sure she makes it home."

"Gotcha." Sonic quickly fell back to sleep.

Cooley took one last look at Sonic's mansion. She sighed. She was ready to go home. She was ready to get Misha back.

Misha hugged Patrick for the last time. She dropped him at the airport so that he could catch his flight.

"So, I will see you in a few weeks," Patrick said as he kissed her on her forehead.

"Yes, you will. I will be waiting." Misha's heart was beating quickly. She was so happy to have Patrick back in her life.

They said their final good-byes, and she headed back to the campus.

She made it into her room and looked around. She noticed all of the pictures of her with the women that she knew. There was a picture of her and Cooley. She realized she was going to have to pack up all of her memories when Patrick came back to town. It was best that she kept her orientation secret. She did not want to lose him.

Still, Misha couldn't help but think about her friends. She thought about all the conversations she had about bisexual women and sike-a-dykes. She always was against women who claimed to be gay, but were actually messing with men. This was what she had become. She realized for the time being it was best to keep her mouth closed. She needed to make sure it was what she wanted before she made the big announcement.

Chapter 24

"I missed you, bruh!" Cooley said, wrapping her arms around Denise. "How was the camp?"

"Man, it was cool as hell. I met some major heavy hitters. I think this pro thing may happen after all."

Denise and Cooley got Cooley's car and headed back to their apartment.

"Did Carmen tell you what happened?" Cooley asked Denise.

"Man, no, I really didn't get to talk much on the phone. They kept us so busy. I swear, Rhonda blew my phone up."

"Fuck that bitch. Anyway, Carmen's mom walked in on her and Nic."

"Oh, shit," Denise laughed. "I bet she had a fit."

Cooley laughed. "Hell, yeah. Nic was mortified. She started panicking and shit. But C said it was all good in the end. Her mother actually respects their relationship now."

"What about Nic's people?"

"Man, I heard they fell in love with her immediately. Nic's mom was calling Carmen her daughter and some more." Cooley sighed. "Man, I am glad to be home. I can't wait to see Misha."

"I bet you can't. So did you hook up with anyone in ATL?"

"Man, nah. And guess who I ran into? Sahara."

Denise looked at Cooley in amazement. "And you didn't hook up?"

"Nope." Cooley smiled. "I told her that I had someone at home."

"Well, it looks like someone's in love."

Cooley looked over at Denise. "You know what, I'll
admit it. I love her. Shit, I can't believe I said that. I'm
such a fuckin' punk."

They both laughed.

Denise made it into the apartment first, while Cooley
got all of her bags from the car. Denise looked around
the apartment. Something didn't feel right. She walked
into her room. She didn't remember leaving her draw-
ers open. She looked around her room. She had a very
uneasy feeling. She heard Cooley yell from her room.

Denise ran into the room and gasped. Cooley stood
frozen at her door, looking at the destruction.

"Oh my God!" Denise said, walking into the room.
The strong smell of bleach hit her nose instantly.

Cooley felt like someone knocked the wind out of
her. Someone hit her where it hurt the most. All of her
hats and clothes were bleached. Her cologne collection
was ruined. She couldn't speak.

Denise didn't know what to do. She looked at Cooley,
whose face had lost all its color. Denise quickly grabbed
Cooley, who immediately collapsed in her arms.

"Who the fuck! Who!" Cooley screamed as tears of
anger ran down her face. She fought to break free from
Denise.

"We'll find out, bruh." Denise tried to calm Cooley
down, but knew it wasn't going to work. She let Cooley
go.

Cooley went on a rampage. She hit the wall so hard
that her fist broke through.

"Cool!" Denise yelled. She couldn't let her mess up
the apartment.

The police finally arrived and surveyed the room. One of the police officers began to ask the same questions again.

"And are you sure no one could have access to a key?"

"Yes, sir," Denise said. "Only three people have keys, and one of them isn't back from L.A. yet."

The police took a report and left.

Denise closed the door and looked at Cooley.

"Man, if I find out who did this," Cooley said, shaking her head, "that person is going to feel pain unlike any other."

"Well, what are you going to do about clothes?"

"That's nothing. I'll get more clothes. Plus, I had a lot of my stuff with me when I headed to ATL. I'll make it. I'm mad about my cologne though. That damn Creed was like a hundred and fifty dollars. Ahhh shit, my Billionaire Boys Club shirt." Cooley held the pieces of her beloved shirt in her hand. "Talk about hitting a nigga where it hurts."

"Well, at least it was a shirt and not your life," Denise said.

"Yeah, but it was a hot shirt." Cooley looked at Denise and cracked a small smile. She knew Denise was right. They were only possessions, but she still was going to work to find out who did it.

Lena looked at herself in the mirror. She felt fat. Lena felt so lonely when Brandon was on the road. She had gotten to the point of doing simple things, like going to the movies. Sometimes Lena would dismiss her staff just so she could do some of their chores. She missed her friends. She missed Denise. She wondered if Denise was back from camp.

Lena picked up her phone to call, but quickly put it back down. She wondered how she would react to seeing Denise. There was only one way to find out.

Lena knocked on Denise's door. She heard music coming from inside. Cooley answered the door in a pair of sweats and a red T-shirt with bleach stains on it.

"Lena, what's going on, ma?" Cooley hugged her.

"Nothing much. I was just in the neighborhood and wanted to stop by."

"What the hell you doing in the hood?" Cooley said. She knew Lena was lying.

"Well, I was just driving around, stopped by the school. Is Dee here?"

"Actually, she isn't. She'll be back soon, if you want to chill."

"Um, that's OK. I guess I'll just talk to her later. Tell her I stopped by." Lena turned around to walk away but heard Cooley call her name.

"Don't be silly. Come on in and see what someone did to my shit."

Lena walked into the apartment. She saw bags of clothes all over the living room. "What happened?"

"Well, someone decided to fuck all my clothes and shit up. But it's all good, I'm always gon' bounce back."

Lena shook her head. She had to admire the fight in Cooley. "Well, if you need anything, let me know."

"Thanks." Cooley sat down in a chair. "Lena, can I ask you a question, between me and you?"

"Yeah, Cool, what's up?"

"Man . . . you know what, don't worry about it. How's married life treating you?"

"It's all right. Brandon is gone a lot," Lena said. She secretly wanted to know what Cooley was going to say at first.

"I bet. So have you talked to Misha?"

"Actually, no. When I got back from my honeymoon I was unable to catch up with her. Then Brandon doesn't really like me going out too much, especially without security."

Cooley looked puzzled. "Security? What's up with that?"

"I guess 'cause of that girl at the wedding. I really don't know what's up with him sometimes. So, how long do you think Dee will be?"

"She should be back any moment."

"Damn, you know what, I left you all's Christmas gifts. I'll come back a little later with those. Let me get on home."

Lena stood up, and Cooley let her out. She rushed toward the steps but met Denise face on.

"Lena."

"Dee."

"What are you doing here?" Denise asked.

"Um, I just was stopping by just to see how you're doing." Lena felt her palms beginning to sweat.

"Did you want to come in?"

"Um no, I left the gifts at home. I'm going to go home and get them."

"Lena, is everything OK? Is Brandon OK?"

Lena sighed. "I'm just a little lonely, that's all. He's gone on the road. I dismissed my staff."

"Well, why don't you come and chill?"

"I think I should get home." Lena smiled. "See you later."

Denise said good-byes and watched Lena until she drove off. She walked into the house to see Cooley still sitting in the chair.

"Did you see Lena?"

"Yeah, she seemed a little off."

"Oh, come on, bruh, you know why she was over here. She wanted another piece of Dee."

"Come on, man," Denise said, sitting on the couch.

"All right, don't believe me. I'm telling you, if it's one thing I know, it's women. She wanted you."

Denise looked at the door. She felt her heart beginning to race. "You think—"

Before she could finish Cooley handed Denise her keys. Denise looked at Cooley and ran out the house.

Lena closed the door to her loft and looked around at the big room. It lacked warmth and love. It felt cold and impersonal. In fact, everything about her house tonight made her tense and frustrated. She just didn't want to be there alone. Tired, she retreated to the cold leather living room sofa and kicked off her shoes. She unwound her long hair from the tight chignon and let it flow across her shoulders and down her back. Mindlessly, she ran her hands through her hair and began to relax.

Lena thought about Denise as the tightness in her body began to release. *How good she looked standing on those steps tonight,* Lena thought to herself. Even through the jacket, Lena could see Denise's athletic build. She recalled how firm and toned her body was and how sexy Dee was in her wife-beaters. She remembered all of those times when Denise worked out in their dorm room, and how she had wanted Dee to take her then. Damn, those wife-beaters!

Lena felt her body relax deeper into the sofa cushions. She could feel the satiny Victoria's Secret lace moisten between her legs. Her body began to tingle as she imagined the feel of Denise's strong hands against her lacy black bra.

She spread her legs open and pushed her buttocks to the edge of the couch. Her body began to undulate as she continued to imagine Denise caressing her warm brown curves.

Lena closed her eyes and raised a finger to her lips and pulled it in as she teased it with her tongue. "Oh, Denise," she moaned, the words spilling breathlessly through her lips.

She slipped her other hand along her thigh of her jeans and edged her way down to the warmth emanating between her legs and rubbed. The moans rose into the hollow echo of the room. Her legs clenched around her hand.

This was tortuous, but she couldn't stop.

She pulled her finger from her mouth and let the palm of her hand roam the silk blouse, grazing her satin-covered nipples as she did. Her body quivered as the tingles sent shivers through her sweet spot. "Oh," Lena moaned softly as she continued to imagine Denise's body above hers.

She reached down and undid her jeans and fingered the lace below, which elicited yet another soft moan from her lips. She pushed her hand under the tight denim fabric and felt the moistness as something stirred within her. She wanted to feel Denise's tongue roaming her tender spots. She wanted to feel the strength of her hands pulling her close.

Lena's body responded to the fantasy. She was soaking wet.

A sudden knock at her door pulled her from her reverie. Shit. Lena straightened her clothes and fastened her pants as she rose to answer the door. With the back of her hand, she pushed the hair from her flushed face. She checked herself in the mirror by the front door before opening it. Absent-mindedly, she reached for the knob and opened the door.

"Dee," Lena said as she saw Denise standing in her doorway. Their eyes locked.

Denise intensely embraced Lena, planting a passionate kiss on her lips. Lena wrapped her arms around her neck as Denise picked her up and carried her into the house. They made it as far as the large rug in the living room.

Denise wasted no time in undressing Lena. Lena pulled Denise's long-sleeved polo shirt off, exposing the white wife beater underneath and smiled.

Denise searched Lena's eyes. She had to have her. She spread Lena's legs, cupped her ass and began to devour her.

Lena lay back, and pushed her body into Denise. She wanted Denise as far into her as she could get.

Denise wrapped her arms tightly around Lena's legs, pulling her closer to her, as Lena unintentionally squirmed to get away from the intensity she was feeling.

The two women were trembling with pleasure.

"Denise," Lena moaned. Hearing her name coming from Lena enticed Denise even more. She sucked on Lena's clit, softly at first, stroking it with her tongue as she did.

Lena could not contain the air that hissed and panted through her lips as the tongue stroked her. She grabbed Denise's hair and massaged her scalp with her fingernails as Denise began to pull with elongated strokes on her clit, her tongue darting in and out of the opening, catching the tartness of Lena's juices as she did.

Denise wanted even more. She buried her face into Lena, pulling her torso closer as she sealed her mouth around the lips of Lena's throbbing, soaking wet pussy. She reached up with her hands and began to rub Lena's breasts and pinch at her nipples.

This was more than Lena could bear. She began to beg Denise, "Please, please, Denise. I want you in me, please."

It was all Denise needed to hear to pull herself away from that wet pussy. She slipped in her thumb and pushed down on Lena's back wall. Lena gasped and tried to force the thumb further in. Denise smiled at the teasing she was giving.

Slowly, Denise withdrew her thumb and positioned herself closer to Lena. She pushed Lena's legs into the air and pulled each ankle onto her shoulders. With her hands firmly planted on either side of Lena, she pushed her body over the girl and began to rub her clit against Lena's.

"Oh, fuck!" Lena gasped as she felt the wet friction press against her. Her eyes became wide, as her hands searched for something to grab hold of. Her mouth lay agape as she pulled first on Denise's wife-beater and then wrapped her manicured fingers around Denise's muscular arms.

She was done. Her ass bucked as her clit continued to kiss and rub against Denise's. She had never felt this sensation before, wet pussy against wet pussy, the friction of clit against clit, kissing, rubbing, and dripping. She felt the commingled juices pouring across her cheeks into her crack. "Fuck. Fuck. Fuck." Lena couldn't control herself.

Denise pulled back slightly and reached under Lena's thigh to insert her middle fingers. She began to stroke Lena as she kissed her. Denise kissed her with the same intensity as when she had eaten her pussy. She forced her tongue deep into Lena's mouth as Lena wrapped her lips around it, stroking it as Denise pushed it in and out.

Denise wanted to prove a point. Lena should be with her. She pushed her body rhythmically against Lena's as she fucked her. Her fingers stroked in and out with same rhythm as her tongue. Lena felt her body being taken over as her orifices were filled. She felt her walls clench down on Denise's stroking fingers.

Denise stroked her harder and faster.

"You want more?" Denise spoke for the first time. Lena couldn't talk. Her only sounds were moans.

"Say it," Denise demanded.

Lena could barely speak. "Yes," she whispered.

Denise leaned into her and said firmly, "Say you want more."

Lena looked into Denise's intense eyes. "More, baby, please, more!" Lena yelled in ecstasy.

Denise pushed in another finger and opened Lena's pussy even wider as she continued to claim her. Lena could feel her pushing against her walls. Her pussy tightened around Denise's hand, fitting her like a glove. Her body began shaking and spasms pulsed through her pussy as Denise continued to rock Lena back and forth on her fingers.

Lena's entire body tightened as the juices spewed over Denise's hand. Her body shook as she called out Denise's name.

Lena's grip tightened around Denise's arms. She couldn't let go. She pushed her body closer to Denise and pushed herself farther down onto Denise's fingers.

"More?" Denise questioned her.

Lena searched Denise's eyes and nodded as she mouthed, "Please."

Denise slowly reached around Lena's ass and pressed a finger into the virgin hole.

Lena couldn't breathe as her body welcomed the violation. She clamped her body onto Denise and began to feverishly ride the fingers pressed into both openings as Denise again pressed her tongue into Lena's mouth.

Denise could feel Lena's walls opening and closing around her fingers and feel the wetness splattering against her own pussy. Her body felt electrified. Her clit began to bulge from all the friction against it. She knew she was about to cum, but she held it as she stroked Lena toward orgasm.

Lena began to call her name. "Denise, Denise, D—D—D—Ahh . . ." Her words trailed off into an orgasmic outburst of cries and curses. "Fuck. Fuck. Oh. Shit. Oh, Denise. Fuck me. Fuck me. Oh."

Denise gave one hard final thrust of her hips as her own orgasm shook her and pushed her onto the trembling woman.

Lena reached up to wrap her lips around Denise's tongue, sucking it like the best dick that had ever filled her mouth.

Denise withdrew her fingers and pressed her body against Lena. She grabbed Lena's ankles and lifted her legs into the air while spreading her open. Denise began fucking Lena's pussy with her enlarged hard clit, banging hard against her before exploding inside her.

Lena screamed once more, "Denise!" before collapsing, spent and out of breath, onto the rug. Her body continued to buck and tremble.

Denise lay down beside her to catch her own breath. She looked over at the panting woman, closed her eyes and exhaled. She had waited so long for this, but it still wasn't everything she wanted it to be. Lena, who had given herself so freely to her, still belonged to someone else. Until that changed, she could not fully claim her. Denise knew she may not have branded her, but she had left her mark.

She leaned up on one elbow and planted a soft kiss on Lena's mouth.

"Lena." Denise looked into her eyes. She felt herself getting weak looking into Lena's big brown eyes.

"Denise." Lena was still struggling to catch her breath and to make sense of what she had just experienced.

"I think I need to go." Denise stood up and put her shirt on.

Lena was speechless, but she knew it was right. She kissed Denise one last time before letting her walk out of the house.

Suddenly the house felt empty again. The warmth and the love had left again.

Chapter 25

"What's up, chicka?" Nic said when she answered her cell phone.

"Nothing much. Where are you?" Larissa asked.

"About to walk into my dorm. Where are you?"

"Come to room 405."

"Whose room is that?" Nic asked as she got on the elevator.

"Just do it."

Nic got off on the fourth floor. She spoke to a few girls who knew her from being with Carmen. She heard music coming from the room. She knocked on the door.

Larissa answered it with a big smile on her face.

"Well, hello there," Larissa said.

"Whose room is this?" Nic asked.

"Come on in." Larissa opened the door and let Nic in.

Nic looked around, surprised not to see anyone else in the room.

"Welcome to my happy home."

Nic's eyes widened. "Word? What happened to ya house and your fiancé?"

"I said good-bye to both." Larissa sat on her large bed. She did what many single-room owners did, pushed both beds together to make one large bed.

"Are you serious? You all right?"

"I have never been better. Nic, I couldn't take it anymore. He was always complaining about me going to school. You know he wouldn't let me get a computer 'cause he didn't think I needed one at home, but then he also didn't want me staying on campus to finish my work. Well, during break I just couldn't take it anymore. I made sure I had a place on campus, I saved up a little money, and I got out. I've never been so happy in my life."

"Well, I'm happy that you're happy." Nic hugged Larissa.

"I owe you so much."

"What do you mean?"

"Nic, you showed me how a girl is supposed to be treated. That nigga wouldn't open a door for me. He wouldn't walk me to my car if it was night time. You treat Carmen and women in general better than most men do. Then they sit up and wonder why women leave for other women."

Nic laughed. "Well, thank you, I guess. But I wasn't trying to break up a home."

"Trust me, breaking up that home was the best thing you could have ever done." Larissa smiled and gave Nic a kiss on her cheek. "You are a lifesaver."

"Oh, shit, so are you. I passed the damn class." Nic gave Larissa another big hug. "I read my paper you know. Thank you so much for fixing it." Nic remembered Larissa helping to type her paper. Larissa actually made it better, and Nic earned an A on her final paper.

"It's no problem. I read it and knew you needed a little push. It was all you in the end."

"Yeah, I admit *Othello* wasn't that bad."

"I told you. So how is Carmen?"

"She's out with her friends."

"So you all are still doing good? No problems at all?" Larissa said, trying not to show her true feelings.

"Yeah, things are going real well right now. We had a real good break. Shit, I gotta get going. We should hook up later."

"Yeah, let's do that. You're welcome here anytime."

"Cool." Nic smiled and walked out the door.

Larissa stared at the door. She wanted Nic to walk back in.

"Oh my God, the dead has arisen!" Carmen yelled as she and Lena ran to hug Misha. "I was starting to wonder if you came back this semester. Why haven't we heard from your ass in weeks?"

Misha took a seat at the table with her two friends. "Girl, I'm sorry. Classes have been killing me. Oh, and I've been going to Atlanta on weekends to look for a job and a place to stay."

"Damn, is anyone staying in Memphis with me?" Lena pouted her lips.

"Hell, no!" Misha and Carmen said in unison.

Everyone laughed.

"The only reason you are staying here is 'cause of that phat-ass crib and that man of yours," Carmen said.

"Yeah, and I bet you she stays at our places more than at her own," Misha added her two cents.

Lena hit her on her arm.

"Hell, the only reason you been home lately is 'cause Brandon got you on house arrest." Carmen was against Lena not taking classes on campus. She never said anything to Lena, but she believed that Brandon was hiding something.

"I am not on house arrest. Brandon is just being careful. He's a star now, and who knows what women are capable of."

"So, where did you tell mister superstar you are right now?" Carmen looked at Lena, who had a guilty look on her face.

"I told him I had some business to take care of. After all, we need to go shopping, don't we?"

"Excuse me, ladies." Just then a very attractive stud walked up to the table. "Haven't I seen you at the club or something?" The woman looked at Misha.

"Maybe. I don't know." Misha looked at the girl. She was attractive. She was around five foot seven with braids like Iverson. Misha noticed the small four-leaf clover tattooed on her neck. She loved the labret piercing she had as well.

"Well, I'm going to say that is a yes. And if I haven't, I would love to maybe go there with you or somewhere else. By the way, my name is Trey."

Lena laughed to herself. Carmen was smiling very hard.

Misha looked at her friends then looked back at Trey. "You know what, Trey, that really sounds tempting, but I am going to have to pass. But, baby, charge it to my head and not my heart." Misha took a sip of her drink.

Trey looked disappointed. So did Carmen and Lena.

"Well, then maybe I will catch you at a better time."

"Maybe." Misha didn't look back when the girl walked away. She didn't want to look and see what she just passed up.

"Bitch, what the hell is wrong with you? That bitch was fine as hell!" Carmen hit Misha on her arm.

"Ouch! And, damn, I'm just not looking for anything right now." Misha took another sip of her drink.

Lena began to smile at Misha.

"What? What are you looking at me like that for?"

Lena started to shake her head. "So, who is the woman that got you so open that you pass up a girl who had damn near every quality on your attractive list?"

"No one." Misha grabbed her bags and got up. "You girls are trippin'. Just because I am trying to focus on school doesn't mean that I am seeing someone. Damn, get off my dick." Misha turned around and walked away to the sound of Carmen and Lena laughing.

"Carmen."

Carmen and Lena looked up to see Neo headed toward them.

She stopped at the table, never taking her eyes off of Carmen. "Can we talk?"

"Um, sure. Lena, I will be right back." Carmen stood up and walked out with Neo.

"Carmen, you know that's real fucked up that you took your friendship away without even letting me know."

"Neo, come on, you know why I did it," Carmen said.

"OK, so you think that just 'cause I had a crush on you that I couldn't be a friend?"

"Could you?"

"Carmen, I am going to tell you the truth. I do have feelings for you. I like Nic, but y'all don't have as much in common as we do."

"You don't know that. I love Nic, and she loves me. That's not going to change."

"I know that. I simply said that if—"

"There is no need for that *if*. And how do you expect me to kick it with you, knowing that you are looking to take my girl's spot?"

"Fine, Carmen. I'm gon' leave you alone. But when that girl messes up, promise you will come see me."

"That won't happen, but I know where to find you." Carmen gave Neo a hug and headed back into the UC.

"What was that all about?" Lena asked.

"Girl, nothing important. Let's get out of here."

***

Cooley picked up her books and headed out of class. She had signed up for the marketing class just to get a little knowledge to complement the experience she'd gained while working at Jam Zone. Cooley was very intelligent and never had problems in school. Most folks were so focused on her swagger they never knew she carried a perfect 4.0 GPA. She ran into Tara as soon as she walked out of the room.

"Well, I told you I was going to run into you again." Cooley smiled.

"I guess you did." Tara smiled back. "So, you take marketing?"

"Yeah, but I don't need to. I just wanted a little more experience for my job."

"Damn, you already got a job? You must be all that then."

Cooley could see Tara was flirting.

"I can't say all that, but I do have a job waiting on me after graduation. So, where is your little boyfriend?" Cooley remembered the little run-in she had last time.

"Oh, I don't know, and I don't think you really care, do you?" Tara said, looking directly in Cooley's eyes.

"No, I can't say that I do. So, what's up with you? Why you with a meat head like that anyway?"

"We have been together for years. He's not that bad, just a little overprotective."

"Well, I can understand why." Cooley grabbed her hand and turned her around. "He got a pretty good prize to protect."

Tara laughed. "I guess. So, anyway, I gotta run. I need to get to my dorm." Tara began to walk away as Cooley watched her. Her mind was telling her no, but something else was telling her yes. She sighed, deciding to listen to her mind this time.

"Cooley."

The sound of the voice made Cooley cringe. She knew she was about to hear it from Lynn. She turned around to see Lynn walking toward her. Lynn was the one person she didn't think about the whole time she was gone. Seeing Lynn's smile made her feel bad.

"What's up, Lynn? How was your break?" Cooley said as she hugged Lynn.

Lynn fought to hold back tears. "It was all right, well, as best as it could have been," Lynn said.

Cooley could tell she was not happy. "I'm sure it wasn't that bad. Look, Lynn, I am sorry about the way things wen—"

"Cooley, I'm the one that is sorry. I should have told you. I just didn't want you to hold that against me and not give me a chance. I hope that you will forgive me and give me another chance. Call me if you want." Lynn forced a smiled and walked off.

"Denise."

Denise heard Rhonda yelling her name.

Michelle looked at Denise and laughed. "Handle that, partner," she said as Rhonda walked up.

"Baby, I have been trying to contact you forever. I understand you wouldn't get at me during camp, but haven't you been back for a while now?"

"Actually, I got back three days ago. We had a game."

"Well, I forgive you."

"Forgive me for what?" Denise asked.

"For not contacting me all winter break. So when can we hook—"

"Rhonda, this isn't going to work," Denise cut her off.

Rhonda's face dropped. "What do you mean? We just said—"

"Rhonda, it was a mistake for me to even consider getting back with you. This is the biggest semester of my life. I don't have time for distractions."

"I'm a distraction?" Rhonda fought to hold back the tears.

"Women, parties, all that shit is distracting. I did not come this far to fuck up at the finish line. Besides, we aren't good together anyway."

"Denise, why you keep doing this shit to me? Why you keep fucking me over? All I'm trying to do is love you!" Rhonda cried.

"I'm sorry."

"No, sorry isn't enough. You are supposed to be with me! We are supposed to be together."

Denise saw the strange look in Rhonda's eyes. She finally saw what everyone else did. Rhonda looked unstable. "Rhonda, please, look, I would like to be friends."

All of a sudden Rhonda looked up and smiled. "Yeah, Denise, friends."

Denise didn't know what to think of the sudden mood change. "You OK with that?"

"Yeah, I'm gonna go." Rhonda smiled and walked off.

Michelle walked up to Denise. They both looked in amazement.

"I told you that girl was crazy," Michelle said.

Denise finally agreed.

"Hey, girl." Cooley hugged Misha as she walked in her dorm room.

"Cooley," Misha said.

Suddenly she realized why she was there. Cooley dropped a bag of gifts on her bed. "These are for you. How was your Christmas?"

"It was fine. Um, Cool, I can't accept—"

"You are too fucking hard to catch up with. I've been by here a couple of times before class started and couldn't get you. Did I tell you that I missed you like crazy, girl?"

"Yeah, well, I actually went to Nashville for a couple of days. Cool—"

"I got you some things I know you're gonna love, especially that bag from Gucci."

"Carla." Misha attempted to talk, but Cooley grabbed her and planted her lips against hers. Misha felt her knees getting weak. She pulled away. "Cooley, look I need to tell you that I don't think it's a good idea for us to hook up."

"What?"

"I changed my mind. It would be a bad idea and I would like it if you left."

Cooley stood frozen in her spot, trying to grasp what Misha was saying. "Mish—"

"Cooley, please just leave."

"Naw, man, what the fuck is going on? What the hell happ—"

"Carla, I don't want you! I don't want to be with you! Now leave!" Misha stormed over to the door and held it open.

Cooley was stunned. She looked at Misha. Her facial expression didn't change. Cooley walked up to the door. "Fine, I'm out." She threw her hands up and walked out the door.

Misha held back tears. Before she could get the door closed, Cooley pushed it open.

"No, fuck that! Misha, what the fuck is wrong with you, huh? We made plans. You think you just gon' keep fucking me over like this? This shit isn't funny!"

"Cooley, I—"

"No, you listen! What the fuck happened to make you change yo' mind, Misha?"

Misha didn't respond.

Cooley's heart dropped. "You know what, fuck this shit! I can't believe I actually believed you were gonna change. You're worse than me!"

"What the fuck is that supposed to mean?" Misha said, offended by the comment.

"It means that at least I'm fuckin' honest. You knew everything I was up to. I told you who I was fuckin' wit. You are worse than half of these scandalous bitches around here."

"Carla, it's not even like that."

"Whatever, Misha. You know what, if you tell me to roll this time, don't fuckin' come back when you change your mind again. So, what's up?" Cooley looked at Misha.

Misha looked at the ground, unable to respond.

"You know what, fuck this." Cooley headed toward the door.

"Cooley!" Misha yelled. "Carl—"

"Fuck you, Misha! Stay the fuck away from me!" Cooley slammed the door and left Misha in tears. She heard her phone ring. It was Patrick's special ring tone, "My First Love" by Avant.

"Cooley," Lynn said when she saw Cooley standing at her doorstep.

Cooley grabbed her in her arms and kissed her.

"I forgive you." Cooley turned around and headed out the door. She walked off, struggling to hold back her true emotions.

Chapter 26

"Brandon, this shit is getting out of hand!" Lena yelled, looking at the new surveillance videos playing in Brandon's office. "The building has security. Why the hell do you need it right at our door like this?"

"Lena, do you forget that I'm a basketball player? Do you forget that I'm one endorsement away from being a true celebrity? Once Pepsi and Nike sign, it's all over. I have a duty to protect you."

Lena did not like all the extra protection. She already began taking telecourses so that she didn't have to go on campus. She seldom got to drive her car because Brandon wanted her to always have security.

"Brandon, this is crazy. I don't see any of the other basketball wives with all this shit. There's something going on that you aren't telling me, and I want to know what the fuck it is!" Lena was furious.

Brandon sighed. "Baby, I've received a few threats. And that psycho girl from the wedding still hasn't been found. She already approached you once. What happens if you are alone and she sees you? I'm not willing to take that chance."

Lena was horrified. "Brandon, you said that she was just a overzealous fan. Now you're saying that she is some kind of stalker." Lena couldn't believe what she was hearing.

"I don't really know what she is, but I'm not going to take that chance. I won't be able to live with myself if anything ever happened to you." Brandon hugged Lena.

Lena wrapped her arms around Brandon. "I understand what you're saying, but this is still ridiculous. I don't want to feel like a prisoner in my own home, and that is what I feel like. From now on I am going to go some places on my own. If Carmen and Misha are with me, then I don't need the bodyguard or the driver. I am going to take my car and go with my friends."

Brandon knew he was not going to win the fight, so he gave up. Lena left his office and went to take a bath. Brandon watched her leave then closed his door. He quickly snatched the phone and left another voicemail.

"You'd better be not answering the phone because you've gotten out of town. If you come anywhere near my wife, I'm going to make sure you pay." He slammed the phone down, realizing he was in a real mess.

Cooley stared at the computer screen. She and the other night owls typed away on their various midterm projects and papers. Cooley loved coming to the computer lab in the early morning hours when there weren't many people out. She decided to take a break from her paper to check her Facebook page. She had twelve new messages, twenty-four new friend requests, and seven new comments.

Cooley read the comments. It was the usual: girls trying to flirt via Facebook. She read through her messages. They were mostly from men, so she quickly deleted them. All of her friends were deleted, since she'd never heard of any of them. She never understood why people sent friend requests and didn't take the time to say hello at all.

Suddenly, her Yahoo! Messenger alert popped up. She had a new instant message.

Sexykitten4u: Hey Cooley

Cooley looked at her friends list; this was someone she didn't know.

KillaCooley: Who is this?

Sexykitten4u: Someone special

Cooley was about to press ignore when another message came through.

Sexykitten4u: Want to know who I am? Come around the corner to your marketing classroom.

Cooley decided to take a chance. She grabbed her bag and headed to the class. Cooley could see a shadowy figure sitting in the far corner. She went to turn the light on.

"Don't turn the light on. Just lock the door and come over here," the seductive voice instructed.

Cooley instantly recognized the voice. "It's about time you got at me, Tara," Cooley said as she walked up on Tara.

"How did you know it was me?" Tara said, as Cooley grabbed her butt.

"I never forget a sexy voice." Cooley kissed Tara on her neck. "So, what's the business?"

"I want you to fuck me. Can you handle that?" Tara said as she sat on top of the desk.

Cooley laughed. "Girl, you gon' need to ask yourself that question when I'm done." Cooley pulled down Tara's little dress. She didn't have on any underwear, which made things easier for Cooley.

Cooley began to devour her breasts, licking over her erect nipples.

"Fuck the sweet shit, Cooley. Fuck me now," Tara demanded as she took Cooley's hand and placed it on her wet pussy.

"Damn, girl, let me do my thing," Cooley said as she rammed two of her fingers in Tara, causing her to jump. "See, be careful what you ask for."

Cooley grabbed hold of Tara's ass and pulled her toward the edge of the desk. She pushed the girl's legs open wide, and as she slid her body between them, she began to finger-fuck Tara like she had a real penis. Tara's body twitched each time Cooley hit her G-spot. "Oh, yes, harder," Tara moaned.

Cooley turned her over and pressed her chest down against the cool, hard desk. She began to hit it from the back. She got off watching Tara's plump ass shake each time she pounded the soft flesh harder. Tara's whole body began to shake as Cooley felt her juices running down her arm.

Tara turned around and smiled. "Well, well, I must say I didn't expect that," Tara said as she pulled up her dress.

"Never underestimate me," Cooley responded as she pulled Tara close to kiss her.

Tara turned her head.

"No kissing. I have a man, remember." Tara smiled. "But I will be in touch soon."

Cooley stood shocked as Tara headed toward the door. "Yeah, you be in touch. Maybe I'll answer."

Tara looked over her shoulder. "Trust me, you will." She walked out of the door.

Cooley didn't know what to think. She smiled. The cockiness turned her on. She was going to get Tara again.

Cooley pulled up to her apartment. She cursed to herself when she saw Lynn sitting in her car.

"Hey, girl, how long you been waiting?" Cooley said.

"Well, about an hour, but I left and got some food. I figured you got caught up on your paper." Lynn smiled as she walked up the stairs.

Cooley watched Lynn walk. She realized she needed to take care of that situation. Lynn was a nice girl, and Cooley didn't want to hurt her.

"So, Lynn, are you seeing anyone else right now?" Cooley asked as they walked in the apartment.

Lynn turned to Cooley. "Why would I be seeing someone else? Why would you ask me that?"

"I just wondered. I mean, you know, I date other people, so I wanted to make sure you were meeting others as well."

Lynn wanted to scream but she held it in. "Well, there is one other person, but she don't have anything on my *papi*," Lynn smiled.

"That's cool." Cooley headed back to her room.

"Shit," Lynn said to herself. She fought back tears. She was in love and she knew it.

"So, what are we going to watch?" Cooley asked as she walked in the kitchen. "Lynn, what's wrong with you?"

"Cooley, I will be honest with you. There is no one else. We've been seeing each other since the first week of school, and I figured things were going to change from this dating-other-people thing."

"Lynn, I told you from the beginning, I wasn't looking for a relationship."

Lynn put her hand on Cooley's arm. "I know, but I thought you would change your mind eventually. I mean, I am the one that you have mainly been with. What am I not doing that is making you go to other girls?" Lynn felt the tears forming in her eyes.

"Lynn, it's not like that. I just don't want to be tied down right now. If it is too much for you, then we may need to end this now," Cooley said as she wiped the tear that fell from Lynn's eye.

"No, I'm good. I just wonder why I never seem to be relationship material."

Cooley looked confused by the statement. "Lynn, what does that mean?"

Lynn lowered her head. "'Cause every time I try to be with someone, they don't want me. I can cook and clean, but nothing else. At first I thought it was just 'cause I wasn't giving it up, but obviously it's more than that."

Cooley put her arms around Lynn. "Lynn, you are good enough; you just caught me at a time when that's not what I am looking for. In a little less than two months, I'll be moving to Miami. I don't want to tie myself down when I know what kind of life I'm 'bout to be part of. But anyone should be proud to have you as their piece." Cooley gave her a forehead kiss, hoping that Lynn took the excuse.

"You are a very special woman, Carla. When you finally decide to settle down, I know you are going to make the girl very happy. I hope I will be that girl one day."

Cooley ignored the comment and headed into the living room. She realized she had a serious issue on her hands, but she didn't want to deal with it tonight.

Chapter 27

"Tammy?" Cooley looked at the frail woman standing at her door. She almost didn't recognize Denise's mother. She noticed the big purple lesion on her forehead and a smaller one on her neck. She realized instantly they were the same kind of spots that Mystque, a famous drag queen, had before she died from AIDS.

"Come in," Cooley opened the door for Tammy.

"Hi. Um, Carla, is Denise here?" she said, looking around the nice apartment.

"Um, no," Cooley responded. She couldn't believe the state Tammy was in. "She should be home soon. Tammy, can I get you something to drink? Please have a seat."

Tammy hesitated, but sat down anyway. "Um, I guess I can come back if I need to."

"No!" Cooley exclaimed. "Um, no, she will be home real soon. I think you two really, really need to talk. I'm gon' fix you somethin' to eat, OK?" Cooley headed into the kitchen and snatched the phone to call Carmen.

"Carmen, get over here now. Tammy is here, and I think she has—"

"AIDS." Carmen finished Cooley's sentence. "I know. I saw her at the last Life Support meeting before I left for break."

"Why didn't you tell me and Dee?" Cooley snapped.

"Because she needed to be the one to tell Dee, but I am on my way. I know Dee is going to need us."

Cooley hung up the phone and brought a plate of Lynn's most recent leftovers to Tammy. "Tammy, how long you had the package?"

"Carmen told you?" Tammy said as she took a huge bite of the food.

"No. I'm not a dumb ass though. The lesions told me. How could you keep this from Dee?"

"I didn't want to complicate her life." She paused as Denise walked in the door.

Denise took one look at Tammy and laid into Cooley.

"What the hell is this woman doing in our house?" Denise yelled.

"Dee, you need to chill out!" Cooley yelled back.

"Fuck that! Get the fuck out!" Denise said as she opened the door.

Tammy stood up, but Cooley grabbed her arm.

"Bruh, close the door and sit down. Look at her. She's sick."

"I don't give a fuck if she's sick," Denise spat but instantly felt bad for saying it. She turned and looked at Tammy. She saw the spots on her face and neck. "What the hell do you have?"

"The package," Tammy said as tears rolled down her eyes. "I don't expect you to do anything. I just needed to give you these papers." She handed Denise a thick envelope. "It's my insurance papers. Mama took out a few policies on me a long time ago. She wanted to make sure I was covered."

"Mema knew you had it and didn't tell me?" Denise said as she sat down in the chair. She couldn't believe what she was hearing.

"Yes, baby, she didn't want to worry you." Tammy sank back down on the couch.

The door opened, and Carmen walked in. She could feel the tension in the air. "Is everything going OK?" Carmen glanced nervously at Denise.

"No, Carmen, everything is not all right. This woman, who has done nothing for me my whole life, walks in and tells me she is dying."

"Dee." Carmen didn't expect Denise to be so cold. Cooley was shocked as well.

"What!" Denise jumped up. "Look, you didn't want to tell me because you knew I was busy. Well, I'm still busy. I told you the business after what you did to Mema's house."

"Bruh!" Cooley tried to interject, but Denise cut her off.

"No, Cool! Nothing has changed. Why the hell should I have to deal with this? You know I realized a long time ago that I couldn't worry about you anymore. I used to wake up in cold sweats in the middle of the night as a child after having a dream about you dying. I dealt with the thought of you coming up dead every day when I was younger. You have never been a mother to me. Hell, you've never been anything to me. I don't even know your middle name!"

"Dee, she's your mother!" Carmen yelled. She felt herself becoming upset by Dee's attitude.

"No, C, my mother died last year. I'm out." Denise stormed out of the apartment before anyone else could say anything.

Tammy sat on the couch. Her face was covered in tears. She got up, but Cooley stopped her. "Tammy, where are you gonna go? Give her some time. She'll come around."

Tammy smiled. "Carla, everything she said is right. I dug my grave a long time ago. I just wanted to tell her I was sorry and give her these papers. When I die I don't want nothing fancy. I just want to make sure that Denise gets to keep as much money as she can."

"Will you be at Life Support this week?" Carmen asked Tammy.

"I'll try to make it. She is real lucky to have you all for friends." Tammy hugged Carmen and walked out of the apartment.

Carmen and Cooley looked at each other. Cooley sat down on the couch and looked at the spot where Tammy just sat. "You know something, Carmen? I can't blame Dee for her reaction."

Carmen looked at Cooley. "How can you say that? She was..."

"Carmen, when my dad died, I wouldn't go see him in the hospital up until his final days. I was so angry with him. For years he always put women in front of me. He would leave me at home with random bitches so he could go off with other girls. One of his women was my first. We had a big argument about him never being there for me when he started getting sicker. We were able to make up, but I do regret not being there during the beginning of the end. But, honestly, if my father had never been around, if my father had picked crack over me, if my mother did what Dee's mother did to that house, I don't think I would have given a fuck either." Cooley looked up at Carmen. "I'm gonna go work out." She kissed Carmen on her head.

Carmen was speechless. She sat there and absorbed everything that happened. She wondered what her reaction would have been if she was in the same situation.

Cooley knew the main reason she would never be with Lynn was because of her horrible sexual performance. Cooley had a lot on her mind after the incident with Tammy. She wanted to take all her emotions out on Lynn. Cooley still hadn't been able to get more than forty-five minutes out of her before she was tired. No matter how much she tried to spice it up, sex with Lynn was boring. Cooley felt herself becoming very restless.

She looked over at Lynn. "I'm heading on campus for a while."

Lynn turned over in the bed. "Cool, it's four in the morning."

"Yeah, I know. I got a lot of things on my mind. I want to check if Dee is in the gym, and I got a paper to finish. You know I prefer to go to the lab in the wee hours of the morning. I need to finish my paper, and I'm not sleepy. I'll be back in a few hours."

Cooley soon found herself standing in front of Misha's room. She thought about calling one of her old random pieces of ass, but she was actually glad that she had weeded them all out of her life. She knocked on the door and right away heard Misha swearing.

"What the hell do you—" Misha looked at Cooley standing at her door. "Oh, something better be seriously wrong."

"Misha, I don't know what's wrong with me. I was driving and just ended up here. Can I come in?"

Misha reluctantly let Cooley enter her room. Cooley looked around the small room. They had a lot of memories there. Misha was in the same room that she had last year. Cooley noticed she hadn't put her rainbow flag back up, and the pictures of them were missing, but she figured they would be gone.

"Misha, I have a problem."

Misha sat down on her bed and tried to wake up more. "What's going on?"

Cooley looked at Misha. She realized how beautiful she was, even in a bandana and old shirt. "Denise's ma is dying of AIDS."

"Oh my God. How is she doing?" Misha said and scooted next to Cooley.

"Dee isn't doing anything. She isn't dealing with it. After all the things her mother has done to her, she can't seem to forgive her right now."

"Cooley, I'm sorry. Is there anything I can do?"

"No, the shit just got me thinking about things. You know I've slowed down so much, and I have you to thank for that. But that brings me to my other problem: you. I'm still a little gon' over you, and I don't know what to do about it."

Misha looked up at Cooley. She still had feelings for her, but her feelings for Patrick seemed to be just as strong. "Cooley, I care about you too, but that doesn't mean we need to be together again."

Cooley shook her head. "I don't think I want to be in a relationship anymore. That shit is for the birds. But I don't want to be just your friend, and I don't want to be your woman."

Misha stood up. "Oh, I get it. You want to be a fuck buddy. A homie lover friend. Fuck you, Cooley, I ain't about to be one of your precious pieces of ass!" Misha started to let Cooley out her door when Cooley grabbed her arm.

"Misha, you should know me better than that. For your information, I have not been fucking around. I had more ass thrown at me during Christmas break than ever, but I didn't jump at it. Misha, I'm out of that stage in my life. I owe that to you."

"Cooley, you fucked a girl the day after we broke up. You aren't out of the stage. You're just taking a break." Misha could feel her heart pounding. She couldn't bear being so close to Cooley. She knew that she still loved her.

"Misha, what do you want from me? Don't you know I would have done anything for you? Hell, I did."

Misha sighed. "Yes, Cooley, you did a lot, and I do admit that you tried. But it just wasn't enough. I don't want a complicated relationship. I don't want drama. I still have bitches looking at me crazy from last year."

"Misha, that was your problem, not mine." Cooley countered. "You let them bitches run our relationship. I let the shit go. I was like, fuck all of them, but what everyone else thought was too damn important to you."

Misha looked at Cooley. "Cooley, I admit that I let the women enter my head. Maybe I wasn't secure enough in our relationship. But, truth be told, if we were to be together again, I still wouldn't be secure enough in our relationship. Being with you is too much work, work I don't necessarily have time to do."

Misha's words hit Cooley like a blow to the chest. "Damn, kid, I never looked at it like that."

"Plus, Cooley, you're headed to Miami after this semester. I'm headed to Atlanta. If we have problems dealing with this local, we surely can't do a long-distance thing. So, we should just be friends and call it a day." Misha looked down at Cooley. She knew that wasn't the whole truth. The truth was that she had a relationship already. She had Patrick waiting on her in Atlanta.

"I guess you're right. Man, you know that girl Lynn. She really is digging me, but I can't even get down like that. Plus, she is not good in bed."

Misha laughed. "What? A girl not living up to your standards?"

Cooley grinned at Misha. "Well, after you, my standards have gotten pretty high. The girl can't even last an hour."

Misha looked at Cooley. She knew Lynn was crazy about Cooley. "Carla, that girl Lynn, I know she really likes you. I'm warning you in advance. She is in love. If you know that she is someone that you are not going to keep around, let her go. Unlike your random bitches, she seems pretty nice, and you don't need to dog her out."

Cooley stood up. "I ain't dogging her out. I have only fucked two other girls since I've been messing with her, one being you. And, besides, I told her from the beginning that I ain't looking for anything serious."

Misha frowned at Cooley. "Cooley, remember that actions speak louder than words. Now, I have a class in the morning, so you gotta go."

"Can't I stay here with you?" Cooley read Misha's expression that clearly said no. "For old times' sake?"

Misha knew it wasn't a good idea, but she decided to let Cooley stay.

As soon as they got in the bed, it was on. Cooley had her head in between Misha's legs licking her clit like a lollipop.

Misha didn't realize how much she missed lesbian sex. She lay back and let Cooley go at it. Cooley knew her body well. Every touch had meaning. Every stroke had purpose. She knew where all of her spots were.

Misha pulled on Cooley's head as she arched her back up and pushed Cooley farther into her bush. Cooley went to town. She slid her long tongue in and out of the narrow opening while she pulled on Misha's ass cheeks. She wrapped her lips around Misha's throbbing clit and sucked as she flicked the tip with her tongue.

Misha purred, "Yes, baby." She'd forgotten the feeling of having such an accomplished female lover between her legs. Cooley continued to remind her.

Cooley reached one hand up and caressed Misha's soft belly before reaching for her hardened nipples. She continued to explore the terrain of the woman's body and began to stroke Misha's long neck.

The vulnerable feeling of Cooley's strong hand pressed against her neck and her mouth firmly pressed against her pussy sent Misha's body into convulsions.

Cooley was just getting started. Misha tried in vain to escape, but Cooley grabbed her thighs and held her firmly as she continued to devour the hot molten fluid pouring from Misha's pussy. Her tongue darted in and out, pushing against Misha's walls.

The woman squirmed beneath her and felt the wet juices flowing into her crack and soaking the sheet beneath her.

Cooley was in her glory. With her eyes clamped shut, she ate like it was her very last meal and Misha was ten courses.

Misha succumbed to Cooley's Killa Cap and flailed along the mattress until Cooley had her fill.

Several orgasms later, Misha wanted to return the favor. She had the urge to eat some pussy, and Cooley was what she had a taste for. She pushed Cooley down and headed down south.

Cooley quickly stopped her. "Hell no, Misha. Only my love and woman can do that shit to me." Cooley never let girls go down on her. Only one had ever succeeded, and now that same girl was trying again. "So unless you are planning on being my wife, then hell no."

"Selfish ass," Misha said, disappointed that she couldn't taste Cooley again. She laid down next to Cooley and let her wrap her arms around her. "Cooley, this is the last time this ever happens," Misha stated. She had begun to feel guilty about cheating on Patrick.

"I hear you," Cooley said as she drifted to sleep. She had every intention of fucking Misha again.

***

Cooley woke up that afternoon. She realized she forgot all about Lynn, until she saw her car in the lot. Cooley thought quickly as she opened her door. The smell of freshly made waffles hit her nose. She saw Lynn standing in the kitchen cooking.

Lynn turned around when she heard the door open. "God, Cooley, I was worried sick about you."

Cooley looked down at the floor. "Man, I'm sorry. It got so late that I ended up crashing at Misha's dorm room, since it was the closest."

Lynn's face dropped. "You crashed with your ex?"

"Yeah, she doesn't have a roommate, so I slept in her extra bed." Cooley realized that she was explaining herself like she was her girlfriend. "Anyway, it really doesn't matter. I'm just glad I got my paper done."

Lynn dropped her spatula. "Cooley, I think it does matter. You were out with your ex all night. You didn't call or anything. I didn't know what had happened to you. And to hear that you were with your ex. Damn, how you think that makes me feel?"

Cooley looked at Lynn. "Lynn, I told you already what the deal was. Now you can accept it or you can not. But at least I'm explaining it. I don't have to do that." Cooley walked to her room.

Lynn followed. "You know it's not that you have to explain. But you should tell the girl that you are sleeping with that you are going to go fuck with some other girl."

"I told you I wasn't fucking her. Lynn, this conversation is over. I didn't fuck her. But, even if I did, you obviously forgot that you ain't my woman. I'm single and can do what I want."

Lynn was pissed. "Oh, you're single and can do what you want now? Well, I am the one that is here almost every night. I am the one cooking and cleaning up your damn apartment. When you're tired, who massages your back? I do everything in my power to please you and this is how you repay me, by throwing up the fact that we aren't official? Fuck you, Cooley!" Lynn grabbed her bag and began to pack up the clothes that she left at Cooley's place.

"See, Lynn, I told you that you weren't ready for this. I told you that I was not looking for a relationship. Stop trying to change the rules now!"

"I am not changing the rules. I just want a little respect!" Lynn yelled.

"I do give you respect. Damn, Lynn, you're here all the time. I kick it with you more than any other woman. I can't offer you anything more than that, so if you want more, you need to go ahead and leave now."

Lynn stopped packing her things. "Cooley, I don't pressure you to make me your girl. We have been messing off for almost a year and you still treat me like we just met. Dammit, haven't I proved myself to you yet?" Lynn dropped her head.

Cooley let out a sigh of frustration. "Lynn, it's not about proving yourself. I am not looking for a relationship. I am moving to Miami after graduation. I don't want to be tied down. You knew the rules from jump."

Lynn's face dropped. She sat on the bed. "Let's just drop it. I have a class. I'll talk to you later." Lynn walked out the room, leaving her bag lying open on the floor.

Cooley knew she had to take care of Lynn soon.

As Lynn walked, she thought about her situation with Cooley. Her mind was telling her to leave but her heart was telling her to stay just a little longer. Lynn had heard stories about Cooley's first love. She hated that Misha left Cooley so damaged, but she knew she had the means to make Cooley happy. She wasn't ready to throw in the towel just yet.

Chapter 28

Carmen turned the television on the campus news station to work on a report for class. She noticed the ad Chi Theta put in about their spring step show. The news of the women's basketball team winning the title covered the station. Pictures of Denise holding the championship trophy made Carmen smile.

"Hey, baby. I'm back," Nic said, walking in with a bag of food.

"Good. 'Cause I'm hungry."

"We interrupt this news report to bring this special report. Breaking news. A girl has been stabbed fourteen times by her lover in Reed Hall."

The announcement caught Nic and Carmen's attention.

"We are unsure of the actual details, but sources say that it was a lovers' dispute gone bad. According to witnesses, the accused caught her female lover with another woman."

"Cooley." Carmen grabbed her phone. She always wondered if Cooley was going to end up hurt. She breathed a sigh of relief when Cooley answered the phone.

"We just have news that the victim was twenty-three-year-old Tameka Haroldson, a senior."

Carmen's body froze. She couldn't hear anything but Tameka's name over and over.

Nic tried to shake her out of it, but was unsuccessful.

Carmen jumped up. "I have to go."

"Carmen, no!"

"Nic, I have to go see if she is OK."

"That ain't your job."

Carmen looked at Nic's stern expression.

"Nic, I want you to trust me on this, please."

"Carmen, if you go, I won't be here when you get back."

"Nic, you don't understand."

"Carmen, don't put me in this situation. You don't owe her anything. Why the fuck you trying to go see her?"

"Nic, please trust me on this. I need to go."

"You don't need to do anything. You want to go. Fuck it. Do what you want. I'm out." Nic grabbed her coat and stormed out the room.

A big piece of her wanted to go after Nic, but Carmen knew what she had to do. She grabbed her keys and headed to the hospital.

"So, Rhonda, you know why you are here, correct?"

"Because you all don't have any faith in me." Rhonda folded her arms. Her mother had called her to come home for a party. When she got there, her doctor and two large men were sitting in the living room.

"Rhonda, you know you are supposed to come to your meetings every other week. Now we worked with you by doing them every other week instead of every week. We haven't seen you in a month, and you never picked up your prescription.

"Those pills make it hard for me at school!" Rhonda said to her doctor.

"Rhonda, we have been through this. The pills make it OK for you to be at school and living on campus in the first place."

"Doc, I am fine. I am doing fine."

"Rhonda, if you are not going to cooperate, we are going to have to take you out of school and put you back in the academy."

"No!" Rhonda stood up. She looked at the two large men. She knew she needed to sit back down.

"She's seeing a girl," her mother said.

"Mother!"

"Some basketball player." Her mother dropped a bunch of pictures and articles on the coffee table.

Rhonda was mortified. "You went through my dorm room? How could you!" Rhonda began to tremble.

"You weren't answering calls. I knew something was wrong. There was a whole drawer full."

"She's my girlfriend. Doesn't everyone keep pictures and accomplishments of their partners?"

"Rhonda, you know that we discussed you not dating anyone," the doctor said firmly. "I think that I am going to have to suggest putting her back into the academy."

"Noooo!" Rhonda jumped up.

One of the men grabbed her.

"I love school. School is the only thing I do love. Don't take it from me."

Rhonda's mother's eyes filled with tears. "What about if she moves back in with me? Could she stay in school?"

"I don't know. Rhonda hasn't been following the guidelines. She could put herself and others in danger again."

"I'm not, I'm not. Let me go to school. I'll come to meetings and take my pills, I promise," Rhonda cried.

The doctor and her mother looked at her. "This is the last time, Rhonda. You mess up again and you are back in the academy."

Rhonda calmed down. She agreed. She did not want to go back to the institution. It would keep her from Denise for good.

Larissa jumped out of her bed when she heard the beating on her door. She opened it, and Nic stormed in. Nic fell down on the bed and put her hands on her head.

"Nic, what's wrong?" Larissa ran over to Nic, not realizing she didn't completely close her door. She had never seen Nic cry.

"Carmen went to see that bitch! After I asked her not to, she still went. She just doesn't give a fuck!" Nic said as tears fell down her face.

Larissa fell to her knees in front of Nic. She wrapped her arms around her. "Sweetie, please don't cry. Nic, you deserve so much better."

"Damn, why she just don't get it? Why she just don't understand? I been driving around for hours. I got back to the room and she still wasn't there. She just don't give a fuck about me."

Larissa continued to hold the sobbing Nic. "It's amazing to me how stupid women can be. A bitch can have the fucking moon, and they still want the stars and sun. Nic, you are the most wonderful person I have ever met. You deserve someone who is going to love you for who you are and not be trying to creep with some nothing-ass person." Larissa looked up at Nic.

Nic looked into Larissa's eyes. Before she knew it Larissa pressed her lips against hers.

Chapter 29

"Well, it seems like you're going to live." Carmen helped Tameka take a sip of water.

"If you call this living." Tameka reached down and touched her leg. She couldn't feel anything. The doctors said the knife had severed her spinal chord. She was paralyzed from the waist down. Tameka choked up at the thought of never walking again.

"You will be OK. I promise." Carmen smiled weakly. She had waited in the hospital for hours until the doctor said it was all right for her to go in for a few minutes. She didn't know what to expect. She'd called Nic several times while she waited, but Nic never answered the phone.

"Carmen." Tameka looked at her. "Why did you come?"

"What do you mean?"

"Come on, you know what I mean. It's not like I deserve to have you here."

"I really don't know." Carmen looked at her phone; there were still no calls from Nic.

"You really love her, don't you?" Tameka said.

Carmen nodded as tears rolled down her face.

"I do, and I think I may have lost her. She really didn't want me to come."

"Carmen, thank you for being here for me, but I can't let you lose her. She's good for you. Go get your girl."

Carmen realized Tameka was right. "Tameka, I wish you well. I hope you have a full recovery." She grabbed her jacket and ran out the room.

Carmen made it to her room. Nic wasn't there. She called Nic's phone again. "Nic, please, baby, come home. I really want to see you. I know you're mad, but please let's talk about it. I'll be at Cooley and Denise's place." She waited a few more minutes and headed out the door.

Nic quickly pulled away from Larissa. "Why'd you do that?"

"Nic, didn't you want it as much as I did?" Larissa said as Nic moved away from her.

"No, Larissa, you're my friend. You're straight!"

"Things change."

"Not shit like that."

"Nic, I knew I was in love with you last semester. I've wanted to kiss you for a long time. I thought you wanted to as well."

"Larissa, I'm sitting here telling you about Carmen, and you thought that's what I needed? I love Carmen. Oh my God, Carmen!" Nic ran to the door.

Larissa grabbed her by the arm. "Nic, don't go back to her. You can stay here with me. You deserve so much better."

"Larissa, I gotta go." Nic ran out of the room.

Carmen walked into her dorm room. She hoped that Nic would be there, because she'd never showed up at Denise and Cooley's apartment. Carmen was relieved when she saw Nic sitting on the side of the bed.

"Baby, I know you're pissed. Let me explain. I—"

"Carmen," Nic said.

"I don't know what I was thinking. I just wanted to make sure she was OK. I kinda felt responsible—"

"Carmen, please," Nic said. "I have something I need to tell you."

Carmen looked at Nic's face. She had never seen her look so stressed. "Nic, please don't be that mad at me. Please don't leave."

"Larissa kissed me."

Carmen's whole body went numb. She couldn't move. The words kept repeating in her head. "What?"

"Carmen, don't be mad. It wasn't what you—"

"You kissed another girl? That's how you decided to get back at me? You kissed another girl!"

"Carmen—" Before Nic could finish her sentence, she felt a stinging slap on the left side of her face. They faced each other in silence.

"So it's like that?"

"You fuckin' with another bitch. Hell yeah, it's like that."

"I'm not fuckin'—"

"Fuck you, Nic. You're just like Tameka."

Nic felt her anger rising. "Oh, you really didn't just say that shit! Carmen, you been waiting on that, huh? Been waiting to find a reason to compare me to that bitch! You don't give a fuck about me. You only care about her. Go be with her then, Carmen. I'm never gonna be good enough anyway!"

"Nic!"

"Fuck this!" Nic grabbed her keys and headed to the door.

Carmen instantly regretted what she'd said, but she didn't want to back down. "Fuck you, Nic. Go be with your bitch. Go fuck her! I fuckin' hate you!" Carmen yelled as the door slammed behind Nic.

Nic ran around the track three times to clear her mind. A big piece of her wanted to run back to Carmen, but another part was tired of dealing with the damage caused by another woman. She realized her heart belonged to Carmen and it wasn't going to change.

She headed back to her room, hoping that Carmen was still there. She walked in and found Carmen's books and many of her clothes missing.

Nic picked up the phone.

"Hey," Misha said.

"Misha, have you talked to Carmen."

Misha walked out of her dorm room and whispered, "Nic, she's here."

"I'm on my way."

"No, Nic, she's too upset right now. Give it a day. She'll be back. Y'all love each other. Just give it a little time."

Nic knew Misha was right. She hung up the phone and lay on her bed.

Larissa's ring tone began to play. Nic pressed ignore and sent her a text message.

Don't contact me again.

Chapter 30

Rhonda hadn't left her room since going to her mother's house. She didn't know what to do to get Denise back. She lay on her bed listening to Patsy Cline's "Crazy" over and over as loudly as the radio could play. She heard a knock on the door but didn't respond.

"Rhonda, this is Kim, the RA. If you don't answer the door, I am going to come in." Rhonda continued to ignore the door.

Kim unlocked the door and walked in. The smell of rotting food caused Kim to cover her nose. "Oh, hell no! Girl, you can't have this room like this," she said as she turned the music down.

Rhonda snapped when she didn't hear Patsy anymore. "What the fuck are you doing in my roooom-mmm?" she screamed.

Other people started coming around.

"What are you doing here?"

"Chill out, Rhonda," Kim said, putting her hands up. "I'm resident assistant. I can come in whenever I think there's a problem, and there is."

"Get out of my room!" Rhonda pointed to the door.

"Rhonda, you need to drop the tone. What the hell is wrong with you?"

"Get out! Get out!" Rhonda continued to yell.

Kim knew the situation could get volatile. "I'm calling security on you." Kim walked out the room.

Rhonda slammed the door. She looked around her room. She knew she was about to be in trouble. If security came she would be shipped back to the mental health facility for good.

She followed Kim into the hallway. "Kim, please don't call security. I'm just going through something. I was dumped." Tears rolled down Rhonda's cheeks.

"Rhonda, we all have been there. I've been dumped before. But you can't let your room get like that. If you get bugs, we all get them."

"I'll clean it up immediately. Thank you." Rhonda walked away.

Kim walked to Rhonda's suite mate's room. "Hey, Dayza."

The thick, red-boned woman looked at Kim. "Is she gonna stop?"

"Yeah, I talked to her."

"Thank God. 'Cause I thought I was going to have to kill the crazy bitch." Dayza smiled and closed her door.

"You know I'm supposed to be kicking your ass right now." Cooley laughed as she walked in Nic's dorm room.

"Cooley, it's been three days. She hasn't contacted me. What's going on?"

"She's pissed off. Man, what the hell happened?" Cooley said, sitting in the desk chair.

"Larissa kissed me. I was talking to her about Carmen going to see Tameka and she fuckin' kissed me. I pulled away immediately and came back here."

"So you didn't fuck her?"

"Hell, no. I didn't even kiss her. She kissed me."

"Man, I'll talk to Carmen. You know she got issues."

"Yeah, but why she taking shit out on me? I ain't Tameka," Nic complained. "She actually compared me to her."

"Man, just let her cool off. I'll talk to her. Now that I know you didn't fuck the girl, things will be a'ight. Let me grab some of her clothes, and I'm outta here." Cooley picked clothes out of Carmen's closet.

"Tell her I love her."

"I will." Cooley closed the door behind her.

Nic felt her world falling apart.

Denise opened the door and smiled as Stephanie walked in.

"You wanted to see me?" Stephanie smiled.

"Yeah, I did. Um, I wanted to talk to you about . . . well, you know." Denise smiled back.

"Dee, there is nothing to explain. I understand where you were coming from. It actually made me respect you more. No love lost. But, trust, when school is out, I'm gonna get you," Stephanie boasted.

Denise laughed. "Dig that then. I hear ya."

"So, are you ready for the games?" Stephanie asked as she sat down on the couch.

Denise sat down next to her. "I guess. I really don't seem to care one way or the other."

Stephanie looked at Denise in disbelief. "You don't care? Dee, these are the last games of our college careers. For some it's the last time to truly play ball. And you don't really care?"

Denise thought about Tammy. "I guess I just have a lot on my mind. But I feel you on that."

Stephanie sighed. "Man, this is my last time to shine. My last time to make a good impression. I want it so bad, Dee."

"I know you do, and I'm going to do all I can to make sure you get your shine on."

Denise leaned over and kissed Stephanie. "Damn, my bad. I just really wanted to do that."

Stephanie blushed. "Well, by all means, continue."

They embraced each other, sensually kissing until they were interrupted.

"Now that's what I am talking about. That's some *Love and Basketball* type shit," Cooley teased as she walked into the room. "It's about damn time. Now let me go save this other damn relationship." Cooley walked out of the room.

"Not as glad as I am." Stephanie kissed Denise again. She stood up. "I better get back to the dorm. I got to get some studying and packing done."

Denise walked Stephanie to her car. "Look, as much as I wanted to do that back there, we probably shouldn't do it again until after the last game."

"Well, in that case . . ." She hugged Denise and kissed her again. "I just needed one more."

Denise watched as she drove off.

Rhonda hit her steering wheel. "I knew that bitch was trying to take my girl," she said, looking at Denise going back toward her apartment. Rhonda had been watching from across the street for weeks, waiting to get proof. She watched Stephanie drive off. "Bitch, you got me fucked up." She peeled off, leaving skid marks on the pavement.

"Carmen, go get ya girl," Cooley said.

"I knew you were going to be on her side," Carmen said and snatched her clothes from Cooley.

"Carmen, you buggin'. Nic didn't do shit wrong. Now you on the other hand—How the fuck you gon' go see that bitch when you know how Nic feels about it? How you gone put her in that situation."

"I just had unfinished business."

"You realize the last time you had unfinished business you ended up getting back with Tameka? How is Nic supposed to feel, knowing you did it once before? Put yourself in her shoes."

Carmen knew Cooley was right. "Was she OK?"

"Hell, naw. That girl look like she ain't had a bath in days." Cooley looked around the room. "Hey, where's Misha?"

"She left for Atlanta yesterday." Carmen could see the hurt in Cooley's eyes. "So when are you two going to work things out?"

"That ship has sailed. We can only be friends, maybe fuck every now and then. I'm not opening myself up to her again."

"To just her, or anyone?" Carmen said.

Cooley didn't respond.

"Well, go get ya girl." Cooley kissed Carmen on her forehead and walked out the room.

Carmen picked up her keys to go to Nic but paused. The image of Nic kissing Larissa entered her head again. She put her keys down. She couldn't do it.

Misha looked at Patrick. He was definitely a handsome man. She knew she was wrong for letting Cooley sex her, but she felt so good. She wondered if Patrick was going to be enough for her, or if she would always want to sleep with women, especially Cooley.

"Misha, is something wrong?" Patrick said, noticing she wasn't eating her dinner.

Misha quickly snapped back to reality. "No, baby, everything is fine. Just one of my friends is going through a lot right now. Her mother is dying."

"Damn, baby, I'm sorry to hear that. Is there anything I can do for them?"

"No . . . but, Pat, I think I'm going to take a break from coming down every weekend. All my friends are trippin' about me not being around. It's our senior year and they hardly see me. And with this going on, I need to be there for her and them."

Patrick didn't like Misha's decision, but he respected it. "I understand, baby. How about I come up there every weekend?"

"Pat, you have work, and you know they are going to trip if you aren't available and something important happens. You spend most of your time when I'm here in the office."

Patrick took a sip of his beer. "You're right. I guess I can go a few weeks without you. And in a few weeks I'll come down. I think it's time for me to meet your crew anyway. I really want to meet Brandon Redding and Denise Chambers."

Misha knew that he couldn't meet them. "Baby, we'll see, but don't make any plans yet. They're both very busy people."

Patrick studied Misha's facial expression. "Misha, why is it that you don't want me to meet your friends?"

Misha was shocked. "What do you mean?"

"Just what I said. When Lena was in town, you didn't want me to meet her then. And now you're telling me I can't come and meet them. Why are you trying to hide me? Or is it you're the one hiding something?" Patrick responded.

Misha could hear the concern in his voice.

"Patrick, it's not that. I would love for you to meet Carmen and Lena. There is something that I haven't told you, and I didn't know how you would react. Carmen is gay. Nic is not a man, but her lover."

Patrick couldn't believe it. "Are you saying that fine-ass woman is a dyke? Damn."

His words cut her like a knife. "Can you please not use that word? And, yes, she is gay."

"I'm sorry about the dyke thing, but hell, I just never would have thought such a beautiful woman would be gay. That's a shame."

"Why is it a shame?" Misha was waiting for this. She could see what he truly thought.

"Nothing, baby. I'm just shocked. Tell me, have you ever been with a woman?"

Misha almost choked after that comment. "What!"

"I'm just kidding. I know you would never go that way. But, seriously, I do want to meet them all. Maybe around graduation, since it's only a month and a half away."

"Maybe." Misha took a bite of her food, unsure of what to do. She knew now that she had to keep it from Patrick. She hoped she didn't have any more lapses. She was going to have to try to stay away from Cooley, the main girl who still knew how to get her hot.

Chapter 31

Denise stood at the bus with Michelle. It was time for the last set of away games before the NCAA tournaments. She was going to be on the road for two weeks. The bus began to load, but they still didn't know where Stephanie was.

The coach walked up to them. "Ladies, let me get your attention. Something has happened."

Denise and Michelle looked at each other as coach continued. "Stephanie . . . Stephanie was hit by a car in a hit-and-run."

"What!" Michelle yelled.

"Coach, what happened? Is she gonna be OK?" Denise said as her heart dropped.

"She was driving down Winchester last night and someone hit her. The police think the person was drunk, because it looks like they hit her more than once."

"Is she going to be OK?" Michelle said.

"Honestly, it's too early to tell how her extensive injuries will affect her, long term. But I have talked to her. Her main concern, believe it or not, is us winning this championship."

Denise's body felt tense. The news seemed surreal to her. She knew she had to get hit after leaving her house. "Man, all she wanted to do was play."

"Tell me about it," Michelle added. "Man, this doesn't even seem right."

Denise and Michelle got on the bus.

"You want to stay in my room now?"

"Yeah, that's a plan," Denise said. She couldn't shake the feeling that something was terribly wrong.

Carmen walked into the Life Support meeting. She looked around, but there was no sign of Tammy. As the meeting was about to begin, she noticed a woman slinking into the room. She breathed a sigh of relief. It had been weeks since the incident, and Denise still hadn't come around. Carmen used the Life Support meetings to check on Tammy. The fact that she was there let her know she was still alive.

"Tammy, how are you doing?" Carmen asked as she hugged her. She could feel Tammy's ribs.

"Making it, I guess. I feel real bad today. How is Denise?"

"She's fine. She's on the road with the team right now. They have the last set of away games before tournament time."

Tammy smiled. "She is going to go pro?"

"I'm not sure, but everyone thinks so. If not in America, she definitely will be picked up overseas. They tried to get her in Spain and Italy last year."

"That makes me happy. I want her to get as far away from this city as she possibly can. I have something to share with you." She handed Carmen a piece of paper.

Carmen opened it and found a picture and an address.

"That's Denise's father."

Carmen's eyes widened. She studied the picture of Denise and her mother and father. They looked so happy together. "Why are you giving me this?"

"The truth is, her father didn't run out on her like she thinks. I was using drugs and he found out. He tried to make me stop, but I wouldn't. Finally he gave up. He threatened to take her from me, but I took her and left for Little Rock."

Carmen couldn't believe what she was hearing. "Then why does she think—"

"Because that's what I told her. That's what I told everyone. When I moved back to Memphis I told Mema that he ran off on me. It was a lie."

"But why wouldn't he try to find her?"

"I don't know. But I do want you to find out. I would like to make that up to him, give him the chance to know her."

Carmen shook her head. "Honestly, I don't think she's gonna go for that. I know my friend."

"Well, just try. Maybe you can contact him first."

"I don't know." Carmen realized things were getting to be too much for her.

"It's up to you. But if she ever mentions him, please give her that address. He doesn't know that I have it."

Carmen nodded her head. They headed back to the meeting. Carmen realized that three familiar faces were now gone. She knew one day soon that would also be the case with Tammy.

Cooley looked at her phone. It was Tara. She pressed ignore. She had lost her mojo after the night with Misha.

She hadn't had sex since, and didn't want to.

Lynn handed Cooley a drink and sat down next to her.

"Baby, is everything OK?" Lynn said as she scooted closer to Cooley.

"I'm good," Cooley said, staring absently at the television. She knew Lynn was trying to entice her, but she had long lost interest in sexing Lynn. Lynn rubbed Cooley's hand against her nipple. It was rock-hard.

Cooley sighed and moved her hand. "Lynn, not to-night."

"What the fuck is wrong with you?" Lynn stood up and protested. "You haven't touched me in weeks ever since you got back from sleeping at Misha's place. Are y'all fucking again?"

Cooley looked at Lynn. Her anger was amusing. "Girl, sit down. I don't want to have sex. I am not having sex with anyone."

"I don't believe you. You love sex too much to not be getting it from somewhere."

"Lynn, damn, I am telling you I'm not having sex with anyone. And even if I was, it's not your business."

Cooley quickly felt a slap to her face.

"Not my business? I sit up here and play wifey with your ass all year, and you tell me that it's not my business? Well, if you're fucking someone else, just tell me, and I'll roll out. I'm not endangering my life for you or anyone else!" Lynn stormed back into Cooley's room.

Cooley followed. "What the fuck is your problem, huh? Do you know how many girls would love to be in your place? For your information, I haven't been fucking anyone but your ass. I give you all my time. What the fuck else do you want?"

"How about commitment? Yeah, you are with me all the time, but when we go out, I'm introduced as your friend. I'm tired of being your friend, Cooley. I want more."

"I can't give you more, Lynn! Damn, why you acting new? We've been through this before!"

Lynn started packing things that she had in her own drawer. "You know what, that was cool at first, but it's been damn near the whole year. Hell, we acting like we together. Why can't you just say the damn word?"

"Because I don't want to be in a relationship!" Cooley snapped. "I don't want to be tied down."

"And you think I like the idea of being replaced? With this shit, I can be replaced at anytime."

"If I was to call you my girlfriend, you could still be replaced." Cooley couldn't believe how angry she was becoming. It was just like with Misha. "Look, fuck this shit. I told you before, I'm not ready for a relationship. I'll be leaving for Miami soon. I told you on more than one occasion to date other people besides me."

"You know what, if that's what you want me to do, fine. I'll talk to you later." Lynn stormed past Cooley.

Cooley wanted to tell her to stop, but she knew it was best to let her go.

Chapter 32

"So, when are you going to tell me about the mystery woman?"

Misha looked up from her book when Carmen made the comment. She still hadn't told her friends about her lifestyle change.

"There is no girl. I told you that." Misha quickly took a sip of her drink. Things were becoming harder to hide. Patrick was coming to town as much as she was going to Atlanta. She hoped that she wasn't spotted out. Misha knew she was wrong, but she decided to hide it until she moved to Atlanta, where she was not known for being a lesbian.

"OK, so exactly what has you glowing and disappearing every weekend? Lena and I never see you anymore."

"I know, girl. I miss y'all so much. But I'm trying to get things settled in Atlanta. I've been looking for apartment and learning about my new job."

Carmen was not buying the excuse. "Yeah, OK, but I never saw a job give a girl a glow like that." She looked at Misha and winked.

"Yeah, well, whatever. You need to be worrying about Lena and not about me. At least I'm leaving town. That girl is practically on house arrest."

"Tell me about it. It seems Brandon thinks someone is going to try to mess with her or something. We had to take a car with a driver and a bodyguard the last time we went out."

"I still think he's hiding something." Misha thought back to the incident at the church.

"Yeah, me too, but I hope that she gets her ankle bracelet off soon."

Carmen and Misha laughed.

"I guess y'all are talking about me."

Carmen and Misha turned around to see Lena. They exchanged hugs.

"How on earth did you get away?" Carmen asked.

"I just left. I want to go get my hair done and get pampered without a damn bodyguard."

"Well, the life of a celebrity wife," Misha added.

Lena frowned. "Yeah, celebrity, my ass. I won't think of myself that way until I do a red carpet or two."

They laughed.

"Well, I was just stopping by, I have to get to the beauty shop."

All three stood up.

"Yeah, I need to go pack as well."

They all went their separate ways.

Cooley stood in front of Misha's door. She wanted to knock, but something was stopping her. She turned around and headed down the hall.

A familiar voice called her name.

"What's going on, Dayza?" Cooley said, looking at the woman.

Dayza would always help Cooley out of binds when they were suitemates freshman year. As suitemates their rooms were conjoined by a bathroom. If Cooley had a girl over and another one showed up, Dayza would let the first girl leave undetected through her room.

"Nothing much. Just heading to my room. I haven't seen your ass around the dorm."

"Oh, shit, girl, I moved off campus last summer with Dee. How you doing? Still curious?"

"Fuck you, bitch. Man, you need to come into my room. I gotta tell you something dealing with Dee." Dayza never had the urge to be with a woman until she met Cooley. She used to hear the sounds the girls would make when sexing her. She could also tell how sprung the girls got over Cooley. It made her curious, but she'd never acted on it.

"What about Dee?" Cooley walked into the room and noticed pictures of a guy all over her room. "This must be ya man."

"My fiancé, actually." Dayza held her hand out and flashed a small ring.

Cooley hugged and congratulated her. "Girl, I've missed you. Especially being next to my room. The girls I've shared bathrooms with have been a mess since you, especially the one across from me now. You know her ass too."

Cooley laughed. "Who?"

"Rhonda Marshall. Bitch is crazy as hell. Girl just be yelling for no reason. Don't no one be in the room with her. And she be playing the craziest music all loud and shit. She flipped out the other day. Kim went in and tried to see what was up. Girl was whacked." Dayza shook her head.

"Are you for real?" Cooley looked at the bathroom door that linked the two rooms. "What happened when she flipped?"

"She ain't been back since. Kim was going to call security on her, so she ran out. Man, Dee better be glad she left that one alone. You should see her room. She is like some type psycho for real. Man, I tried to find you a while back after some real crazy shit."

"What the hell happened?"

"Cooley, a few months back I came home and she was just crying hard in my bathroom, right. She was yelling, 'Denise, Denise,' so I opened the door to see if she was OK. She was standing in the mirror crying a river. I glanced over at her room, and she had all these candles lit around a picture of Denise. When she realized I was there, she stormed into her room and slammed the door."

Cooley looked at the bathroom door. "Get the fuck out of here. I knew that bitch was psycho."

"Hell, yeah, I don't know what her deal is, but she is bugging."

Cooley looked at the bathroom door again. "Can I use your bathroom for a second?"

Dayza nodded her head.

Cooley walked into the bathroom and closed the door.

Cooley looked at the door to Rhonda's room. She knew that she now had a chance to find out the deal with Rhonda. She put her ear to the door to see if she could hear anything. She turned the knob to see if it was unlocked. It wasn't. Cooley pulled out one of her credit cards in an attempt to pop the lock.

Dayza walked into the bathroom. "I knew what your ass was up to. Give me that shit." Dayza took the credit card and popped the lock instantly.

"Damn, did you get in my room like that?" Cooley laughed.

"I didn't need to get in your room. I could hear everything."

They opened the door and gasped.

"Shit. I gotta get my camera out the car." Cooley ran out. She returned with her camera in hand.

"Look at what I found." Dayza motioned.

Cooley looked in a drawer and saw a large pile of articles and pictures of Dee. "Look at these. It's like she was stalking her." Cooley looked at the pictures of Denise leaving the gym and talking to Stephanie.

"Oh my God. Talk about fatal attraction," Cooley said as she looked around the room. She noticed something over by her sink. Cooley felt rage coming over her as she picked up her favorite pair of Gucci shades. Cooley knew instantly who messed up her clothes. "Oh, this bitch is going down."

"Look, Cooley, the bitch is a certified nutcase." Dayza held up a bunch of prescription bottles. Dayza read one of the labels. "Lithium. She must be bi-polar. I don't know about the rest of these."

"Look, I got all I need. Let's roll out." Cooley placed her shades in her pocket. "Ms. Rhonda is going down."

Chapter 33

Denise looked up at the hospital sign and took a deep breath. Her heart began to pound as she walked up the stairs. She had promised herself that she wasn't ever going back to that hospital. But now she had a good reason, Stephanie.

Denise got on the elevator. It was the same elevator she used all the time to come see Mema. She touched the seventh floor button and fought back the urge to cry. She quickly pushed the button for the ninth floor. She made it around to Stephanie's room. As soon as she opened the door she felt better.

"Hey, you," Denise said as Stephanie smiled at her.

"Hey, superstar. You played your ass off, girl." Stephanie smiled at her friend. They had been getting to know each other better. If Denise ever asked, she planned on saying yes.

"Yeah, it was OK. Would have been better with you out there." Denise sat in the chair next to Stephanie's bed. "Stephanie, I don't know what to say."

"There's nothing to say besides, a drunk driver ruined my chances of ever playing ball again." A tear rolled down Stephanie's face. "I may not be able to walk right again."

Denise's heart was breaking in front of her. She had always taken her skills for granted, never realizing they could be gone the next day.

Denise grabbed her hand. "I guess you're going to have to come home with me, so I can take care of you." Denise smiled.

Stephanie turned red. "Last thing you need to do is worry about a handicapped chick." Stephanie smiled back.

"Steph, you know it's not like that. I got your back always."

"Well, you won't have to this go-around. Maybe it's just not in the cards for us, Dee. My mom is coming to get me tomorrow. She's taking me back to Texas, where she moved."

Denise looked at Stephanie's face. She was getting butterflies. She hadn't felt them since she met Lena. "Stephanie, it scared the shit out of me when coach told me you were in the hospital."

Stephanie's heart to began race. "It scared me waking up in the hospital," Stephanie admitted. "Man, you just never know how things are going to change. It's like there are so many things I wish I would have done before this happened. Some people I wish I would have actually gotten to know. Man, when it happened I thought I was about to die 'cause the person just kept on hitting me over and over. The bad thing is that I thought to myself that if I was about to die I wish I would have apologized to some people, and spent more time with people." Stephanie looked at Denise. "You never know what turns your life is going to take."

Denise thought about what Stephanie was saying. "Steph, please don't lose touch with me."

"Of course, not."

Denise kissed Stephanie on her forehead. "See you around, Superstar." Stephanie smiled as Denise walked out the room.

Denise headed out of the hospital, but heard someone calling her name. She turned around to see Nurse
Paulette, the nurse who had taken care of her grandmother while she was in the hospital.

"Yeah, Ms. Paulette, how are you doing?" Denise said
as she hugged the small, older woman.

"I am doing just fine. I see you are doing well too.
Caught a piece of that basketball game the other day.
Are you going pro?"

"Well, hopefully. There are going to be a few people
looking at me during the tournament."

"I am so proud of you. You are such a strong girl. I
don't know how I would be able to go to school, play
sports, and deal with my mother in the state your mother is in. I just came to tell you that they moved her to the
twelfth floor, you know, since she has gotten to the point
that she is."

Denise didn't know what to say. She didn't want Paulette to know that she didn't even know her mother was
in the hospital. "Oh, thank you. Do you know the room
number?"

"1218." Paulette put her arm on Denise. "Now, I want
to warn you that she has gotten pretty bad this week. I
know that you probably don't want to hear this, but you
need to start getting preparations ready. There is no
way to come back now."

Denise nodded. She felt a twinge in her stomach realizing that Paulette just told her that her mother was
about to die. Denise hugged Paulette again and headed
to the twelfth floor.

As she made it off the elevator her hurt and anger
started to set in. She passed by many rooms, all quar-
antined. Denise looked at the door, knowing Tammy
was on the other side. She went to turn the handle, but
stopped. She turned around and walked away.

Chapter 34

"Well, I guess you're doing a good job here," Denise said approvingly as she looked around Mema's house. Shemeka had transformed it since the last time she was there. It looked like a home again instead of a crack house.

"Yeah, well, I did the best I could do. I had to keep the kids out for a while to clean, but it's home for us now." Shemeka was gleaming with pride. She was happy with herself.

Denise sat down on the sofa. There was no more plastic on it. She laughed to herself thinking of how Mema kept plastic on all the furniture. She sighed, thinking of how much she truly missed her grandmother. "It feels like I can feel her in here."

"Yeah, I know. I felt so funny sleeping in here the first few nights." Shemeka laughed.

"It was like she was watching me, wondering why I was in her bed."

"Shemeka, I must say that I am proud of you. You are really getting yourself together," Denise replied. She was glad that she and Shemeka were not fighting all the time.

"Yeah, it took a little while, but I'm all good now. My daddy wanted to move in, you know. I told him no. He wasn't too happy about that." Shemeka looked at Denise. She had her head down in deep thought. "You know, Denise, we can't really choose who our parents are. I love my daddy, but I know he is good for nothing. But if something was wrong with him, I would be there for him."

Denise sighed. She knew what Shemeka was getting to. "I know what you are getting at—"

"Do you?" Shemeka cut Denise off. "Do you know that your mother is going to die any day now? I saw her the other day and she looks terrible. I think she is trying to hold on until you come."

"I can't do it, Meka. Just yesterday I was standing at the hospital door. Man, I tried to go in, but I couldn't. She did that to herself." Denise tried to hold back her tears. "I can't forgive her. She did too much."

Shemeka sat down next to Denise. She put her arm around her. "Denise, you have a lot to look forward to in your life. You are going to go pro and do big things, but you will never truly be happy until you let go of all the bullshit. Hold on." Shemeka got up and headed to the back room.

Denise stood up and walked over to the mantel with all of the family pictures on it. She noticed a picture of her mother when she was younger. She was very beautiful before she got into drugs.

"Here it is." Shemeka handed Denise a book.

"This book is what got me to this point. I was at the library with the kids and a woman handed me this book. She said it changed her life, so I read it. This book helped me get over all the pain that I was holding in. I was finally able to get over all the hurt from my mother and my father and all those trifling men who left me with these kids.

"Your mother had the good sense to leave you with Mema. My mother had me in crack houses with her. I never told anyone, but she pimped me out for drugs one time when I was fifteen. She let her ex, Dante, rape me. Then I ended up getting pregnant by the monster. That's why I just took over my own life when I had my baby. You know who saved me from my mom?"

"Mema?"

"No, your mom. She saw me in the crack house once and went off. She got into a fight with my mother and everything. She got me out of there and took me to my father's house. It wasn't much better, but he didn't keep me around the shit, like my mother."

"Shemeka, I didn't know." Denise hugged her crying cousin.

"Well, now you do. My father only came around when it was convenient for him, and my mother didn't care about anything but drugs. Your mother cared enough to leave you in a positive environment, and to stay away so you could grow up differently. You gotta let that pain go."

Denise felt the tears start to flow from her eyes. She knew Shemeka was right. She took the book from Shemeka and headed out the house. She had some unfinished business to take care of.

When she got in the car she looked at the book. Shemeka had given her *In the Meantime* by Iyanla Vanzant.

Cooley was ecstatic when she left the school pharmacy. She had to flirt to get the information she needed, but she was successful in the end. She held the papers close to her body.

Cooley noticed a group of girls walk into the University Center. She glanced over at the women, obviously new sorority girls. They all were so happy to have on their sorority letters.

She smiled when she saw one girl in particular leave the group and walk over to her. "I thought you wanted to be a Chi Theta," Cooley said to the girl.

"Yeah, well, I changed my mind. AKA was the best choice for me, considering my mother is an AKA," Tara said as she popped the collar on her sorority shirt.

"Well, congrats. Y'all must be coming out."

"Yeah, in front of the university apartments. Are you going to come?"

"Maybe. I'll try to get out there."

Tara smiled. "I've been missing you, Cooley. I didn't think you were serious about never seeing me again."

Cooley laughed. "I told you I was. How's your man?"

"He's fine. He can't do me like you do."

"Of course, not." Cooley smirked. "It was good seeing you, shorty."

Tara put her hand on Cooley's. "Cool, how about one more time before the school year is out? After that I will never bother you again."

Cooley looked at Tara's frame. Even in jeans and a T-shirt she could see her unbelievable figure. "I'll think about it. How about that?"

Tara smiled. "I'll take that. Just don't think too long." She ran off when she heard her sorority sisters calling her name.

Cooley laughed to herself. It even boggled her mind why girls fell for her as hard as they did. She thought about the one girl she wanted to be with, Misha. If only she could get her back.

Cooley's eyes widened when she noticed Lynn walking in to the U.C. with another stud. She felt a little twinge of jealousy when she saw the girl put her arm around Lynn.

Lynn's whole body froze when she saw Cooley sitting at the table. She excused herself from her date and walked over to Cooley. "I didn't know you were going to be in here. I would have nev—"

"You don't have to explain to me. You don't answer to me."

Lynn's faced dropped. "I know but—"

"No buts. So you did have a chick on the back burner, huh?" Cooley said, trying to stay calm.

"No, Cool, it's not like that. I just met her a few days ago. She asked me to come to the student movie with her tonight."

Cooley shrugged her shoulders. "I guess so. Go be with your li'l lame-ass date. When you're finished you know where to find me. I'm heading home." Cooley packed up her books and headed to the door.

As soon as she made it home there was a knock on the door. Lynn had stood her date up and headed to Cooley's house.

"What you doin' here?"

Lynn looked up at Cooley. "I don't want to be with her or anyone but you. I can't give you up that easy."

Cooley opened the door all the way and let Lynn in.

Lynn threw her arms around Cooley. "Please, Cooley, I just want you to know how much I care about you. I know you don't want a girlfriend, but don't you realize that I love you?"

Cooley didn't know what to say. She knew she cared about Lynn, but it wasn't the same way she felt about Misha. "Lynn, I love you too, but I'm not ready to commit to anyone. I can't make that commitment with you."

Lynn stopped listening after she heard Cooley say she loved her. She never expected to hear her say those words. "Well, I'm not going anywhere. Now, can you make love to me, please?" Lynn seductively walked back to Cooley's room. She decided that night she was going to let Cooley do whatever she wanted to her. After all they were in love.

Cooley was shocked by Lynn's openness.

They finally had sex for hours. Lynn let Cooley have complete control over her body. Cooley finally was satisfied after the sex with her.

They fell asleep in each other's arms.

Chapter 35

Lena sat under the dryer reading an *Essence* magazine. She was excited to read it because she wanted to see what number Brandon had gotten on the "25 sexiest athletes" list. She was gleaming with pride as she looked at her man. She knew things were about to take off now that he was considered sexy in print.

Someone walked toward her dryer. She figured it was her beautician coming to check her hair. "Is it dry?" she said, not looking up from her magazine.

"Um, I'm not here to check your hair." She looked up to see the woman who crashed her wedding.

Lena raised her dryer. She looked at the woman. "What do you want?" Lena felt her anger rising.

The other women in the shop began to watch and wonder what was about to go down.

"Look, I'm not here to fight with you. I just came to give you this." The woman dropped a packet on the floor. "You can pick it up by having this ticket. Have a nice life." The woman hurried out of the shop.

Lena grabbed the packet and opened it. Her heart began to race as she looked over the documents. She felt like she was about to have a heart attack.

"Girl, is everything OK?" Her beautician walked up to her.

Lena held up a picture. "I gotta go." She ran out of the beauty shop with rollers still in her hair.

***

"Who is it?" a weak voice whispered as the door opened.

"Tammy?" Denise said as she walked into the dark room.

"Denise?" Tammy slowly turned her head to see her daughter standing there.

Denise gasped at her mother's presence. "Yeah, it's me." She walked closer. Her whole body began to shake as she looked at her mother's sunken face and the lesions covering her face and arms.

"What are you doing here?" Tammy asked. "How did you know where I was?"

"Carmen told me that you weren't in Life Support. She told me that she'd been up here to visit you. I see you're hanging in there."

"I didn't think you wanted to see me. I wouldn't want to see me if I was you." Tammy turned her head away from Denise.

Denise fought back tears. "Why'd you hide this from me for so long?"

"I didn't want to complicate your life anymore than it was. You were busy with school, basketball, and taking care of Mama. I didn't want you to have this on your mind as well."

Denise looked down at her mother. She knew she was right. Denise was dealing with a lot during her first years of college. If she'd known about Tammy, she may not have been where she was then. "You got it from using?"

"I don't really know. I was hoin' and using. It could have been either one." A tear fell from Tammy's face.

"How long do you have left?"

"A few more weeks at the most."

"Damn!" Denise yelled as she hit the tray sitting next to her.

"Denise, listen to me. I don't want you to think about me. There will be a package sent to your house by Mema's attorney. It'll contain all you need. I don't want a funeral at all. I don't even want you there. You play basketball and go on with your life. I never was there for you, and that was my biggest mistake. But, Denise, I love you so much, and I only want what's best for you."

"How am I supposed to concentrate on the tournament or school with this on my mind?"

"Denise, there's nothing you can do. There is nothing anyone can do but me. So I'm doing what is necessary. Leave my room and never come back. You play ball and win that tournament and go pro. That's the only thing I can do for you now."

Tears rolled down Denise's face. "I can't just leave you here. You're still my mom."

"No, Mema was your mother. I'm the woman who had you. I was never there for you, and I regret that. But you need to do what is best for your future, and watching a junkie die ain't it. Now please, Denise, leave my room." Tammy turned her head toward Denise again.

Denise looked at her mother. She sucked up her emotions and walked toward the door. She turned around and looked at Tammy again. She called her name.

"Yes, baby?" Tammy said as she turned back around toward Denise.

"I forgive you for everything." Denise walked out the door. As soon as she made it to the elevator, she broke down.

Carmen opened the door to her room. Nic wasn't there. She felt her heart breaking. "No, no. I fucked up."

"Didn't expect to see you here." Nic walked into the room.

Carmen turned around. "I figured we needed to talk."

"We needed to talk two weeks ago. You didn't seem to care then!" Nic realized that she didn't do anything wrong.

"Nic—"

"Fuck you, Carmen. I told you not to go. I begged you not to go!" Nic was furious. "You want to look at the fact that La kissed me. What you did was ten times worse than a girl kissing me that I didn't even kiss back."

"I, I had to—"

"You know what I did when she did that? I fucking left the room and told her to never contact me again. That bitch cheats on you constantly, treats you like shit, and you run off to be with her. You leave me to go be with her! You ought to be glad I didn't fuck!"

"Nic, I had to go," Carmen cried.

"No, you didn't!" Nic yelled.

There was a knock on the door. She opened the door to see Lena standing there.

"Lena, what's wrong?" Nic asked.

Carmen walked to the door and saw the bloodshot eyes and dried tears on Lena's face.

"I didn't have anywhere else to go," Lena said as she began to sob. "Everything's over." She fell into Nic's arms.

Nic carried her into the room.

"Lena, talk to me. What's going on?" Carmen said as Nic put Lena on the bed.

She couldn't speak. She just handed Carmen the package that the girl gave her.

***

Lena's heart had dropped when she opened the package at the beauty shop. Inside were pictures of Brandon and this girl. She saw a picture of him putting his head to the girl's pregnant belly. The girl had also given her the child's birth certificate and social security card. Lena saw a letter with her name on it. She'd opened it when she got in her car.

Lena,

I know you are going to despise me for the rest of your life. I understand. I was the other woman who was with your man. I now know it was the biggest mistake I ever made. Brandon and I were together for three years. I didn't know about you until you arrived at Freedom. That's when I found out that Brandon had a main chick, and it wasn't me. But by then I loved him and was determined to keep him. Love makes you do some fucked up things, including get pregnant by a man who will never really love you.

Yes, the baby is Brandon's. As you can see from the birth certificate, Brandon took full responsibility for him. He even named him Jonathan Brandon Redding. I just knew that the baby was going to change things between us, but I was wrong.

Suddenly Brandon got a conscience and realized he wasn't going to lose you for anyone, not me or his own child. I do admit that he loves you very much, and he has paid me to get out of town. The only thing is that, per his contract, he paid ME to get out of town, but not his baby. So, I am leaving Jonathan with you and Brandon. It may be selfish, but I know that he will have a better life with you and Brandon than he will ever have with me.

I know that you probably don't want your husband's bastard child, and I'm sure that divorce is on your mind. But I want you to know that I was the only one. Brandon loves you and told me that he was never going to do this again to you. You are a lucky woman in the end. I had him part-time, but you have him forever. You can pick John up at Nanny's Day Care. I have enclosed paperwork signing over my rights to you. I have already signed them.

Lena closed the letter. She began to cry as she looked at the picture of the baby. It was the same picture she saw in Brandon's desk.

Something told her to forget it, but she couldn't. She picked the child up from the day care and headed back to her house. When the baby began to cry she broke down. She told the housekeeper to watch the child. She packed some of her things and left her home.

"That sorry son of a bitch!" Carmen yelled as she looked over the items in the package.

"I left the baby at my house with the housekeeper. I had to get out of there," Lena said.

"It's fine, Lena. We're here for you. Is there anything you want?" Carmen said.

"Yeah, Lena, you can stay here with us," Nic offered, looking at Carmen.

Carmen looked at Nic and turned back to Lena.

"No, this is the first place he is going to come. I don't want to see him. I want to go somewhere he can't find me."

All three of them knew there was only one place Brandon didn't know about.

Chapter 36

Denise lay down on her bed. Cooley sat in the chair next to her.

"Man, I know you are hurting right now, but I believe she did the right thing. Denise, you've come too far to give it all up now."

"Man, it's like I feel like I'm going to hell if I don't go spend all the last days with her."

"Naw, bruh, it's not like that at all. You're doing what she would want you to do. You staying here isn't going to help her live longer. You did the best thing you could do. You let her know that you forgave her. That's all she ever wanted."

"You know I got a call from the New York Liberty. They want me to come to their camp this summer. They want me."

"Hell, yeah. That's what I'm talkin' about. Shit, I wish you was gonna be closer to Miami. But, hell, we gonna be ballin', so we can visit each other." Cooley laughed as she tried to take Denise's mind off of Tammy. "Man, only a few weeks left."

"Yeah, I know. God this has been a long-ass year. I can't wait to fuckin' graduate and get the hell up out of here."

Cooley knew the time was right. "Bruh, there is something I have to show and tell you." She headed to her room and came back with a large envelope.

"What's all this?"

"Well, I'm only telling you this because of your safety. Man, I told you Rhonda was crazy, but you don't even know the half of it."

"Don't start that again."

"Dee, for real. Look, Dayza is Rhonda's suitemate. She told me that Rhonda be like yelling your name and listening to crazy music and shit. She said that Rhonda spazzed out after you left her alone the last time. She was like going off and shit to the R.A."

"For real?" Denise looked troubled.

"Man, for real. She said that Rhonda like rolled out and didn't come back 'cause they were going to call security on her. So we broke into her room."

"You broke into her room?" Denise said.

"Well, kinda. We just kinda popped the lock. Look, man, the important thing is what I found. Check this shit out." Cooley threw all the documents on the bed.

Denise started to look at the pictures and information.

"Man, the girl is fucked up. I did a check on her, and the bitch is bi-polar and manic depressive and some more shit."

Denise continued to look through the pictures. She noticed the picture of the drawer filled with info on her. "Is this in her room?"

"Hell, yeah. She got like a collection on you and shit. Oh, and look what I found at her crib." Cooley pulled out her shades. "You know what that means."

"Your room." Denise put her hands on her head. "How the fuck did I end up with the nutcase?"

Cooley laughed. "Kinda crazy, huh? The tables are turned for once."

Denise looked at Cooley. She was right.

"Man, I'm glad you found this shit out. I better not see that girl. She been up in my crib and shit. We need to get the locks changed."

"You bet not see her? Man, if I see her, I'm gon' beat the black off of her. Look what she did to my damn clothes. But I hear she hasn't been to her room in a while."

"Well, you know what, C, fuck it. I'd rather she stay away than attempt to come back into my life for any reason."

"I feel you on that."

Suddenly they heard a knock on the door. They both walked to the living room as Carmen opened the door with her key. Nic was carrying Lena.

"What the hell happened?" Denise exclaimed as she grabbed Lena out of Nic's arms.

"I'll explain everything. Take her to your room, please," Carmen said as she paced the floor.

Denise carried Lena to her room. Lena was crying hard. Denise couldn't make out anything that she was saying. She put Lena in her bed and headed back into the living room.

"You are fucking bullshitting!" Cooley yelled. "What the fuck did I tell y'all!"

Denise sat in silence trying to absorb everything that Carmen said. She was furious.

Carmen noticed the look on Denise's face. "Dee, don't even think about it," Carmen warned.

Denise just looked at her.

"Brandon is a bold muthfucka, I tell you. How the fuck he gon' let this shit happen? See niggas don't think shit out at all," Cooley said as she sat down on the couch.

"Well, I don't know what Lena is going to do," Carmen said.

"So, I guess she'll just stay here for a few days until she clears her—"

Cooley quickly interrupted Carmen, "Hell, no, she won't stay here! Man, Brandon ain't finna send people up here to get his wife. She need to go home and deal with that shit. She knew what she was getting into when she married his ass."

"Cooley, come on, that's fucked up!" Carmen yelled.

"No, it isn't. Come on, C, you know good as I do that Brandon already got static with Dee over Lena. If he finds out that his loving wife ran to the arms of Denise, he's going to be ready to pop off."

"He doesn't know where y'all live," Nic added.

"And he is a fucking superstar. He can find out where we live and anything else he wants to find out. I ain't down with this. Denise, say something!" Cooley yelled.

Denise raised her head. "She can stay here until I leave for Nationals. I'm sure she'll calm down in a few days." Denise got up and walked to her room.

Cooley cursed, but knew she had lost.

"Lena?" Denise said as she walked into her room.

"How could he, Denise, how could he?" Lena said. She finally stopped crying as hard, but tears were still streaming down her cheeks.

"Lena, I don't have the answer to that. But just try to get some rest. You want something to eat?"

Lena shook her head. "Thank you for letting me stay here. I heard y'all in the other room."

"It's no problem, and you know it. Now go to sleep."

Lena turned over and closed her eyes.

Denise headed back into the living room.

Cooley came out of her room with a bag in her hand. "I'm gonna stay at Lynn's tonight, a'ight. You can sleep in my bed." Cooley gave Denise daps and opened the door.

***

Misha finished packing her bags to go home. When she got off the phone with Carmen, she knew Memphis was where she needed to be right then. Misha couldn't believe Brandon had a child.

"You ready, baby?" Patrick said as he walked in the room.

Misha closed her suitcase. "Yeah, I am." She threw her arms around Patrick. "I am so sorry about this."

"No, baby, I understand your friends need you. I'll be praying for Lena and her situation."

Misha kissed Patrick. She that she had made the right decision. Patrick was her future. She was able to do what many women couldn't do: she was leaving the gay life behind her. "I love you so much."

"I love you too. Now let's get you on that plane."

Nic and Carmen drove in silence until Carmen broke. "I just can't believe this night."

"Yeah, it is real fucked up," Nic responded. "I feel bad for Lena."

"I know, and I can't believe that woman left her child like that. Nic, I know you're mad at me." Carmen shook her head in disbelief.

"Carmen, don't. I don't want to talk about it. I understand why you went. You needed closure."

"Nic, I'm sorry."

"Carmen."

"I felt guilty."

Nic looked at Carmen. "What do you mean? Guilty for what?"

Carmen began to cry. "I did that to her. I wished for her to experience the pain that I felt. I wished it all the time. I . . . I wanted her to be hurt."

"Baby, you can't put that on yourself. Carmen, that is not your fault. Tameka did that to herself."

"But I wished it on her. I should've been careful what I wished for. I never really wanted her or anyone to truly get hurt."

"It is not your fault. Why didn't you talk to me about this?"

"Nic, you get so emotional when it comes to her. I didn't want to make you mad."

"You made me mad by doing what you did."

Carmen put her hand on Nic's leg. "Baby, please, I am sorry. I need you. You make me whole."

Nic wrapped her arms around Carmen. "Baby, I love you more than I've loved anyone in my life. Just let me love you, Carmen, damn!"

"I've never had anyone to treat me the way you do."

"Carmen, if you just let me in. Baby, I'm not trying to hurt you. I just want to make you happy. I just want to give you all the love that you give to everyone else in your life. You don't deserve anything less. Let me love you, Carmen."

Carmen closed her eyes as Nic held her tight. Finally, she let go. The wall built around her heart finally broke down. "I love you, Nicole."

"I love you too, Carmen. I'm not going anywhere."

Denise heard Lena's footsteps heading toward her direction. She watched as Cooley's door opened. Lena stood there wearing nothing but a T-shirt.

Denise sat up in the bed, watching as Lena walked closer and climbed on top of her. Lena planted a sensual kiss on her.

Denise pulled back. "Lena we don't need to—"

"Denise, please, I need to feel good. You're the only person who makes me feel good. Please don't say no." Lena kissed her again. Lena straddled Denise. She began to grind against Denise's pelvis.

Denise wrapped her arms around Lena and returned the kisses. Their tongues stroked each other and aroused all of their senses.

Denise ran her hands down Lena's back, slowly pulling her shirt up over her head. She looked at Lena's perfect naked body sitting on top of her. Lena's breast sat up perfectly as though they were inviting Denise to devour them. She did.

Denise grabbed Lena's long ponytail and pulled her head back. She slowly sucked on Lena's neck as Lena continued to grind against her pelvis. Denise ran her hand down the front of Lena's neck until she reached her breasts. She just wanted to feel her. She massaged her breasts, using her index finger and thumb to play with Lena's nipples. They quickly became erect.

Denise slowly ran her tongue around Lena's right nipple, licking circles until she placed the whole nipple in her mouth. She sucked on Lena's breasts, keeping everything slow. She was not going to rush this experience at all.

Lena's body responded pleasurably. Denise could feel her own body becoming more and more excited with every touch.

Denise slowly picked Lena up and placed her on the bed. She stood up and held her hand, out. As soon as Lena grabbed her hand Denise scooped her up in her arms. She carried her to her room and laid her on the bed.

Denise undressed.

Lena had never seen Denise completely naked before. She studied Denise's curves. She didn't realize she had so many. She looked at the curve of Denise's ass. Her pussy reached the height of its wetness.

Denise pulled out a box. She took out her latex manhood and strapped it on. She looked over at Lena who had positioned herself in the middle of the bed. Denise put one knee on the bed as she raised Lena's leg. She licked her way to Lena's inner thigh, leaving her name branded on her leg forever.

Denise slowly opened Lena and felt her wetness. She smiled at how wet she made Lena. She slowly stroked her index finger in and out, using the index finger to entice Lena's clit, until Lena begged for her to taste her.

Denise gripped Lena around her ass and pulled her closer to her. She indulged in her sweetness. It had never been that sweet before. Lena continued to grind her pussy against Denise's tongue. Denise was impressed.

Lena's body jerked as she moaned, climaxing from the intensity of Denise's mouth and lip action, but this time Denise wasn't finished.

Denise stood up and placed a condom on her manhood. She prepared to enter Lena when Lena, stopped her.

"No, let me." Lena stood up and pushed Denise on the bed.

Denise watched in excitement as Lena mounted her. She slowly straddled the strap, beginning by slowly grinding. Lena slowly increased her speed.

Denise bit her lip. She had never been so enticed by a woman in her life. Lena definitely knew how to ride. The grinding against Denise's pussy caused her legs to tense up. Denise wrapped her hands around Lena's ass as Lena body-worked the strap.

Lena's breasts bounced up and down as she got more and more into it. She threw her head back and moaned.

She wanted more. She took more. Denise tried to maintain, but let out moans of ecstasy. Denise rose up as Lena continued to work her. She licked the sweat from Lena's stomach. She planted kisses all over Lena until they both could not take anymore and came.

Denise and Lena got in the shower together. The warm water hit their heads as they kissed and rubbed each other. Denise had to taste her again. She picked Lena up and placed her on her shoulders.

Lena placed her hands against the top of the ceiling as Denise penetrated her again with her tongue. Lena's legs gripped Denise's head as she came.

"Shit, Lena!" Denise yelled. "You cutting off my circulation."

They both laughed.

Denise put her down gently.

"My bad." Lena wrapped her arms around Denise and kissed her again.

They dried each other off and got into bed. Denise wrapped her arm around Lena's naked body. Neither of them needed clothes.

Denise kissed the back of Lena's neck. "I could lay like this with you forever," she whispered in the sleeping Lena's ear.

Slowly, Denise fell asleep.

Lena placed her hand around Denise's hand. "I could too," she whispered.

Chapter 37

Denise stood in front of the crowd of high-school seniors. The college was hosting a women's high-school basketball camp. Denise loved working with the young women trying to make it to where she was. She listened to her coach talk about how different college basketball was from high school. The coach called Denise to the front. Many of the girls' eyes widened, staring at Denise as though she was some sort of star.

"I prefer to answer questions, so feel free to ask," Denise said.

The young women's hands flew into the air. They started with the question everyone wanted to know: Was she going pro? Denise evaded the question, stating that she hadn't chosen what option she wished to take at that time, but that she was happy she had options, due to getting a college degree. She used that to begin talking about how important college is. Most of the women listened, but there were a few who were uninterested in anything besides the hope of going pro.

The side gym door opened. The bright light coming in made it difficult to see who was entering. Denise continued to talk until the focus was no longer on her, but on the tall pro basketball player that entered. The girls whispered and screamed as Brandon walked closer.

The coach, very surprised to see him, gave him a hug and introduced him to the crowd.

Denise headed to the bleachers next to Michelle.

"Guess you can't compete with that," Michelle stated since the girls were no longer interested in hearing from her.

Denise took a sip, trying to ignore Brandon, who was talking to the girls about the exact same thing she was just saying. She thought about Lena. "Nah, I think I can take the dude."

"Dig that then." Michelle laughed.

Just then the coach called for Denise to come over. Denise knew trouble was ahead.

"Yeah, what's up, coach?" Denise said. She tried not to make eye contact with Brandon, but could feel him eyeballing her.

"Nothing much. Brandon wants to speak to you, so y'all can take my office." The coach smiled.

Brandon and Denise headed into her coach's office. Denise watched Brandon sign autographs and take pictures with a few girls. He quickly excused himself and headed toward the coach's office. Brandon gave her an evil look as he passed her.

Denise shook her head. *Here we go.*

Two days had passed before Lena finally decided to check her voice mail. The messages started out calmly and ended horribly.

Hey, baby, I'm on my way home. See you soon, boo. Lena deleted the first message.

Brandon seems shocked in the second message. Bae, where the hell are you, and why are most of your things gone? Why the hell aren't you answering your phone? Lena, what the fuck is going on!

Lena could hear the baby crying in the background. Brandon was panicked now. *Lena, baby, I know you*

*are pissed, but please come home and let me explain.
Baby, don't do this. I'm so sorry. Just please answer
your phone. Please. I need you, please, baby. I'm
sorry!*

Lena started to feel worse with each passing message. Brandon sounded like he was completely distraught. *Baby, I'm dying without you. I can't eat. I can't sleep. I'm not whole without you. Baby, please.*

That message broke Lena's heart. She began to cry, wondering if Brandon was all right. She turned around and looked at a picture of Denise. She began to feel guilty. She knew she was no saint. She fell for Denise and let her have her body. She knew it wasn't as bad as what Brandon had done, but one sin isn't worse than the other.

She looked down at her ring. "For better or for worse." She knew what she had to do.

Lena heard the front door open.

"Knock, knock."

Carmen and Misha walked into the house.

"Hey, girls," Lena said as she hugged both of them.

Misha hugged Lena. "I'm so sorry I wasn't there for you. When Carmen called me, I took the first flight I could get."

"It's OK. I'm going to be OK."

Carmen poured them some wine. "Yes, we are all going to be OK."

Lena looked at Carmen. "Are you OK?" Denise had informed her of the situation with Nic.

Carmen sighed. "I'm great. Nic told me everything. She's such a strong woman. I don't know how she held all of that in for so long. But we're going to be just fine, and we are going to make it. Have you talked to Brandon yet?" Carmen said as she and Misha looked at Lena.

"No, I haven't talked to him. I know he is freakin' out right now. I just can't talk to him right now."

"I feel you on that. Fuck him. Make his ass sweat," Misha responded.

"Lena, what do you think you want to do?" Carmen said as she handed Misha a bottle of water. "I mean, are you going to get a divorce?"

Lena stared at the wall. "Why does this have to be happening to me? I never thought I would be considering divorce, especially not this early. I haven't even called my mother. She's gonna flip out, but I know she's gonna tell me to stay."

"Why do you think that?" Misha said, disgusted by the thought of a mother telling her daughter to stay in a bad marriage.

"Because that's what high-society wives do. They turn the other cheek. Hell, I've been turning the other cheek for years now." Lena looked at Carmen and Misha. She knew they both knew she was telling the truth.

"I always knew that Brandon cheated on me. I knew the whole time I was in Atlanta and he was here that he had to be getting it from someone. I know that on the road he's probably meeting a groupie or two, but I was content knowing I'm number one. But to know that this was an ongoing relationship, he was treating her like a girlfriend, not a groupie. He had a child by someone other than me. I've lost out on the chance to have his first-born because he already has a child."

They sat in silence thinking about the situation. "You know, back when I found the picture of the little boy, he could have come clean then, but he lied. I would feel ten times better if he would have just told me then."

"Well, we are here for you, no matter what you decide to do." Carmen placed her arm around Lena.

"Yeah, if you want me to get some homies from the neighborhood to kick his ass I will," Misha joked.

They all laughed.

Denise made sure to keep her defensive stand just in case Brandon wanted to get out of place with her. She could tell Brandon had been going through it. His eyes looked completely worn out.

"Denise, where is my wife?" Brandon said calmly.

Denise looked through him.

"Denise, tell me."

"I don't know," Denise lied nonchalantly. She could tell Brandon was close to blowing.

"Look, I already called Carmen and got cursed out a few times. I know she isn't in the dorms. No one has seen her. Now the only place I haven't checked is your place, and I just bet that's where I will find her." The aggression was present in his voice. "Now are you going to tell me where to find my wife, or am I going to have to do it the hard way?"

Denise felt herself becoming angry. "Man, don't come to me like that. You fucked up, and you have the nerve to come threaten me? You really have lost it."

Brandon slammed his hand against the coach's desk. Denise didn't flinch.

"Damn, Denise, I'm losing it. I need to talk to her. She isn't answering my calls. Now her voice mail is full. I just need to talk to her and work things out. I love her." Brandon sat down in the chair.

Denise could tell he was seriously hurting. "Look, Brandon, I don't know where she is for this very reason. You're predictable. She knew you would come here looking for her."

"Really? I wonder why she figured that. Y'all think I'm some sort of fool!" Brandon knocked over a chair and ran up to Denise.

They were standing face to face, but Denise didn't back down.

"Oh, is that right, huh? You men are all the same. You want to look at me 'cause ya girl left. Look at your muthafuckin' self," Denise said gravely. "You fucked up, not me!"

Brandon turned around and put his shades on. "I know the deal on you."

"What's that supposed to mean?" Denise questioned.

Brandon turned back toward her. "I know you've always wanted her. If I find out you had your dyke-ass hands on her, I'm going to kill you."

It took everything in her not to hit him. "Is that the best you can do, Brandon? You think a threat means anything to me? You're pathetic. You're married to a fuckin' diamond, but you go around fucking glass-ass girls. But you want to threaten me? Get the fuck out of my face."

"Yeah, well, it's my diamond. I can wear it. Hell, I wear it out nightly." Brandon smirked as he opened the door. "You'll never have it." He walked out the door.

"That's what you think."

Denise grabbed her things and headed out of the gym. She looked at her missed calls. One of the numbers looked very familiar. She called it back.

A young woman's voice answered, "St. Francis Hospital. How may I help you?"

Chapter 38

Rhonda peeked around the corner to see if anyone was coming. She walked in the back door and quickly ran up the dorm stairs. She was lucky. There was no one out on her floor. She quickly opened her door and went in.

"Bitches," she said as she noticed people had been in her room. Her bed didn't look the same. Nothing looked out of place, so she just let it go.

It felt good to lie in her dorm bed again, but it didn't have anything on the bed in the hotel she had been staying in for days.

She picked up a picture of Denise. "Oh, baby, I miss you. I know you have to be missing me." She planted a kiss on the picture. "We'll be back together soon."

She slowly drifted off to sleep.

"What's going on?" Cooley asked Dayza.

"Shhhh," Dayza hushed Cooley and pulled her into the room. "She's back."

"Oh, really?" Cooley felt the anger rising in her. "That bitch is about to pay."

"No, Cooley, you can't do it like that," Dayza said, grabbing Cooley's arm. "They will know I was involved. It can't be now. And how you expect to get those pill bottles back in there now with her there?"

"Look." Cooley pulled out her wallet. She handed Dayza one hundred dollars. "I need you to put these back whenever you know she's left. If by any chance she tries something, I got you."

"I don't give a fuck about her. I can take her in my sleep. I'm worried about getting kicked out of school."

"Day, you're a senior. You'll be out of school in another week," Cooley said.

Dayza realized she was right.

"Trust me, that bitch isn't going to get wrong with you."

"I got you."

They shook hands and Cooley left.

Cooley looked at Rhonda's door. She fought the urge to knock on it. *In due time that ass is mine.*

Denise got out of the elevator. This scene had become old to her. She made it to the nurse's station. "I got a call. My name is Denise Chambers."

The nurse's facial expression said it all. "I am sorry to inform you, but your mother has passed away."

"I figured that much." Denise was sad but didn't cry. "What do I need to do?"

Denise spent the next hour filling out paperwork.

"This was in your mother's room." The nurse handed Denise a bag of her mother's possessions.

Denise noticed a thick envelope addressed to her. Her heart began to beat quickly when she saw her grandmother's attorney's name on it.

Denise opened the package and found information alerting her about her mother's insurance policies. Mema had taken out three life insurance policies on Tammy years ago and had them paid up when she died. All together, the policies left almost $70,000.00 dollars to Denise.

There was a letter addressed to Denise. She sat back on the couch and read it.

Denise,
There are so many things that I want to say to you that I just don't know how to. If you are receiving this letter I have finally left this earth. I know that I have never been there for you, and hopefully I can make up for it when I get to heaven, if I go to heaven. I have always loved you and only hoped I did the best thing for you. I wanted you to grow up in the most loving environment possible, so I left you with Mema. I don't regret that decision when I see the woman you have turned out to be. My only dream is that I could have lived to see all of your dreams come true. I have messed my life up and hope that you will never follow in my footsteps. I just hope that you realize that I always did love you, and that never will change.

When I met your father he was a wonderful man. He got me back in school and helped me graduate. But then I was introduced to crack. He tried to get me off of it but I was hooked. He couldn't take it and so he left. I was so angry with him for leaving that I changed your name back to Chambers so that you wouldn't have his last name. That is a decision I have regretted till this day.

I am telling you this because I was so angry that I told you that he walked out on us. He didn't leave. I made him leave. He wanted to be there for you, and I wouldn't let him. You have every right to never forgive me for that. I wanted you to know that you are not an only child. Your father had a son before he met me. His name is Tony Matthews. Last time I checked he still lived in South Memphis with his family. His phone number is 901-311-1242. I encourage you to meet him. I hear he has a child.

I hope that time will heal all your pain that I have caused you. I hope that you will get any and everything that you ever want in life. I love you, Denise.

Your mother.

Denise closed the letter and held it to her heart. She decided that she was going to give her mother a small memorial service.

"I think I have decided to go home," Lena announced as the credits to *Imitation of Life* rolled.

"Damn." Carmen wiped a tear from her eye. She always cried on that movie. "Are you sure?"

"Yeah, Lena, there is no need to rush the decision," Misha added.

"Ladies, you know I'm not innocent either. I've been having sex with Denise. That's cheating too. If Denise was a boy we could have ended up in the same situation. I love Brandon, and if anyone is going to be there, it's going to be me. So tomorow I'm going home, but I'm going to make him sweat for the rest of the day."

They all laughed.

"That's so wonderful. I think that Brandon has learned his lesson. Poor boy sounds a mess on the phone. I say hold out until you get a rock like Kobe's wife," Misha said. "All of us are going to get exactly what we want. You and Brandon are going to be OK, Nic and Carmen are going to get married, and I am going to be paid in Atlanta. Give me some more wine." Misha held out her glass. She still hadn't told them about Patrick.

Carmen poured more wine. "Girl, I swear this drinking wine totally helps with my cramps."

"Shit, what day is it?" She looked at her calendar, gasping.

"What's wrong with you?" Carmen said, taking another sip of her wine.

Lena looked at both of them. "I'm late."

Michelle walked out of the gym and headed toward her dorm. She heard someone beep a horn at her. She turned around to see a white Mercedes. She pointed at herself, wondering if the person was honking for her.

Brandon rolled down the window and nodded.

"Hey, Brandon, what's up."

"Nothing much. Your name is Michelle, right?"

"Yeah."

Brandon nodded his head. "Yeah, I've seen you play. You got skills, yo'."

Michelle smiled. She took it as a major compliment coming from him.

"Look, you know Dee, right? I just got the good news from her that she's going pro."

"Word! Dee didn't even tell me that," Michelle smiled.

"Yeah, I want to deliver a gift to her, but I forgot to get her address. Do you by any chance know what apartments?"

"Yeah, of course." Michelle wrote down the address and some quick directions.

"Thanks for this." Brandon handed her some folded bills.

Michelle smiled at the three one-hundred-dollar bills. He drove off before she could thank her.

Chapter 39

"OK, so I bought three tests," Carmen said as she sat down on the couch.

"OK, I don't want to do this," Lena said as she paced the floor. She couldn't believe she might be pregnant. She wasn't ready to be a mother.

Misha looked at Lena. "Girl, if you don't go in that bathroom and take that damn test." She handed Lena the test.

Lena looked at them. "I don't want to take it alone." She looked at both of them. "You bought three tests."

Carmen laughed. "Girl, that would be a waste of ten dollars. If I'm pregnant, it would be Immaculate Conception."

"I don't care. I want y'all to take it with me."

Misha grabbed a test. "Fine. I'll go first." She walked into the bathroom as Lena headed into Cooley's bathroom.

The three girls waited for the tests to finish. Carmen smiled. "I'm gonna be an auntie. I just know it."

Lena frowned. "I don't think I'm ready to be a mother. Just 'cause I decided to go home doesn't mean that we're all right. We have a lot of things to work through."

Misha looked at both of them. "Lena, you would be a great mother." Misha thought about Patrick. She knew one day he would make a great father.

Cooley walked into the house. "What's up, y'all?" She looked at Misha and smiled. "Hey, Misha."

"Hi, Carla." Misha looked down at the floor. She still couldn't believe she let Cooley have her body again.

Cooley laughed. "You know only my most special girl can call me by my birth name."

"OK, Cooley." Misha smiled.

"You can call me Carla." Cooley winked at her and walked to her room.

Carmen laughed. "When are you going to realize that y'all are meant for each other?"

"What the hell!" Cooley yelled.

The three girls realized all three pregnancy tests were in her bathroom. They got up but Cooley walked into the living room. "Damn, did you have to take them in my bathroom?"

"Sorry, bro, we didn't know you were coming home," Carmen apologized.

Cooley shook her head. "Well, congrats, Lena."

Lena's heart dropped, "One was positive."

Cooley smiled. "Actually, two of the three were positive. I'm guessing buying that majority wins." She headed back to her room.

The girls stood in their spots, completely shocked by Cooley's statement.

Misha ran into the bathroom. She looked down at the three tests: Lena's and hers were both positive.

Carmen and Lena quickly followed. They both looked at Misha, who was holding her test.

"Misha?" Carmen said as she looked at her friend.

Lena looked at Misha. "Misha, how?"

Misha's heart was pounding. The whole room began to spin. She was pregnant.

Cooley looked back at the girls. Misha looked like she had seen a ghost. Cooley quickly realized what was going on. "Misha, you pregnant?"

Misha began to cry. She didn't know what to say. She turned around and looked at Cooley who was more shocked than the rest of them. "I—I have to go." Misha ran out of the room before anyone could stop her.

Carmen looked at Cooley. She could see the hurt in her eyes. "Cooley, are you OK?"

Cooley stood there looking at the pregnancy test that Misha dropped. She turned around and ran out of the door as well. Carmen tried to catch her but couldn't. She ran back inside and told Lena that she had to go follow Cooley.

Denise walked into the apartment to find Lena's bags packed by the door. Anger quickly set in as she remembered the chat with Brandon earlier. Lena came out of the back completely dressed.

"You going back to that fool?" Denise yelled.

Denise's anger caught Lena off guard. "Dee, I have—"

"So, what the fuck, huh, Lena? You fuck me then go right back to him. I can't believe I let you do this shit again!"

"Dee, you don't."

"You know what, you can roll. I'm tired of loving someone who doesn't love me back!"

Lena looked at Denise. "You love me?"

Denise looked at Lena. "Lena, are you that clueless? Lena, I have been in love with you since last year. I've been sitting back letting you put this train wreck on my heart, but I can't do it anymore. If you're going back to him, go, but don't bring yo' ass back over here when he fucks up again!" Denise stormed into her room and slammed the door.

Lena was in shock. Denise had never talked to her like that before. She felt her heart breaking as well. She lightly knocked on Denise's door. "Dee, I'm pregnant."

The door slowly cracked open. Denise walked out with a look of amazement on her face. "What?"

"I'm pregnant. I just found out." A tear fell from her eye. "Denise, a big piece of me wants to stay here with you, but another piece is telling me to go home to the father of my unborn child."

Denise put her hand on Lena's stomach. Her heart was breaking. "You're right."

"Denise, you will never know how much I care about you."

"Please, Lena, don't say anything else. Just go. Besides, your boy came to talk to me today."

Lena turned around in shock. "Oh my God. What did he do?"

"Nothing. He is real fucked up right now. I could see it in his eyes," Denise said.

Lena looked down. "Denise, you are the best friend a girl could ever have, and whatever girl you end up with is going to be the luckiest girl in the world."

"I'll always be there for you." Denise stood up and hugged Lena. For the first time she didn't feel that romantic spark between them.

They heard a knock at the door.

"That's probably Carmen. You won't believe what else happened," Lena said as she opened the door. She gasped when she saw Brandon standing there fuming.

Misha closed the door to her dorm room. She was drained. What had happened? She grabbed her stomach. She was holding Patrick's seed. Misha sat down on her bed and pulled a tiny box out of her purse. She opened it and looked at the three-karat diamond ring.

Patrick asked her to marry him over dinner their last night. Misha didn't know what to say, so she said she needed some time. She knew that wasn't the answer he expected, but he accepted it. Misha knew that she loved Patrick, but she didn't know if she loved him enough to be married to him.

Misha thought about the look on Cooley's face. She knew she had broken her heart. Misha began to cry. She didn't know what she was going to say to Cooley. She owed all of her friends an explanation. Misha heard a knock on her door. She opened it to find Cooley standing there.

"Carla," Misha said as Cooley walked into her room.

Cooley looked around the room. She noticed that Misha took down all of her pride paraphernalia. "So, the new switch in your ass was from some nigga!" Cooley couldn't explain the feeling she had. It was new to her.

Misha froze. She didn't realize how much Cooley loved her. "I'm so sorry, Cooley. I didn't mean for y'all to find out this way."

"Misha, what the fuck is going on?" Cooley looked at Misha's desk and noticed the ring. She picked it up and looked at Misha.

"He's my first love. The only man I have ever loved. We saw each other at Lena's wedding, and things just went from there."

"So, that's why you wouldn't get back with me. You went and got with some dude. You're engaged to a man?" Cooley felt her temper starting to flare

"I haven't said yes to him yet. But now, now I am going to tell him yes."

Cooley looked down. She felt tears trying to form in her eyes, but she quickly fought them off. "Have a good life, Misha." She started to walk out of the room.

Misha grabbed Cooley's arm. "Cooley, please. I don't want you out of my life."

"What the fuck you mean, you don't want me out your life? You picked some nigga. You been fucking some nigga and fucking me at the same muthafuckin' time! How the fuck you gon' do me like this? I fuckin' love you and you fuck me over again!"

Misha's heart dropped when she saw the first tear fall from Cooley's eye. She grabbed Cooley and pulled her into her arms.

"Damn, Misha, why the fuck you doing this shit to me!" Cooley cried. She was no longer the hard masculine Cooley. She was Carla, a girl whose heart was broken.

"I love you too, Cooley, but—" Before Misha could finish her sentence Cooley kissed her. Cooley wasn't going out that easily.

Misha wanted to resist, but she couldn't. She gripped Cooley tighter. Cooley raised Misha's skirt up and inserted her fingers inside of Misha. Misha let out a moan. Her nipples instantly became erect. Misha closed her eyes and let Cooley do her job.

Cooley stroked Misha's wetness. "No nigga can fuck you like this, Misha. No nigga can get you this wet."

Misha let Cooley have her body. She closed her eyes as Cooley fingered her, causing nectar to run down Cooley's hand.

"You know you love me. Say you love me!"

"I do love you," Misha cried. Misha thought she heard Patrick's voice in her head. She opened her eyes when she saw that Cooley had stopped. Misha turned around to see Patrick standing in the door, holding a dozen red roses.

Chapter 40

"Baby!" Lena exclaimed when she saw Brandon standing at Denise's front door.

Brandon looked at Denise then looked back at Lena. He quickly ran into the house and hit Denise.

Lena cried out for them to stop. Denise and Brandon were going head-to-head, fighting in the middle of the living room. Lena didn't know what to do. She was too small to break the fight up between them.

"I told you to stay away from her," Brandon yelled as he threw another punch at Denise, who ducked and hit him with a right hook.

"Brandon, Denise, stop it please!" Lena yelled as she tried to grab Brandon's arm. Everything went black as she met his elbow instead.

Denise and Brandon instantly stopped when Lena hit the floor. Fear struck both of them as Brandon ran to pick her up.

"Baby, Lena, baby, wake up," Brandon pleaded frantically as he tried to get her to open her eyes.

Denise grabbed some water and dabbed a few drops on Lena, causing her to open her eyes. Lena looked at both of them. Suddenly she let out a loud screech and grabbed her stomach.

"Lena!" Denise yelled at the sight of her friend in pain.

Brandon was frozen in one spot.

"Brandon, you gotta get her to a hospital." Denise hit Brandon to snap him back to reality. "Brandon, get her to a hospital. She's pregnant!"

Brandon's face dropped. "Oh my God, what have I done?" Tears rolled from his face. Brandon quickly picked Lena up in his arms and carried her out of the room. He continued to call her name.

Denise stood there, not knowing what to do. She looked around her shattered living room. She wanted to follow, but something told her to stay.

"Patrick!" Misha yelled as Patrick walked out the door. She put her pants on and ran after him. Misha caught up with him as he made it down to the front; she could hear him calling for a cab. "Patrick, please wait!"

"Misha, what's going on?" Carmen yelled as she ran up to the dorm.

Misha flew right past her.

"Get the fuck away from me, Misha. Now I know why you couldn't say yes to me. You're fuckin' with another man!" Cooley ran out of the dorm after Misha.

Carmen tried to grab her arm, but couldn't get her in time.

Misha grabbed Patrick's arm. "Pat, please it's not what you think. Carla doesn't mean anything to me," Misha said, oblivious to Cooley's presence.

Cooley froze when she heard Misha's words.

Carmen caught up to Cooley. She could see the pain in her friend's eyes.

Patrick turned toward Misha. "Carla? Carla? That was a fucking dyke?"

Misha could see the anger growing in him. "Patrick, please listen to me. I am so sorry. I am sorry."

"Fuck you, Misha!" Patrick yelled, causing many people to look at her. Patrick turned and looked at Misha with disgust. "I can't believe you did this, Misha. I loved you."

"Pat, I love you. I only want to be with you."

"I can't tell, with what I just saw!"

Patrick turned to walk away.

"Patrick!" Misha yelled. "Patrick, I'm pregnant!" Patrick stopped in his tracks and turned around.

Misha looked at him. She hoped it wasn't too late.

Chapter 41

"You're what?" Patrick turned around when he heard those words come out of Misha's mouth. He slowly walked back to her.

"I'm pregnant, Patrick," Misha said as tears rolled down her face. She never expected things to come out this way.

"Are you sure?"

"We took tests today. I have to go to the doctor to be sure, but my test came back positive. Patrick, just give me a chance to explain."

Misha noticed that something had caught Patrick's eye. She turned around to see Cooley walking toward her car. Patrick sped past her and ran up on Cooley.

"Pat, no!"

Before Misha could catch him, Patrick's fist met Cooley's face.

"Hold up!" Cooley said as she ducked past the rest of Patrick's attempted blows.

Misha grabbed Patrick's arm. "Baby, please stop."

"You been fuckin' with my woman!" Patrick yelled at Cooley.

"She was my woman before she was yours!" Cooley snapped back.

"Bullshit!" Patrick broke free from Misha and attempted to hit Cooley again. Cooley ducked, causing Patrick to lose his balance and hit the ground.

Cooley stood over Patrick. "Look, man, I don't know you and you don't know me. But I tell you one thing, you never have to worry about seeing me with yo' bitch again."

Cooley's words cut Misha like a knife. "Bitch?" Misha snapped at Cooley. She couldn't believe she just called her out of her name.

Cooley turned her anger toward Misha. "You heard me! You got this nigga trying to fight me and shit over your lying ass. I thought you were gay, Misha. Remember, you don't even fuck with bisexual bitches? But looks like you're just like them. A bisexual bitch!" Cooley walked over to her door.

"Cooley, that's fucked up. You don't even know the situation," Misha pleaded, forgetting Patrick was standing there.

"I don't give a fuck!" Cooley said as she got in her car. "Go be with that nigga. I'm out." She slammed her door and sped off.

Misha stood there looking at the spot Cooley's car was in. She suddenly remembered that Patrick was still there. "Pat," she said as she realized he was walking away. She grabbed his arm, but he pulled away.

"Misha, how could you? I thought you loved me. You're gay? You have been gay this whole time?"

"After you left I was gay. I've been messing with women ever since you left. But when you came back in my life, I realized I still loved you. I want to be with you."

Patrick snapped, "I can't tell. You practically lost it when that chick called you out. Misha, I don't think you know what you want!" The thought caused Patrick to go from angry to hurt.

Misha and Pat stood outside. The dorm steps were filled with onlookers wondering what was about to happen next.

"Can we take this inside?" Misha asked, not wanting anyone else in her personal business.

"No, you need to tell me something now. Do you want to be with me only? Can you give up women?"

Misha looked at Patrick. Her heart told her to say yes.

"I—I don't know," Misha stammered. She could see Patrick's face drop in front of her.

"Well, I guess we are done here." Patrick turned around and walked off.

Misha wanted to move, but she couldn't. Her whole body was frozen. She had lost everything.

Brandon and Lena stared at each other in silence. Lena could see the fear and hurt in his eyes. "Brandon, where is the baby?"

Brandon sighed and shook his head. "At the house with the nanny."

"And the mother?"

"Got people looking for her, but they haven't found her yet." Brandon wiped a tear from his eye. "Baby, I am so sorry."

Lena reached her hand out toward him. "Brandon, how could you do this to me? I was supposed to be your baby's mother. I was supposed to be the only one." Lena put her hand on her stomach. "Now we're waiting to find out if I've lost my baby because of you." Lena felt herself getting upset. After his fight with Denise, she woke up to find herself in a hospital bed.

"I'm sorry, baby. I don't know what to do or say. I fucked up so bad and then to find out you were with her. I, I just lost it. I thought you—"

"So, because you've been cheating on me and dogging me out, you thought I was going to go and fuck off on you in retaliation! Even if I was, could you blame me? It's not like you wouldn't have deserved it!"

Brandon sat there in tears, like a little kid listening to his mother yelling at him.

"I always knew you were fucking off on me. I always knew that you had side flings. But, no, you had a relationship with this girl, and she had your baby. You don't give a fuck about me!"

Before Brandon could respond, the doctor walked in. "OK, I am happy to say that you are stabilized and that you did not lose your baby. I am placing you on immediate bed rest for the next few weeks, just to monitor your activity though. No stress, you hear me?"

Lena and Brandon nodded in response.

"Don't worry, doctor, I'm not going to let her lift a finger." Brandon stood up and shook the doctor's hand.

"Great. Well, I will send the nurse with the release papers. Remember, Mrs. Redding, no stress, OK?"

Lena nodded, knowing that stress was something she was bound to have.

When the doctor left the room, Brandon looked back at Lena. "I know right now there is nothing I can say. I love you, Lena, and I have always only loved you. I fucked up big time, and I'm willing to spend my lifetime making it up to you. Just don't leave me. I can't be without you." Brandon fell to his knees at Lena's bedside. "You're my earth."

Lena wasn't trying to hear him. "We'll keep the baby until you find the mother. I will come home so I can rest. You know, the funny thing is, I was coming home to you today. Then you had to come show your ass."

"Baby, I fucked up. I was so lost. I didn't know what to do. Then that girl told me that you were with Denise, and I lost it."

Lena turned her head to Brandon. "What girl?"

Brandon looked up at Lena. "Denise's ex-girlfriend. She told me that she caught you all together, and I lost it."

"What!" Lena got up out of the bed. "Brandon, that girl didn't catch me with anyone. She was trying to start some shit."

Brandon grabbed Lena by her waist. "Look, I know you're angry, but no stress. You're coming home, and we can deal with this later. I will take care of Denise."

Lena looked at Brandon. "I just want you to know that it's Denise that kept us together. She told me to go back to you. Think about that." Lena walked out the room and went to sign her papers.

Brandon stood in one spot, realizing he had made a big mistake.

Chapter 42

Denise couldn't get off of the couch. She had too much in her head for one day. She heard the door open. Cooley and Carmen walked in.

"What the hell happened in here? Why the fuck are you bleeding?" Carmen said as she ran to the bathroom. She came back with a cold towel.

"Well, Brandon and I just got into a fight."

"What the hell is going on today?" Carmen said.

Cooley sat on the couch next to Denise. "Man, I just got into it with Misha's fiancé," she said in disbelief.

"What?" Denise was confused. "Please don't say anymore. I got too much going on now. Tammy passed."

Carmen put her hand over her mouth. "Dee, are you all right?"

"Lena is in the hospital. Brandon hit her."

"What!" Cooley and Carmen both said.

"It was a mistake. It happened while we were fighting."

"Oh my God. Let me call her." Carmen headed into the kitchen to call Lena.

Cooley looked at Denise. "What the fuck is going on, bruh?"

"Tell me about it," Denise responded. "My mom died, Misha is straight or bi or something, and Lena is pregnant. What the fuck is really going on?"

"Oh yeah, Misha is pregnant too." Cooley began to laugh hysterically. "And don't forget about your stalker."

Denise began to laugh too.

Carmen came back into the room and looked at them, wondering what was wrong.

"Lena is OK. The baby is OK." Carmen sat on the couch. "This is some strange shit."

Cooley stopped laughing. "Man, y'all, out of all the women who I have been with, the one that I fall in love with leaves me and starts to fuck with a man. Karma is a bitch, I guess."

"Yeah, and out of the women that I actually start to deal with one is psycho and the other is married with a child on the way." Denise had to laugh. "Shit. That's supposed to be your ass, Cooley."

Carmen began to laugh as well. "My friends. I swear I need to write a book."

Cooley and Denise laughed with her.

Nic walked into the apartment, looked at the three of them, and wondered what was wrong with them. "What did I miss?"

The question made everyone laugh harder.

"Nothing, man, have a seat," Denise said motioning for Nic to take a seat in the chair. "So, are y'all OK?"

Carmen sighed. "We will be. Isn't that right, baby?"

Nic smiled. "That's right. How are Lena and Misha?"

Cooley rolled her eyes.

Carmen frowned at her. "Don't act like that now 'cause you got played. It wasn't like y'all was together or anything. Misha is grown. She can do what she wants to do and who she wants to do."

Cooley couldn't respond. She knew Carmen was right. "Man, I got played."

Everyone started to laugh again.

Denise stood up. "I can't believe that nigga came up in here trying to jack."

Carmen smirked. "Whatever, Dee. Don't act innocent. We all know what you been doing with his gal."

Cooley began to laugh again. "Damn, that's right. That nigga had an ass-kicking for you, just for the wrong reason."

"Yeah, whatever."

They all laughed. That's all they could do.

Chapter 43

"Hey, sweetie," Misha said as she walked into Lena's bedroom.

Lena smiled. "Hey, girl. Come over here and lay with me."

Misha walked over and climbed onto the bed.

"Do you want anything?"

Misha shook her head.

"Well, how was the doctor's appointment?"

Misha felt tears forming in her eyes. "I'm pregnant. And I have lost the only man and only woman I have every truly loved. I fucked up."

Lena placed her arm around Misha. "I can't lie, baby, you fucked up. But if you love that man, you need to go to him. But if you know that you are not going to be fully satisfied, then you need to let him go."

Misha knew that Lena was right. "Lena, I have never been so happy before in my life. When I am with him, I am happy, just like when we were kids. But at the same time, I still am attracted to women. I don't know if I am going to slip up again like with Cooley."

"Misha, I understand," Lena said as Misha laid her head on her lap. "I am, after all, in love with a man and a woman."

Misha raised her head up. "Denise?"

"This doesn't leave this room," Lena said as she lowered her voice. "I love Brandon. I truly love Brandon. But after being with Denise, I admit that I love her too.

I wanted so much to be with her. She makes me feel like I have never felt before. But I made the decision that here is where I am supposed to be. I value my friendship with her too much to jeopardize it again. And I love Brandon's lying ass so much that I am willing to give him a second chance."

"But why would you think you couldn't be with Denise? You know she loves you too."

"Because my heart truly belongs to Brandon. She only holds a piece of it. Brandon holds the most. If he didn't, I wouldn't still be here. So, Misha, you need to figure out who truly has your heart, Patrick or the lifestyle."

Misha laid her head back down on Lena. She knew that she was right. She had a decision to make, but she wondered if it was too late to turn back.

Cooley sat in Lynn's dorm room. She looked around at her desk. She had pictures of them in frames. Cooley laughed at a picture that Lynn took of her sleeping. She realized that Lynn really did love her. She just didn't feel the same way. Cooley loved Lynn, but she was not and never would be in love with her.

Lynn walked into the room in her robe. "Just give me a few minutes to get dressed." She pulled the robe off in front of Cooley.

Cooley looked at her body. It was nice, but it wasn't the best she had seen. "Lynn, why do you like me so much?" Cooley asked.

Lynn turned around and looked at Cooley. "What do you mean?"

Cooley looked down at the picture of her sleeping. "Just what I said. Why do you like me so much? I'm just an average type of nigga. I ain't worth shit. So, why you choose to be with me, even though you know we ain't together?"

"Cooley, I don't know. There's something that I see in you, I guess. That first day at the bookstore, I felt this attraction to you that I don't usually feel with anyone. I knew then that you were going to be someone special in my life."

Cooley looked at Lynn. She could tell that she meant it. "Lynn, after graduation I'm leaving for Miami. I'm moving there, and I'm going to be in a very fast-paced industry. I kept telling you, we aren't together, because I didn't want you putting too much into me. I don't know what the future holds, and I didn't want you to ever place all your marbles in my bag."

Lynn pulled her shirt over her head. "Cooley, I hear you. I do admit that I don't want you to move 'cause I care about you. But I've been looking into some things, and maybe things will work out. I have faith that one day soon you'll realize how much I love you and give yourself to me completely."

"I don't see—"

"Just let things happen, Cooley. Stop thinking so much and just go with things. That's what I do." Lynn smiled.

"Lynn, seriously, I'm telling you this as a friend. You gotta think with your brain, 'cause the heart and emotions get people into trouble. No matter what happens with us in the end, I just want you to know that I do value you as a friend."

Lynn didn't know what to think about Cooley's statement, but she just smiled and let it go.

They headed out the door to the movies.

Chapter 44

A week had passed, and Misha found herself standing on Patrick's doorstep.

Misha was sitting in her dorm room packing up all of her belongings. She found a picture of herself and Cooley together. They had taken it right after she crossed into Chi Theta Sorority. Usually she got butterflies when she looked at that picture, but this time she felt nothing.

She turned and looked at a picture of herself and Patrick. It was taken at Lena's wedding. She looked at him in his suit and her in the bridesmaid's gown. They looked beautiful together.

Emotions began to flood through her body as she realized that she had made a big mistake. She constantly tried to contact him, but he would never answer her calls.

After she had filled up his voicemail on his cell and home phone, she realized there was only one thing to do. She borrowed Lena's car and drove to Atlanta. Now, here she was, standing on his doorstep.

Misha rang the doorbell a few times. She looked in the garage and saw Patrick's car in there. She realized he just wasn't coming to the door.

"Patrick!" she yelled at the top of her lungs. "Patrick, I'm not leaving until you come out here!" Misha realized neighbors were starting to look out their windows, but she didn't care. She rang the doorbell again, until she heard the door unlock.

"What are you doing here, Misha?" Patrick stood in the doorway blocking her so that she couldn't come in.

"I need to talk to you. You wouldn't answer the phone."

"I don't think we have anything to talk about." Patrick went to close the door when Misha yelled out.

"Patrick, it's you. You have me and my heart. I want to be with you and our baby."

Patrick opened the door back up. "Why, Misha? Just a week ago you were kissing a fucking woman. Why you want me now?"

"Patrick, I can't lie and say that I don't have an attraction to women. Just like you will always be attracted to other women, I will too. But it's about acting on it. I don't have the urge to act on it. I love you and you only. You have held my heart all these years, and you still hold it."

Patrick looked at Misha. "How can I know that in a few months you won't want to go sleep with a girl?"

"Because you love me, and I love you. Just like I know that you are not going to go sleep with another woman. It's trust. I trust you."

"I don't think I trust you anymore, Misha. I saw a girl doing you!" Patrick yelled.

"I know, and it was a mistake. I was emotional and it happened. But, baby, I promise you it will never happen again." Misha grabbed Patrick's hand. "Please give me the chance to make it up to you. Let me earn your trust back."

Patrick looked at Misha. He shook his head. "I'm sorry, Misha, but I can't. It's over. I'll be there for you and the baby, but I can't be with you. Now, please leave." Patrick slowly closed the door, leaving Misha in tears.

Lena and Brandon sat on the couch watching *Law and Order*.

Brandon looked over at Lena. "Lena, I want to ask you something."

"Yeah?"

"Baby, I fucked up, more than once. You've been there for me through it all. But I can't help but have the feeling that you have tip-toed out on me at least once."

"Bran—"

"No, let me finish. If you have, I can't blame you. I haven't been all I should be to you. Yeah, it may hurt for you to tell me, but I would rather know than not know. So, we can start over fresh."

Lena looked at Brandon. She knew she needed to tell him the truth. She turned to tell him everything about her relationship with Denise. "Brandon, you're right. I deserved to go out and mess around, but I promise you I haven't."

Brandon's face lit up. He kissed her on her forehead. "I love you so much, baby. I'm going to get a water, you want something?"

Lena nodded.

Brandon headed to the kitchen.

Suddenly Lena heard a baby crying. She had been in her room for weeks and had almost forgotten there was a baby in the house. She followed the sound to the guest bedroom. The nanny was giving the baby a bottle.

"May I?" Lena asked the woman, who gladly handed the little boy to her. She held the baby in her hands and fed him the bottle. Lena lit up inside. For the first time, she truly felt motherly.

"You look so beautiful doing that."

She turned around to see Brandon standing in the door, smiling. "He is a beautiful baby," Lena said as she caressed his soft curls. "What's the status on the mother?"

"Still haven't found her. They think she may have left the country," Brandon said as he walked closer. "I guess we got some things we need to talk about."

"Yes, we do." Lena sat down in the rocking chair. "Brandon, I love you, and I want to make this work."

Brandon's face lit up. "Baby, are you serious? I will do anything."

Lena smiled. "First, we are going to go to counseling. Second, you are going to do what you have to do to get legal custody of this boy. We are going to raise him."

"You really want to raise him?" Brandon questioned.

"Yes, he is going to be our baby's big brother. We will raise him as our own. And there is one more thing. You need to apologize to Denise for what you did."

Brandon sighed. "You're right, I do owe her an apology. I will do it when she gets back in town." Brandon kissed Lena on her forehead. "Lena, you are my earth, you know that."

"Let's hope you don't forget it again." She raised her head up so that he could kiss her on her lips. Things were finally looking positive.

Chapter 45

Denise sat in the chair with her cap and gown on. Graduation was bittersweet for her. She was happy that she finally did it, but the one person she wanted to see her graduate was not there. A tear fell from her face as she thought about her grandmother. She knew she had to be smiling from heaven.

Denise walked across the stage. People in the stands roared as they called her name. Denise turned her tassel to the other side. She felt intensely proud of herself. She quickly snapped the graduation picture at the bottom of the stage.

Denise yelled as they called Cooley and Carmen's names. She couldn't help feeling proud of them as well. They had experienced and endured so much together over the years.

At the closing of the ceremony, the class stood up and threw their hats in the air.

Denise didn't throw her hat. A picture of her grandmother was taped to the inside. She pressed the cap to her heart instead.

"Bruuuhhhh!" Cooley yelled as she hugged Denise.

"Y'all turn around and let me take a picture," Carmen said, wiping the tears from her eyes.

"She been crying all day," Cooley said.

"I'm sorry, I can't help it," Carmen said as she snapped the photo.

"Leave my baby alone," Nic said as she wrapped her arms around Carmen. "Let me get a group picture of you all, the three amigos." Nic snapped the picture of the trio.

"That was beautiful."

They turned around to see Lena standing there.

Carmen had Nic snap a picture of her and Lena. Denise watched as Lena smiled for the camera. Their eyes met. Lena walked up to Denise.

"Hold up, let me get a picture of you two," Carmen said.

Denise wrapped her arm around Lena as they posed for the picture. She felt a warm sensation take over her body.

"Let's give them some privacy," Cooley said. "Besides, I want to meet Nic's family. I know it's gotta be some sexy girls in it."

"Hey, stay away from my cousins, Cooley!" Nic yelled as they ran off.

"Dee, I am so proud of you." Lena smiled.

"Thanks. I'm a little proud of myself."

"Dee, I just wanted to tell you—"

"Lena, please don't. Don't apologize, don't tell me how you feel, just don't do anything. My heart can't take much more right about now."

"So, do you think we will ever be able to be friends again?"

Denise shook her head. "Lena, you mean a lot to me, and I will never forget you. You are going to be a great mother, and I know your baby is going to be the most beautiful baby in the world. But I can't be friends with you. I can't be friends with the woman I'm . . . that I'm in love with." Denise hugged Lena. "I wish you nothing but the best."

Lena fought to hold back tears. She didn't want to let go. "I wish you the same."

Denise finally let go.

Lena watched her walk away. Denise never looked back.

Misha threw her gown and cap on the bed. She was glad the graduation was over. She broke down crying when Cooley walked across the stage. She didn't stay for pictures. She didn't have any family to be with. She realized she'd lost her chance to have a family again.

Misha looked around her dorm room. Everything was packed. She was supposed to leave for Atlanta the day after graduation. Now she had no idea where she was going to live or go. She heard a knock on her door. Misha opened the door to find Cooley standing there.

"Look, I am not in the mood right now if you are coming to yell at me," Misha said as she walked back into her room.

Cooley closed the door behind her. "I ain't here to yell. I'm here to apologize. I'm sorry about that incident. I admit that I was hurt. I reacted real badly." Cooley sat on the bed next to Misha.

"I'm sorry about everything too. I don't know what's wrong with me." Misha began to cry.

Cooley wiped the tears from her face. "Nothing is wrong with you. Everyone fucks up from time to time. So, are you really pregnant?"

Misha nodded. "Yes, and he doesn't want to have anything to do with me, unless it's dealing with the baby."

Cooley looked at Misha's facial expression. She realized that she had truly lost Misha. "You really love him. I can tell."

"I do, Cooley. I can't even lie. I have loved him for years. He was my first, and I wanted him to be my last. But I fucked it all up." Misha buried her head into Cooley's chest.

Cooley put her arms around her. For the first time she was in complete friend mode with Misha.

"Now I know how Dee felt about Lena." Cooley sighed. "He'll come around. Just give him some time. You will be OK." Cooley stood up. "I gotta go. See you tonight at the party, right?"

Misha shook her head. "Yeah, I'll be there. Cooley, thanks for this."

"Anytime." Cooley put her shades on and walked out the door. She finally let Misha go, and it hurt like hell.

Chapter 46

Cooley pulled out all the stops for the graduation party. She called in some favors with Super Sonic and had her perform at the party. The party was in the campus ballroom, which was also a big surprise. It was definitely the party of the year.

Cooley saw Lynn walking toward her. "What's up?" Cooley hugged her when she walked up.

Lynn smiled. "I have something to tell you later." She kissed Cooley on her lips and headed off toward her friends.

Denise walked up and put her arm on Cooley's shoulder. "Have I told you that I am proud of you?"

"Why is that?" Cooley said to her friend.

"Because while I have been up here dealing with drama, you have been in chill mode with a great girl. You have totally impressed me."

"Don't read anything into Lynn. I am not with her. I'm still single." Cooley smiled.

"Yeah, OK, well, I am still proud of you. We did it. We made it through school, and we are going on to do big things." Denise hugged Cooley.

Carmen walked up behind them and wrapped her arms around them. "I love you guys so much!" she exclaimed. Carmen had been sentimental since they got to the party.

"We love you too, boo boo," Denise said as she kissed Carmen on her forehead.

"I don't know what I am going to do with you all so far away—"

Cooley quickly cut her off. "Damn, C, not tonight. We're supposed to be partying. Save that shit for tomorrow." Carmen hit Cooley on her arm and gave her a kiss on the cheek.

The party continued through the night. All of the Greek organizations were present. The sororities were doing their strolls, and the fraternities strutted through the crowd.

Cooley caught the eye of Tara, who was in the middle of the AKA stroll line.

Tara excused herself from the line and walked over to Cooley. "So, I guess I didn't get it before your graduation. Is it still too late?" Tara asked seductively.

Cooley looked at Tara. Her body was banging in her low-cut shirt. "There's a possibility I can still let you cash in that rain check." Cooley winked her eye.

Tara smiled. "How about meeting me at my room in thirty minutes?"

"I'll see you then." Cooley turned around and headed toward Denise. "Dude, I will be back in a little bit. I gotta go handle someone."

"All right. Be careful," Denise warned as she continued to dance.

"Cooley!" Lynn ran out the door when she saw Cooley walking out with Tara. She caught them right in time.

"Lynn, what's up?" Cooley said nonchalantly.

"What are you doing?" Lynn said.

Tara stood to the side to see what was going to happen.

Cooley walked up to Lynn. "I'm about to go kick it with her."

"But what about us?"

"What us? Lynn, how many times have we gone through this?"

"So, you mean to tell me it really is that simple for you? You can just go off and be with the next girl after spending all this year with me?"

"Lynn—"

"Don't 'Lynn' me. Cooley, I have held out for you all this damn time."

"I told—"

Lynn quickly cut Cooley off again. "Don't tell me what you told me. Your actions spoke a hell of a lot louder than your words!"

Cooley wanted to hug Lynn and apologize for hurting her, but something in her was holding her back. "Look, you knew the deal when you got into this with me, so I don't know why you acting new. I'ma holla at you, shorty." Cooley turned around and grabbed Tara's hand.

"One day someone is going to get you for the hurt you have caused me, you cold bastard!" Lynn yelled as Cooley walked down the steps.

Cooley ignored the comments.

Dayza headed out her door to go to the party. She noticed Rhonda walking out of her door as well.

"Rhonda, I didn't know you were back. How are you doing?"

"I'm fine," Rhonda snapped. She was in a rush to get to the party to see Denise.

"Oh, well, I was worried about you." Dayza played her role. "You goin' out?"

"I'm going to the graduation party."

"Oh, OK. I'll be there too. Shit, I left my wallet. I guess I'll see you there."

Rhonda walked off. She didn't have time to wonder why Dayza was finally speaking to her. She hurried down the steps.

Dayza waited for her to disappear before running back into her room. She pulled out a credit card and quickly popped the lock on the door. She placed the pictures they had taken back into the drawer.

"What the fuck are you doing in my room?" Rhonda yelled as she rushed toward Dayza.

"Back, back, bitch!" Dayza said, holding her guard.

"What were you doing with my stuff? I'm calling security!" Rhonda yelled.

"Yeah, OK, you do that. And when you do, I will tell them how you have been stalking Denise Chambers. I'll let them know how you broke into their apartment and fucked up Cooley's clothes."

Rhonda froze. "How you know all that?"

"Bitch, you're busted!" Dayza said. "Cooley is going to blow the lid wide open on your ass. Denise is never going to talk to you again!"

"No, stop it! Shut up!" Rhonda yelled. The room began spinning. She couldn't let that happen. She had to stop Cooley.

Rhonda ran out of her room but froze when she saw Cooley walking with a girl she knew named Tara. Her first reaction was to go hurt Cooley, but then she realized something. Tara had a boyfriend, and Cooley had a girlfriend.

Rhonda took the steps to her dorm room to avoid running into them. She peeped around the corner and watched Tara pull Cooley into her room. Rhonda's eyes brightened. Maybe she was going to have her revenge after all.

Rhonda headed into her room and pulled out the campus directory. She knew Tara's boyfriend's name. She quickly found his dorm number.

A male voice answered the phone.

"Is this Tyrone?" Rhonda tried not to laugh.

"Yeah, who is this?" Tyrone said, trying to figure out who was calling him so late.

"Let's just say a good friend. Look, your girl is in her dorm room right now with a dyke. She is getting her pussy ate, and the girl is making her moan more than you ever could."

Rhonda hung the phone up. She knew her work was almost done.

She picked up her phone again and called Lynn's number. She got the voice mail; she realized she must still be at the party. Rhonda was about to hang up when she heard Lynn say her cell phone number on the message. She quickly hung up and got on the computer.

Rhonda went to send her a text message via the Internet so that it could not be traced.

Cooley is fucking a girl right now in Jefferson Hall room 603.

She pressed send. Rhonda lay back on her bed. Vengeance would be hers.

Chapter 47

The party finally ended around three o'clock. Denise looked around for Cooley, who never made it back to the party. The whole gang decided to head to the dorms together, since Denise's car was parked at Jefferson, where Nic and Carmen lived.

"That party was off the chain!" Carmen said as she wrapped her arm around Denise.

"Yeah, it was. Where the hell is Cooley?" Carmen questioned, realizing Cooley wasn't with them.

"You know Cool. She is fuckin' someone right about now. She told me she was going to hook up with someone, but I figured she would make it back to the party, since she planned it."

"Well, you know Cooley. What the hell?" Carmen noticed a crowd of people in front of Jefferson Hall. "I wonder what's going on."

Dayza saw Denise coming. "Dee, it's Cooley. Dude is beating her up."

They all ran up to see Cooley on the ground getting stomped by a large football player. Denise and Nic ran to pull the guy off of Cooley.

He turned and hit Nic.

Soon both Nic and Denise were pounding him.

Carmen quickly attended to Cooley, helping her get on her feet. Cooley, filled with adrenaline, ran to jump in as well. They kicked him until they got him on the ground.

"How the fuck did this happen?" Denise asked, catching her breath.

Dayza looked at the dormitory door. She saw Rhonda peeking out, smiling. She pointed up at the door. "That bitch called dude and told him Cooley was fucking his girl."

Cooley looked up and saw Rhonda's face go from happy to terror-filled.

Rhonda turned to run toward her room.

"That bitch is mine!" Cooley yelled as she and Dayza ran up the stairs.

Denise and Nic ran after them.

"Shit." Carmen threw her hands up over her head and followed.

Rhonda struggled to get her door open. She made it in thinking she was safe, until a strong kick to the door caused her to fly into the wall. Cooley stood menacingly over her. Rhonda was terrified.

"So yo' ass wanna play?"

"I didn't do nothing!" Rhonda yelled.

"You broke into my crib. You fucked up my clothes. Bitch, you fucked up big time."

"I didn't—"

"Shut the fuck up."

"Yeah, bitch, I told you that yo ass was toast!" Dayza yelled as Denise and Nic ran into the room.

Denise pulled Cooley back. "Bruh, let it go. She ain't worth it."

"Fuck that, Dee! This bitch got the game wrong."

No one noticed Rhonda standing up.

"Oh shit!" Dayza yelled as Rhonda slipped into the bathroom. "That's OK. You can get her through my bathroom."

Rhonda was cornered. If she could get out of the bathroom she could get to a knife to fight her way out. A shiny object caught her eye, a razor. She picked it up.

Misha couldn't go to the party. She just couldn't bear it. She cried in her lonely room. She held her stomach, unable to believe the mess she had gotten herself into. She heard a loud crash as two of her boxes came tumbling down. "Great, just my luck," she said and got up to pick up the broken boxes.

"Can I help you with that?"

Misha froze in her spot when she heard the familiar voice. She turned around to see Patrick standing there.

"What are you doing here?" Misha said as she stood up.

Patrick walked closer to her. "Misha, did you mean everything that you said when you came to my house?"

Misha nodded her head. "I meant every word of it. I love you, Patrick."

"I watched you graduate," Patrick said as he came even closer to Misha. "I couldn't stop thinking how proud I was of you. I realized that I can't stay mad at the mother of my child. I can't hold anything in your past against you. If you're bisexual I'm sure we can get over it, if you really want to be with me."

"I want to be with you more than anything in the world."

"How do I know you aren't going to want a woman again?"

"Patrick, I can't lie. I am attracted to women. But that attraction has nothing on the love that I have for you. When you came back into my life, I knew it was the right thing. I love you so much."

Patrick looked her in her eyes. "Then I guess you need to put this on." He handed her the ring he had previously offered.

Misha felt tears rolling down her face. "Are you serious?"

Patrick laughed. "Baby, I love you, and I am willing to give it another shot. I need you and our baby in my life. I don't care about your past. I want to worry about our future."

Misha threw her arms around Patrick and gave him a sensual kiss. She never wanted to let him go.

Misha and Patrick lay on her bed making passionate love. Her phone began to ring. She ignored it as she rode her man like a prized rodeo champion. It rang over and over again.

"Shit . . . babe-babe," Patrick stuttered from the hurting Misha was putting on him. "Who the fuck is that?"

She looked at her phone. She had six missed calls.

It started to ring again. It was Carmen again.

"What, bitch!" Misha's heart dropped when she heard Carmen crying uncontrollably.

Nic took the phone from Carmen. "Misha, come to the Med. There's a problem."

"I'm on my way." Misha got up and started getting dressed.

"What's going on?" Patrick asked as he got out of bed.

"I don't know. Come on. Something's happened. My friends are at the hospital."

"Shit, well let's go." They quickly hurried out of the room.

Chapter 48

"Come in here." Tara grabbed Cooley by her shirt and pulled her into the room.

They went at it.

Cooley threw Tara on the bed and began to rip her clothes off of her.

Cooley hadn't had any wild sex in a long time and was ready to play. She grabbed Tara's breasts and began to lick on them. She sucked on the nipple until it became erect and hard. She quickly made her way to the other one, ensuring they were both nice and hard.

"Shit!" Tara yelled as Cooley picked her up and sat her on top of her face. Tara began to ride Cooley's tongue like a cowgirl. Tara hit the wall as she began to climax from Cooley's intense tongue action. She didn't know what Cooley did, but the mixture of vibrations and licks caused her to lose her mind.

Tara came, but it was not the end. Cooley turned her over and began to hit it from the back. Tara couldn't believe that fingers were giving her so much pleasure. But it wasn't until Cooley's tongue began to fuck her pussy from behind that she began to erupt. Her juices rained on Cooley's tongue as soon as Cooley stuck her finger in Tara's ass.

Ready for round three, Tara climbed on top of Cooley and began to grind on her. Cooley held both of Tara's breasts in her hand, stroking them as Tara bumped and grinded on her.

"Oh, Coooo—" Tara screamed as her door flung open.

Before she could say anything, Tyrone pulled her off of the bed and began to pound on Cooley. Tara let out another scream as she saw Cooley's face become a bloody mess. She tried to grab Tyrone's arm, but he turned around and punched her. She hit the wall and fell unconscious to the floor.

Tyrone picked Cooley up.

"Let her go!"

Tyrone turned to see Lynn standing in the door.

She ran in and pulled his arm off of Cooley.

Tyrone dropped Cooley, and she fell to the floor. "I don't need this shit." He ran out of the room to escape.

Cooley managed to stand up. She looked over at Lynn who was putting all the pieces together. Her look turned from worry to anger when she realized Tara was naked.

"Lynn," Cooley said.

"I can't believe you!" Lynn's whole body began to tremble from rage.

"I'm sorry you had to see this," Cooley said as she wiped the blood from her mouth with her shirt.

"I knew it. So this is why you couldn't fuckin' commit. After all the shit I did for you! All I put up with. You go fuck this bitch!" Lynn slapped Cooley on her already bruised jaw.

"Lynn, calm down. You know we're not together."

Lynn snapped, "Don't give me that bullshit! I have been there for you all this damn time, and this is how you repay me. I transferred to Miami University so I can be close to you, and you go and fuck some other tramp." Lynn began to pound on Cooley.

Cooley stumbled, trying to block her blows.

"Lynn!" Cooley called her name, but she was in another world. Cooley tried her best not to hit her. She pushed Lynn into Tara's desk.

Cooley turned around when she heard Tara moan.

Tara finally woke up from hitting the door.

Cooley helped her to her feet.

Suddenly she heard Tara scream. Tyrone ran back in and started hitting Cooley.

Cooley managed to duck from an incoming blow, causing Tyrone to lose his balance. She ran out of the room and halfway down the stairs.

She made it outside and attempted to catch her breath, but Tyrone knocked her down the stairs.

Cooley turned around so that she could face him head-on. She wasn't going to go out without a fight.

They began to fight again. A small crowd formed around the dorm to watch.

Suddenly, Tyrone hit Cooley squarely in her nose. The blow knocked her to the ground.

She blacked out and didn't wake back up until Carmen pulled on her.

Now they sat outside of Rhonda's bathroom door.

"She's got my door barricaded or something," Dayza said running back into Rhonda's room.

"That's OK," Cooley said. "You gon' have to come out soon, bitch!" Cooley yelled as she pounded her clenched fists on the door.

"Let me handle this," Denise pleaded with Cooley. She knocked on the door. "Rhonda, this is Dee. You need to come out of there."

The sound of Denise's voice was music to Rhonda's ears. "Dee, are you alone?"

"Yeah, Rhonda, I had everyone else leave. Look, I just want to talk to you, so we can figure some things out."

"I don't believe you. I don't think you're alone."

"How can I prove it to you? You have to trust me."

Rhonda knew Denise would never lie to her. She slowly opened the door. "Dee."

Before she knew it, Cooley had grabbed her, locking her hands behind her back. "Bitch, you are going down."

"Cooley, not so hard" Denise said, pulling Cooley back.

Cooley lost the grip on Rhonda, which allowed her to get free. Rhonda ran and grabbed a knife out of her dish holder. She turned and faced them.

"So, you're a liar, Denise!" Rhonda said with a look of rage in her face.

Everyone in the room took a defensive stance and watched her.

"Carmen, get out of here now!" Nic yelled to Carmen without taking her eyes off of Rhonda.

"I'm getting security." Carmen ran out of the room.

"Rhonda, put that shit down now. It's not that serious," Denise said.

"Yeah, I think it is. Y'all gon' try to jump me and you gon' tell me to put it down. I loved you, Denise, and this is how you do me!"

"Rhonda, please," Denise pleaded. "Don't do something you are going to regret."

"The only thing I regret is loving you for so long."

"This girl is crazy," Cooley said under her breath.

Rhonda lunged toward Cooley.

"No!" Denise pushed Cooley out of the way, causing Cooley to head face first into the edge of Rhonda's desk.

Nic grabbed Rhonda and forced the knife out of her hand. Security arrived quickly and grabbed Rhonda. She screamed the entire way out of the building.

Everything was a blur. Cooley slowly focused her eyes. She felt the side of her face; it was wet. She looked down and saw something red on her hands. As her eyes came into focus she saw the blood on her hands. It was her blood. She could hear someone yelling in the background, but couldn't make out the name. Slowly it started making sense. The voices were yelling Denise's name.

Cooley squinted her eyes to see what was going on. She saw Carmen on the floor, holding someone. As her eyes focused she saw long, black hair. Denise was on the ground. Cooley looked at the puddle of blood next to Denise.

"Bruh?" Cooley said.

Nic tried to tell her to sit down but she couldn't.

Cooley struggled to get up. She had to get to Denise. She stood up, and everything immediately started spinning. She saw a bright light. Then everything went black.

Chapter 49

Lena and Brandon jumped when they heard her phone ringing. She quickly answered it to silence the tone. All she could hear was loud voices. They sounded like people yelling and crying.

"Carmen?" she said, knowing it was Carmen by the ring tone.

"Lena, it's Nic. Man, something real serious happened. You need to come to the Med."

Lena could hear the seriousness in Nic's voice. "Nic, what happened?"

"Lena, there was a fight. Cooley is hurt and Denise . . ." Nic couldn't finish talking.

Lena felt her body tense up. "Nic, please what about Cooley and Denise?"

"Lena, it doesn't look good for Denise. You need to come."

Lena's whole body began to shake. Brandon quickly grabbed her.

"Baby, what's going on?"

Lena started crying hysterically.

Brandon grabbed the phone from her and continued to talk to Nic. "We're on our way."

Lena couldn't move. Brandon put her pants on her and carried her to the car. Lena cried the whole way there. Terrible images flooded her mind of Denise being hurt bad, or worse.

Lena jumped out of the car as soon as Brandon pulled up in front of the Med. She didn't wait for him. She ran in.

"Denise Chambers. Where is she?"

"Ma'am, we need you to calm down. Do you know her birthday?"

"Where the hell is she?" Lena yelled as she hit the desk.

"Lena!" Nic yelled.

Lena ran toward Nic. "Where is she? Where is Denise?" Lena cried. "What's wrong?"

"Lena," Nic struggled to get her words out. "Denise. Denise was stabbed."

Lena felt her whole world crashing around her. Her legs gave out, but Nic caught her. She heard Nic calling her name, but she couldn't speak.

"Lena, we don't know what is going to happen yet. They are operating on her now."

"Take me to her. I need her! I need her!" Lena cried. Nic helped her toward the operating room.

Carmen jumped up when she saw Lena. Misha and Carmen held Lena. They comforted each other.

Nic's heart was breaking. Carmen was in so much pain, and there was nothing she could do for her.

Brandon quickly joined them. Nic and Patrick filled him in on what was happening. They waited together.

Two hours later the doctor came out of the two large doors. His grim look didn't make them feel any better. "Is there any family here?"

"Yes, I am their sister," Carmen said.

The doctor looked at Carmen in disbelief. "Ms. Wade has suffered trauma to the right side of her head. The most she will probably have is a permanent scar. She will be all right, but for now needs to rest."

"What about Denise?" Lena asked.

The doctor's face became very stern. "Ms. Chambers lost a lot of blood, but we were able to stop the bleeding. The next twenty-four hours are very critical."

"Can we see them?" Carmen asked.

"You can see Ms. Wade, but I strongly ask that you not excite Ms. Chambers too much." The doctor gave a smile.

Carmen and the others headed toward the back.

Lena grabbed Carmen's hand. "I'm going to see Dee."

Carmen nodded.

Lena walked into the small hospital room. Tears began to pour from her eyes as she looked at Denise on the bed. Denise looked so helpless. Lena's knees started to get weak. She quietly sat in the chair next to Denise's bed, and slowly reached out and held Denise's hand. A surge of energy ran through her body.

"Dee, I hope you can hear me," Lena whispered. "You get better, OK? I, I need you to get better." The tears continued to run from her face. "You are strong, and you're going to make it through this. I only wish I could be as strong as you." Lena's voice began to tremble. She struggled to get the words out. "Denise, I don't know what I would do if you weren't in my life. You can't leave me. I love you so much. I, I am in love with you."

Lena heard the door creak. She turned around but did not see anyone. Lena jumped when she felt pressure on her hand. She looked down. Denise's hand was squeezing hers. Lena smiled. She knew everything was going to be all right.

As soon as the doctor gave the OK to go visit Cooley and Denise, Brandon had headed to the cafeteria to get Lena some water. He finally realized how close the group was, and that, regardless of orientation, they were Lena's first true friends.

He walked back to room 406. He didn't want to be loud, so he slowly pushed the cracked door open and paused. Lena was talking to Denise. He didn't want to disturb, so he stood there listening through the crack. He heard her tell Denise that she loved her. She paused. Just as he was going to open the door, he heard her say something else. "I am in love with you."

The light from the hall way suddenly was blinding. Brandon stared at the closed door. He knew he should be mad, but he wasn't. All he could do was stare at the wooden door. His wife was inside. She'd just told another person that she was in love with her.

Brandon took a step back from the room. The statement was replaying over and over in his mind. He threw the cup of water away and walked toward the bathroom. Brandon splashed cool water on his face. He needed to stay calm. All sorts of questions rushed into his mind. Were they sleeping together? Did Lena no longer love him? Had Denise been sleeping with Lena all along? Rage began to set in.

Suddenly, a small voice began to speak to him. *If she did stray, could you blame her?*

Brandon walked back toward the room. He saw Lena walk out of the room. She was so beautiful to him. She was carrying his child.

Lena looked up at Brandon and smiled. "Denise grabbed my hand. I think she is going to be all right." Lena wrapped her arms around him.

A quick image of Denise touching Lena's naked body flashed into his mind. He tried to shake it off. "That's wonderful, baby. Do you know how long you want to stay here?"

Lena looked at Brandon. He had a strange look on his face. "Bae, are you all right?"

Brandon gave a smirk. "Yeah, I just was thinking about you and my baby."

Lena smiled. "You're right, we probably should be heading home. Let me go say good-bye to Carmen."

Brandon watched her walk away. As soon as she turned the corner, he entered Denise's room. He looked down at Denise, who looked like she was in a peaceful sleep. "Denise." She didn't move. Brandon shook his head. "I just want to say . . ."

There were so many things he wanted to say. He wanted ask her if it was true, if she had slept with Lena. He wanted to know how she could make Lena want her. He wanted to tell her never to come around his wife again.

Brandon looked down at Denise. "I just want to tell you to get better. My wife . . . she really . . . she really cares about you a lot."

Brandon couldn't speak anymore. Tears began to fall. In his mind he knew it was true. He also knew he couldn't blame anyone but himself. He knew that he could never tell Lena what he heard. He also knew he was going to have to work overtime to keep his wife and to make her love him again.

Chapter 50

Misha heard the rustling of Cooley's bed sheets. She opened her eyes to see Cooley tossing and turning. She jumped up and put her hand on Cooley's arm.

"Carla, what are you doing?" Misha asked.

Cooley slowly opened her eyes. Everything was a blur. All she could see was white walls. She turned her head. A face began to come into focus. She soon realized it was Misha. Cooley licked her dry lips. Her voice crackled as she spoke. She cleared her throat. "Denise?"

"She is fine, Carla." Misha smiled. "You were having a bad dream again."

Cooley looked at Misha. Slowly, images began to come in her head. She saw Denise lying in blood.

Cooley rose up but quickly fell back down. "Fuck!" Cooley yelled. She had been out of the hospital for a week, but Denise was still in.

"Cool, are you all right?"

"Where is Carmen?"

"Carmen and Nic are at the hospital with Dee. They have been staying with her while I stayed with you."

Patrick popped into Cooley's head. "Where is your dude?"

"At the hotel."

"Well, I guess that wasn't a part of my nightmare."

"No," Misha said.

Cooley looked away. "Damn. I gotta pee."

Misha helped Cooley up. Cooley slowly walked to the bathroom. She turned to wash her hands in the sink. She paused when she saw the large bandage on the right side of her face. She rubbed her hands against the dressing. She remembered everything now. "I guess karma finally caught up to me."

"Don't say that. You didn't deserve this." Misha walked over to Cooley. She put her arm around her waist.

"Misha, I've done some fucked up things in my life. I've treated women real fucked up. I finally have to deal with the consequences of my actions. But, Dee, she ain't done nothing wrong. I would have preferred to die than have anything happen to her. It's all my fault."

"Carla, it's not your fault. It's Rhonda's fault."

"Misha, there would have never been a situation if I wasn't trying to be up to my old self. Dee would have never had to go to that room if it wasn't for me. I can only hope she will forgive me. I want to go see her."

"You sure you up for all of that?" Misha asked.

"Yeah, I am. I gotta see my bruh."

Vivid memories of the night continued to haunt Cooley. She was filled with emotion as she walked into the hospital. She had almost lost her best friend.

"Hey, bruh. Dee, look who's here."

Cooley's heart tore apart when she saw Denise lying in the hospital bed.

Denise smiled when she saw Cooley and Misha. "Bruh, I was wondering when you were going to get up out of your bed," Denise teased.

Cooley smiled. "You know how I do it. Gotta sleep in." She didn't want to ruin everyone's mood, so she held her feelings in.

"I missed you, bruh," Denise said.

"Man, you will never know." Cooley grabbed Denise's hand. She tried to hold back but couldn't. "I am so sorry, bruh."

"Cool, come on now. I'm gonna be OK. You're gonna be OK. Fuck it. We got big things to do."

A nurse walked in the room.

"You here to tell me I can go home?" Denise said to the nurse and smiled.

"Oh, you know you aren't going anywhere." The nurse smiled as she checked Denise's machines.

"I'm so happy to have my crew here with me again," Carmen, said hugging Cooley.

"Well, I'm sorry to spoil your moment, Carmen, but I have to go."

"Oh, you are headed to Atlanta tomorrow morning right?" Carmen hugged Misha. "I'm going to miss you so much, girl."

"Aww, me too, but you know I am going to get out to L.A. while I am still sexy."

"I hear that."

"You're going to Atlanta?" Cooley asked.

Misha could see the hurt in Cooley's eyes. "Yeah, I'm moving there."

"Good luck." Cooley gave Misha a hug. She didn't want to let go, but she knew she had to.

"Bye, everyone." Misha headed out the door.

Cooley yelled her name, causing her to turn back around.

"Misha," Cooley said, walking toward her. "Just know, you were the first. Misha, I will always love you. Remember that." Cooley kissed Misha on her hand.

Carmen and Denise were surprised by Cooley's statement.

Misha smiled. "Same here."

They let go.

Misha walked out of the room and out of Cooley's life.

Cooley turned around to see them looking at her. "Yeah, that's right. A nigga said the *L* word."

Everyone started laughing.

"Fuck y'all, man." Cooley laughed as she sat back in her chair.

They talked and laughed the rest of the night.

Chapter 51

Denise pulled her shades off as she looked down at the tombstone in front of her. "Well, I guess we both knew this day was going to come." She wiped tears from her eyes. "I know you always tell me to be strong, but you can't blame me at this point." Denise smiled as she read her grandmother's name on the tombstone.

"I hope I made you proud of me. That's all I really ever wanted to do." She placed the creamy white orchids she bought on the grave. "I really wish you were here with me. I love you so much, Mema. I hope I will continue to make you proud. Well, I am out of here, headed to the big New York. I know you're watching out for me, so I'm not worried. I am about to take New York by storm." Denise placed her hand on the tombstone. "I love you, Mema." She stood up and walked a few graves down.

"I love you too, Tammy." She placed a single rose on the resting spot of her mother. She walked back toward the car, where Cooley was waiting.

"You ready to go, bruh? Damn, check that out," Cooley said, looking at the sky.

Denise looked up to see a full rainbow spread across the blue sky. She smiled. "Yeah, bruh, it's time to go."

Lena tried not to think about Denise leaving town. She knew she couldn't go to the airport because it would be too hard on her. The television was now watching her. Vivid thoughts of Denise were rushing through her mind.

She remembered their first meeting in their dorm room. Denise caught her as she was about to fall out of a chair. That was the first time their eyes met.

Thoughts of Denise working out in their room came. She could see Denise's magnificent body, especially the tribal tattoo she had on her arm. It was always Lena's favorite tattoo.

"Baby, I know you told me to stop buying shit for the nursery, but I couldn't help myself," Brandon apologized as the doorman and maid brought in his numerous bags.

Lena didn't hear anything he said. All she could hear was Denise's voice.

"Lena?" Brandon said, noticing that she did not respond. He walked over to her on the couch. "Lena?"

Lena looked up at Brandon. "I have to go." She jumped off the couch and headed toward the door.

Brandon grabbed her arm. "Where the hell are you going?"

"I have to go say good-bye," Lena said, quickly grabbing her purse and keys.

"Naw, you ain't got to go nowhere." Brandon stood menacingly in front of the door.

"Brandon, let me go. I just need to..."

"What, Lena? You need to tell her again that you're in love with her?" Brandon looked at Lena.

Lena's entire body froze.

"Like I said, you ain't goin' nowhere."

Lena looked at Brandon. She could see he meant every word. Denise's face entered her mind. She thought about never kissing Denise again, never feeling Denise's skin. "I'm going."

"Lena, walk yo' ass out that door if you want." Brandon walked away from the door. "Go ahead and do it. Just leave ya key here. And, on the way, call ya family and explain that you walked out on me for a woman. For a muthafuckin' woman!" Brandon punched the wall so hard, his fist went through it.

Lena jumped.

They both stared at each other in silence. Lena dropped her purse on the table. Brandon walked away to the bedroom. Lena knew things would never be the same.

Brandon's body froze when he heard the front door close. He ran out of their bedroom to find Lena gone. Brandon went to grab the door when his son began to cry. He turned the doorknob as the little boy cried harder. Brandon turned around and walked back to the nursery.

"I don't know what I am going to do without you two." Carmen's tears had left wet spots on Denise and Cooley's shirts.

"Carmen, we're gonna see you soon," Cooley said. "I'm gonna come out to L.A. right after I'm completely settled."

"Denise, call me as soon as you make it," Carmen said.

"I will, Carmen. Y'all better get on the road before your mom starts to panic." Denise heard the call for her flight over the intercom. She looked at Cooley, Nic, and Carmen. "I guess this is it."

"Don't say that," Carmen said. "This is just a see-you-later."

"Dig that." Denise gave Nic daps and hugged Cooley and Carmen. "Bye, peeps." Denise walked toward the walkway. She looked back one more time. A piece of her knew that Lena wasn't going to come, but she wished she was wrong. She took a deep breath as she walked through the gates.

They watched from the window as Denise boarded the plane and took off.

Denise looked down at the view of Memphis from in the air. She sighed. "Good-bye, Memphis. Good-bye, Lena." She closed her eyes and exhaled.

Cooley hugged Carmen one more time. "Well, I guess I'm next."

"If you want us to wait on you, we can," Nic said.

"Naw, I'm good. Y'all get on the road—What the hell?"

Everyone turned when Cooley noticed a familiar face running toward them.

"Lena?"

"Where is Denise?" Lena panted. She was out of breath from running down the concourse.

"I'm sorry, sweetie. She already left."

"Nooo! I didn't get to say good-bye!" Lena yelled. She looked out the large picture window at the sky. She wanted to cry, but couldn't. She turned around to see them staring at her. "I guess I was too late. I better go." Lena turned around and headed back toward the door.

No one knew what to think about her. They watched as she headed back to her car.

"Well, we better get on the road. Your mom ain't about to kill me," Nic said to Carmen.

"You're right. Carla, take care of yourself in Miami. Don't make me come there and hurt you."

"Trust me, boo, I'm gonna be on my best behavior." Cooley grinned. "After all, I do have a permanent reminder." She pointed to the scar on her face that she would have to live with forever.

Carmen smiled and gave Cooley another hug. They said their final good-byes and parted ways.

***